Praise for
WHEN HARRY MET MOLLY

"A delectable debut…I simply adored it!"
—Julia Quinn, *New York Times*
bestselling author of *What Happens in London*

"At once frothy and heartfelt, *When Harry Met Molly* satisfies! This book is better than dessert!"
—Celeste Bradley, *New York Times*
bestselling author of *Rogue in My Arms*

"Kieran Kramer pens a delightful Regency confection…a wonderfully bright debut."
—Julia London, *New York Times*
bestselling author of *A Courtesan's Scandal*

"A delicious romp that will keep you laughing. A fun heroine and a sexy hero make this a delightful read."
—Sabrina Jeffries, *New York Times*
bestselling author of *The Truth About Lord Stoneville*

"I couldn't put it down…a charming delight!"
—Lynsay Sands, *New York Times*
bestselling author of *The Hellion and the Highlander*

"A wickedly witty treat…an exquisite debut!"
—Kathryn Caskie, *USA Today*
bestselling author of *The Most Wicked of Sins*

"*When Harry Met Molly* is a delightful, page-turning read! New author Kieran Kramer will capture both your imagination and your heart."
—Cathy Maxwell, *New York Times*
bestselling author of *The Marriage Ring*

St. Martin's Paperbacks Titles by
KIERAN KRAMER

When Harry Met Molly

Dukes to the Left of Me, Princes to the Right

Cloudy
with *a* Chance *of*
Marriage

KIERAN KRAMER

St. Martin's Paperbacks

This is a work of fiction. All of the characters, organizations, and events portrayed in this novel are either products of the author's imagination or are used fictitiously.

CLOUDY WITH A CHANCE OF MARRIAGE

For information address St. Martin's Press, 175 Fifth Avenue, New York, NY 10010.

ISBN: 978-0-312-37403-7

Printed in the United States of America

St. Martin's Paperbacks edition / May 2011

St. Martin's Paperbacks are published by St. Martin's Press, 175 Fifth Avenue, New York, NY 10010.

10 9 8 7 6 5 4 3 2 1

To Steven, Margaret, and Jack with all my love

ACKNOWLEDGMENTS

Thanks, as always, to the incredible duo of Jennifer Enderlin and Jenny Bent! And my deep gratitude goes as well to *all* the wonderful people at St. Martin's Press, including Loren Jaggers, Eileen Rothschild, Anne Marie Tallberg, Brian Heller, Sara Goodman, Danielle Fiorella, and Matthew Shear. I'm so honored and proud to be a St. Martin's Press author.

Thanks also to my family, friends, and even my town for always supporting me and making my life rich. Special hugs to Starla and Johnny Davis, Rob and Mary Beth Harlowe, and Brindy and Gary Scott, my dear friends and neighbors. A shout-out to Dr. David Castellone, our family physician, and his staff at Palmetto Primary Care. For a decade now, you've given us a ton of TLC. And finally, I'd like to thank the teachers, staff, and administrators of Dorchester District II schools for watching over my children all these years and helping them become smarter, kinder people (and giving me time to write). Bless you all.

Cloudy
with *a* Chance *of*
Marriage

CHAPTER ONE

Books were Jilly's great escape, but unless she chose
to use them as missiles—which she'd considered but
decided against as they were her source of livelihood
now—even they couldn't save her from the unpleasant
task before her. She must stop the loud goings-on at
the dead end of the cobblestone lane once and for all.

She walked up from a murky bed of fog that swirled
thickly about her knees onto the front steps of 34 Dreare
Street and knocked on the door. The sprawling three-
story house was situated on a scrap of lawn at a right
angle to her own shop. A tattered skull-and-crossbones
flag hung listlessly against the roofline while a piece
of wood painted with the words HOUSE FOR SALE
leaned against the aged foundation.

No answer.

She knocked again and heard bumping noises and
several loud male voices, one of them singing off-key.

Finally, the door opened wide. A gorgeous man with
golden hair, dressed only in a cambric shirt and faded
trousers, lofted his golden brow. "Thank God, it's you."
His voice was like honey. "Miss Jones." He swept a
slow, warm gaze over her.

Of all the nerve!

Jilly was so taken aback by what she could only call his brazen *maleness,* she didn't know what to say.

He chuckled. "I thought you might be the constable."

And then he smiled and winked, as if he'd just asked her to meet him in the garden at midnight.

She blinked, which she was wont to do when she was flustered. "And . . . and how would you know I am Miss Jones?"

"Because you look terribly angry."

He certainly didn't. He looked the opposite. He looked happy, damn his hide.

"May I assume you're the thoroughly undisciplined Captain Arrow?" she demanded to know.

"The very same." He took out a cheroot and lit it. She'd meant her remark as an insult, but he made unruly behavior seem like an appealing state. "I only forgo discipline when I'm off duty, you know. What can I do for you . . . Miss Jones?"

Really. He was too much. Did he honestly think a woman with any brains in her head would fall for that kind of nonsense?

"Stop saying my name as if—" Oh, dear. She couldn't finish that sentence, not if she were to remain a lady.

"As if what?" He gave her a wide-eyed, innocent look.

"Never mind." She forced herself to inhale a breath through her nose. "There's a man hanging out of your upstairs window."

Now it was his turn to give a short laugh. "Lumley, probably."

She blinked. "Aren't you concerned?"

"No," he said around the cheroot. "It's a trick of his."

"Well"—she shook her head and tried not to make her hands into fists—"I find it hard to work when I see a man hanging upside down out a window."

Captain Arrow gave her a charming grin. "You're not getting angry again, are you, Miss Jones? We moved onto Dreare Street on the same day, after all. That's a special connection, don't you think?"

She huffed. "Your sign makes clear you've no intention to stay. I do plan to make this my home. And I'm not angry. I want—"

"You want what?"

Very well. She *was* angry.

"I want to be able to look out my window and not *see a man hanging upside down, that's all!"* She flung an arm in the direction of her store. "Who's going to have a pleasurable browse for books when my neighbor holds parties night and day? You and your cohorts had just better not introduce any fallen women to the mix, or I'll call the constable myself."

"We already have," he said, his expression angelic, "but the ladies leave discreetly through the rear so as not to cause a stir."

Jilly gasped. "How dare you! The sooner you sell this place, the better."

"I told you," Captain Arrow said, "after the last letter you put through my door—"

"My fourth," she interjected, running out of breath. "My fourth in six days."

"Yes, your fourth," he replied equably. "I had a courier deliver you a note in return—"

"You call a drunken man who falls through my door a courier?"

Captain Arrow looked abashed—yet somehow not. "This is an unusually complicated house party, Miss Jones. I beg your patience. On the one hand, my friends and I are celebrating my safe return from my final voyage with the Royal Navy, during which I captured a notorious pirate. He was a ruthless murderer, so you must grant—"

"Your noble deeds don't give you license to disturb the peace!"

"Nevertheless," he went on smoothly, "at this house party we're also mourning the fact that I didn't receive the purse I should have. All that pirate gold seems to have vanished into other people's pockets."

"That's your business, not mine—"

"Which brings me to the third reason for the house party. There's hope yet for me to become a rich man. I've suddenly found myself the proud owner of this tidy mansion, and as soon as I procure a buyer for it, I'll be well equipped to make my way through the world as a landlubber. In the meanwhile, the house needs christening, don't you agree?"

She narrowed her eyes at him. "No. I don't. It needs paint. And you're ruining my business."

He chuckled. "*I'm* ruining *your* business? I should

hardly think so. Perhaps your business needs a proprietress with a little more sport in her."

He smiled, and one of his eyebrows flew up in a suggestive manner.

"Why," she asked, ignoring his disgusting display of masculine allure, "would a respectable female wish to be sporting?"

"You'll know once you try it. Come to my house tonight. We're holding a small theatrical evening."

"Over my dead body," she said, even though she adored theatrical evenings. "Let's get back to the point that forces me to venture over here—you're disturbing the peace, sirrah."

"Hardly. We've had no one running naked down the street in the last two days."

"Fancy that!"

"And not a single one of my guests has sung a word of any song outside."

She put a finger to her mouth, pretending to consider his words, then dropped her hand. "You know, you're right. They only sing in the house now—with the windows wide open. And sometimes"—she drew in a breath and said low—*"the singer is wearing only a tricorne hat."*

"That's Lumley again," he said as if he were talking of the weather.

Speaking of which, didn't this unrelentingly cheerful man notice they had bad weather here on Dreare Street? *All* the time?

Jilly's heart was pounding so hard, she needed

support. So she leaned forward and put her hands on either side of the door jamb. Captain Arrow leaned back a fraction of an inch.

"If *I*"—she whispered—"have to come over"—she pulled back to take a breath—"one more time—"

"Yes?" He leaned forward again. "What will you do?"

She closed her eyes a brief moment, then opened them and stared at him. "I'll go mad." It was as simple as that. "I'll go stark, raving mad."

Before he could answer her, she turned around and marched back to her store, directly through a plump cloud of fog that refused to be dispersed by the weak morning sun overhead.

Miss Jilly Jones.

Already Stephen adored her. He always did the outliers. Perhaps because he was one himself. Of course, his new neighbor was doing her best to be true to type. She excelled at appearing bookish. Prim. A bluestocking with no sense of humor. A woman to be avoided at all costs.

But no other prim miss he'd ever met had grasped door jambs and leaned into his face as if she'd like to bite his head off. He was a sea captain used to giving orders, not taking them, by God. This cheeky Miss Jones showing up flinging commands about was something new. Truth be told, he'd never met a woman as unmanageable, which made him admire her a great deal. It also made his blood hot for her. She was a challenge, that one. And Stephen never turned aside from a challenge.

Hadn't he risen to the challenge of being named an Impossible Bachelor not long ago with his three best friends, Harry, Nicholas, and Charlie? And he'd come out of Prinny's ridiculous albeit amusing wager unscathed, unmarried, and as unrepentant a bachelor as he'd ever been.

When Miss Jones left his front step, he instantly determined that he wanted to have a scorching flirtation with her. Other than sell his house, what else did he have to do?

He had a strict rule that he didn't seduce virgins, so bedding her was out of the question. But imagine what creative machinations he'd have to go through just to steal a few kisses! Grabbing a delicious tendril of her hair and wrapping it around his finger would be practically out of the question unless he were good . . . *very* good. And if he could slip a hand up her gown at least to her knee, then his short stay on Dreare Street would go from being mildly entertaining to memorable.

This was one war he'd have to be very cunning to win.

He was crestfallen when she entered the bookstore and pulled the door shut without looking back out to see if he were still there. It was a good move. Pretend indifference to the enemy—shake their confidence. His own strategies would have to be put in place, he realized. Miss Jones was too substantial, obviously, to fall for his good looks alone, a fact which delighted him. Infatuated young ladies bored him.

He wanted a *real* dalliance. A real one, of course, engaged his mind.

And Stephen had a brilliant mind. He chose not to emphasize that point when he was out of uniform. It was something to do with his need to relax, to disengage, to not be the leader always. As captain of a ship in the Royal Navy, he'd always been at the center of things, interconnected by necessity to every man on board. It was an exciting but exhausting way to live.

Perhaps he was addicted to lack of sleep, loud noises, near-death experiences, and chasing enemies. Settling down in a quiet, peacetime navy held no appeal for him, which was why he was leaving it, despite the Admiralty's hope that he'd take command of a man-of-war.

Neither was he tempted to resign himself to a subdued gentleman's existence on land, complete with a demure wife, several adorable children, and a second career in banking or international trade.

Give him lots of money—more than his pension was worth—so he could live beholden to no one. Give him noise and bluster. Boxing and horse racing. Bawdy girls and boisterous men.

His own sailing vessel.

A pied-à-terre in Paris.

Give him something out of the ordinary.

Give him Jilly Jones.

CHAPTER TWO

In the late afternoon of the day of her useless conversation with Captain Arrow, Jilly heard a loud popping noise from his house. She looked up from smoothing a page in her nearly blank accounting book and saw a young man at a second-floor window drop a bag of water onto the pavement.

"Bull's-eye!" the fellow cried.

A roar of approval went up from the group of well-dressed gentlemen gathered on the street.

Jilly sighed. For goodness' sake, when would a constable ever arrive and throttle the lot of them?

"I often wonder," she heard her clerk, Otis, remark to their lone customer of the afternoon, a small, elderly woman perusing a copy of *Pride and Prejudice,* "if Mr. Darcy and Elizabeth had a few secret trysts before they made their nuptial vows." He chuckled and looked into space. "Who could have resisted Darcy?"

"Well," the elderly woman speculated, one hand to her lips, the other balancing the book, "I'm not sure—"

"If," Otis interrupted her in dramatic tones, which made her nearly drop the book, "if Darcy were too

much a gentleman to propose an illicit liaison, then don't you think Elizabeth must have been driven so mad by desire that *she* seduced *him* instead?"

The old woman stared at him.

"It's quite a titillating thought." Otis took the book out of her trembling hands and placed it back on the shelf. "It's our only copy," he confided to her in an earnest whisper. "Let me show you something else."

Dear God. Jilly watched her assistant sway gently down the aisle toward her meager collection of atlases, crooking a finger at the tiny woman to follow him. The shop would be bankrupt within a month if the mayhem persisted at Captain Arrow's house and if Otis didn't learn to *sell books*.

Her father's ex-valet didn't seem able to part with any of them, except for the atlases, but what was Jilly to do? She couldn't cast him out in the cold, for heaven's sake. He'd been devoted to her father and, after his death, her only trusted friend.

"You dress very well for an older man," she heard the little lady rasp, "but you're quite mad. Almost as mad as those people who live next door."

A few seconds later, the bell at the front door tinkled, and the door shut with a loud bang.

"And you have a lovely day, too!" Otis flung after their lost customer with all the sarcasm a frustrated, impoverished bookseller could muster. "That atlas was just the thing for you, if you'd only listened to reason. And how dare you call me an 'older man'? I'm not a day over thirty."

"Otis," Jilly called in a warning voice.

He'd been thirty for as long as she could remember. He twisted around to face her, his large feet crossed in outrageous saffron-colored shoes, his tailcoat swinging madly.

"But Lady Jilly!"

"Miss Jilly," she corrected him.

"Oh, dear," he apologized. "But what am I to do? She wouldn't have appreciated *Pride and Prejudice*. She has no fire in her soul. I'm saving it for someone who has spirit, style, and good looks."

Jilly blew out a breath. "Some of the worst villains and biggest fools have good looks," she reminded him.

"Yes," Otis returned smugly and touched the nape of his neck.

He believed himself to be quite good-looking, she knew. And he did have mesmerizing eyes, a jolting blue that was quite disconcerting. But he hardly filled his waistcoat, he was so thin. He also had knobby knees, a Roman nose that looked as if it had been broken several times but hadn't, wispy gray hair that circled his ears, and a pate as shiny and bald as a baby's bottom.

"I never said good looks *alone*." He lingered on the last word, which was his tendency. "I also mentioned spirit and style. Or did you forget? Those gentlemen at the captain's house have them in *spades*."

Jilly marched past him with a small square sign, which she placed in the window. "That isn't spirit and style," she said. "That's what happens when you buy a cask of brandy and invite your debauched friends over to drink it with you until it runs out. We must start selling books soon, or we'll run out of money."

The sign promptly fell over, and she adjusted it again until it was right. "I need a ledge beneath the window." She brushed past Otis, wishing she had enough money to ask the carpenter who'd put in the bookshelves to come back and make the ledge. But she didn't. She'd have to make do for a while, until profits started coming in.

Otis traipsed after her. "I abhor what Hector has done to you," he said over her shoulder. "A lady should never worry about money. And she should stay far away from the taint of trade. We may thank Hector for this state of affairs."

"Be that as it may"—she picked up a feather duster and swept it over a line of dictionaries—"please try to remember, the next time a dull, unattractive patron requests *Pride and Prejudice*, to acquiesce and allow him or her to purchase it." She turned and faced him. "*If* you want to keep food on your plate."

Otis made a moue of distaste. "I hate when you get dramatic. Of course I want food. Good food, too. It's been a week since I've had a decent brioche." He put his hand to his mouth, suddenly looking quite hungry. "I suppose I can part with *Pride and Prejudice*. But only—"

"No *but only*s." She strode past him with the feather duster and threw it in a cupboard filled with cleaning supplies, including a bottle of vinegar-and-water and the rag she used to shine the windows and the large, ornate looking glass her father had always had in his library. The rag she used to clean it was one of Papa's old shirts, actually. She had a feeling he'd approve of her new endeavor were he alive to see it.

Comforted by that thought, she wet the rag with the vinegar-and-water solution and rubbed it in great circles around the looking glass. London was a smoky place. But even where she'd made a clean spot, the mirror appeared murky, able to reflect back only the meager gray light slanting through the shop windows.

The bell rang again.

"If you've come back for Mr. Darcy, you can't have—" Otis said in a singsong voice then paused.

"Him," he finished in a whisper.

The glow from the lamp cast over the books went from a watery yellow to a deep, burnished gold in a trice. And no wonder. Captain Arrow, who until this moment hadn't deigned to grace their shop, was now blocking the doorway and the scant light coming through it. Not only that, he was grinning as if he hadn't a care in the world.

Maybe he hadn't, which annoyed Jilly no end.

"Ahoy, Captain," Otis said in an overly admiring voice.

The captain did have particularly gleaming white teeth set off by his swarthy tan, but Jilly did her best to ignore his sterling good looks. "I don't believe we can help you," she told her new neighbor, the rag still in her hand. "We've no brandy here. Only books."

She knew it was self-pity making her churlish, but she couldn't seem to help herself.

"I've come to reinvite you to the theatrics," the captain said, ignoring her slight. "You and your assistant both."

Otis bowed. "You do me a great honor. I am Mr. Otis Shrimpshire, bookstore clerk extraordinaire. And fashion connoisseur." He waved a hand. "Not that it matters. Books are my business now."

Captain Arrow seemed only slightly taken aback. "A pleasure to make your acquaintance," he said in amenable tones. "And marvelous shoes, if I do say so myself, Mr. Shrimpshire."

"Please call me Otis." Otis positively beamed at him.

Jilly pursed her lips. "Thank you for asking, Captain, but we're not interested in attending the theatrics."

"*I* am." Otis elbowed her.

She sent him a dirty look.

"Do come, Miss Jones," Captain Arrow urged her. "One must make merry occasionally"—his face took on a noble, serious aspect—"even a stalwart woman of business such as you."

Woman of business. She was that, wasn't she? It was lovely to hear herself addressed with respect.

And *stalwart*. That was a good word.

"Yes, well—" she began, about to tell him that owning Hodgepodge was a massive responsibility she didn't take lightly, then pulled herself up short.

He was making fun of her, wasn't he?

There was a distinct twinkle in his eye.

"I'd rather be a stalwart woman of business than

one of your silly lightskirts," she snapped at him, and flicked the cleaning cloth at an invisible spiderweb. She would pretend it was the captain's broad shoulder and that he was so cowed by her skill with the rag, he left her in peace and went home and became quiet and subdued for the rest of his life.

"The shocking female who owns this wretched store is right," called an ugly voice from the door.

Jilly's mouth dropped open. She ceased her rag-flicking and turned around to see who had freshly insulted her. A prune-faced elderly woman, her pinched mouth stained in cherry juice, shuffled into the shop and eyed them all with disdain. Her gown was elegant but unfashionable, and a small porcelain figure of a lady looking eerily like her—snooty and grand and diabolical—was hand-painted at the top of the Continental dress stick upon which she leaned.

"Your housewarming celebrations are ill-advised, Captain," the woman continued. "You should take up your command again and go back to sea. The sooner the better."

Jilly would have smiled triumphantly at the captain, but she was far too wounded by the woman's scathing rhetoric about herself to bother.

"Do tell me you three simpletons already knew that despite its exalted location in Mayfair, Dreare Street is considered an unlucky address," the crone uttered, her words slithering out like a curse.

There was a dreadful stillness.

What a thing to say! Otis gave a small cry and blinked madly. Jilly wanted to speak, but once again, she couldn't find her voice. Captain Arrow appeared completely unperturbed. Perhaps his having dealt with pirates had something to do with that.

The woman thrust a withered finger toward Jilly. "You, Miss Jones, are the first to buy here in over thirty years. And Captain Arrow, you're the first person to voluntarily accept your inheritance. I know for a fact that your second cousin thrice removed attempted to give the house to at least three other distant relatives of yours. None of them wanted it because it's on Dreare Street."

There was a beat of awful silence. Jilly's head felt as if it would burst.

"No!" Otis flung a hand to his brow. "*Why*, God? Why us?" And he drew out an outrageously oversized lace handkerchief with which he covered his face and proceeded to burst into tears.

"That's the silliest thing I've ever heard," Jilly said to the woman, her indignation of monumental proportions. "We live here now. And we refuse to believe such nonsense."

She'd already had her fair share of bad luck. She refused to have more.

"Nonsense?" The woman walked over the threshold. "Did you, the owner of a bookstore with a ridiculous name, say *nonsense*?"

Jilly's eyes widened, but she nodded. That small figure at the top of the cane seemed to stare malevolently at her.

The woman stamped her walking stick and shook

Jilly out of her trance. "Lady Duchamp doesn't deal in nonsense. She's too clever. And she knows that one should avoid fools."

"Yes, but who are *you,* madam?" Otis asked.

The woman narrowed her eyes at him. "Why, Lady Duchamp, you idiot." She turned to Captain Arrow next. "You're disgustingly handsome. Aware of it, too, aren't you? I'm sure you think staring at me as if you can see my underthings will charm me. But I'm not charmed. Not in the least."

Jilly shared a look with Otis. Otis almost giggled but didn't.

Thank God.

Captain Arrow stepped forward and kissed Lady Duchamp's hand. "I find that women with tongues like adders usually have good reason for their vitriol, or at least did at one time. Consider me a friend should you ever need one, my lady."

"Pah," is all she said back, then lowered her brows. "I am the oldest resident on this street and the most put-upon. I despise everyone who lives here and only wish they had more bad luck than they already have. I hope a tree falls through your shop window in a storm, young lady, drenching all your books, and as for you"— she shoved a finger at Captain Arrow's chest—"you and your loutish friends . . . I hope the pox visits your house and kills you all."

"What about me?" Otis looked terribly offended at being left out.

Lady Duchamp pointed the end of her stick at him.

"You, sir, are already so pathetic, I can think of nothing to worsen your lot in life. You are the epitome of failure and misery."

Otis looked well satisfied with the insult.

The old woman turned on her heel and walked away at a snail's pace. They could have easily gone after her to deliver their own insults, but Jilly knew—and apparently Otis and Captain Arrow did, as well—that such a harpy would be impervious to any barbs.

Another beat of silence passed, broken only by the sound of Otis whimpering into his handkerchief again. Finally, he lowered it and looked accusingly at Captain Arrow. "You're a sailor, and sailors are terribly superstitious. What do you plan to do now that you know Dreare Street is unlucky?"

Captain Arrow shrugged. "Sell the house as always."

"But who will want it?" asked Jilly. "Who'll want to buy a house—or books, for that matter—on an unlucky street?"

She felt such despair, she wasn't sure that she wouldn't burst into tears at any moment. But then she remembered how useless tears were, and the despair hardened into a knot of defiance in her stomach.

Captain Arrow looked at her with the bland confidence of a man who seldom encountered misfortune—or if he did, quashed it. Perhaps with a broadside of cannon fire, or a saber, at the least.

"One can thwart any superstition by employing one's wits," he said. "I've defied every nautical superstition there is without mishap. I've set sail on Friday, thrown a stone into the sea, stepped on and off a ship left foot first, and conversed with a ginger-haired person before boarding, all to no consequence. It shall be no different on Dreare Street. I'll sell the house and be on my way in no time."

"You navy captains are so demmed confident!" Otis cried.

"And so should you be," the captain insisted, slapping Otis on the back. "It's a waste of time, putting credence in luck and superstition. One simply needs to use one's own resources, and the world is your oyster. Is it not, Miss Jones?"

Of course, Jilly was reluctant to agree with him in any way, but she must. Here she was, the proud owner of a bookshop because she'd gone after what she wanted, which was wrong, according to the vicar in her home village. She was supposed to do only what the men in her life told her to do.

"You're correct, Captain," she said. "There *is* no such thing as bad luck. We make our own fortunes. Therefore, I declare with complete certainty that Dreare Street is *not* unlucky. Just because there's an inordinate amount of fog in the morning, and a man next door who's a disturbance to the peace, and no customers in Hodgepodge, and an evil old woman with a frightening walking stick—well, that doesn't mean it's unlucky. All that can be dealt with, I assure you."

She crossed her arms and glared at her handsome neighbor. Woe to anyone who interfered with her plans for Hodgepodge. There was too much at stake for her to capitulate.

Thoroughly unruffled, Captain Arrow looked at her with a devastating smile on his well-defined lips—the kind of smile that would make any other woman swoon—and a slow-burning gleam in his golden eyes. It was as if he found her the most appealing woman in the world.

No doubt he looked at every woman that way, so Jilly refused to be flattered, even though her breath was a bit short and something depraved inside her wanted to eat him up, like a delicious pudding one licked off the sides of the bowl when no one else was looking.

She must suppress that thought immediately.

"Excuse me, Captain. I'm busy." The rag-snapping had lost its luster, so when her eyes lit upon a book of poetry, she determined to read a line. *Any* line. She opened it to a random page, held it beneath her nose, and read:

To His Coy Mistress,
by Andrew Marvell

Had we but world enough, and time,
This coyness, Lady, were no crime.

My goodness! She felt scandalized, but better that than be required to look at Captain Arrow. She allowed herself to peek at a few more lines:

My vegetable love should grow
Vaster than empires, and more slow;
An hundred years should go to praise

Thine eyes and on thy forehead gaze;
Two hundred to adore each breast,
But thirty thousand to the rest—

"Enjoying yourself, Miss Jones?" Captain Arrow's honeyed tones broke through her reverie.

She slammed the volume shut, her face flushed and her temples damp. What a naughty poem! The captain would no doubt adore it.

"No," she said. "I'm *not* enjoying myself." And she shoved the book back beneath at least ten others and made them into a neat pile. "I'm organizing my shop. It's exhausting, time-consuming work."

"All the more reason for you and Otis to come with me now," her golden-haired nemesis said. "My friend Lumley has mixed a fine rum punch to fortify us during the performance. I assure you, our lady friends are absent, and every man is clothed"—Jilly turned scarlet—"and on his best behavior."

Otis straightened his cravat. "I'm going."

Jilly stomped her foot. "No, you are *not*."

Otis stomped his foot back. "Come now. We need to welcome our new neighbors."

"But we're the new neighbors, too," Jilly said.

"Exactly," Captain Arrow replied, and held out his well-clad arm. He'd taken the time to put on a coat, a fine one that fit him like a glove. His cravat, she couldn't help but notice, was a sartorial miracle. "An entertaining skit and one small cup of punch while you watch, Miss Jones. Perhaps we'll bring better luck to Dreare Street if we all share a toast to it."

She hesitated. Toasting their new abode did seem like a fine idea. Her father had taught her to toast when she was a small girl. Perhaps the ritual of toasting was just the tonic she needed to keep her more anxious thoughts at bay.

Besides, the captain's boots were shined so bright, she could see books reflected in them, which was a pleasant sight. Her determination to avoid the man was temporarily forgotten.

"Oh, very well," she said, removing her apron. "Just one small skit and a cup of punch."

It had been so long since she'd indulged in any amusements.

Too long.

Since well before she'd married the odious Hector.

She took the captain's arm and prayed she'd continue to believe he wasn't charming or intelligent in the least. She didn't need a neighbor who would make her wish she wasn't trapped in a bad marriage to an awful man. And she most definitely didn't want a neighbor who would uncover her secret—

That she was a runaway wife hiding from her husband.

CHAPTER THREE

"Here is your seat of honor, Miss Jones," Stephen said as he guided her to a faded armchair in the parlor where the theatrics were to be held. He handed her a glass of punch. Their fingers tangled, and she flinched ever so slightly.

"It's quite mild," he assured her, pretending not to notice her reaction to his touch. It was a good sign, even if she did think she abhorred him. "I'm directing this piece, so I shall leave you two to be our audience. We invited Lady Duchamp and several other neighbors, as well, but no one responded."

"Then they are *fools,* Captain," Otis said. "This is a lovely home. It's large and rambling—quite lopsided, in fact—but it's full of people with spirit, passion, and style."

"Do you agree, Miss Jones?" Stephen couldn't resist asking her.

"I suppose I must," said Miss Jones tartly, "if the compliment will hasten you back to your duties as stage director."

He chuckled. "You're rather a spitfire, aren't you?"

"I'm nothing of the sort," she said, and tossed her head.

He exchanged a look with Otis, who rolled his eyes, and left them. But from his position behind a potted palm near the front of the room, he watched Miss Jones focus on the stage. She was as guarded as ever, a vertical line on her brow. She took a tentative sip of the punch, and then several more.

No wonder. It *was* a delicious punch, Stephen's own recipe.

Miss Jones's eyes widened when he drew the curtain back and the actors appeared. His friends were dressed as women with coconut breasts, grass skirts, and awful wigs (all of which Stephen had accrued in various ports).

Miss Jones leaned forward in her chair and watched the players avidly. Her eyes sparkled at their witty repartee, which Stephen had written on a piece of foolscap that same morning. And then she laughed—a big, light, airy laugh—and clapped her hands madly at the conclusion.

Much to Stephen's surprise, she'd turned out to be the type of audience member any playwright or actor would yearn for. In appreciation for her enthusiasm, the actors, led by Lumley, drew her up on their makeshift stage, which was really nothing more than an area of the drawing room emptied of furniture and rugs and flanked by standing candelabra. She immediately fell into the part they desired her to play, Queen of the Coconut Girls.

Otis begged to be allowed onstage as well, hopping

up and down in his seat, so Lumley called him up and urged him to play the King of the Fire Dance.

Then someone began playing a set of small, primitive drums Stephen had purchased in the islands.

It was at that point, when Miss Jones began a lively dance, a wreath of flowers sliding off her head, that he realized his prudish neighbor was a bit tipsy. Of course, he'd planned for that. He'd had designs on her since he'd first seen her, but now—

Now he wasn't so sure he should pursue them, at least that evening, not when she was in her cups.

Timing was everything. He knew that from the war. And now Miss Jones was pushing him out of the way to get to the window on the second floor so *she* could drop a bag of water on the target painted on the pavement outside 34 Dreare Street.

He was surprised he hadn't noticed earlier that she had vivid black eyebrows made for drama. And glossy black hair done up in a tight knot begging to be unraveled. Her eyes, the startling violet-blue color of pansies, stared up into Stephen's own with obvious pleasure.

"Watch this, Captain!" she cried lustily, and leaned out the window with her paper bag of water. The sun was just setting behind the massive holly bushes at the top of the street.

Plop.

"Bull's-eye!" She yelled her delight then drew her head back in the window. "Another! Get me another!"

Lumley and his cohorts raced to get her another bag while Otis clapped madly.

Stephen yanked Lumley to a stop. "What in bloody hell did you put in the rum punch?"

Lumley shrugged. "The usual."

"The usual? For a *lady*? I said to make it strong but not *that* strong. Just enough to make her somewhat malleable to the suggestion that she's out of order expecting us to be as goody-goody as she."

Lumley had the grace to blush. "Well, you can't taste the rum. Not with all that delicious coconut milk and bits of orange in it," he said defensively and paused. "I like your Miss Jones. She's the most sporting female I've ever met. You should do everything you can to stop being such a vast annoyance to her."

Stephen glowered at him, but Lumley didn't seem to notice. His impatient, determined expression suggested he had more important things on his mind, such as filling paper bags with water. He moved on to do Miss Jones's bidding.

"I think it's time you went home, Miss Jones," Stephen said in his best captain's voice.

She frowned. "Whatever for? We've all night. Stand aside, Captain, and let the true merrymakers have their way."

She looked at him as if he were the dullest man on earth.

Stephen wasn't used to being considered dull. In fact, the assessment quite wounded him.

And he also wasn't accustomed to insubordination. He hadn't tolerated it on board navy ships, and he certainly wouldn't in his own house.

"Your store," he said to Miss Jones. "It needs tending."

"What do you know about it?" she said, flagrantly defying him. "*I'm* the proprietress of Hodgepodge. I make all the decisions there."

Well, then.

He turned a steely eye to Otis. "Doesn't the store need attention, Otis?"

"Surely not, Captain." Otis was wide-eyed. "It's closed for the day." And he turned his back on him and went skipping off to assist Miss Jones.

Good God. What was happening here? Whatever it was, Stephen didn't like it. He didn't like it the way a sailor doesn't like a red sky in the morning, which signaled squalls ahead.

He maneuvered himself closer to his two guests, which involved squeezing in between them at the window.

"It *is* a late hour," he lied. Somehow without elbowing anyone in the ribs, he managed to take his watch out and observe the face in an obvious manner. "And I've got an early-morning meeting. Do go home now, Miss Jones. You'll escort her, Otis?"

About an inch from Stephen's face, Otis gave a sloppy salute. "Demmed right, Cap'n."

That was better. Sort of.

Stephen gradually moved out his elbows so neither one had any room left and waited for the two of them to figure out his silent message. Somehow, they never did—Miss Jones almost hit him in the eye with her own elbow—but after three more *plops,* she'd had enough and decided to go home.

"Not to tend to Hodgepodge," she said, eyeing him askance when she rose from her perch. "But because I'm tired."

She took Otis's arm, and he patted her hand. "I am as well. I think."

Stephen watched the two of them walk ahead of him toward the stairs. But Otis's shoe, adorned with gaudy rubies and pearls no doubt made of paste, had lost a heel, a fact its owner hadn't noticed until now. He was so busy looking for it, he knocked over a small table, whereupon a tumbler of punch fell and hit him on the head.

Miss Jones screamed when her friend sank in a heap to the floor.

Stephen immediately went to him, checking Otis's head and bending over to listen to his breathing and his heart. He stood and grinned at Miss Jones to reassure her. "Don't worry. He didn't feel a thing, and I think he's snoring, actually, so he can't be too bad off. I'll get Pratt to escort him home later. *You* need to go home now."

"Are you sure he'll be safe for the nonce?" Miss Jones surprised him when she took Stephen's much larger hands between her own and squeezed. "He's my very special friend, Captain. Nothing can happen to him."

Stephen—master flirt, commander of warships— was touched by her simple devotion to her eccentric companion. "He'll be fine. I promise."

"All right, then," she said brightly, and dropped his hands. "We can go."

Out on the street, he couldn't remember the last time a female had looked at him so—with utter trust. Women often looked at him with nary a bit of inhibition, as she was doing now, as well. It stirred his blood. But the trust part disconcerted him. It made him feel noble, especially as she still had flowers in her hair and looked in need of saving.

"It was a fine party." She yawned, and her bodice almost burst open with the effort, exposing the tops of her breasts. "What a shame it's over."

He thought back on the past week. He'd seen the way she'd peeked through her shop window to observe the boisterous goings-on taking place at his house. No one looked that often without wishing they were somehow involved in the merriment themselves.

"Tomorrow is always another day for a party," Stephen said, suddenly encouraged—encouraged in a heated way—by her bodice and by her unusual complacency. He was a man, after all, a man who'd recently been on a long voyage with no women to charm him.

They stopped outside her door.

She looked up at him, and he was tempted—tempted even though if he were being sensible, he knew she was all wrong for him.

All wrong.

But the primal part of him reminded him she wasn't *all* wrong, was she? He saw her lips, plump and pink and half parted. Why shouldn't he kiss them?

Encouraged even further by her utter stillness—so unusual for an unmanageable miss—he leaned in an inch—

And she stepped back an entire foot. Definitely out of kissing range. Even out of hugging range.

Miss Jones opened her door, pulled it almost shut behind her, and peeked out. "I enjoyed the evening!" she said airily, and gave him a brilliant smile.

He had that same utterly lost feeling he'd had the first time he'd let a line accidentally slip through a cleat, leaving a sail flapping uselessly in the wind and out of his reach.

"I'm, ah, glad you enjoyed the punch," he said. "It's a special recipe from the islands."

"Oh." That grin again. "It was delicious. But the fumes made my nose prickle, so I poured some into the dead potted palm near the stage after the performance."

"You mean when you were dancing and dropping bags of water . . . ?"

She nodded. "I was simply having fun. I think. I'm not quite sure. I've never had punch before. I feel—"

"Yes?" She had a certain longing look in her eyes that made him want to rip the door open and kiss her.

"I feel—" She hesitated and bit her lower lip. "I feel like . . ."

Dammit all, she felt as if she wanted to kiss him. He could tell.

She lifted her chin and suddenly looked noble and passionate, like Joan of Arc. "I feel like reading," she said.

Reading?

She nodded avidly. "Oh, yes. I do it every night before I go to bed."

Bed. She shouldn't have said that. He imagined her in a high-necked cotton night rail with a long row of buttons.

She let out a pleased sigh. "Yes, every night I read."

Of course, on the ship, he read every night, too. But he'd much rather read the curves and sighs of a warm, willing woman, any day.

"I'm reading mythology this week," she went on. "I adore Hermes."

"The messenger god?" Stephen was doing his best to turn away from thoughts of undoing her buttons one by one.

"Yes." She grinned. "The book I'm reading now has impressive illustrations of him. In one picture, he's standing with his fists on his hips and one knee bent, and he's laughing. It's as if he's looking straight at me."

Stephen saw her eyes turn dreamy, and it wasn't about *him*. It was about that damned Hermes.

"I suppose you're not in your cups, then, if you can read about the gods tonight." He scratched his head, most disappointed.

"Me?" Her nose wrinkled. "In my cups? Whyever would I be?"

Stephen felt extremely guilty of a sudden. "No reason."

"I'm beginning to think you had a secret plan," she said stoutly. "I should have stayed more on guard this evening."

"I'm a wolf, am I?"

She closed the door a fraction of an inch. "We both know what you're after, Captain."

He moved forward and said into the crack, "Come back out here, Miss Jones, and tell me what that is."

"No," she replied in confident tones. "You already know."

He sighed. "Can't you be complacent again? As you were just a minute ago when you were yawning?"

"Complacent?" Her pitch rose a notch.

"Yes, dammit all. Complacent." He felt like knocking his head against the shop's stone wall.

"I knew it!" she cried. "You were trying to ply me with punch, so I'd stop complaining about the noise from your house. Either that, or so I'd become another one of your fancy women."

"Miss Jones." She'd guessed correctly, of course.

"Don't 'Miss Jones' *me*." She huffed. "You're a sore loser. You could at least admit I'm right."

"Very well." He blew out a breath of frustration. "You're a shrewd woman. Impossible to fool."

"And you're an intelligent man to recognize that fact."

All evening he'd been thinking about the moment their fingers had met around that glass of punch. She was ripe for a man's touch, and he was heady with longing to be that man.

"Now let's go back to how you looked when we were navigating the corner," he said in a husky whisper. "Happy. Sporting. *Kissable*."

There was a beat of silence, but it was cut short by

her predictable bluestocking gasp. "You should be ashamed of yourself," she hissed through the crack. "I told you I've no need to be sporting for you or anyone else. Nor shall I kiss you. *Ever.*"

The crack in the door became even smaller, but he noticed she didn't shut it completely.

He leaned on the jamb and saw her eye, unblinking but narrowed. "It would be so much easier for both of us if you'd fall in line."

That same eye grew wide and offended.

"Not in a million years," she declared. "How can I sell books when you persist in tomfoolery? I enjoyed being Queen of the Coconut Girls and dropping those bags of water very much. But I'm wise enough to know there's a time and a place for making merry, and doing so every night and day on a street where many other people live and work is not the time *nor* the place." She paused a beat. "Good night, Captain. Please send Otis back when he's feeling better, with both his shoes *and* his missing heel."

She shut the door in his face.

In his face.

Stephen could hardly believe it. If anyone had done that on board his ship, they'd have been thrown into the ship's brig. And when they were let out, made to scrub the decks with a tiny scrub brush until they gleamed.

Jilly leaned against the bookshop door and took a deep breath. Captain Arrow was a dangerous man. Thank God he was leaving Dreare Street soon.

Dancing on stage had made her giddy with delight. So had dropping bags of water out the window. Even walking home with the captain had made her happy. Possibly because he was breathtakingly handsome. And funny. He'd made clever jokes all night long, the kind that sometimes took a minute to ponder because his sense of humor was so dry.

Of course, she'd ignored them. She didn't want him to think he was entertaining in the least.

She was on to his strategy: he'd confessed it himself. He wanted her to fall in line, to make her more malleable, to turn her over to his way of thinking. He believed one could take part in revelries whenever one wanted to, whether one had obligations or not. He wanted her to stop complaining and join his party indefinitely!

Thank God she'd not succumbed.

"Oh, dear," she muttered, and put her fingers to her lips. She couldn't help thinking about how close she'd come to seeing things his way, when he'd put his mouth so close to the crack in the door and said the word *kissable*.

For a split second, she'd had visions of them doing just that. But then she'd remembered.

Hector.

She was married already, and to a cruel, stupid man—a distant cousin, actually—who'd delighted in making her miserable while running through her father's fortune. From his deathbed, Papa had acknowledged Hector was a crude sort of man, but he was also the true heir. He was kind to marry Jilly and not force her out of her own home, wasn't he?

Jilly shuddered. If only Papa had known Hector's true nature. He was the opposite of *kind*.

But it's all right, a stalwart voice in her head reminded her. *At least you're free of him now.*

Jilly's mother had owned a small property independent of her husband's estate. Thanks to the discretion of her family attorney, Hector had known nothing about it. Jilly had sold it off, along with a steady stream of precious family heirlooms, behind Hector's back, to raise the funds to buy Hodgepodge.

And then she'd run away—in the middle of the night.

She'd been terrified, but the closer she'd come to London, the more exhilarated she'd become.

It was a new life for her. A new life for Otis, too.

Now she yawned and crawled into bed, comforted by the thought that someday she'd be able to go long lengths of time without thinking of her husband.

But she found she couldn't sleep, and not because she was thinking of Hector. She was thinking about Captain Arrow again. They'd never gotten around to making those toasts to Dreare Street, had they?

"And we probably never will," she whispered softly to herself. "Not if his aim is to ply me with punch."

Even as she said it, she felt regrets about what couldn't be. Because the evening had been unlike any she'd ever known. Diverting, joyful.

With many *plops*.

She thought back to the sheer exuberance she'd felt dropping those bags of water. And before that, the dancing between the flaming candelabra, surrounded by men in grass skirts.

Hector would have hated every minute of it.

But thinking of him again made Jilly's chest tighten with fear and loathing, so she closed her eyes and clutched her coverlet close, only to slip into a dream about coconuts and drums.

CHAPTER FOUR

The next morning, a slant of sun—real sun—peeked through Stephen's window. He felt as comfortable and lazy as the ship's cat that used to sleep on top of his charts on his desk in his cabin.

"Late to bed, late to rise," he said out loud, his humor fully restored in spite of his rejection by Miss Jones the evening previous, "makes a man—"

Makes a man what?

Happy?

Relaxed?

He threw off his quilt, and—

The bed promptly collapsed on the floor.

What the devil?

Thoroughly jolted, he was now at a ridiculous angle, his head down, and his feet up. Gingerly, he rolled off the side of the mattress. He'd just bought the frame from a well-respected furniture dealer. It was sturdy and new, of the finest maple.

He leaned over to examine the legs at the top of the bed. Good God, they'd fallen through the floor! Two floor planks had given way. No doubt the gaping hole accounted for the shouts coming from below in the breakfast room, where Pratt, his former ship's cook, had been charged with the daily morning chore of frying up a rasher of bacon and several dozen eggs, as well as toasting a loaf of bread and making a pot of tea.

Stephen froze, wondering if his legs were to go through the ceiling next. Carefully, he walked over the seemingly sturdy planks to the door of his bedchamber and looked back at the slanted bed.

Odd, that. Very odd.

He shrugged. Nothing he could do about it at the moment. Might as well have breakfast, if there was any left that didn't have plaster in it.

"You've got woodworm in a beam." One of his friends winced as he looked up at the hole in the ceiling through pince-nez missing a lens; it had been lost last night in a playful brawl on the roof. "One rubbery creature fell on my toast."

Gad.

The other men looked near to being sick.

"I'm sure it's only in that portion of the beam," Lumley added, his face rather green and his eyes a bloodshot red. "Otherwise, we'd be seeing it everywhere. And we haven't."

Stephen eyed the row of beams above his head. The others, if in good condition, would support the ceiling very well, but his chest tightened, nevertheless. "The executor of my cousin's will told me the house was worn in places, but one doesn't look a gift horse in the mouth. I'd planned to have it inspected at my leisure."

Another friend added a few dollops of brandy to his

empty teacup and drained it. "I'm sure it's fine. Except for that one beam, it appears in excellent shape."

Frying pan in hand, Pratt was none the worse for wear. Always impeccably groomed, this morning he wore one of his more intricately embroidered waistcoats when he slid three eggs and a side of bacon onto Stephen's plate. "No house is, what you call, *perfetto*," he said, kissing the fingertips of his right hand, where several large golden rings sparkled.

The whole table seemed soothed by his smooth Italian accent.

"It's nothing I can't take care of." Stephen picked up his fork and looked round the company as if daring anyone to disagree.

"Aye," whispered one dapper fellow who'd had both eyebrows shaved off but didn't know it yet. "If I were you, Arrow, I'd hire a reputable carpenter, the best in London."

There was a low, miserable chorus of assents.

Stephen was aware none of the men at the table had done an ounce of hard labor in their lives. They were all sons of noblemen, accustomed to having everything done for them by servants and skilled laborers— especially Lumley, who was so rich, if a coin fell out of his pocket he could hire someone to pick it up for him if he wanted.

Stephen poured himself a glass of beer and gulped it down. "I can take care of my own house. Besides, I've nothing else to do while I wait to sell it."

Except win over a certain bookshop owner.

Not that *that* was going well.

"Did you happen to notice this street is unlucky, Arrow?" one of the men said in a wary voice. "A chimney sweep told me so last night when he directed me here. I was on Curzon and actually passed by Dreare Street without seeing the entrance. Someone needs to cut back those large holly bushes out there."

Stephen gave a short laugh. "Yes, I heard only yesterday the street's unlucky. But we've seen no evidence of it, have we?"

Everyone looked up at the hole in the ceiling.

"Forget that," Stephen said with disgust. "We're men of action, not puppets of Fate. One small rotten beam doesn't make a place unlucky."

The other bleary-eyed men of action agreed that this was so, but not until Stephen swept his intimidating captain's gaze over them.

"Speaking of action," said a freshly wakened gentleman limping through the breakfast room door with nothing on but breeches and mismatched boots, one a tasseled gray leather and the other a deep black. "Who's driving up this early in the day? I thought the next carriageload of lightskirts wasn't arriving until after sundown."

Stephen went to the window and peered out. A respectably dressed young woman was getting out of a coach, and she was followed by an older man and woman.

Who were they?

The young lady wore a cape over a fussy white gown with bold green braid and too many matching plumes atop her bonnet. She looked up at the house, and Stephen saw she had a sweet face but an unfortunate squint. A square-faced older woman with broad shoulders spoke crossly to her, which no doubt was why the girl's smile instantly disappeared.

The man had three chins, an overdone waistcoat, and a silk hat squashed so hard on his head, his ears stuck out. He looked about him with an air of superiority that made Stephen dislike him on sight.

Stephen strode to the front door. "How may I help you?" he called out to them, rather dreading their answer. All three had a determined look about them.

He was in no mood to deal with house buyers today, not with that wormy beam and the chunks of plaster on the dining room table. And it didn't sit well with him that Miss Jones was outside her store, no doubt pretending to wash her windows in order to spy on the goings-on at his house.

The girl smiled broadly. "We're your family, Th-tephen Arrow." She spoke with a great lisp. "Dith-tant, of course, on your father's th-ide. But family nonetheless."

His heart clenched. The only person he considered real family was dead. Mama had been gone several years now, and there was no one else save that cousin who'd left him the house, and he was on his father's side of the family. If these people were, too, they weren't family by his definition of *family*.

He prepared himself to dismiss the trio, but as he'd learned the value of diplomacy in the navy, he'd do his best to be halfway charming about it.

Now the gentleman looked at Stephen with a haughty eye. "I am Sir Ned Hartley. This is my wife, Lady Hartley, and our daughter, Miss Hartley. My third cousin is the late Earl of Stanhope."

Stephen, at very guarded attention, knew very well who the Earl of Stanhope was. "Your point is?"

Sir Ned's lips thinned. "My point is we're staying here with you while we're in Town."

Stephen scoffed. "Hardly."

So much for diplomacy.

Lady Hartley gasped, and Sir Ned narrowed his eyes. "You've received notice from your attorney. He assured us you signed for the letter."

Stephen blinked, but just once.

He *had* signed for a letter. It had come the day he'd arrived at the house, but he'd forgotten all about it as he'd been working hard at opening a stubborn cask of Highland whisky with a very dull blade. He did remember inviting the courier in for some drinks. The man had obliged and stayed half the evening.

Stephen had no idea where the letter was at the moment.

"The letter stated that we plan to stay at 34 Dreare Street for the length of the Season," boomed Lady Hartley.

Stephen clenched his jaw to keep from wincing. Surely he could find something to like about the woman. Her thunderous voice certainly complemented her broad-beamed physique and thrusting bosoms the size of world globes, the kind found in schools around the country. And education was a good thing, wasn't it?

He knew he was grasping at straws, but it was the kindest observation he could produce about her.

"You can't, I'm afraid," Stephen explained. "I plan to sell the house immediately."

"Immediately?" asked Sir Ned. "You have a buyer?"

"Not yet, but I soon will." It was his latest mission, to find that buyer. "There will be people traipsing in and out all day, no doubt, kicking the corners of the fireplaces, peering into all the rooms. We're in Mayfair, so I expect someone will come along and purchase the place within the week."

"But Cousin," Miss Hartley lisped, her voice tinged with disappointment, "it's our opportunity to get to know each other."

Stephen's heart sank like an anchor disappearing into the briny deep. Miss Hartley had that look in her eye—the one that suggested she might already be halfway in love with him. He called it the Bedazzled Virgin look. He was old enough now to be quite tired of it. It was the reason he avoided Almack's and other places where sweet young girls gathered.

Sir Ned yawned. "As for the sale," he drawled, "I don't anticipate a buyer any time soon. Everyone knows Dreare Street is unlucky."

"If you know that," Stephen asked testily, "then why would you stay here?"

Lady Hartley laughed. "My husband doesn't protect his inheritance by being careless with his money. If he can save a tuppence, he will."

Sir Ned beamed as if he'd been highly complimented. "Yes, well, there's plenty of room here for all of us. We hardly have to encounter each other. No doubt we keep different company." He looked Stephen up and down as if he were riffraff. "You can take your meals at your club."

"I prefer to eat at home," Stephen said. "Not that it matters to you. We've had an enlightening conversation, but I'll have to ask you to be on your way. I'm expecting a houseful of guests later today."

Feminine houseguests who enjoyed making merry at all hours and for no reason at all, unlike his staid neighbor, Miss Jones.

"I brought another copy of the letter in the event you'd make trouble." Sir Ned pulled a piece of paper out of his pocket and handed it to Stephen.

It hurt his eyes to read the lines, but he scanned it and saw that it was authentic. In it, the attorney declared that the baronet, his wife, and daughter were permitted by a codicil in the will of Stephen's deceased cousin to stay at the house during the Season.

His chest tightened with resentment.

Lady Hartley tossed her head. "We hear you've been named one of Prinny's Impossible Bachelors." A flock of birds flew out of a tree at her earsplitting pronouncement. "But I'm warning you, Cousin"—she pointed a finger at him—"all manner of merrymaking must cease immediately. Miranda will be sheltered from wayward behavior. In fact, shame on you for not wearing a cravat."

Stephen looked down. Yes, he was only in a shirt and breeches, but dammit all, it was only noon.

"Although I'm sure you mean well, madam," he said evenly, "what I wear is none of your business. And I've no intention of letting you stay, even if we are"—he swallowed—"very distantly related."

Sir Ned stuck out his lower lip. "Well, we've no intention of leaving." He held out both arms, and his wife and daughter took them. Together, all three began walking up the stairs toward the front door.

"We've rights, and we know the law," sniffed Lady Hartley.

Miss Hartley—Miranda—looked down at the ground, her cheeks pink. Perhaps she was embarrassed by her parents' effrontery.

Stephen sighed. And here he thought being given a house as a gift was a lucky thing! Which reminded him—

He might still have a way out of this quandary.

"Just this morning," he said, "my bed fell through the ceiling. I can't vouch for the safety of all the beams."

Sir Ned and Lady Hartley exchanged glances.

"So much for your immediate sale." Sir Ned chuckled. "No one will want to buy an unsafe house."

Touché.

Stephen felt grimmer than he had in years. "But surely that's enough to convince you to go to a hotel."

Lady Hartley looked at him with something akin to pity. "Do you really think a man who's prudent with his funds would be cowed by such a small crisis?"

"I suppose not," Stephen said through gritted teeth

just as Sir Ned forced himself between Stephen and the door.

Stephen was so stunned at the man's loutish behavior that Lady Hartley pushed past him as well, her breasts shoving hard against his chest, a gleam of something quite recognizable—and unsavory—in her eye.

He was left alone with Miss Hartley.

"Where are the servants?" she asked in a meek voice, her *s*'s hissing.

Poor thing. She probably had no idea her mother was a lascivious creature.

"I've only Pratt, my cook," Stephen replied. "And he's inside, plucking chickens."

She lofted her brows. "But who shall watch after us?"

"Captain Arrow does a splendid job of that," came an amused feminine voice from across the way. "Why, he's had many a guest over the past week, and not one of them appears unhappy in the least. He's a fine host."

Miss Jones.

Stephen narrowed her eyes at her. "Thanks for the recommendation."

"My pleasure," she said with an angelic smile. She held another rag in her hand, and her jet-black hair fell in little tendrils about her face.

Miss Hartley squinted Miss Jones's way. "I don't believe we've met," she said, not unkindly.

Miss Jones put a hand on her chest. "Why, I'm Miss Jones, the owner of Hodgepodge, which I hope will soon be the most visited bookstore in London. Do come by and take a look at our selection."

"I'm Mith Hartley." She blushed. "My father says books are for daydreamers."

"Not to contradict your father, but is there something wrong with daydreaming?" Miss Jones asked with an annoying amount of spirit. "Whether you're lost in a fairy tale or in a theory on chemistry, daydreaming about possibilities is rather enjoyable, in my view."

Miss Hartley folded her hands. "Father says he prefer I gain wisdom and experience through life."

"Then you've come to the right place," replied Miss Jones with a cheerful grin. "You'll get a lot of that sort of thing over there at Captain Arrow's."

"Is that so?" Miss Hartley asked excitedly, her *s*'s becoming even more pronounced.

"Most emphatically," Miss Jones answered with a pert smile.

Stephen was feeling less cheerful by the second. "Shall we go in, Miss Hartley?" He held out his arm.

"Yeth," she lisped. "It's unfortunate Mith Jones thpeaks her own mind and doesn't look fashionable in the least. I like her, but Mama wouldn't approve."

Stephen was tempted to laugh at the ridiculous nature of that comment, but he'd no one to appreciate his feeling, except Miss Jones, and she was in his bad books for interfering, wasn't she?

He took a look back at her.

She winked.

Good God. He'd been winked at by women before, but it was because they'd wanted either him or the coins in his pocket. Sometimes both. But she was mocking him, wasn't she?

It simply wasn't done. He was either too commanding or too charming to be mocked except by his very
closest friends, Lumley, Drummond (formerly Lord
Maxwell), and Traemore.

Stephen's spirits hit dead low, like the tide. But he
couldn't wait for time to restore them. He must take
action.

First things first. He'd assess the situation with the
Hartleys further. So without any sign of the reluctance
he felt, he held the front door open for Miss Hartley
and forced himself to follow her into the breakfast
room. He entered just as Sir Ned held a jewel-encrusted
quizzing glass to his bulbous eye and raked the company lounging about the table with a scornful glance.

"Begone with you, gentlemen," the jowly baronet
ordered in an ugly voice. "And don't bother gathering
up your things."

"We've nothing to gather," retorted one of the men
with a chuckle, and looked down at his own rumpled
shirt. "This is a party. We slept in the clothes we
came in."

"You're disgraceful heathens, aren't you?" Lady
Hartley announced with keen interest.

Sir Ned lowered his quizzing glass and bestowed a
fawning smile upon the party. "Demme. Didn't notice
you're wearing boots by Hoby and coats by Weston.
See here, lads, sorry about the rude send-off. Stay as
long as you'd like. I've got a daughter here to marry
off, and she has a large dowry. Most of you pups from
good families waste all your blunt on extravagance

and could use an infusion of wealth, couldn't you? Miranda's your girl."

Miss Hartley blinked several times and went to the window to look out, but Stephen guessed she was really attempting to disguise her embarrassment.

He understood her angst very well. This couple was truly awful—

And both he and Miss Hartley were related to them.

The houseguests' expressions, depending on the measure of alcohol still flowing through their veins, registered varying degrees of shock and disgust at Sir Ned's vulgar speech and Lady Hartley's indifference to her daughter's comfort.

There was the quick pushing back of chairs by a few alert young men, followed by the slower rising from the table of the still impaired, and then the tromping of feet heading past Stephen toward the front door.

All his friends were leaving.

And as they streamed by him, he told himself, *There's no such thing as bad luck.*

No such thing.

He trailed after the last man, the one limping in the mismatched boots, and wished he could leave, too.

On the front step, one of the more sober fellows slapped Stephen's shoulder. "You poor sod. You'll be married off to that Miranda in no time, eh?"

Stephen was too depressed to make a reply.

Another friend stopped and shook his hand for far too long. "This is a bad business, old chum," he hiccuped.

"That it is," Stephen said glumly, hardly noticing that his fingers were still caught in an enthusiastic pumping of hands.

"Down the steps now, Bertie." Lumley shoved the man aside and turned to Stephen. "What's the world coming to when anyone with a piece of paper from an attorney can simply walk into a house and take it over? I'll send a message to the fancy girls—tell them not to bother coming this evening."

Stephen watched his friends leave as fast as their pickled legs could carry them, some faster than others. But all slowed to an amble once they were far enough away from his house, away from the unwelcome house-guests.

He sighed. It was a damned shame his house party was to end well before its time.

And then he had another bad feeling, one that made him look to his right.

Miss Jilly Jones was now inside Hodgepodge, staring out the shop window, her mouth agape. When their gazes locked, she pressed her lips shut and looked boldly at him, then slowly lifted the rag she kept perpetually in her hands and rubbed a slow, triumphant circle around the panes of glass, blocking her face from his sight.

Good thing. He was in no mood to deal with the smug smile he could swear he saw curving her lips.

CHAPTER FIVE

Jilly stayed busy in the midst of having no customers by washing her windows, dusting her books, and baking scones for the neighbors. She left the scones on their doorsteps with a brief note of introduction and the announcement that complimentary tea and scones would be provided to anyone who entered Hodgepodge that week. After that, they'd be sold for next to nothing to discerning readers who should feel free to sip, eat, and read to their hearts' content at the bookstore during business hours.

When she wasn't attempting to drum up business, she was writing a novel. She'd only just begun, but it was going to have a dastardly captain in it who married the ignorant daughter of a mushroom—who wore a silk hat smashed upon his ears so that they stuck out—and a giant woman who spoke so loudly, windows rattled.

Quill to mouth, Jilly mused on what their dozen children would look like. She already knew how they'd behave: rudely. And they'd be cursed with seriously good looks so that no one ever felt sorry for them. And people *should* feel sorry for them, Jilly felt with all her heart, for these children would have sad excuses for parents.

Perhaps the woman who lived next door to the children would take them under her wing and teach them manners—she'd even take them to the seashore each year because she would be a very rich bookshop owner patronized by all the gentry and the Prince Regent himself.

Diligently, Jilly wrote a whole half page describing the scene in which the captain and his awful wife forgot Christmas Day. But when the cuckoo clock chimed two, she looked up from her scribbling. Otis was out, for far too long, looking for the perfect pair of secondhand shoes to go with his pink and white striped waistcoat, the one he'd found at Captain Arrow's house the night of the theatrics. It had been adorning a bust of Admiral Lord Nelson on the stair landing, and when no gentleman there could claim the illustrious garment as his own, Otis had taken it with Captain Arrow's blessing.

Poor Otis. Books weren't his passion. Fashion was. But he was trying, and he was always so supportive of her.

Jilly heard the shop door open and wished she could be entirely excited at receiving a customer, but part of her was always prepared to see Hector. Yes, it was a shame, but it was the way things were. She knew as long as she lived, she'd never be completely free of him.

So when a breathtakingly lovely girl peeked in the door, she released a discreet sigh of relief. The girl had rich brown hair, the color of chocolate, pulled back in a luscious, loose knot, and a dimple on either side of her mouth. Her best asset was her eyes, which were large and sea green.

"Hello," she said to Jilly with a shy smile. "I'm Susan Cook. I live down the street."

Jilly put her quill down and stood. "It's lovely to meet you, Miss Cook." She smiled, too, excited that someone—especially someone other than Hector— had come into Hodgepodge! She was beginning to despair that anyone on the street was friendly.

A small boy, no more than four, popped out from behind Susan. He had her same button nose and a wide grin. "I'm Thomas," he said in a robust manner, although Jilly couldn't help noticing his legs were thin. "You make good scones. Could we have some more, please? And some butter and jam, too, if you don't mind."

Susan's mouth became a round O. So did Jilly's. And then they both burst into laughter. Thomas did, too, although Jilly could tell he had no idea what was so funny.

"Thomas!" Susan rubbed his head with a palm. Her tone was stern but fond. "We don't go about begging. Be glad with what you got from Miss Jones. You don't ask for *more*."

"I don't mind a bit," said Jilly. "I promised them to anyone who walked in, didn't I?" She couldn't help wondering if the lad got enough to eat. In fact, she was so charmed by Thomas's cheeks turning pink with embarrassment she said, "Wait here. I've not only got scones ready at the moment, I've got something else."

She went to the rear of the store and opened a door between two bookshelves, which led onto a small corridor. On the right was her office and down from that, Otis's bedchamber. To her left was the staircase leading to the living quarters above the shop: her bedchamber and a spacious front room she shared with Otis each evening.

Picking up an orange sitting next to a ledger in her office, she brought it out to Thomas. "Here," she said. "My friend Otis got this for me as a special treat, but I'd much rather give it to you."

Thomas's eyes widened. "Thank you very much."

"You don't have to do that, Miss Jones," said Susan warmly.

"Please call me Jilly." She smiled again. "And it's my pleasure. I hope Thomas and I will become fast friends."

Thomas clutched the orange in both hands and beamed up at her.

"I can see you already are." Susan sighed and looked shyly at Jilly. "I hope we can become friends, too. I'd love for you to call me Susan."

"Oh!" Jilly's heart swelled with happiness and she squeezed her new friend's hand. "I hope we can, as well."

Susan's mouth thinned into almost a grimace. "I don't know if you'll want to, Miss Jones, once you realize"—she looked back at Thomas and then at her again—"Thomas doesn't have a father. We're alone in the world, you see. I never married." She swallowed. "I would have if—"

She broke off and hung her head. "My family won't talk to me. I—I'm trying to make it on my own as a seamstress. I tell everyone I'm widowed, but it's not true." When she looked back up, her eyes were glassy with unshed tears. "I don't know why I told you the truth. Maybe it's because you're the first woman on the street to show me any kindness. Bringing us scones like that."

Jilly sighed and shook her head. "Women can be hard on their own sex, can't they?"

"Yes, they can," Susan agreed.

"It's all right," Jilly soothed her. "Of course we can be friends. I'm a woman alone, too, if you don't count Otis, an old family friend who's more like an uncle to me. He'd protect me from harm if he could, but some-how . . . I think I might protect him more."

They both chuckled together again.

Susan wiped at her eyes. "It's a relief to be honest with someone, I can tell you that."

Jilly felt a pang of guilt. She wished she could be honest, but it was simply too dangerous for her to do so.

Thomas tugged on his mother's skirts. "When can we go, Mummy? I want to see the tree with the new green leaves."

"Oh, yes," Susan said. "Spring's here, thank good-ness."

"Yes, and more leaves will pop out soon, won't they?" Jilly knelt before Thomas. "And have you no-ticed? The birds are singing."

Thomas leaned close to Jilly's ear. "No one sings like Mummy at bedtime."

Jilly couldn't help giving him a hug. "I'm sure she's the best singer in the world."

Thomas nodded solemnly. "She is."

Susan glowed with the contentment of a happy mother. "We'll come again," she said at the door.

"Please do." Jilly dared to give Susan a tentative hug, which her new friend returned unequivocally.

"See you soon," Susan said, beaming.

When mother and son left hand in hand, Jilly looked after them with a twinge of envy. She'd wanted a child. But Hector . . . Hector hadn't been able to father one. She guessed it was probably the main reason he'd been angry at her all the time.

It wasn't meant to be, that stalwart voice in her head reminded her.

And a good thing, too, because Hector shouldn't have had any children. He'd have been an awful father.

She gulped, banished all thoughts of the family she'd always wanted but would never have, and put away her quill and paper. She wasn't in the mood to write anymore, but what could she do now? Hodgepodge was as ready as it would ever be for customers. It was so clean, she could eat off the floor. The inventory was quite impressive, as well. The books ranged from old Latin texts to the most recent novels. The corner which held a few cheery tables and chairs was pristine. Her small living space upstairs was tidy, and a beef stew she and Otis would share for dinner simmered over a low fire.

Everything was in order, even the street. Outside, it was eerily quiet without Captain Arrow's friends around. She couldn't say she missed them—no, indeed. But until now she hadn't noticed how no one came down Dreare Street if they could help it. And the neighbors kept to themselves.

Lady Duchamp, Jilly was sorry to say, lived directly across from her. The old hag occupied the biggest mansion on Dreare Street and kept numerous servants. Every morning Jilly saw one of her footmen bring the carriage around and help his mistress into it. She always returned almost an hour later.

Where did she go? Jilly wondered.

And then there was her new friend Susan, who lived at the other end of Dreare Street and ran her seamstress shop, which appeared to have as few customers as Hodgepodge did.

Jilly had also seen a man who appeared to be an artist lugging a bag of rolled canvas home to his shabby studio. There were several colorless families, too, who lived in colorless houses and didn't appear interested in her or themselves. They were just existing, she guessed, going to work, coming home—the ones that had to work, that is. She'd seen a couple of these bland families who were well off enough, judging by their carriages and clothing and number of servants, but they didn't look *happy*. Or excited about anything.

Every sort of person lived on Dreare Street, she thought. Rich, poor, working class, and titled. Until now, all of them had seemed depressed—except for Captain Arrow. But now, he did, too. His face when those encroaching people had walked into his house had been rigid with disapproval. Yet they were still there, weren't they?

Too bad Dreare Street wasn't a thriving, bustling neighborhood street like the other ones Jilly had been on in Mayfair. When she'd inspected the building, she'd been assured that the pedestrian traffic was so low because it had been raining buckets the two days she'd come by to visit.

Ironically, the rain was what had made her fall in love with Hodgepodge. Everything had seemed so cozy inside. She'd even felt safe from Hector. It was why she'd told the broker she'd seen enough.

The shop on Dreare Street was to be her home, her safe haven. It was her portal to a new life.

Now she walked outside to straighten her flower beds. Thank goodness, she thought, that Susan had come in today. Jilly had been about to give in to the feeling that her instincts had been wrong about buying Hodgepodge. She was so glad she hadn't surrendered to such a gloomy thought—

At least not yet.

Bad luck.

All of Stephen's friends said he was having *terribly* bad luck.

"It's so bad you need to do a special tribal dance or some such thing to reverse it," Lumley said at their club the afternoon of the Hartleys' arrival at Stephen's house. "I think you picked it up in the islands."

"No, it's that street," another friend conjectured. "It rots. After all, it's called Dreare Street."

"As in *dreary*." A third friend flicked Stephen on the side of the head.

Stephen brushed him off like a pesky fly.

"Abysmal Street would be a better name," another friend commented, laughing loudly in his ear.

Stephen had gone to his club for comfort, and he'd left with a ringing ear, a throbbing temple, and the conviction that perhaps his friends were—dare he say it?—right.

For the first time in as long as he could remember, he was in a quandary that didn't seem to have a solution. The baronet and his wife were cold, humorless people, scheming to marry off their daughter, probably to him—and they were ensconced at his house.

His private abode.

The place where he wanted to be himself . . . to do what *he* wanted to do.

And Miss Hartley! Well, she was the last woman on earth he'd want to marry, no matter how sweet and lacking in guile she was.

In disgust he'd gone to his club to forget them all. But that hadn't happened, obviously. When he returned home before dusk, he found Sir Ned and Lady Hartley waiting for him, like spiders in a web, in the drawing room.

"We want to tell you something of importance," said Sir Ned. "After a discussion with my wife, we've decided that Miranda will entertain your suit. Marrying

you would save us a great deal of time and expense.
We could go home tomorrow and stop in Canterbury
for the special license."

Stephen was silent with shock, but then he thought
to ask, "Miss Hartley, don't you care to experience
the Marriage Mart?"

Miss Hartley blushed and stammered, "W-who am
I to question my parents?"

"Don't worry about not being her equal, Arrow,"
Sir Ned said. "I have enough money and titles to
make up for your lack of either."

"We can fudge the truth," said Lady Hartley. "On
tour, at least. We can claim you're a baron or earl and
no one would ever know the difference."

"I'm not interested," Stephen said. "I'm already . . .
pursuing someone else."

"Who?" asked Miss Hartley.

He glanced out the window and saw Miss Jones
working in her flower beds.

"Miss Jones," he said, and immediately realized
his desperation had caused a lapse in his usually im-
peccable judgment.

No one would choose Miss Jilly Jones, the owner
of Hodgepodge, as a possible wife. She was too unmanageable. Wives were supposed to be meek, which
was why he'd never marry. Stephen wasn't fond of
meek women. They bored him.

"I'm sorry," he corrected himself. "I meant to say
I'm interested in pursuing, ah, another woman. Several doors down. Miss Jones's *friend*."

"What's her name?" Miss Hartley lisped.

Stephen started. He hadn't thought of a name, of course. He was about to say "Sarah Pimsdale," which sounded like the name of a perfectly manageable miss when Sir Ned interrupted him.

"Right," the baronet said with a cocky grin. "Too late to cover it up. You want to marry Miss Jones." He looked at his wife. "Who's Miss Jones?"

Lady Hartley merely shrugged and stared daggers at the world. It seemed the news had put her in an awful pout.

Miss Hartley rushed to the window. "You're looking at her right now, aren't you, Captain?" She pointed at his ebony-haired neighbor, who was now pulling weeds. "*She's* the one who's stolen your heart. Miss Joneth, the bookseller."

"Before you even had a chance to get here, dear Miranda," Lady Hartley muttered, then turned to her husband. "Do something, Ned."

Sir Ned's chins began an almost imperceptible jiggle, and a keen light shone from his eyes. "Right you are, my love." He adjusted his coat and stood. "I'm off to see the lady, Captain Arrow. Take us to see Miss Jones."

"Why should I?" He went into full-fledged defensive mode, backing up toward the drawing room door, and then to the front door, to block Sir Ned from leaving.

"Stand aside," said Sir Ned, approaching him with a determined, if very short, stride.

What was Stephen supposed to do? If Sir Ned challenged him, he certainly wasn't going to fight the man. He was too old. It would be unsporting of him to land the stubborn fool a facer.

Right now he could only hope the baronet would be intimidated enough to turn around.

But he obviously wasn't. He tapped Stephen in the chest. "I want to become acquainted with the woman who's blinded you to Miranda's charms."

"Absolutely not," Stephen said, looking down at him. "Miss Jones has no idea I'm pursuing her."

Lady Hartley marched over to him and angled her head at Miss Hartley. "Enough with pursuits, Captain. You can stand completely still with Miranda. She's right here, waiting. And you won't have to worry about lining your pockets before declaring yourself."

"I'd really rather you stay out of my private business." Stephen glared at them both.

"Let's go, Arrow," Sir Ned urged him.

Stephen realized he must change tactics. His unfortunate relative would find a way to confront Miss Jones sooner or later. So he opened the front door a crack. "I'll let you through," he told the baronet, "but if you interfere with my plans to woo her, there will be hell to pay. Am I making myself clear?"

Finally, Sir Ned paused. But he wasn't terribly cowed. He still had a fervent light in his eyes. "Very well," he acceded. "But if I find she can't hold a candle to my Miranda, I'm going to sit up with you tonight, lad, and we'll discuss your future over a bottle of port. You could have quite a cushy life as my son-in-law."

Stephen couldn't bear to hear any more. "I'm going to let you out now," he said. "But first, I'd like a few moments with her myself. Then you may join us."

He opened the door all the way and headed to Hodgepodge, Sir Ned gasping behind him.

Stephen whirled around. "Remember," he warned the baronet, "wait here."

Sir Ned actually stopped. Now all Stephen had to do was tell Miss Jones to go along with his ruse that he had plans to pursue her. Pursue her for what, he couldn't say. She wouldn't approve of a scorching flirtation, and marriage was out of the question.

He'd remain as vague as possible.

It shouldn't be too difficult.

Good God, of course it would be difficult!

The street, as usual, was deserted. Miss Jones had left her flowers and gone back inside.

Stephen strode into Hodgepodge so fast, the door flew back on its hinges. "Where is she?" he asked Otis.

Otis looked up with a grin. "Hello, Captain. We're closed, of course. But you're always welcome. Things have been quiet at your house this afternoon."

Miss Jones, who was sweeping the floor, looked over her shoulder at him. "A refreshing change," she added.

Now was not the time to spar with her, so Stephen let the comment pass.

He was pleased to see she looked almost disappointed.

"How may I help you, Captain?" she asked coolly, and put aside her broom.

He raked a hand through his hair, reluctant to reveal to her that he was in an untenable situation. "My unexpected—and unwelcome—guests have ruined all my party plans," he confessed. "It's because of them that I'm calling upon you now."

"Do tell," Otis urged him, a concerned wrinkle on his brow.

"It's not good." Stephen braced himself and looked Miss Jones square in the eye. "They want to marry me off to their daughter, so I told them I was interested in pursuing your acquaintance." He inhaled a breath, then went on. "Of course, they think I mean marriage."

Her eyes flew wide and she put a hand over her heart. "That's impossible!"

"I understand I didn't ask your permission to tell such an untruth," Stephen said with an attempt at a grin, "but surely the idea's not *that* outrageous."

"Oh, yes it is." Miss Jones's face was bright red.

Otis looked almost as unsteady as his mistress. "I do believe I'll brush my spare coat," he said, and left through the rear door of the shop.

"I heard today from Otis, who heard it from a shopkeeper on Brook Street, that you're an Impossible Bachelor," Miss Jones said, her fists on her hips. "That title only confirms my suspicions about you."

Stephen felt a momentary pique. "It's not my fault Prinny chose me for the title, but what has that to do with anything anyway?"

"First of all, you'd never be pursuing any woman with any remotely honorable intentions," she replied instantly, "and second, I wouldn't in a million years *allow* myself to be pursued by you."

"Oh, is that all? We can work around *that*."

"Oh, really?" Miss Jones picked up the broom again and held it close to her chest. "What you're asking of me is too much, Captain." Her voice was fervent with disapproval. "I can't possibly allow it."

He'd been prepared for her to object. "They're here for only a little while," he soothed her. "Life with them is going to be difficult enough as it is, but if they think I'm eligible to court their daughter, it will be so much worse. I told them you have no idea I want to pursue you. You may act ignorant of the whole matter."

"If that's true, why did you bother even telling me?"

She wouldn't give him an inch, his shrewd neighbor. "Because I wanted you to understand why I'll be acting rather *warm* toward you in their presence. And there's always the chance the obnoxious Sir Ned might say something denigrating about my supposed quest to have you. He'd no doubt like to dissuade your interest. I didn't want you caught off guard if that happens."

Miss Jones's brows almost crossed over her nose. "Why don't you simply move out while they're here?"

"I can't. I've got repairs on the house to make before I sell it. I've got to stay."

She said nothing, merely pinched her mouth shut.

"I know you have no reason to help me," he said, "but I appeal to your sense of charity. And if there's ever anything I can do for you in return, I promise, on my word of honor, I will."

"No," she said into his eyes.

He would wager it was a favorite phrase of hers.

Sir Ned strode into the store then, the tips of his ears pink. "So, Miss Jones, you're the favored one," he announced.

She gave him a warm but wary smile. "May I help you?"

The newcomer looked her up and down. "I understand Captain Arrow has his eye—"

"On those atlases. *Do* go and look them over for me, Sir Ned." Stephen spun the man around and gave him a light shove in the direction of the oversized tomes.

Thankfully, the man, once pushed, kept going, like a boat shoved away from a dock.

When the baronet was out of hearing, Stephen returned to his appeal to Miss Jones. "Please," he begged her in a low whisper. "Please go along with it. Otherwise, my life will be a living hell."

"Not forever, it won't." Her cheeks were rosier than usual. "Besides, there are other women you could have chosen for your imaginary pursuit. How about one of your fancy ladies?"

He stared at her, at a loss to answer the question. "I saw you outside with your daffodils, and at that crucial moment, it never occurred to me to think of anyone else. Of course, several seconds later I did, but by then it was too late. They'd latched onto you."

He wouldn't tell her he'd been thinking about her before he even saw her—all day, as a matter of fact.

She stared at him a long moment and then sighed. "Very well, Captain. I suppose saying yes won't do any harm. I can feign ignorance of your intentions, after all. But I'll have you know—I do this with a great deal of misgiving."

He released a pleased sigh. "Thank you."

Now that the pressure was off, he wasn't able to help noticing she looked extremely fetching in her pale pink gown.

"But someday soon I might need a favor, and you'll do whatever I ask," she said, "or I shall tell your houseguests the truth, that you're making this charade up."

"You're blackmailing me." He could hardly credit it.

"Don't worry." She gave him an impish smile. "What could I ask from you? Not much, I assure you. But I shall enjoy thinking on it."

"Captain," called Sir Ned excitedly, "what's the farthest place you sailed on your last voyage?"

Stephen never took his eyes off Jilly's. "The Horn, Sir Ned, the Horn," he called back to the man.

Looking rather smug, Miss Jones stood waiting for his answer.

"Under duress," he murmured, "I accept your offer. But I have a requirement of my own."

"And that is?" She was toying with him. And toying with him was damned near close to flirting, even if she didn't recognize that fact.

"If you want my assistance," he said, "—and you must, for judging from your expression, the prospect of subjugating me to your whims absolutely delights you—you can't tell the neighbors my pursuit of you is contrived."

She looked up at the ceiling then back at him. "Very well. I agree. Except for Otis. I tell him everything."

"Agreed."

They shook hands quickly, at the precise moment the door to the shop was thrown open.

Stephen dreaded turning around. What if it were the crying Miranda? Or her moaning mother?

Thank God it was only Lady Duchamp. "Captain Arrow, the top-heavy matron on your front doorstep is spitting nonsense," she drawled, "something about your being here to pursue Miss Jones. I shall feel compelled to box her husband's gigantic ears if she's told me a lie."

Stephen drew himself up. "It's no one's business but mine and Miss Jones's, my lady."

Lady Duchamp looked at Miss Jones. "Has he proposed marriage?"

"No." Miss Jones's mouth was a bit white.

"Well?" Lady Duchamp stared accusingly at Stephen. "Whyever not, if you're pursuing her? Do you have reservations, young man, about commitment?"

"As I said, my lady, it's—"

"Hellooo? Is she in here?" Lady Hartley thankfully interrupted, her voice calling like a foghorn from outside. *"Miss Jooones!"*

Miss Hartley, her hands clamped to her ears, peered over her mother's shoulder into the shop. "Oh, ith lovely!" she exclaimed.

Lady Duchamp curled her lip at the new arrivals.

"I don't consort with mushrooms," she said. "I'm leaving."

Miss Hartley blanched as Lady Duchamp made her way past her by nudging her in the stomach with the tiny porcelain woman at the top of her frightening walking stick.

But Lady Hartley batted the cane away. "Get that thing away from me!"

"Watch yourself!" Lady Duchamp warned her.

For a few seconds, a small struggle at the top of the stairs between both titled ladies took Stephen's attention away from Miss Jones's delicate profile, which he'd been admiring while she wasn't looking.

But the old harridan and her swinging cane were soon out of the way, and Lady Hartley and Miss Hartley finally entered the shop. Miss Hartley smiled sweetly at Miss Jones, but her mother eyed Miss Jones's modest pink gown and appeared to find it wanting.

"It's come to my attention you're the object of Captain Arrow's pursuit," Lady Hartley said. "Are you?"

Miss Jones deigned to smile at her. "I don't know. Am I?"

"Impertinent girl!" The matron reddened, but then her gaze turned hopeful. "You mean you're not the captain's intended?"

Miss Hartley bit her lip and appeared most interested in the answer, as well.

Bedazzled virgins often were.

Miss Jones looked at him with a twinkle in her eye—a most unexpected twinkle—and shrugged.

"Captain Arrow has never declared himself," she said in a breezy manner.

Lady Hartley turned to Stephen. "Well?"

"A man likes to choose his own opportunities," he said grimly. "*Not* be pushed about by interfering women."

"All I know," said Miss Jones to the ladies with a confidential air, "is that he follows me about like a lovesick puppy." She giggled. "He's quite adorable, if you like that sort of thing."

Lovesick puppy?

Adorable?

Stephen narrowed his eyes. Miss Jones had adjusted rather well to their so-called impossible and unwelcome circumstances, hadn't she?

Miss Hartley giggled. Lady Hartley looked at him suspiciously.

Which wouldn't do at all. The two women mustn't guess this was all a ruse. He was livid, but he did his best to look like an adorable, lovesick puppy—without losing an ounce of his captain's authority or his bachelor aloofness.

"You appear quite ill, Captain Arrow," said Miss Jones, her voice concerned but her eyes alight with amusement. "Are you all right?"

"Never better," he choked out, and sped off.

He would wring Miss Jones's neck later.

He found Sir Ned with his nose still in the atlas. "Purchase the thing," Stephen told him. "And leave."

Instead, Sir Ned trotted to the counter, the book

hugged close to his chest. "I think I shall simply borrow this book for a while. I'm living right next door, after all."

"I'm sorry, but I need to *sell* that atlas," Miss Jones said.

Sir Ned glared at her, dropped the book on a table, and stalked out of the shop, his wife and daughter right behind him.

Miss Jones looked at Stephen with dismay. "Sir Ned and Lady Hartley are awful."

"Yes, they are."

She didn't even seem to hear him agree with her, which was a rarity she should enjoy. But now that everyone had left, she was like a balloon with no air. In their short, fiery acquaintance, Stephen had never seen her so despondent.

He didn't like seeing her this way. She was far too appealing to sink so low.

"I think it's best you go now, Captain," she said quietly.

He felt guilt slap into him like whitecaps on the side of a dinghy. "You may not want to masquerade as the object of my affections," he said, "but you certainly got some enjoyment out of the charade a moment ago. So why are you upset now?"

She took out that damned dusting cloth and began to wipe it over a tabletop. "Because this deception of yours was thrust upon me. It's a waste of my valuable time, and I regret allowing you to interfere with the running of Hodgepodge."

"Miss Jones, forgive me for noticing," he said gently, "but it's not as if you're bombarded with customers."

She wheeled on him. "I know that. But I'd rather spend time on my priorities than on yours. I couldn't care less if Sir Ned and Lady Hartley attempt to snag you as their daughter's husband. But I do care about making my bookstore a thriving business. And—"

"And what?"

She bit her lip. "It's highly improper, our arrangement. What if—"

"What if what?"

She shook her head. "Never mind."

Gently, he took her arm. "Are you worried I might take advantage of you? Perhaps even kiss you?"

He could see her swallow. "Would you?" she whispered, and looked up at him.

A taut silence stretched between them.

"No." He did want to kiss her, of course. "I would do nothing without your permission."

She nodded, apparently relieved, which was a new circumstance for him. Most women craved his kisses.

"Let's look on the bright side," he said. "Perhaps we could both work to increase your business. Helping Hodgepodge thrive would help me, as well."

Her face brightened. "How?"

"I could do some chores for you. My houseguests will see I'm here . . . which will confirm their belief that I'm pursuing you."

He thought about his beam that needed fixing. It

would have to wait another day or two, maybe even a week, before he could get back to it.

Miss Jones appeared to consider the idea. "I can't think of anything I need, except—"

She closed her mouth again.

"What?" he asked her.

"It doesn't matter. I need some carpentry work. But I've no supplies and won't be able to afford any for a while."

"I've got a shed full of tools and whatnot. What did you require exactly?"

He saw a spark of hope flare in her eye. "A window ledge," she said. "I want to put books in the window for passersby to look at."

"And a cat," he added. "Everyone will want to come in and pet it."

"Yes. I *love* cats." She was leaning on the counter, looking out onto the street. He thought she looked quite enchanting, the way she spun a tendril of sooty hair wistfully around her finger and smiled at the thought of a cat. "I haven't had one in several years."

"Why not?"

"Oh." She sat up. "No reason."

Funny. Her eyes were shadowed, as if she'd said something wrong.

He decided to ignore the awkward moment. "There's a stack of planks in the shed, too," he said. "I don't know how old they are. They might all be rotten. But I'll look about and see what I can produce to help you."

"Thank you," she said, casting her eyes down.

A strange awkwardness descended upon them.

"You're welcome." He dragged his hand across the counter and patted it once. "See you tomorrow."

"See you," she said quietly.

Stephen was shocked to discover he wasn't dreading the prospect.

CHAPTER SIX

The next morning, Jilly was glad to see Captain Arrow arrive with some carpentry tools, nails, a wide, long plank, and some small pieces of wood.

"Good morning," he said, but he sounded a bit guarded, a remnant of that strange awkwardness between them the day before.

"Thanks for coming." She felt equally reticent, although she didn't know why she should worry. Their agreement was quite simple, and she actually trusted him to keep his side of the bargain.

"How are your guests today?" She was very aware they were alone. Otis was upstairs washing the breakfast dishes.

Captain Arrow shrugged. "I left before they awakened. They'll be up soon enough, I suppose."

She wanted to tell him she was excited about the plank he'd found. But she also didn't want him to think she was impressed with him in any way. After all, the only reason he was making her a window ledge was because he'd entangled her in his problem, and it was a most inappropriate ploy, considering the fact that she was already involved in her own deception.

Which was inappropriate, too, but it was *hers*.

When Captain Arrow didn't seem to notice her understated reaction to his arrival and became immediately absorbed in the task she'd set before him, she felt a bit bereft.

Why didn't he care that she was ignoring him?

She began to regret her cool manner. She wanted to know what every piece of wood was for and how long the task would take. She couldn't wait to get her books on that ledge!

Diligently, he worked on. His legs, arms, and back bristled with power—and a hint of danger—as he measured. Even so, when he carried some materials outside, the shop lost some of its coziness. Jilly couldn't help staring while he shaped the ledge with his shaving tools on the pavement. Part of her wanted him to come back inside so she could talk to him, although why, she didn't know.

She was a married woman.

And *he* was a rake. Not once had he shown interest in her books, either.

The perfect man, in her view, was someone who knew as much if not more about books as she did.

Again—not that it mattered. She was married. Romance was not to be hers. At least she had her freedom, the greatest gift she could ever want.

Nevertheless, the captain was very handsome. She couldn't stop taking peeks, pretending to herself that all she cared about was observing his progress. Once he turned around to her and grinned knowingly, as if he could read her most private thoughts.

She'd drawn back then, determined not to look any more. And luckily, something happened to divert her.

Otis arrived downstairs and let fly with the feather duster, while Jilly looked into the last crate of books she had to shelve. It had taken her all week to get her purchased inventory catalogued and put in the proper bookcases. The books in this particular crate had been left by the previous owner in his attic.

"My goodness." She turned a small, leather-bound journal over in her hands. "It's a diary."

Otis put down the duster and looked at the journal with her. "It belonged to someone named Alicia Maria Fotherington, who lived"—he started, which made her start, as well—"almost two hundred years ago!"

Jilly's heart thumped madly. She loved a good story.

"I wonder *where* she lived," she said, and quickly thumbed through the first several pages. "My goodness." She looked up at Otis. "She lived here, on Dreare Street, in Captain Arrow's house."

"You don't say!" Otis exclaimed, and walked to the window and looked first at the captain, who was busy sanding a small piece of wood, and then at the house. "Was she married?"

Jilly bit her lip. "I don't know, but I plan to find out. It's not as if I don't have time to read it."

Otis made a face. "True. But as soon as you're finished, I want to read it, too." He paused. "Here," he said excitedly. "We have a new customer."

He straightened his coat, and they both watched the

artist from down the street tip his hat to Captain Arrow, who acknowledged him with a friendly greeting.

The fellow wore a faded coat, boots that had seen better days, and a sheepish grin on his boyish countenance when he arrived at the door.

"Hello," he said in a strong but kind voice. "I'm Nathaniel Sadler. Thank you for the scones. They were delicious, Miss Jones."

"You're very welcome, Mr. Sadler," Jilly said. "We have plenty more. And please call me Jilly."

"I'm quite full at the moment, but thanks." He grinned. "And I'd be most obliged if you'd call me Nathaniel."

"Nathaniel, then," she said. "And this is Mr. Shrimpshire, my assistant."

"Otis to artistic geniuses," Otis explained. "I've seen your paintings in your window."

Nathaniel thanked him for the compliment, and the men shook hands.

"I didn't come in sooner because"—Nathaniel hesitated—"people don't mingle on Dreare Street."

"I wonder why?" Jilly truly couldn't fathom it. "In the country, we got to know all our neighbors very well."

Nathaniel shrugged. "Most people don't mingle on any streets in Mayfair, actually. You'll have a lord living next to a dress shop on one side and an attorney's office on the other. People don't speak unless they're with people like themselves. But here on Dreare Street, the residents are even more isolated from their neighbors." He looked at them from beneath a fringe of wavy black hair. "Lady Duchamp does her best to quash any signs of friendliness between us."

"That's obvious," Otis said. "She's not a very happy person."

Nathaniel winced. "She's a widow. Perhaps that accounts for it."

Jilly liked that he was a compassionate sort and began to get an idea, a very *good* idea. Somehow she wanted him to meet Susan.

"Do you—would you mind if I looked through your books?" he asked.

"Not at all," she replied warmly.

He scratched his head. "I don't have any money to buy one. But I do love to read."

Those were the perfect words to say to a lover of books. "You go right ahead and browse," Jilly said. "And if you see one you like, please take it as a gift from one neighbor to another."

What was one book between friends? She wasn't making any money anyway.

Otis made a face at her.

She quelled him with a glance.

Nathaniel blushed. "That's very kind of you. Perhaps someday I could paint a small portrait of the exterior of Hodgepodge you could hang in the shop." He looked around at the blank walls.

"I'd love that," Jilly said with enthusiasm. "I'd also be happy to hang any other paintings you might have. They could be for sale here."

His eyes brightened. "Really? I've had no luck finding a patron in London. You'd be doing me a great service. That is . . ." He looked around. "Do you get many customers?"

She shook her head. "I'm afraid not. And I must confess that's one reason I'd like to hang your paintings. Perhaps they'll attract more clients. At the very least, your canvases would make the shop far more attractive."

"So true," echoed Otis. " 'A thing of beauty is a joy forever.' " He paused for dramatic effect. "Shelley said that. In fact"—he preened—"I'm an expert at all sorts of poetry. Shall I show you his work?"

Nathaniel shrugged. "Why not?"

"Um, I believe Otis meant to ascribe that quote to *Keats*." Jilly cast an apologetic look at her assistant.

Otis reddened. "Oh, yes. Keats. Doesn't he wear outrageous cravats? And his hair à la Brutus?"

"I've no idea," Nathaniel said. "He's an amazing poet, that's certain."

"Tell me about yourself, Nathaniel," Jilly asked. "What brought you to Dreare Street? Have you always lived here?"

His cheery face took on a rather grim cast. "I arrived here two months ago as the student of a great painting master. He was planning an exhibit for me, which he claimed many well-known art collectors would have attended. But he died three days after we arrived. Lady Duchamp allowed me to continue renting his studio if I paid the same amount plus a quarter more—for the master's dying so inconveniently on her property. I must say the place has wonderful light."

"I didn't realize Lady Duchamp owned your building." Jilly was aghast at the old woman's callousness and unbridled greed. "So what happened to you after your friend died?"

Nathaniel's eyes darkened with sadness. "All his connections disappeared, and I was left to fend for myself. I've been trying ever since to find another patron."

Jilly sighed. "I'm so sorry you've lost your friend and are having a rough time of it. Do you—do you believe the rumors that Dreare Street is unlucky?"

"Yes." Nathaniel chuckled.

His answer was so flatly delivered, Jilly couldn't help laughing herself.

"Well," she said, leaning closer to him, "perhaps if we keep talking to each other here at the store, Lady Duchamp won't notice that we're all cheering up. Please do come by any time. I'll look forward to chatting with you."

"I shall." He gave her an infectious grin. "Thanks again, Miss Jones. It does get awfully lonely on Dreare Street."

A wonderful picture of Susan and Nathaniel together flashed in her mind. He was a man with a compassionate heart, and she was a woman who could benefit from some tender understanding.

They'd be a perfect couple, she decided. But she'd put away her brilliant idea until later.

Nathaniel spent a few minutes quietly browsing, and Jilly couldn't help feeling pleased at how engrossed he was in the books.

"I can't pick a book out today," he said. "There are

so many interesting ones. I'm leaning toward the one about the canals in Venice, but I'll come back again very soon to take another look. How's that?"

"I'd love if you visited *every* day," Jilly replied. "Consider Hodgepodge your home away from home."

"Why, that's very kind of you," he said, looking genuinely moved.

When he left, Jilly realized that was exactly what she did want: a home. A family. A sense of belonging. Hodgepodge could provide that for her *and* for other people on the street. She simply had to stay the course.

Stephen came back inside with the piece of wood that would become her new ledge, and her heart lightened.

"I'm only here a moment," he said breezily.

Her heart promptly sank. "All right, then."

He was on his haunches now, testing the ledge beneath the window. She tried to ignore how manly he was, how focused he was on his craft and on making a ledge for her shop. He didn't have to try so hard—she wasn't even paying him, and one might even say he'd been coerced—yet he was making a tremendous effort.

Which was quite charming of him.

Think of something else, of someone *else!*

She smiled. "Do you need my help, Captain?"

"No, thank you," he replied politely, although she noticed he didn't even look at her.

Blast. When he was near her, she couldn't concentrate on other things. His golden hair glinted—who could look away from that? And his hands. They were strong hands with tapered fingers. They looked quite capable.

How would they feel around her waist?

Think of something else! "Captain—"

He paused in his work and cast a glance at her over his shoulder. "Yes?"

Oh, dear. She could tell she was interfering. "Nothing." She bit her lip. "I'm sorry."

A beat passed. "I'm not," is all he said. He tossed her a quick grin, lowered the ledge to the floor, and stood.

Her heart raced even more. What had he meant by that? And was he going to come over to the counter to speak to her? Because if he was, she was backing up.

She cast a furtive glance around for her dusting cloth.

But she didn't need it. He came nowhere near her.

"I'll be working outside again," he said.

She felt that odd disappointment settle over her when he went out the door.

However, she couldn't think about *why* he affected her so because a few seconds later, a long, pale woman entered the shop. Jilly had seen her before, coming out of her fine home on Dreare Street with two long, pale children, a boy and girl of about fifteen, and her florid-faced husband, a man who appeared to take life very seriously in his tight cravats and multilayered black cape.

"Welcome to Hodgepodge," Jilly promptly stated. "May I help you find something?"

When the woman turned to her, Jilly was shocked

by the desperation she saw in her eyes. "I'm your neighbor, Lavinia Hobbs." The woman swallowed. "And if I don't find a receipt for the perfect soup, I'm afraid—"

"What?" asked Jilly, her heart lurching and her pulse racing.

Mrs. Hobbs lowered her hand. "I'm afraid we'll have a very dismal dinner."

"Oh." Jilly let out a small breath.

Was that all?

She noticed the lady's eyelids were red-rimmed. Jilly daren't ask her why, but she wanted to show she was concerned. "May I help you search?"

The woman nodded, misery surrounding her like a cloud. "I'd be grateful to find a receipt for turtle soup."

"Come with me." Jilly's tone was warm but brisk. "That should be no trouble."

Mrs. Hobbs followed silently. Jilly did her very best to cheer her by thumbing through several volumes on cookery with her. After ten minutes or so, her pale neighbor did appear in better spirits. They'd found a delicious-sounding receipt for turtle soup in one book, which Mrs. Hobbs decided to purchase.

At the counter, while Jilly wrapped the volume in brown paper, Mrs. Hobbs smiled thinly. "Thank you for the scones. I was quite surprised to receive such a token of generosity. Of course, Mason was quite suspicious of it."

"Mason?"

"My husband. He thought you wanted something." Mrs. Hobbs waved a hand. "His family is so grasping, you see. He came into a great deal of money a few years ago, and we moved to Mayfair with such high hopes."

Her voice trailed off wistfully, and there was an awkward silence.

"Is . . . is everything all right, Mrs. Hobbs?" Jilly asked.

Mrs. Hobbs swallowed hard. "Of course."

"Are you sure?"

"Yes." Mrs. Hobbs hesitated, then added, "I mean, no. Not really. Things are . . . *not* all right."

She gulped.

Jilly held the string she was tying still. "I'm sorry to hear that," she whispered. "I'll be happy to listen if you need an ear."

Mrs. Hobbs let out a deep sigh. "I do, actually."

"I promise to keep your confidence," Jilly said, with the warmest smile she could manage.

Mrs. Hobbs stared at her a moment. "Very well," she said. "The truth is, Mason lost his inheritance. Almost every penny. He invested in a tea company that was attempting to rival the power of the East India Company, and his company failed. We're struggling to survive."

Jilly laid her hand on Mrs. Hobbs's long, pale one. "I'm so sorry."

Mrs. Hobbs pulled her hand back and gave a little sniff. "We'll be fine," she averred. "I did have to fire the cook, and Mason's in a terrible mood all the time these days, but if I make a good dinner—"

She stopped, put her hand to her mouth, and gave a

little sob. "The thing is, Miss Jones, I'm a terrible cook. All my life I have been. I don't know if I can manage."

Jilly came out from behind the counter and squeezed her hand. "I'm sure your turtle soup will be delicious."

Mrs. Hobbs squeezed back. "I just can't seem to do anything right anymore," she whispered. "Neither can the children."

"Well," Jilly said, a bit overwhelmed but touched by Mrs. Hobbs's apparent trust. "Please visit any time you need someone to talk to. And send the children, as well. Even Mr. Hobbs, if he's a reader."

Mrs. Hobbs moved away and stared out the window. "He only reads the papers for the financial news." She shrugged. "He thinks reading anything else is silly."

Jilly joined her at the window and saw Captain Arrow sawing through a small, thick block of wood as if it were butter. Something in her middle warmed in a totally irrational fashion.

"Don't worry about Mr. Hobbs," she said. "Let reading be *your* form of entertainment." She took Mrs. Hobbs's hand again and tugged her to the shelves. "Come with me."

Mrs. Hobbs actually chuckled. "Miss Jones, you *are* bossy, aren't you?"

"Yes, I am, but only about books." She grinned and pulled out a small book of silly limericks and jokes and handed it to Mrs. Hobbs. "Here. You and the children read this when you're blue. I'm sure you'll find your spirits will improve right away. And once they do, don't let anyone, especially Mr. Hobbs, dampen them for the rest of the day. All right?"

"All right." Mrs. Hobbs smiled, a small, hopeful smile which warmed Jilly's heart. "I will. But Miss Jones, somehow I doubt you're only bossy about books." She threw a sly glance at Captain Arrow. "You managed to get our new neighbor to work for you, a man who's done nothing but enjoy himself with his friends—until now."

"Oh, well." Jilly coughed lightly. "He probably tired of constant diversion. And some men love carpentry, don't they?"

Mrs. Hobbs chuckled again. "Perhaps it's something else he loves—the sight of a certain bookshop owner."

"Mrs. Hobbs." Jilly couldn't help being shocked at Mrs. Hobbs's teasing. A very secret part of her was even pleased by it.

A wicked secret part that she would suppress.

Mrs. Hobbs said nothing else, merely left with a smile on her face and her shoulders rather thrown back, a sign of renewed confidence which pleased Jilly no end.

Ten minutes later, Stephen walked back into Hodgepodge with the small wooden blocks, determined to show Miss Jones he had more substance than she gave him credit for. This window ledge was going to be the best piece of carpentry work she'd ever seen. Not only that, he would show her he could be civilized, mature, and focused when he felt like it—but only when *he* felt like it. Not when he was told to be. Now that he'd left the navy, he no longer had to worry about commanding officers. He was his own man.

His *own* man.

"Would you like something to eat?" She looked at him only a moment before looking away.

He couldn't countenance it. Miss Jones was more nervous around him than she'd ever been before. "No, thank you—"

"I insist, Captain. For all your hard work."

"But I'm not hungry—"

"Captain Arrow." Ah. Now she was back to her old self. She speared him with a look that dared him to defy her. "Accept my hospitality, the way I accepted yours at your theatrical evening."

So much for his being in charge. "Very well," he agreed. "If you don't mind fixing me something, I'll be happy to eat it. It would mean I won't have to go back to my house and the company there. No offense meant."

"None taken," she said. "Otis has prepared a noonday meal already."

"Shall I eat it here, in the shop?"

"How hospitable would that be?" She gave him a rather forced smile. "Why don't you and Otis eat first, upstairs, while I watch the store, and then I'll follow? I'd rather stay here in case we get a customer."

"Suit yourself." He put his tool belt aside and followed. When she opened a door between two shelves on the back wall to a small corridor behind it, he noticed her slender neck and had a sudden desire to put a kiss on it.

You're foolish, he told himself. What drove the desire in him to kiss a hard, unmanageable woman like Miss Jones?

Otis started in his chair when they entered the office.

"My goodness," he said, lowering his book, "I was just getting to one of my favorite parts, when Elizabeth goes to Darcy's mansion with her aunt and uncle—and Darcy spies them there!"

"Yet he treats her with great respect," said Stephen with a chuckle. "He could have made her feel completely out of place, but no. He's in love. Supposedly, men in love forget all the good reasons they have to be annoyed with the object of their affection and forgive her everything."

Miss Jones turned her head to stare at him. "You've read *Pride and Prejudice*?"

Stephen arched a playful brow. "Of course. What else does one have to do on a ship but fight wars, clean decks and tackle, eat, indulge in an occasional rum with one's shipmates—and read?"

"Well said, Captain." Otis slapped his book shut and stood.

Miss Jones still looked stunned. "But you've shown no interest in the books in Hodgepodge," she told him.

Stephen lifted his broad shoulders. "There's a time

for reading . . . and a time for indulging in merry-making with one's friends."

Otis chuckled. "Clearly, in your world, those times don't overlap."

"No, they don't," he said. "Now that the parties are over, thanks to my houseguests, perhaps there *will* be a time to read. I'm sure you agree, Miss Jones, when one is alone, reading is as diverting as any good friend or party."

"I do agree." Miss Jones blushed as pink as the inside of a conch shell.

"Miss Jones?" Stephen was amused to see her so prettily discomfited, but he couldn't fathom why she was.

But too soon she seemed to recover. "Why don't you and Otis go have some lunch?"

"I'm not at all hungry," Otis said. "I'll watch the shop, and you and Captain Arrow enjoy a meal together."

Miss Jones hesitated, but then she said, "Would that suit you, Captain?"

"Yes," he said, noting that she wasn't looking directly at him. "We can talk about literature. Which of the ancient Greek playwrights is your favorite?"

She told him with a great deal of enthusiasm as they traipsed up the stairs. He enjoyed listening to her spout her obviously well-educated opinion so happily. He also enjoyed seeing her from behind, and he didn't feel a bit guilty about it. They were talking about cerebral things, so why should a man feel guilty for enjoying viewing a woman's shapely rear through her gown, and perhaps imagining what she looked like without that gown on her pleasingly rounded form?

Of course, she being a maiden, they really shouldn't spend time alone in her living quarters, but she'd already flouted convention by running her own bookshop, hadn't she?

She must have read his mind. "I'm aware that it's rather improper for us to be here in my private quarters without a chaperone," she said a bit stiffly. "Which is why we shall dine al fresco, where we'll be in full view of the entire street."

"Oh? I didn't know you had a balcony."

"I don't," she said. "But we do have the roof, if you don't mind climbing."

She pointed to a set of rungs on the wall.

Stephen looked up and saw a trapdoor. "I don't mind at all," he said. "Shall I go first?"

She blushed, no doubt understanding that if she went first, he'd be able to see up her skirts.

"That's an excellent suggestion," she said. "You go ahead with a blanket. You'll see just where to place it." She reached into a cupboard, withdrew a cheery quilt, and thrust it into his hands. "I'll follow behind with the food and drink."

"Good plan," he said, and clambered easily up the rungs. When he pushed on the roof door, it gave with a mighty squeak. Above his head, he saw the usual gray skies that hung above London.

Once on the roof, he saw the perfect place to sit, a

rim of bricks surrounding the chimney. The bricks would make an excellent bench with enough room in between the people reclining there to place a picnic. And yes, if neighbors chose to look up from their windows or the street itself, they'd be able to see the two of them on the roof.

He laid the blanket down and walked closer to the edge. Dreare Street from this vantage point didn't look so bad, even with the bits of fog still clinging to a street lamp and a large tree in Lady Duchamp's yard. He gazed down at his house and wondered what Sir Ned and his family were doing. Probably bickering.

Behind him, he heard Miss Jones climbing the rungs, and he got on his knees to grab the food, the drink, and then her hand. When he pulled her up, she grazed his chest with her own soft one before falling back.

"Oh, my!" She looked up at the sky with a pleased grin on her face. "I see some blue."

It was a small spot of color but just cause for celebration—and a good way for him to avoid thinking about the fact that they'd just come into very close contact.

He picked up the jug of water, and Miss Jones carried the basket and cups to the brick bench.

She poured water into their cups and dispensed bread and cheese. "There," she said, looking well pleased. "I do enjoy a picnic."

Her eyes were bright, he noticed. She'd never looked prettier, especially with that shaft of sunlight piercing her hair, turning its black color almost blue.

"Everything's better outside," she said. "Isn't it?"

Did she have any idea how appealing she was when she smiled?

"Yes," he said. "Everything. Especially a kiss."

CHAPTER SEVEN

It happened so fast, Jilly didn't have time to think. Captain Arrow's pupils darkened, and next thing she knew, he leaned toward her.

She didn't back away. She couldn't. It was as if she were riveted to the spot, lost in the dark depths of his eyes, the irises rimmed with gold.

And then he was kissing her with his warm, seeking mouth. He pulled her into a different world, a new place where she was no longer Jilly, runaway wife and bookseller, living in London.

But she stayed in that world willingly. How could she not? She was sharing a blissful, heady moment with a handsome, virile man, one who made her heart beat fast and her limbs melt like butter—

Who made her forget to think.

She'd never been kissed this way.

Ever.

She didn't know a kiss could be so—

Perfect.

When he gave a little groan in his throat and pulled her closer, she delighted in the sensation of being held so closely to his broad chest, his hand pressed posses-sively on her lower back.

She wanted more.

More.

"God, you're beautiful," he whispered, and kissed her neck.

Oh! How sweet of him. Hector had never compli-mented her.

Hector!

She opened her eyes wide and pushed him away. "We can't do this."

"Why not?" His voice was low and husky. "No one's looking up from the street, and I've seen nary a curtain move."

She felt almost desperate to stay right where she was, but instead she shook her head and scooted away.

"No." She felt shaken to the core by her lapse. "I'm not one of your easy women. I—I can't do this. I don't *act* like this."

She told herself her heart was beating wildly be-cause she was angry at him and shocked at herself—not because she wanted to kiss him again.

He followed her and tucked a tendril of hair behind her ear. "A man who doesn't try to steal a kiss from a pretty miss at a rooftop picnic is remiss in his duties as a man."

He had the regretful, lost look of someone whose desire has gone unsated, even though he also sounded amused. Confident. The way an Impossible Bachelor likely always was.

It was the lost look that touched her. She felt adrift of a sudden, too. Everything in her ached to be with him that way again—to kiss him, to be held by him, to mingle breaths and feel his skin against her own.

But she mustn't. She must protect her identity at all costs.

"What a silly sentiment," she forced herself to say.

She knew very well she couldn't kiss him again.

She was Jilly Jones, bookseller.

Prim, *unavailable* bookseller.

Yet another part of her still reveled in the kiss and in the fact that he'd called her not only *beautiful* but *a pretty miss*. Hector had never referred to her as such.

"Is it a silly thought?" The captain arched a brow. "If it is, I want to be silly always."

Heavens. She wished he would say something annoying—not something appealing. She looked away from his golden eyes and the intensity of his heated, hungry gaze.

He wanted more.

So did she.

It was like a fire between them that she'd have to pretend didn't exist. Not only that, she'd have to douse it somehow.

She stood and walked a few feet away. "Now tell me about yourself," she said to the line of rooftops across the street, then dared to look back over her shoulder at him. "How did a Lothario like you come to be a captain in the Royal Navy?"

He bit into a hunk of bread and, while he was

chewing, smirked at her. "Rather obvious change of subject, Miss Jones. Are you sure you'd not like to go back to the other?"

She turned to face him, her arms now crossed over her chest. "What happened just now can't happen again. *Ever.*"

"Ever?" He had a glint of mischief in his eye.

Damn him for not believing her!

She took a deep breath. "Ever," she said flatly. "If you want me to stay on this roof with you—if you want to continue speaking with me at all—then you'll respect my wishes."

He took a swig of water, all the while looking directly into her soul, it seemed. Could he tell she harbored a secret? That she was a wanton to have kissed him so willingly?

"All right." His expression was clear and untroubled. "I'll respect your wishes."

"Good," she replied.

Yet somehow she didn't feel as if he'd promised her the same thing she'd asked.

She sank down on their crude seat and tore into her own piece of bread in a fairly uncivilized fashion, rattled and frankly indifferent to the social niceties at the moment. Captain Arrow hadn't observed them, had he?

Kissing her in broad daylight!

What if any of the neighbors had chosen that moment to glance at her roof?

Thank God none apparently had. She stretched out her legs in relief that *this* time, she probably wouldn't suffer any consequences for using poor judgment.

"What are you doing, Miss Jones?" The captain cast an admiring eye at her hemline.

Goodness. Her ankles were showing.

"Enjoying the weather until you noticed," she said crossly, tucking her feet back under her gown. "Now tell me your tale."

"Yes, madam." His voice was sleek. "The story goes I was born the son of a poor fisherman and his wife. But I never met my father."

"What happened?" Everyone should know their father if they possibly could, she thought, and felt a tad regretful for being harsh with him.

"My mother told me he drowned one summer during a torrential gale. I arrived two months later."

"I'm so sorry," she whispered.

He gave a careless smile. "It's quite all right." He threw one buckskin-clad leg up on the brick ledge and leaned back against the chimney, the portrait of a healthy male at ease. "I had an idyllic childhood. Lots of neighboring men stood in as fathers. We were close in my village. But one day the fun came to an end. An earl who lived nearby decided to send one poor boy to Eton, along with his son, who was supposedly a weak sort. My mother said the earl hoped whoever he chose as a charity case would serve as that boy's protector."

"That's not such a bad idea."

"No, it seemed reasonable enough. At any rate, the village elders recommended that I accompany the lad. The earl interviewed me and then agreed to send me. I had no desire to go, but my mother gave me no choice. I was educated at Eton, was never called upon to assist the weak boy—who seemed perfectly healthy to me—and when he and my own friends later left to attend Oxford or Cambridge, the earl's largesse rightfully ceased. I went to sea instead. From there a captain took me under his wing. I saw a great deal of action during the Wars, so I quickly rose up through the ranks. Anybody would have—I just happened to be in the right places at the right times."

"Don't be so modest, Captain. I'm sure your skill had much to do with it."

"Now you're being kind," he said.

"Not at all," she replied. "I don't believe in false flattery."

"Neither do I," he said. "This scone is delicious."

She smiled. "It's an old family recipe."

"I saw you deposit some on other neighbors' doorsteps."

"I'm sorry I didn't give *you* any," she said tartly, and felt her cheeks heat. "But I couldn't reward you for your bad behavior."

He laughed. "That's quite all right. Had I known what I was missing, I would have piped down."

"Really?"

"No." His eyes crinkled at the corners. "It's a shame to extinguish a very good party."

"I knew you'd say something like that," she said, charmed in spite of herself. "Now go on about your story."

"There's nothing more to it," he said. "The Wars are over. That pirate I always wanted to capture is now sitting in a gaol, thanks to me and my crew. I'm ready to start the next phase of my life."

"What an interesting tale," she said. "You became a great success, just as your mother had hoped."

"Yes, it does sound like a nice story, doesn't it?"

Jilly noticed a trace of bitterness in his voice. "What's wrong, Captain? Was it traumatic being sent away from home without your permission?"

"It's not that." His eyes were half lidded of a sudden. "Recently, I found out the real truth about my birth. Well after mother died, a village elder wrote to tell me that the earl who sent me to Eton, Lord Stanhope, was my father. That's when I found out that I'd inherited this house on Dreare Street. The whole village knew my situation and conspired to keep it a secret from me. They invented the tale of the father who drowned at sea."

Jilly put a hand to her mouth. "I'm so sorry. To be lied to all these years—it must have been terrible to find out after your mother's death."

Stephen shrugged. "I thought I knew my mother and all those people in my village. But every time I went home to visit, every time they smiled at me and patted me on the back"—he stared across the street at Lady Duchamp's house—"they were concealing the truth."

There was a beat of silence, broken by the faint sound of a broom seller hawking his wares on Half-Moon Street.

"I'm sure they did it to protect you," Jilly said, realizing full well she was deceiving him now.

But she must, she reminded herself.

She had no choice.

Nevertheless, she felt terribly guilty.

"I'm certain they thought they had my best interests at heart," he said cheerfully enough, then stood, lit a cheroot, and inhaled upon it. Blowing a plume of smoke, he looked back at her. "I'd have been better off knowing the truth. It may hurt, but at least it allows you dignity."

"I imagine you were very dignified, Captain, in your uniform." She couldn't believe she'd blurted that out. Because she *had* imagined him in uniform.

She blushed to the roots of her hair.

He laughed. "In my uniform, yes, I could play the part as well as any naval officer. But you've seen me out of uniform. You know that given a choice, I choose the undisciplined road. You and others on Dreare Street might say I choose impulse and feeling over caution and reason. And I do."

"But that's because you don't know what the truth is anymore," she said.

He gave her a long look.

She stared back, refusing to be cowed.

"You're not only a beguiling bookseller but a perceptive one, too, aren't you?" He reached out and rubbed a scratchy thumb over her chin.

She stepped back. "If you insist on flirting with me, Captain, I'll ban you from the store."

He dropped his hand. "But how will I do your bidding then?"

"You're mocking me, sir." Her heart was still

pounding from his touch and now he had a look in his eyes that made her knees weak.

He chuckled. "You've got it all wrong. I admire you and your independence. Tell me more about yourself."

The rumble of a carriage coming down the street saved her from having to answer. They went closer to the edge of the roof and peered down.

"Perhaps it will stop at Hodgepodge," Jilly said, leaning farther out for a better look.

"Not so far." Captain Arrow grabbed her arm and pulled her back against his stomach.

For a brief second, she allowed herself to rest in the crook of his arm. Something wild and wicked in her wanted to lean even farther back against the man, but she forced herself to straighten her spine. "Captain?"

"Yes?" he said into her ear.

"You can unhand me now."

"Very well. But only if you take a step back with me."

They did, in tandem, and he released her. She pretended she didn't care one jot that he'd held her and she'd liked it.

The carriage did, indeed, stop in front of Hodgepodge. Part of Jilly was glad. And the other part was regretful. The part that was glad urged her to move toward the hatch leading down to her living quarters. She couldn't afford to think about the part of her that wanted to stay on the roof with the captain.

From the front of the store, Stephen watched as a small, gray man got out of the carriage, his expression as stern as a schoolmaster's. Stephen followed his instinct to go to the door ahead of Miss Jones and Otis. There was something about the man's eyes he didn't like.

The visitor stopped in front of him, a black leather satchel at his side, and looked up at him. "You're in my way," he said dryly.

"I know that," replied Stephen. "What's your name, and what business do you have here?"

"Captain!" Jilly said behind him. "Please let our customer inside."

"He's not a customer," Stephen called back, his eyes still on the man.

It was a statement, not a question.

The man looked at him without flinching. "If it means I may enter the shop, then yes, indeed, I *am* a customer." He gave Stephen a false smile. "My name is Mr. Alastair Redmond."

"What's your business here?"

"That's between Miss Jones and me."

Stephen narrowed his eyes at him. "I'll let you in, Redmond," he said, "but watch your step."

"Right," the man answered with a world-weary sigh. "I've heard that before."

Stephen reluctantly stepped aside, and Mr. Redmond walked up to the counter, where Jilly stood with a nervous smile pasted on her face.

Did she sense as well as Stephen did that this sour-faced man was the bearer of some sort of bad news?

"Are you the owner of Hodgepodge?" Mr. Redmond asked her, his voice reedy.

Otis gave a small cry, but then he pursed his mouth and proceeded to fumble with his shoe. He almost had it off, and—

"*Otis,*" Jilly whispered.

He looked at her, his eyes filled with fear and something else—the determination to slay a giant.

She shook her head.

He slowed, then stopped removing his shoe.

Stephen considered the scene before him. Why on earth would Otis remove his shoe unless he were about to use it to defend Jilly? Stephen didn't like the man, either, but he had no idea who he was. Was Otis simply following Stephen's lead? Or did he have reason to expect trouble at Hodgepodge?

This possibility only put Stephen more on guard.

Jilly looked back at Mr. Redmond. "Yes," she said, as if she were about to go to the guillotine. "I am Miss Jones."

Otis bit his thumb.

"Very well." Mr. Redmond reached into his coat pocket. "I'm here to give you this." He handed her a piece of paper. "It's a legal document regarding your property."

Without looking at the paper, Miss Jones held it to her mouth and gave a little giggle. Then Otis followed suit. They looked at each other as if their lives had been spared.

Otis lowered his brows and Miss Jones drew herself up.

"I see," she said with the gravitas one would expect

from a business owner. But her mouth still showed a bit of laughter at the corners, and her eyes, palpable relief.

What disaster had she averted?

Stephen had a great craving to know. If he had a special affinity for unmanageable ladies, he had even more of one for unmanageable, *mysterious* ladies.

"Leases on this street haven't been renewed in years due to an oversight," Mr. Redmond said. "Either pay the new fees, or move."

The lightness in Miss Jones's expression vanished. "But I own this house."

"Yes, she does." Otis came to her and laid a hand on her shoulder. "So go away, little man." He raised his chin. "Please see him out, Captain Arrow."

Stephen would have liked to pick up Mr. Redmond by the back of his jacket and sling him into his carriage, but he knew it would probably only bring more trouble to Hodgepodge.

"You need to explain yourself clearly," Stephen said to him. "And waste no time. Our patience is short, and justifiably so. This sounds like another government ploy to raise taxes."

"It's no ploy." The little man's voice sounded smug as he looked around at them all. "Didn't you know the actual dirt beneath the homes and businesses of Mayfair is owned by someone else?"

"That's terrible!" Jilly cried.

"Are you sure about that?" Stephen demanded to know.

"Yes, I'm certain," Mr. Redmond replied.

"You don't have to be so demmed happy about it."
Otis crossed his arms over his chest and went into a
full pout.

Mr. Redmond lifted one brow and looked at Stephen. "If you live on this street, the same particulars
of this document will apply to you. I'm starting on
this corner and working my way around to distribute
copies to everyone."

"The hell you say," said Stephen.

"Bluster all you want," Mr. Redmond said in a
bored voice and pulled out a sheaf of papers. "What's
your name?"

"Arrow," replied Stephen in a testy voice.

Mr. Redmond sifted through his stack and removed
a single sheet. "Read it and weep."

Stephen yanked it from his hand and stuffed the
paper in his shirt pocket.

"You'd best examine the document well." Mr. Redmond was cool. "Anyone who's late may have the
land leased out from under them."

"You can't mean that," Stephen said.

"I do." The man didn't blink.

"What would happen to the person who owns the
house?" Jilly asked.

"You'd be told to move." Mr. Redmond sighed as if
he were terribly tired of having to go over this devastating news with yet another dimwitted Londoner.

"But you can't very well move a house," Otis insisted.

The man shrugged. "The house could be brought
down and a new edifice put up. The destruction of the

home would be your loss, of course. However, this is Mayfair. Who can't afford to pay their lease in the wealthiest part of London? I say if you can't afford to live here, it's your own fault."

Miss Jones sank onto a stool. "Why didn't anyone tell me about this lease situation when I bought Hodgepodge?"

"They probably didn't want you to know," Mr. Redmond said. "Either that, or they'd forgotten themselves. As I said, this lease renewal is long overdue. Thankfully, someone brought it to the attention of the proper authorities."

"Someone?"

"I've no idea who," he said. "All I know is that it's true. Dreare Street is in arrears."

"Everyone is?" Captain Arrow asked.

Mr. Redmond nodded. "Everyone. Now if you'll excuse me, I must finish alerting the neighborhood."

"Don't let us keep you," Otis said.

Mr. Redmond brushed by him, and Otis shrank back. When the man left, he pulled out a handkerchief. "Excuse me." He buried his face in the floral fabric. "I've got to recuperate."

He gave a loud sob, threw open the door to the back corridor, and ran to his room.

Stephen saw Jilly's face was pale when she stared at the paper in her hand and then slowly folded it into a tiny square.

"Will you be all right?" he asked her.

"I think so," she returned stoutly, but he saw her fingers tremble. "What will you do?"

"I'll have to pay it. I can't afford to have someone else come in and take the land from me. Then I'd not be able to sell the house. They could pull it down, do what they want with it. I'd be left with nothing. Nothing but my pension."

Miss Jones took a breath. The air was heavy between them.

"You're afraid of something," he said. "Something that happened before you got this news."

Her full, rose-pink lips thinned. "Why would you say such a thing?"

He shrugged. "Because you let your guard down at the theatrics. The difference between that woman and the bookshop Miss Jones is remarkable. And when Mr. Redmond walked in, Otis was about to clock him with his shoe—and he didn't even know who the man was."

"That's silly," she said with a sniff, and played at stacking books on a table. "Otis is eccentric."

Stephen watched her attempt to appear relaxed. But she couldn't do it. Her knuckles were white.

"And as for me at the theatrics," she went on, "I told you, I realize there's a time and a place for fun, and that night was one of those times."

He reached out, pried her hands off the books, and grasped her fingers. "I want to know everything about you." Her hands were so small and delicate in his. "Tell me."

She pulled her hands back, and her dark brows lowered dangerously. "That wouldn't be appropriate, Captain." Her voice was cool—although he sensed fear in it, too. "I'll see you tomorrow when you're able to work on the ledge."

"Very well," he said.

She was a terrible liar. She *was* in trouble. She'd been afraid of Mr. Redmond for her own reasons, and he was determined to find out why.

CHAPTER EIGHT

"It's time to get serious about selling books," Jilly said to Otis over supper that night. "We need money, and quickly."

He paused, his fork in the air. "I hate to suggest this, but perhaps you shouldn't have *me* selling the books."

Good. He'd finally realized what she'd known all along. "Yes, well, we both know a female shopkeeper is anathema to some people," she said. "Then again, so is a man who wears the kinds of shoes you do."

She grinned and looked down at his feet. Today he had on turquoise slippers, each adorned with a single, short peacock feather on top. They were absolutely shameless.

"The point is," Otis said, looking up from admiring his footwear, "I'm too emotionally attached to the books. I thought I adored only shoes, but the books—they're like my children, too, even the ones I haven't read. Their covers are grand, their pages smell sweet—in a musty, bookish way—and their titles are enchanting. *Candide. Don Kicks Oat.*"

"*Don Kicks Oat?*"

"You know, the one about the Spaniard and the windmills."

"Ah, *Don Quixote*!"

"The very same," Otis replied, unruffled, and drank a swig of beer.

"I can appreciate that sentiment," Jilly said, "but we've got to do better."

Otis put his tankard down and shook out his sleeve so that the lace showed to advantage. "You'll sell all the books now," he insisted. "I'll stick with cooking, baking our daily scones, cleaning both the bookstore and our private living quarters, running errands, and keeping an eye on the latest fashions on Brook Street."

"Fair enough." Jilly smiled. "But even if I take over the selling of the books, we haven't the customers to purchase them."

"We need more people strolling by," Otis agreed. "I do my best to attract notice with my waistcoats and shoes, but it's not been enough. Especially if it's foggy, as it is almost all the time. Who can see me through the shop window?" He cast a glance at her gown. "We're going to have to work on your appearance, my dear."

"Me? Why?"

Otis pursed his lips. "Now that you're incognito, you've lost that *je-ne-sais-quoi* you frankly never had but were on the cusp of having—if you'd only let me spend your clothing allowance."

"I put it away to buy Hodgepodge."

Otis sniffed.

She gave a little laugh. "You must agree purchasing Hodgepodge was more important than my looking lovely for Hector."

Otis shrugged. "Put that way, I must agree."

"Besides," she said, "you yourself said the fog gets in the way of people admiring your waistcoats and shoes. We have to have a plan that works not around my fashion sense but the fog."

"And the street's reputation for having bad luck," Otis added with a shiver.

"And our lack of time. I'd have to sell half my inventory, at least, by the time Mr. Redmond comes round again, to make the kind of money I need to pay off the lease, and I just won't have the hours in the day to do so."

Jilly bit her lip. Three large obstacles to success: bad weather, superstition, and a shortage of time. What could one do about any of them?

"We can't accomplish this enormous task by ourselves," Otis said in a soft, hesitant voice. "We need people to help us. But we're all alone in this world, aren't we, Miss Jilly?"

"We've got each other," she said firmly, and grasped his hand.

He nodded and gave her a misty smile. "I'm here to protect you. You do know that, don't you?"

"Of course," she said, although she was simply indulging her dearest friend. There was no way on earth Otis could protect her from Hector or anyone else. Throwing a shoe at Hector's head—or the head of one of his minions, as Otis had at first supposed Mr.

Redmond to be—wouldn't stop her ogre of a husband from dragging her back to their village.

"We'll come up with a plan to save Hodgepodge." She kissed Otis on the cheek. "I'm off to bed now. I want to read some of Alicia Fotherington's journal."

In bed, she opened the diary and began to read about the young lady of good family who'd married a prosperous man named Lyle Fotherington and moved to Dreare Street two hundred years earlier.

It's a happy place, this street, Alicia had written, *and prosperous. Fat-cheeked children, smiling mothers, fine gentlemen, and pleasant shopkeepers abound. Lyle's servants welcomed me with a bouquet of flowers picked from the back garden. The house is brand-new. Lyle had it built for us. It's small but elegant, standing at the end of the street as if a sentinel over the rest of the houses. I believe I shall have great good luck in my new life as the wife of such a kind man.*

Jilly's heart warmed toward the woman. She remembered when she, too, hoped for the best from her marriage.

She felt guilty continuing to read when her candles were in short supply and she could ill afford more any time soon. But the words of the long-gone mistress of 34 Dreare Street fascinated her.

The bustling street fair is the highlight of my week, Alicia painstakingly put down in her tight scrawl. *Every Wednesday I go down one side of the street and up the other with my cook and lady's maid, bargaining with the vendors and exchanging greetings*

*with our neighbors. We always come back to the house
with the merriest grins on our faces. I purchased a
fine bolt of rich damask which will become my gown
for the Christmas ball and supper. And tonight Cook
roasted a plump rabbit she bought at the fair. Lyle
was well pleased, except for my cheeks, of course.
They were pink from lingering too long in the sun.*

The sun!

How fortunate Alicia Fotherington had been.

Jilly read only a few more pages, laid the book
aside, and dutifully blew out the taper on her simple
bedside table. As she drifted off to sleep, she thought
about Alicia and how happily she'd lived on Dreare
Street so long ago.

What a different place it had been then!

Sunny. Happy.

Prosperous.

Heavens. Jilly sat bolt upright in bed, and with shaky
fingers, felt for her matches and lit her candle again.
Springing out of her sheets, she wrapped herself up,
grabbed the taper, and walked into the sitting room.

Otis was attempting to repair his shoe, the one he'd
lost at Captain Arrow's, by the light of the dying fire.

"I have an idea," she announced, her heart beating
fast with excitement.

"What?" Otis held the shoe up and squinted at the
newly fixed heel.

"Maybe we don't have a family, but we have all our
neighbors, don't we?" Jilly began to pace behind him.

Otis's brow furrowed. "Beyond the artist and the
seamstress you told me about, and Captain Arrow,

they're not very friendly. Lady Duchamp is a veritable devil."

"I know, but we should have a meeting—a meeting of the whole street. Everyone else has to produce the money to pay off the lease, too. At dinner, I was thinking only of how to solve Hodgepodge's financial woes, but no doubt *all* the businesses—indeed, all the residents—on Dreare Street are suffering."

"True, but what about the residents who have plenty of money?" Otis laid aside his shoe. "We also have people like Captain Arrow. He wouldn't mind leaving Dreare Street, and I'm sure he's not the only one. Why should they bother to help us?"

Jilly thought about Mrs. Hobbs's long, pale face. "Captain Arrow will help us because he needs to sell his house. And the others may help simply because . . . it's dreary here on Dreare Street."

"It is!" cried Otis, pushing out his chair and standing. "It would be such a pleasure to look out and see people walking up and down enjoying the weather." He raced to the window and flipped back the curtain. Jilly could see the evening fog swirling about the sputtering gas lamps across the street.

"All right," he said, turning back to face her, "mayhap *not* enjoying the weather but perhaps enjoying each *other*."

"Yes." Jilly chuckled. "Not to mention that if the others ever want to join Captain Arrow and sell their homes, they'll have a much better chance to do so if the street appears prosperous."

Otis clasped his hands beneath his chin. "Oh, my,"

he whispered happily. "We'll all get together and have a wonderful time making Dreare Street flourish. Do you think we could get rid of the fog?"

"I don't see how that's possible." Jilly sighed. "I suppose we're in some sort of valley between the neighboring streets. The fog simply rolls in and stays."

"That's a demmed shame." Otis strode to a looking glass and adjusted his cravat. "But even with the fog, we can still be a happier street. What shall we do?"

"A street fair." Jilly was so excited, she wanted to do a little jig.

But Otis's face fell. "Those aren't common anymore, especially in Mayfair."

"That's a good thing," she replied happily. "It will be a special event."

"What if we're not allowed?"

"Who would tell us no?"

"Perhaps the Lord Mayor of London."

"We'll not worry about that quite yet. Let's think about the fair. I need you, Otis, to be as enthused as I. Please." She paused. The fire crackled loudly in the hearth. "Don't be afraid."

Otis grinned. "Very well." He clasped his hands together. "We'll have booths to sell things."

"Yes. All sorts of things." Jilly laughed. "First thing tomorrow, we'll make a sign."

"You and your signs." Otis waved a careless hand. "If no one walks by, no one will see it. What you need to do is . . . employ a town crier." His voice cracked with excitement.

"We can't do that."

Otis clapped his hands. "Yes we can. I've got a lovely scarlet jacket and a black tricorne hat. You have a bell. Now we have a town crier. Get the bell, Miss Jilly. Posthaste! I'll be right back."

The man was deadly serious. By the time Jilly had found the bell on the mantel, her faher's ex-valet had groped his way through the dark to his room and arrived back upstairs kitted out in his version of a town crier's uniform.

"Tomorrow," he said fervently. "Tomorrow begins a new age for Dreare Street."

"Yes," Jilly said, adjusting the shoulders of his jacket. "Tomorrow we shall tell everyone about the street fair."

"We'll make loads of money." Otis rang the bell.

"And if it's a success, we'll hold another one."

Then Jilly had a brilliant thought: she was in a position to demand Captain Arrow act as a partner in creating the street fair. There'd be booths to construct, at the very least, and someone would have to organize the neighbors. Who better to do that than a ship's captain?

If for some odd reason he balked at the idea, she'd remind him he had no choice but help her—if he wanted her to continue pretending to be the object of his affections, that is.

CHAPTER NINE

Early the next morning, Stephen woke up to the sound of shrieking.

He was now sleeping in a different room, one on the ground floor, until the beam beneath his bedchamber was repaired. Fully clad in breeches and shirt, he tried to jump from his bed to see what was the matter, but he was detained by a feminine hand pushing on his chest.

"Hello, Captain." A well-endowed woman lay next to him in a filmy cotton shift.

"Lady Hartley!" It was like waking up to a nightmare. "What in God's name are you doing in here?"

She smiled. "I've been waiting for you." She leaned forward with her thin, dry lips parted, but he yanked the sheets down and scrambled around her out the bottom of the bed.

"Your daughter is screaming." He was vastly annoyed, but he held his temper in check. "I'll deal with you later."

He didn't wait for a reply but raced upstairs to the second floor to find Miss Hartley in her bedchamber pointing at the ceiling with a shaky finger.

"Bats," she lisped. "Loads of them. They just flew in the window and . . . and disappeared. Where'd they go?"

Sir Ned was snoring loudly in the bed in the next room.

Stephen crept closer to the beam Miss Hartley pointed at and saw bats clinging to its far side. One by one, they disappeared into the attic, obviously through a hole in the beam.

Good God, another rotten beam. Was the whole house to fall down around them?

"You'll have to find another bedchamber," Stephen said, well aware that now two bedchambers in the house were uninhabitable. Not a good thing if you wanted to sell a house.

Miss Hartley gave a small sob. "I was so frightened. Where's Mother?"

He felt himself color. "I don't know. Sleeping, presumably. Or awake. Who can say?"

"What if the bats have gotten to her?" Miss Hartley scurried off, presumably to look for her mother.

But she ran right into Pratt, who was coming up the stairs with a magnificent, bejeweled sabre.

"My goodness," she said, "where did you get a sword like that?"

"It belonged to my great-grandfather," he said. "Stand aside, *per favore, bella*." Pratt immediately put her behind him and held the sabre out in a defensive stance. "I will defeat the thing that makes you shriek like a demon."

"It's all right," Stephen told him. "It was only bats."

"Thank you anyway," Miss Hartley told Pratt softly. She trembled just a little.

Pratt lowered the sabre, looking almost disappointed. "Come with me." He put his arm around Miss Hartley's shoulders. "I will feed your mouth delicious flavors—crisp toast with golden butter and yellow plum jam, savory fried eggs, and sweet, milky tea—so you forget your fear."

"I'd like that." Miss Hartley smiled.

Stephen strode past them down the stairs, pulled on his coat, hat, and Hessian boots, and went out into a dense fog. Even though the daughter was all right in her own way, he hated living at 34 Dreare Street with the reprehensible Hartley parents.

And he hated the fog.

He was off to the attorney's office to see what could be done about the Hartleys *and* the house, which obviously hadn't been inspected recently.

There was nothing he could do about the fog.

He could kick himself for signing for the house without checking its sturdiness himself, but who was he to say no to an inheritance? Particularly when the pirate loot he'd been relying on to finance his new life had been unfairly taken from him mere days before he'd learned of the house?

He'd gone only a few steps onto the street when he smelled a delicious odor—frying bacon. And it was coming from the first floor of Hodgepodge.

He saw the vague shape of Otis leaning out the window. "Come up for breakfast, Captain! London isn't even awake yet. Where could you be off to so early?"

"I've got business at my attorney's office," he said. "But you're right. I'm too hasty. No doubt he's not there yet."

Otis chuckled. "So wait here with us. The shop won't open for another hour and a half. We've got tremendous news to tell you anyway."

Otis did sound rather lively for so early in the morning.

"I'd enjoy that," said Stephen, "if it's all right with Miss Jones."

"It *should* be all right with Miss Jones," a whiny masculine voice called out from a window at his own house, "since you're courting her. But what kind of food shall I break my fast with here?"

Stephen gritted his teeth.

Sir Ned.

He was, sadly, awake.

Stephen turned toward the large shadow hanging out one of his windows. "Pratt will take care of you."

"Bah!" called another voice through the fog.

This voice came from in front of Lady Duchamp's house, and it was the old crone herself. Stephen hadn't realized it until just now, when a break came in the mist, but a horse and carriage waited before her house, and she was inside the carriage, at the window. She was apparently going on her regular morning outing, wherever that was.

She leaned on her cane. "You're a poor excuse for a host, Captain Arrow. And that baronet and his harpy of a wife are up to no good, mark my words."

"Who is *she*?" called Sir Ned, his voice thick with fury.

Lady Duchamp's carriage began to roll down the street.

"Arrow?" Sir Ned yelled again from his window. "You'd better set her straight! Arrow, are you there? And what are you going to do about the bats?"

Stephen ignored him and slipped through the fog to the front door of Hodgepodge. Otis had come downstairs and was waiting to let him in. The familiar odor of books comforted him, and that delicious bacon smell had wafted down from the first floor. He realized he was hungry, he hadn't read a good story in a long time, and he was anxious to finish the ledge.

It felt good to have such simple cravings.

Of course, his craving for Miss Jones was much more primal. He looked forward to seeing her this morning.

"Miss Jilly is finishing up the toast," Otis said, as if reading his mind. "Come upstairs."

Stephen was taken aback by the man's appearance. He was dressed in a tricorne hat and red coat and was carrying a bell, like a town crier. "What's going on?"

Otis stood tall. "We have an important announcement to make to Dreare Street," he said in a dramatic voice. "But first, we must eat."

Upstairs, Miss Jones was bending over the fire and holding a slice of bread on a poker.

She looked over her shoulder, her cheeks pinkening at the sight of him. "Good morning, Captain."

He'd never seen a more alluring sight. "Good morning, Miss Jones."

She seemed struck dumb by his presence, but then she stood straight with her poker and toast. "We've much to discuss," she said rather breathlessly.

"Do we?" He'd rather not discuss. He'd rather *do*. Kissing, that is. He wished it could be more, but he knew a scorching flirtation was all he could allow.

"*Captain*." He felt reprimanded with that word alone.

"Yes, Miss Jones?"

She let out a huff of air. "You need to stop being so . . . so—" She waved her poker and toast.

"Stop being so what?" He pretended he had no idea what she meant. But he knew she wanted him to stop looking at her the way he'd looked at her on the roof the afternoon previous.

"Are you asking him to stop being so spirited, good-looking, and stylish?" Otis interjected.

"Of course not," said Miss Jones crossly. "Forget I even spoke. Here." She thrust the poker toward Stephen. "Grab a plate and take this. We've plenty of butter and jam."

Stephen did as he was told. After he'd slathered the toast with both butter and jam, he sat down at the small table and began to eat. Otis ate a piece of toast as well and then remembered to pass the bacon, which Stephen took with thanks.

Otis looked back between Miss Jones and Stephen and chuckled. "My, my," he said, and wiped his mouth with a linen serviette.

"What are you on about?" Jilly asked her assistant.

Otis merely shrugged and kept chuckling and eating his toast. Stephen couldn't help it—he knew that Otis was aware of the tension between Stephen and his mistress. He gave a short laugh, too. Which made Otis chuckle more.

"I need you to be serious," Jilly said to Otis in her primmest manner. "And you, as well," she said to Stephen.

Stephen stopped chewing. "I'm perfectly serious, Miss Jones."

Otis giggled again.

"No you're not." Miss Jones narrowed her eyes at Stephen. "I know what you're thinking."

"Do you?" He cast a sideways glance at Otis.

He knew they were being like two little boys, but it was an amusing diversion, especially when one wasn't allowed to give in to impulse and damned well kiss the girl.

"Yes, I do know," his beautiful neighbor said, "and you're putting our futures in peril by refusing to listen."

"But you haven't said anything," Otis declared in his sauciest manner.

Miss Jones pursed her lips. "I'm saying it now."

Stephen sat up straighter. "Do go on." He did his best to intimidate her with the face he'd used when facing the enemy at sea, the one that had set his own sailors trembling in their shoes—but she merely put a hand on her hip and stared him down with her violet-blue pansy eyes.

Good God, he could get lost in those eyes. But at the exact moment he had that delicious feeling, her pupils sharpened dangerously, and he looked away.

First.

What was the world coming to when he looked away first? And from a female other than his own mother? It had never happened before.

And damned if it would ever happen again.

He looked back at her, intending to impress her with his best fierce expression, but it was too late. As if his lowered brows and steely-eyed glare meant nothing, she was already on to putting another hand on her hip and opening her mouth to deliver a big speech.

He knew it would be a big speech. Women always nagged men with big speeches.

So he retreated to his own little world, a world that consisted of her breasts, straining against her laces, her pale, delicate neck and the creamy expanse of her shoulders, and the plate of bacon, which still had two slices on it.

"Captain," she said. "You're to partner with me in conducting a street fair."

And then there was dead silence.

Whatever happened to the big speech?

He returned his gaze to her face. "I'm afraid that's impossible." He could hardly take the remaining bacon now, a fact which set his jaw on edge.

Miss Jones blinked several times. "You must." She began to pace in a small, tight circle. "We have no choice but to try."

"Why?"

She turned to face him. "To make money to pay the overdue leases."

Otis pushed himself up from the table and took his bell with him. "Now we've got that out of the way, I'm going outside to call the neighbors over."

And then he scampered down the stairs.

Stephen pushed his chair back. "I'm leaving. Thank you for the toast and bacon."

"Captain." Miss Jones stood in front of him, her chin in the air. "I did you a favor, now it's your turn to return it."

Stephen looked down at her. "People don't conduct street fairs in London anymore."

Miss Jones bit her lip. "But they used to have a street fair here on Dreare Street."

"*Used* to. They don't anymore."

She looked so bereft, he felt almost regretful about bursting her bubble. "I know many of us have money woes," he said. "But a street fair won't cure them. You've no idea how much is involved in conducting one. It's a major undertaking. And I, for one, don't have time to make it happen. I have a house to repair."

He turned to go.

"You have to help me," she blurted out. "You made a promise when I agreed to allow you to pursue me."

He turned back around. A few beats of tortured silence went by. What could he say, other than that she was right?

"You're right," he said. "I *am* pursuing you." He lifted her chin and had a brilliant thought. A morning kiss would be a nice thing to have, especially one from Miss Jones.

"No, Captain," she said, her face flushing pink. "You're not really. It's all a ruse."

"That kiss on the roof was no ruse."

"Yes, well, that was a mistake." She blinked several times.

"Was it?"

Her lips parted prettily. She wanted to kiss him, too. He saw it in her eyes.

Out the window, they both heard the bell ring and Otis cry, "Urgent meeting at Hodgepodge regarding the overdue leases! Commencing immediately!"

And sadly, Miss Jones took a step back. "We need to focus on my plan. Trust me, Captain. It will work."

The empty space she'd left near him—and that ringing bell—irritated him enough so that all his good humor vanished. "Why should I trust your judgment over my own?" he demanded to know.

It was a ludicrous idea—especially when a man needed a kiss.

Miss Jones looked at him steadily. "Because I found that diary and got the idea for the street fair from it. It was meant to be. It was . . . good luck."

"I don't believe in luck." And he didn't.

"Nor did I," she replied, "but I've realized something recently." Now she grew agitated but in a delicious way—all breathy and warm and appealing. "We resort to luck when we worry that someone or something else is going to snatch the future we crave away from us. That's why I believe in luck now, Captain. I'm desperate. And I suspect you are, as well."

"I'm not desperate, Miss Jones."

Other than being desperate for *her*.

"Aren't you?" She was impertinent, asking him such a question with a daring little arch to her brow.

Of course, she'd no idea how provocative her statement was.

He thought of other ways—other than longing for her—in which he could be desperate. The idea of sitting on Dreare Street while his house crumbled around him came to mind. And of all the money he didn't have yet that he'd have to spend to fix it. And the days, weeks, months, and perhaps years it would take to sell it afterward.

It was a dismal prospect.

Very dismal.

"I . . . I might be a little bit desperate," he admitted. "But not enough to take orders from anyone."

She cracked a smile. "We'll see about that. Come on!" She beckoned him with a hand.

"I'm only going to stay and listen because we both made an agreement," he told her in his firmest manner, the one he'd always used to negotiate the enemy's surrender. *"Together."*

But she either didn't hear him or ignored him.

She was already running down the stairs and calling Otis's name.

CHAPTER TEN

Jilly expected to see some neighbors appear at Hodge-podge after Otis performed his duties as the street crier, but she wasn't prepared to see so many of them arrive that the bookstore was crammed to overflowing within minutes.

Otis reappeared with his bell at the front door, positively beaming.

The crowd, Jilly noted right away, seemed nervous. Everyone stood looking at each other warily. A very few conversed in low tones, but most people acted as if they didn't know each other and rather regretted coming.

Jilly went to Otis.

"Well done," she told him, refusing to give in to nerves. She squeezed his hand. "Please leave the door open. Anyone else who arrives will have to listen from there."

His cheeks were bright red with excitement. "It was remarkable. I barely began ringing the bell and speaking when people started pouring out of their houses. It was almost as if they had been waiting for the announcement. As if they knew something must be done to help Dreare Street. Of course, no one could see where they were going through the fog—it's particularly thick today—but I kept ringing the bell, and they found us."

Jilly was just as excited. "I'm going to do my very best to bring us together."

"You will," Otis said. "I'm sure of it."

She turned back to the crowd and gently eased her way through before stopping at the counter. It was time to address Dreare Street. She would need to lead her neighbors into a major resolution. It would require that she be bold and convincing.

But no matter how tall she stood, she still couldn't be seen by some people near the shop windows.

"Here," Captain Arrow said, "Stand on this." He brought over a sturdy chair. "I'll stay beside it to make sure you don't fall."

"Thank you," she said, acutely aware that his hands were at her waist when he lifted her up.

But she was angry at him. He hadn't truly committed to assisting her in this endeavor. He'd made it clear he thought it was a stupid idea and he was only here because she'd threatened to reveal that his pursuit of her was a mere ruse if he didn't cooperate.

She needed more than halfhearted support. She needed him to believe her plan could work.

So she'd have to convince him, too, wouldn't she?

"Hello, residents of Dreare Street," she said, and tried to control the trembling in her voice. "Thank you all for coming. I realize I haven't met all of you, but I'm glad—*so* glad—you're here."

Most people just stared at her. A few smiled, among them Nathaniel, Susan, and Mrs. Hobbs. From the door, Otis mouthed something and made some earnest gestures she didn't understand. She could swear he was pretending to ride a horse, and then he made a face as if he'd sucked on a lemon.

She couldn't see Captain Arrow's face as he was next to her. But she sensed his reluctance to be there.

Introduction over, Jilly took another breath and launched into her main point. "We're here this morning because Dreare Street is in crisis. We're in arrears. We must all pay an overdue lease on the land beneath our homes, and for many of us, this will be a severe hardship."

"That's right!" a man called out.

She wasn't sure who'd said that, but there was a smattering of applause in response.

Good, she thought. *They want out of this fix, too.*

She smiled. "I'm glad we're in agreement on that point. Because I believe we'll need everyone's cooperation if we're to solve our financial woes. But there's something else I think is just as important to repair"— she paused—"and that is the doleful atmosphere on Dreare Street."

There were a few intakes of breath and one or two murmurs.

"It can't be done," croaked one elderly man in a fine vest of gray silk that had seen better days. "I've been here my whole life, eighty years. Dreare Street is dreary, and that's the way it's always been and always will be."

There was a murmur of agreement.

Everyone looked sadder than ever.

Jilly caught Captain Arrow's gaze and couldn't read it. It was completely neutral, and she guessed he was probably biding his time until the meeting was over. His indifference annoyed her no end—not that she had time to think on it at the moment.

She must address the elderly man's concerns.

"Said with all due respect, but you're mistaken, sir." Her tone was bright. She wouldn't let Captain Arrow's or anyone else's skepticism keep her from her purpose. "Two hundred years ago, Dreare Street was a bustling, thriving community."

It seemed everyone's mouths dropped open at that statement.

"That's impossible!" cried Mrs. Hobbs.

"Im-*possible*," echoed her red-faced husband.

Nathaniel held up his paint-stained hand. He must have come straight from his easel. "Pardon my asking, Miss Jones, but how would you know what Dreare Street was like two hundred years ago?"

She heard a familiar whimper—she swung her gaze to Otis and saw him puckering his mouth more than ever, as if he were sucking on two lemons, not one. He angled his head toward the door.

It was Lady Duchamp. She was already waving her cane about, the one with the tiny porcelain figurine on top, and making a path toward the front of the crowd.

How could Jilly not have noticed her absence?

The old lady's mouth was as puckered as Otis's had been.

So that was what he'd been trying to tell her—that Lady Duchamp was on the way. She must have just returned from her mysterious morning outing in her carriage. Of course, Jilly couldn't object to her presence. She was a neighbor and should be at the meeting as much as anyone.

"What's going on here?" Lady Duchamp demanded to know.

"A meeting," someone called out.

Lady Duchamp made an ugly face. "I don't approve of meetings. Too many people use them to plot against the government. I'll call the constable on you people if you don't disband immediately."

Behind her someone else walked in, the most arresting woman Jilly had ever seen. She had wide, slanted green eyes, high cheekbones, a mass of glorious blond hair, and a bold, aristocratic air.

"Aunt! What's going on?" The beautiful woman looked about the room. "Why are you here with *these* people?" She seemed to see Captain Arrow then, and her irritated expression dissolved and took on a nuance of curiosity. "Oh, very well. We may stay long enough for you to make a general introduction." Her voice had lost a trifle of its scorn.

"This is my niece Lady Tabitha, of the Dorset Bellinghams," Lady Duchamp barked. "She puts all of you to shame."

Lady Tabitha appeared amused for some reason. Probably because every man in the room stared at her goggle-eyed, except Captain Arrow. He was too self-possessed to be goggle-eyed, but Jilly had no doubt he was as moved by Lady Tabitha's beauty and presence as the rest of the males in the room.

Lady Tabitha seemed to have eyes only for Captain Arrow when she said, "I do hope I'll be entertained while I reside on Dreare Street."

Jilly seethed inside at the girl's flirtatious manner, even though it was no concern of hers if the captain and Lady Tabitha took pleasure in each other's company.

Lady Duchamp angled her cane at Jilly. "What's going on here?"

"A meeting, my lady," Jilly said with dignity, although suddenly she felt plain and frumpy in front of the two latecomers. "Dreare Street is in arrears, and we intend to find a way to pay what we owe."

"It will never happen," Lady Duchamp said. "And I say good riddance to the lot of you."

Lady Tabitha was unmoved by her aunt's vitriol. She merely cocked a brow and gazed around the company with a bemused expression.

Jilly had no choice but to ignore her harpy of a neighbor. "We have another, equally important mission, as well," she told the crowd, "to make Dreare Street a cheerful place to live. Not only will that make all of us happier residents, we might attract more customers to the businesses on the street."

"Bah," the old woman said. "Give up. The fog's never going to go away. No one can be happy in such fog. Not a soul will buy anything in such a fog, either."

"How can you trust the quality of merchandise you

can't see?" Lady Tabitha said with a light chuckle and a mysterious, pointed glance at Captain Arrow.

Jilly noted he met the lady's gaze, but his gave nothing away.

The crowd's murmurs grew louder, until one small, strong voice spoke above the noise.

"But I don't want to leave." It was Susan. "I like my flat. I like Miss Jones."

Jilly's heart warmed.

Lady Duchamp swiveled around to look at Susan. "You should be among the first to leave, young lady. It's not as if you get any business. A seamstress's hands should be blistered and red from all the work she does, pushing needles through fabric, but I suspect yours are soft and white from lack of use. Show them to me."

Susan held up her hand slowly. Her fingers trembled.

"See?" Lady Duchamp's voice was triumphant. "They're too pretty by half."

Susan clenched her fingers and jerked her hand back down. "I'm not ready to give up," she said with feeling. "I'm here to find a way to pay that money. I'm a good seamstress, too, if anyone will give me a chance." She looked around the room. "I also believe there are other kind neighbors here in addition to Miss Jones. I've never found out, but I'd like to. We have a lot of fog here, more than the average London street. But surely a kind word from a friend can outweigh the gloom the fog brings."

Jilly saw Nathaniel over in a corner eyeing Susan with curiosity, just like everyone else.

"I agree, Susan," Jilly said. "We can be a thriving community, the way Dreare Street used to be." She reached into a pocket in her gown, pulled out Alicia Fotherington's journal, and held it aloft. "This diary was written by someone who lived here two hundred years ago. Her name was Alicia Fotherington. I've only just begun it, but from the very start she tells about the happy life on the street. And one of the happiest things on Dreare Street at the time was—"

Good heavens.

Jilly felt as if her stomach had dropped out of her body.

A man had just peered in the window behind Lady Tabitha.

A man who looked like Hector.

Jilly's heart jammed in her throat, making it difficult to breathe.

But then the man angled his gaze to the left and—thank goodness—she saw he wasn't Hector at all, simply a man who looked eerily like her husband.

And then he walked away.

But it could have been Hector, a scary voice inside reminded her. *And next time it might be.*

"What was the happy thing, Miss Jones?" Nathaniel called out.

"Yes, Miss Jones," Susan asked warmly. "What made Dreare Street a nice place to live?"

Jilly felt her mouth open and shut like a fish. The hand holding the diary aloft began to tremble.

"Excuse me." She looked at Captain Arrow, and he seemed to sense her discomfort because he put a hand on her waist. "I feel faint," she whispered.

Immediately, he picked her up and set her on the floor.

Around them, everyone stared and began murmuring words of concern.

"Are you all right, Miss Jilly?" She heard Otis's voice from the door.

"We've no doctors on this street," said Lady Duchamp, "so you'd best hope you're not deathly ill, young lady."

"I'm fine," Jilly assured everyone. She gave a nervous laugh. "I didn't eat this morning. I should have."

Otis stared at her with wide, fearful eyes. Poor man, he could tell something was wrong. He knew she'd broken her fast with that toast, bacon, and a strong cup of tea. But she couldn't tell him in front of everyone else about whom she thought she'd just seen.

Captain Arrow lowered his head to hers. "You look as if you've seen a ghost," he said.

They exchanged a silent look for a few seconds.

"It's nothing," she whispered. "I simply grew faint for a moment. It must be the excitement of having the bookstore full of people."

"I don't believe you," he said in a low tone, "but now's not the time to discuss it. Can you go on?"

She nodded. "Of course."

He gave her a hand—his was strong and reassuring—and she returned to her chair.

"Forgive me, everyone," she said briskly. "I felt faint for a moment, but it's passed."

The truth was, it hadn't passed a bit. She was still buzzing from fear. She was having difficulty even concentrating on the task at hand.

"Now," she said, her voice quavering just a tad, "let me finally tell you what I think we should do, based on what made Dreare Street prosperous back in Alicia Fotherington's day." Her gaze swept the room. "They used to hold a small market here every Wednesday. It was really a lovely little street fair. Isn't that delightful?"

Otis clapped. "Yes!" he cried. "It's very delightful!"

"What's your point, Miss Jones?" Mr. Hobbs asked her, his mouth twisted with impatience.

"I believe *we* should hold a street fair," she answered him in her brightest, most confident voice. But she didn't feel bright and confident at all. She felt frightened. And vulnerable. What if that man had been one of Hector's minions?

Maybe Hector was waiting for her somewhere in London!

"At first, we'll hold just one," she managed to suggest, despite her racing thoughts. "But then if it's a success, we can repeat it."

"This is Mayfair," Mr. Hobbs said in a flat tone. "And two hundred years later. No one holds street fairs anymore."

"Besides which, no one likes the place," Sir Ned said. "Dreare Street's unlucky."

"And there's too much *fog*," said Lady Hartley with a moué of disgust.

Jilly attempted to compose herself. "We can't let a bad reputation or a little weather hold us back," she said. "Think of it this way: we'll raise money to pay our overdue leases. Won't that be wonderful for all of us?"

"Yes!" squeaked Otis.

But no one else said a word.

Jilly forged on. "Even those of us who have the money at hand will enjoy having some of that financial burden removed. We'll split the profits. And with this street fair, Dreare Street will make a name for itself. We'll be prosperous again. *Happy*."

"Speak for yourself," Lady Duchamp bit out.

"All residents," Jilly went on earnestly, hoping everyone was ignoring the naysayers among the crowd, "whether you own a business or not, will be proud to call Dreare Street home."

She leaned back and took a breath, hoping her message had gotten through.

Susan smiled, raised a finger, and opened her mouth as if she wanted to say something.

"Yes, Susan?" Jilly asked hopefully. Finally, someone was going to agree with her!

But Susan seemed to think better of it and put her finger down.

Jilly's heart sank. "Anyone else with a comment?" she asked in faint tones.

Lady Duchamp sniffed loudly, but not a single person spoke.

When Jilly gazed around the room, her spirits plummeted further. To her dismay, some faces, like Sir Ned's and Lady Duchamp's, were scornful. A few, such as Captain Arrow's, Lady Tabitha's, and Nathaniel's, were unreadable. Surely, Jilly thought, if they were enthusiastic, they'd show some emotion, wouldn't they?

But no. They didn't. Captain Arrow's face was the worst of all. She was used to seeing him merry. An impenetrable expression didn't suit him at all.

Some expressions, like that of Mrs. Hobbs, were confused. Still more, like Susan's, were simply sad and worried.

Not a one of her neighbors appeared hopeful.

Jilly stole a quick glance at Otis—

His mouth drooped down, and he was staring into space with a big wrinkle on his forehead. But oh, when he caught her gaze, how he tried to be optimistic! He gave her a wobbly grin and a thumbs-up.

But it was too late. She'd seen his disbelief.

Her stomach tightened into a hard knot of tension. If even Otis couldn't come up with authentic enthusiasm, her idea for saving Hodgepodge and all of Dreare Street must be a disaster. She clasped her trembling fingers in front of her skirt and racked her brain for a solution, but none came.

Perhaps she must face an unwanted truth: her idea was doomed.

CHAPTER ELEVEN

Stephen believed Miss Jones's proposal was as likely to launch as a yacht with no rudder, sails, or crew. But to see this naïve yet well-intentioned campaign fail so quickly bothered him. Perhaps it was because he hated to see Miss Jones disillusioned. He was reluctant to admit it, but he rather liked her optimistic nature. And perhaps he was disappointed because none of these people on Dreare Street had volunteered to be put in their difficult position. They weren't ready to fight their enemy. They were ill trained, taken by surprise—

Vulnerable to attack.

Stephen had made sure his ship's crews were always ready. They'd been trained, and they'd known exactly what they'd signed up for.

The people on Dreare Street were easy prey for the Mr. Redmonds of this world.

It was a pity. But what was he to do? Go about protecting everyone? He couldn't keep being a naval captain on land, urging the population of Dreare Street onward and upward.

No. It wasn't his place. He couldn't take on other people's problems anymore.

He had his own.

"Well, that's that," Mr. Hobbs muttered aloud, hitting his hat on his leg. "This meeting didn't help at all. I'm on my way."

As one, the crowd turned toward the front entrance of Hodgepodge.

"Don't leave!" Otis cried, throwing his arm across the door. "Let's play charades, shall we? I've a book title." And he held up four fingers.

"Four words!" called out Nathaniel.

Otis held up one finger.

"First word!" lisped Miss Hartley, a big grin on her face.

Stephen saw Miss Jones's jaw working hard, and was sorry to see her violet-blue eyes clouded over with distress. But then she looked at him, and those eyes turned almost black.

"What have I done?" he asked her.

She pursed her lips. "You know what." She hopped down from her chair and stormed past him.

He took her arm. "You can't possibly expect—"

She yanked her arm back. "If you've nothing to say to help me, then please—just play charades and leave with the rest of them."

She went over to her counter and bent below it. He heard a cupboard flung open, and saw the top of her ebony head, moving back and forth. She must be putting something in the cupboard and taking something out. Long lashes framed her cheekbones, and her delicious lips pursed as she created two stacks of books.

She always moved things about when she was upset.

Her idea about the street fair didn't seem viable, but Stephen didn't have a better solution, did he?

"There's more to this thing than trying to earn money to pay the lease and keeping the street's spirits up, isn't there?" he told the top of her head. "Maybe you don't even realize it yourself, or maybe you do. But my instincts tell me you're creating the street fair to keep something else at bay—something that's worrying you besides the money. Something you're afraid of."

She refused to answer. But then she looked up, distrust of him evident in her gaze. "Whatever my reasons, at least I'm trying to do something to *help*."

He laughed. "I've done plenty of helping, as you call it, in my time."

"Oh," she said mildly, "is your time over, then? You're awfully young to retreat from the world."

He pushed off the counter, too annoyed with her to speak.

"Fourth word!" called Sir Ned at Otis's antics.

"Second syllable!" called the lively old man in the gray vest, the one who'd lived on Dreare Street his whole life.

His whole life.

And he'd never seen it happy.

Stephen made a split-second decision.

"Otis," he said in a voice he knew would be heard above the crowd noise—it was his captain's voice. Hadn't he planned mere seconds ago never to use it on land again?—"please cease the charades and continue holding the door. I've something of importance to say."

"The Mysteries of Udolpho!" Miss Hartley cried out. Her mother stared at her in shock.

Otis clapped. "Very good, Miss Hartley."

"She's not supposed to read novels!" Sir Ned cried. "They're nonsense."

"Shut up, you idiot." Lady Duchamp poked Sir Ned in the chest with her cane. "I've better things to do with my time than listen to you or Captain Arrow or anyone else in this godforsaken shop. Get out of my way."

She managed to get to the front door, but Otis held fast to the doorknob. "You must stay, my lady. Captain Arrow is a man of passion, style, and good looks. He has something important to relate to all of us."

"You foolish clerk," Lady Duchamp chastised him, "why should any of us listen to the captain? He's more concerned with carousing than he is with the affairs of Dreare Street. If he could sell his house today, he'd depart faster than a ball from a fired pistol."

Stephen saw everyone turn and look at him with a great deal of skepticism.

"Lady Duchamp does have a point." He pulled out a cheroot and lit it on a candle taper. In a moment, he blew a small smoke ring. "Perhaps I haven't shown much interest in Dreare Street." He lowered his cheroot. "But I'm interested now, and that's all that matters."

"Why should we believe you?" a young man asked with genuine curiosity.

Stephen raked a hand through his hair and sneaked a glance at Miss Jones. She was looking at him with her brows drawn and her arms crossed.

Just like a disapproving schoolteacher.

"Oh!" said the old man in the gray vest. "I see how it is. You like *her*." And he pointed at Miss Jones.

"Is that true, Captain?" asked Mrs. Hobbs.

He cleared his throat. How to answer that without inflaming Miss Jones's temper even more?

"He's pursuing her," explained Sir Ned with a great deal of self-importance. "But he's waiting until he sells his house to declare himself. I'm right, aren't I, Arrow?"

"You don't have to answer that, Captain." Miss Jones looked neither right nor left but directly at him, as if she didn't want anyone but him to see her mortified expression.

It was a most uncomfortable moment, made even worse when most of the other women looked at him softly—except Lady Hartley and Lady Duchamp (both of whom were staring malevolently at Miss Jones) and Lady Tabitha. She wasn't looking softly at Stephen at all but with a knowing look, as if she and he were the only two people in the room worthy of any attention whatsoever.

As he often did in crisis, he ignored all distractions, both petty and large, and focused on his purpose.

"Perhaps I'm helping because I like desperate causes," he went on. "And at the moment, I want"—he looked at Miss Jones and thought, *I want* her, *although God knows why*—"I want Dreare Street to prosper."

Miss Jones's scowl lessened by at least half but remained steady.

"More than anything," he added.

She gave him a reluctant smile then, and he must admit, he loved knowing he'd pleased her.

"Let's get down to business," he said. "Does anyone have any idea how to earn that money? Other than Miss Jones's idea for the street fair, of course. If you have a better plan, now is the time to voice it."

It was an uneasy minute. No one spoke. Everyone stared at everyone else. Not even Sir Ned, the know-it-all, had an idea.

And damn it, neither did Stephen. Try as he might, he could think of no idea to save the street other than Miss Jones's.

He glanced at her.

Was she smirking at him?

He believed she was. Reluctantly, he must concede victory to her *and* sound happy about it in the bargain.

Dear God. He felt testy but was determined to be a good sport. After all, it wouldn't be the first time he'd been forced to follow someone else's ill-conceived plan. He'd done it in the navy many a time.

He inhaled deeply on his cheroot and exhaled. "We have less than a month to raise the funds to send Mr. Redmond, the collector, packing. And it appears we'll be conducting a street fair. We've nothing to lose. Have we?"

Almost everyone shook their heads.

"I think it could be fun," Nathaniel piped up.

"I do as well," echoed Miss Hartley.

"My Thomas will love a street fair," said Susan. "I say we try it. Why not?"

"We could have theatrics," said one matron.

"I know of a, hmmm, what you English call an up-and-coming acting troupe who might do it," said Pratt. "They're performing at the Royal Coburg Theater. I shall take Miss Hartley and her parents with me. We shall run these actors to dirt."

"Run them to *ground,* you mean," said Miss Hartley, clasping her hands together.

"Yes, we will find them and not let them go," said Pratt. "Not until they say yes."

His last comment was met with much enthusiasm.

"And we'll need someone with influence to appear at the fair," said one middle-aged man who'd never spoken until this moment. He was a frequent dog walker, but he'd yet to visit Hodgepodge to browse.

"You're so right!" exclaimed Jilly. But which person of influence? she wondered. And how would they get him or her to come?

"Excellent ideas, all," said Stephen. "Any others?"

"Of course, we'll have booths," said Susan shyly. "I'll sell gowns and fancy caps."

"I'll sell my paintings," said Nathaniel.

"I've boxes of china to get rid of," said one lady.

"And I've old silver!" said another.

"I'll cook something," said Mrs. Hobbs. "Meat pies!"

"No you won't," said her husband. "You can barely boil water."

Mrs. Hobbs bit her lip. "But I can try!"

"I'll provide drinks," said someone else, a stout older gentleman. "I make a fine beer in my cellar."

"We need a band," said someone. "My hotel manager knows someone."

"And a children's parade," Susan added with a delighted smile.

As everyone shouted out their ideas, Stephen marveled at the change in Miss Jones. Her odd nervousness was gone. So was her anger. Her eyes were sparkling again.

"All these plans we're making are splendid," she said with a happy smile. "And now I need to know how many of you are in. Please show by a raise of hands."

Otis, Susan, Nathaniel, the Hobbses' children, and Mrs. Hobbs immediately raised their hands. But Mr. Hobbs made his family put their hands back down.

Miss Hartley was next, along with Pratt and several older residents. Her mother nudged Miss Hartley in the side.

"But I want to help," the young lady said.

"You can't do that," her father blustered. "Helping is for the lower classes."

"But I've nothing to do except go to parties all day and night and talk to stuffy people." Miss Hartley turned pleading eyes on her parents. "Please, Mother and Father, please let me do this. And you raise your hands, too. We need to go to the Coburg Theater with Pratt."

Lady Hartley rolled her eyes. "All right," she said. "But we'll involve ourselves only sparingly. Just enough that we can tell amusing anecdotes about these people later."

These people.

Stephen looked around and saw only decent citizens of London. Gad, the Hartleys were a boorish couple. And to think they were sleeping under *his* roof!

By the time Miss Jones finished counting, everyone had raised their hands except for the Hobbs family, Lady Tabitha—who stated that she'd no interest in the fair as she was a guest in the neighborhood—and Lady Duchamp.

The old harridan faced the crowd to vent her spleen once more. "A curse on this street fair," she muttered. "And on all you ridiculous people."

With that, she sailed out. Lady Tabitha directed one last, alluring look Stephen's way, and then she followed her aunt. Drawing up the rear was the Hobbs family. Stephen hated to see Mrs. Hobbs appear so drawn when a moment before, she'd been terribly excited. The children, judging by their sagging postures, were disappointed, as well.

Miss Jones called a wistful good-bye to them, but the unlikable Mr. Hobbs shuffled his family out so quickly, Mrs. Hobbs and the children couldn't return Miss Jones's farewells.

Fortunately, everyone else remained. They were

busy talking about the street fair, what they would do, and how.

Despite the few setbacks they'd encountered with the loss of some participants in the fair, Hodgepodge was bursting with activity, Stephen noted with satisfaction. Miss Jones must have noticed, too. He exchanged a look with her, and she gave him a happy grin.

Then she mouthed the words, "Thank you."

He must admit, against all good judgment, he felt excited himself. And warmed by her gratitude. Craving a kiss from her again, he followed her with his eyes as she made cheerful forays into the different clusters of people filling every corner of Hodgepodge.

"Miss Jones," he whispered aloud, "you're a damned nuisance."

Nevertheless, as annoying as the lady was, he must give her *some* credit. Already he could see a change in the attitudes of the people of Dreare Street.

Hope hung in the air, along with the lingering fog, a wisp of which had been blown into the bookstore by Lady Duchamp's exit.

But still, there was hope.

He felt it as surely as he did the plank floor beneath his feet.

CHAPTER TWELVE

"First things first," Jilly said to Captain Arrow the next day. She knelt near him while he put the finishing touches on her window ledge. "We need booths."

"Wait." He looked sideways at her, an appealing grin on his face, and her heart melted in an alarming way. "I thought you said 'first things first.'"

"I did."

He cocked his handsome golden head at the ledge. "This was first. The ledge. What do you think of my progress?"

She sighed and bit her lip. She was happily surprised to see what a good craftsman he was. Indeed, he'd taken great pains with that ledge. She might even say he'd shown it extreme attention.

"You're doing a good job," she said simply, and stood.

"'Good'?" He cocked a brow. "I'm rather disappointed. Do I sense your words are measured?"

She sighed. "I'm afraid to compliment you too very much in case you think your obligation to me is over. Because of you, the whole world thinks we have an . . . an understanding."

"Ah." He laid down his hammer and stood before her. She had to look up into his gold-flecked eyes. "That would be intolerable, wouldn't it?"

His gaze was too warm for comfort.

"Yes," she said, the word trailing off. "It would. Now, Captain—"

"You call me Captain much too often. Please feel free to call me Stephen."

"I'd rather not." She felt her face heat. "You know very well it's improper."

He moved a few inches closer. "But I heard you call that artist by his given name—Nathaniel."

She blushed. "That's because he's no danger. You, sir, are an Impossible Bachelor. A lady can't be too careful around the likes of you."

She strode to the other end of the window and peered out.

"Expecting someone?" the captain asked in cheerful tones.

A brief vision of Hector invaded her thoughts. "I wish a hoard of customers were coming this way," she said as coolly as she could muster.

He laughed. "You're not afraid of me, Miss Jones. You like me. *That's* what you're afraid of."

"Oh, hush," she said, and glowered at him.

He looked right back at her, with a lazy grin that somehow made her blink repeatedly, like a fussy old maid.

Which she was. Or might as well be since she would never marry again.

"Now about those booths," she said in a deliberate

change of subject. "We can't sell anything at the fair without them. We need *you* to make them."

He rubbed his chin. "I suppose we never put a limit on the number of favors you may ask me."

"No, we didn't." She couldn't help being pleased at her foresight. "It's too late, of course, to change our arrangement."

"Yes," he said thoughtfully. "It's too late. Much too late."

He began walking toward her.

"It is," she agreed.

And then had a very bad feeling.

Because he was looking at her as if he'd trapped her into saying something she shouldn't have.

He stood before her and raked her with a glance that seemed to see right through her blue-sprigged muslin gown. "You agreed to go along with this story of mine. This romantic story of pursuit. Did you not?"

His eyes again. They held her fast.

Her heart began to thump wildly, and she backed up a step. "Yes," she said. "But if you're thinking about kissing me—"

He came forward a step. "When did I ever say that?"

She turned her head to the right. "You didn't have to."

He chuckled, and put a finger under her chin, turning her face slowly back to meet his gaze. "All I'm suggesting, Miss Jones, is that being involved with each other"—he hesitated—"could be a pleasurable thing."

"I'm not interested," she said flatly. "We have an

agreement, and that's what we'll adhere to. Kisses were never mentioned."

"No, they weren't." He kept her gaze, measure for measure, and dropped her hand.

She tried to ignore how good his fingers had felt wrapped around hers. "Back to the discussion about the booths," she said.

"I've already worked on one." He returned to his work at the ledge.

"Really?" She couldn't help but sound pleased.

He looked back at her with a sly grin. "Oh, so now I'm in favor."

"Is it any wonder?" she said, following after him when he stood to get the hammer. "When will it be finished?"

"It already is." He picked up the hammer and let it dangle from his fingers. "Pratt and I were up all night, actually. Lumley came over and lent a hand. We've enough scrap wood and nails to make at least five or six more. That should be enough, don't you think?"

"Yes." She felt shy of a sudden. "Now I know why you look a bit . . . sleepy."

"Now you know."

"I assumed you'd been out at some sort of revelry. I didn't hear a peep from your house."

"Not even the hammering at midnight?"

"No."

"You must have been well asleep." He gave her a look that made her blush.

She had no doubt the man was thinking of her in her bedclothes—or worse, without them on at all. "Yes, well," she stammered, "I was exhausted from worry and excitement, I suppose."

The truth was, she'd been so frightened by the face she'd seen at the window during the meeting, she'd opened Papa's old emergency flask and taken two large swigs of fine French brandy, which had helped her tumble into a very disturbing sleep.

But now was no time to dwell on her fears about Hector. She hadn't even had an opportunity to confide in Otis. Last night seemed hardly the time, not when he was so giddy with excitement about the fair.

"What did Sir Ned and Lady Hartley think of the noise at midnight?" she asked the captain.

"Sir Ned never heard it. He snores too loudly. And that's why Lady Hartley never heard it, either. As for Miss Hartley, well"——he laughed softly—"she sneaked out of the house into the shed and watched us, poor thing. She never stopped talking the entire time we were working."

"My goodness!" Jilly laughed. "I had no idea Miss Hartley had it in her to defy her parents."

"She's sleeping late this morning," the captain said. "Otis must be, as well."

"He is, actually." Jilly was amazed at his knowledge of the goings-on in her household. "How did you know?"

"He was there, too."

"Was he?" Her mouth dropped open. "He left me a note on his door, but he never said why. I assumed he wasn't feeling well."

"Excuse me," a lithe voice called from the back of

the store. "My ears are burning. I'm awake now, I'll have you know." Otis showed himself, looking none the worse for wear. He beamed at Captain Arrow. "Our booth is perfection itself, if you ignore the yawning gaps between the planks. But you're so right. The air flow between customer and selling agent will allow an atmosphere of true commerce to flourish."

"I'm glad you see it my way," said the captain.

"*Our* booth?" Jilly looked at Otis.

He reddened.

"I suppose you haven't had an opportunity to tell Miss Jones your plans," the captain remarked.

"Oh, my. Not yet." Otis looked worriedly at Jilly. "While you tend the store during the street fair, I, er, would like to run a booth. I'll sell my specially adorned footwear—"

"But Otis," she interrupted him. "You can't sell your special shoes. Each pair means something to you."

He laughed. "Of course I won't. I'm going about the street collecting used shoes in good condition today. I shall make new ones. And one of the young men on the street works at the hotel around the corner. He said they've got four big boxes of shoes. It seems people leave them under their beds all the time and never come back to pick them up. He said some don't have matches, but I can make them match, can't I? With a few slaps of paint and feathers and some of those exotic shells the captain brought back from his voyages—"

"Wait." Jilly crossed her arms. "Were many people there last night?"

Otis nodded happily. "Yes, my dear, everyone who came to the meeting was there but you, Lady Duchamp, and that odious Mr. Hobbs and his poor, poor family, who I know want to participate in the fair if that unpleasant man would only allow them. It was quite a festive evening."

Jilly stared at the captain. "Why was I not invited? I thought I was partnering with you in creating this event."

Captain Arrow shrugged. "It wasn't planned. It simply happened."

"I didn't want to wake you, Miss Jilly," Otis said. "You were sleeping like a baby, with Alicia Fotherington's sweet little journal propped in your hands. I had to blow out your candle and take the diary away."

"Oh, dear," she said. "I must have wasted a candle." She trailed off, hating to think about their precarious financial situation.

She'd tell them about the diary instead. "Last night I read all about the second wing Alicia's husband added onto the house in hopes they'd soon have a family. It's the wing closest to Lady Duchamp's."

"I sleep there," Captain Arrow said. "Or *did*." Some fleeting tension seemed to cross his face.

"Is there a problem with that wing?" she asked him.

"No," he said lightly. "None at all. Just a few repairs I have to make."

"Oh." She pushed an annoying wisp of hair off her

cheek. "At any rate, do finish telling me your plans for the booth, Otis."

"Gladly." He clasped his hands together. "In addition to the shoes, I'll sell my signature handkerchiefs. I've already commissioned Miss Susan to make thirty overlarge ones. Today I'll be sifting through her scraps for the fabrics—I see yellows, golds, scarlets, blues . . ." He held up his hand as if he were displaying a shelf of them. "They'll be all the rage, mark my words. Especially if we can get the Prince Regent to come," he added in an offhanded tone, and went to adjust his cravat in the large, oval mirror.

"The Prince Regent," Jilly said with a chuckle. "You have lofty ambitions, my friend."

Otis looked at Captain Arrow. "You haven't told her yet?"

"No." The captain was quite preoccupied with a small, sharp corner on the ledge.

"No one's told me anything." She was beginning to feel quite left out.

"Captain Arrow, Lady Duchamp, and Lady Tabitha are going to a ball," said Otis grandly.

A ball?

The captain?

With Lady Tabitha?

Jilly felt a small twinge of something, although she wasn't certain what it was. Something to do with that left-out sensation again. And feeling plain and frumpy.

"Was Lady Tabitha there last night?" she asked in as neutral a tone as she could muster.

"I told you," said Otis, "everyone was." He looked at Captain Arrow. "Tell her why you're going to the ball."

Captain Arrow lifted his head from his work. "So we can invite the Prince Regent to the street fair. We'll ask him to be our guest of honor."

Jilly was so shocked, she could hardly breathe. "The Prince Regent? Attending *our* fair?"

Stephen stood. "Why not? I know him fairly well. He chose me to be one of his Impossible Bachelors, after all."

Jilly huffed. "What a silly arrangement *that* was. I never heard about it at the time, of course."

"Where were you?" Captain Arrow asked quickly. "Were you not in London?"

Jilly gave a little laugh. "No, actually." She trailed off and looked at Otis. "Otis and I might be called country bumpkins."

"Is that so?" Captain Arrow sent her a penetrating stare. "You've never told me where you're from, or what you did before you bought Hodgepodge."

"It never came up, Captain." She kept her tone light.

"Well?" He was insistent.

She sniffed, inwardly chagrined that for the first time since arriving in London, she'd have to tell the lie she'd practiced with Otis. "We're from Devon."

Somerset, actually, her stricken conscience reminded her.

"And how did you find yourselves in London?" The captain's words were equally light—but she sensed he was more intrigued than he should be.

He'd told her on two occasions now that he thought she was hiding something.

Otis wore an unlikely expression that she thought screamed deception, but to the rest of the world probably signified nothing more than bland attention to an ordinary social inquiry.

"My father died and left me a tidy inheritance." She'd decided long ago to stick with the truth as much as possible. "Otis was his valet and found himself without a job. I asked him to accompany me to London to help me open a bookstore. He's known me since I was a small girl."

"She's always wanted to own her own bookstore," Otis said, rocking on his heels.

"Indeed, I have." She touched the nape of her neck.

"Really," said Captain Arrow.

A few awkward seconds passed.

"Of course, I vowed to protect her in the big city." Otis thrust a hand through the air like a claw and roared like a lion.

Jilly gave a nervous laugh. Another beat of silence went by.

"Right," said Captain Arrow eventually, looking back and forth between them.

"About your plans to meet the prince." Jilly felt it was time to bring the conversation back from where it had veered into dangerous territory. "I must admit I'm rather confused. I thought Lady Duchamp planned on being no help at all with the street fair. Yet she's attending the ball with you?"

Captain Arrow lofted a brow. "It was Lady Tabitha's

idea," he said. "She said Lady Duchamp received the invitation just yesterday, and Lady Tabitha invited me along. It turns out she's quite the sport."

Sport.

"Is she?" Jilly gave the captain a wan smile, remembering that at their very first meeting, he'd told her she required more sport in her.

He nodded once. "She's enthused about the street fair, although she can't say so in front of her aunt. When I mentioned I was about to ask my good friends Harry and Molly Traemore to invite me along on one of their society jaunts—where I'd be sure to see the prince— Lady Tabitha told me I don't have to bother." He gave a little laugh. "I'm actually quite grateful to her. I was looking forward to seeing my married friends, but I'd like to delay the interrogations about my romantic life for as long as possible."

Jilly's face burned when she heard the word *romantic*. He'd said the same word to her a few moments earlier, when he'd given her that look, the one she could tell meant he wanted to kiss her.

Long ago, she'd hoped for romance. Her nurse had always told her that was a silly hope, that well-off people married for practical reasons. But Jilly had believed she'd be the exception to the rule.

Now she realized she hadn't been.

Romance wasn't to be hers.

It was for people without a past haunting them, people who could laugh carelessly and find amusements where they could—people like Captain Arrow and Lady Tabitha.

CHAPTER THIRTEEN

Once again, Miss Jones was attempting to hide how she really felt but couldn't quite manage it. Stephen could tell she wasn't at all enthusiastic about his going to the ball with Lady Tabitha and Lady Duchamp.

But his bookish neighbor wasn't one of his admirers, so she couldn't possibly be jealous of Lady Tabitha. Miss Jones had made it clear, however, that she didn't like the fair plans progressing without her. Perhaps that was it.

Or was she simply a lady who longed to go to a ball?

The more he thought about it, the more he believed the last possibility was the most likely. Every woman wanted to be a Cinderella, didn't she?

"Don't you get your own invitations to routs, balls, and musicales, Captain?" Otis asked in a polite manner. "Surely a person of such style, spirit, and good looks—"

"Certainly I get invitations from my old Eton friends," Stephen interrupted him, embarrassed at Otis's over-the-top flattery but not wanting to seem churlish, either. "But as I said, my married friends don't know I'm in Town yet. Since I've returned from sea, I've holed up here on Dreare Street with friends who, like me, couldn't care less about Almack's and debutante balls."

The bell rang at the front of the shop.

Miss Jones's face lit up when the person strolled in. "Nathaniel!"

Stephen must admit to feeling a spark of jealousy at how happy she appeared to see him.

"Miss Jones!" The artist's face creased into a smile. After everyone exchanged greetings, he said, "I'm back to get my book. I had a chance to look last night after the meeting, and I've decided I want the one about Venice."

"Excellent choice," Miss Jones murmured, and watched him with great interest as he took the book off the shelf.

"I'd like to have it wrapped, if you don't mind," he said and brought it over to her. "I'm going home soon for a brief visit, and I don't want it muddied by travel. I'll be reading it to my mother." He gave a wistful smile. "It's not often she sees books."

Miss Jones laid the book on the counter and sighed. "What a thoughtful son."

Nathaniel blushed.

Stephen watched as she shook her head in apparent wonder at Nathaniel's heroic qualities and went about wrapping the book in brown paper, all the while talking to him about Venice and how she'd love to see it someday, too. When she was done tying the book with string, she handed it back.

"Take it with my compliments to your mother," she

said with a smile that would have left any man with a beating heart breathless.

"Thank you." Nathaniel tucked the package under his arm and looked over at Stephen and Otis. "Lads, we enjoyed ourselves last night, didn't we?"

"That we did," said Otis.

"Your booth is next," Stephen added.

"I'd help you with it," Nathaniel said, "but I'm busy painting—I hope I can sell something at the fair. I'm beginning to wonder if I have any talent. No one's buying."

"You're tremendously talented," Miss Jones insisted. "I especially like your bold use of color."

"Do you?" Nathaniel's eyes seemed to soften when he looked at her.

And no wonder, Stephen thought. Already, Nathaniel had been declared the best son in the world, and now he was possibly the greatest painter. Any man would like to be so sincerely complimented.

Stephen found he wanted more compliments from the bookseller for himself, ones that weren't measured. Miss Jones wasn't made to hold anything back. Yet with him, she did suppress something. He saw it in every line of her being.

The seamstress, Susan, came into the store with her young son, Thomas, just as Nathaniel was leaving. They crossed paths at the front table, where Thomas stopped to examine a book with paintings of birds.

"Look at these," he said to Nathaniel, and pointed at the pictures. "I like the one with yellow on its wings."

"That's a goldfinch," said Nathaniel with an awkward smile and a nod at Susan.

Susan smiled back rather shyly. "Good morning."

Stephen recognized a mutual interest there. So did Miss Jones, obviously—she looked back and forth between them with a delighted smile on her face.

Nathaniel made his farewells, and Susan and Miss Jones exchanged a happy greeting.

"I hear you're working with Otis on a project for the street fair," Miss Jones said.

"Indeed, I am." Susan looked at Otis. "I came by to tell you I found two ladies on Dreare Street willing to darn lace on your handkerchiefs, Mr. Shrimpshire."

"That's excellent news," Otis declared. "Please call me Otis."

"Very well, Otis." Susan cocked her head in the direction of her shop. "If you're ready to see the fabrics I have, we can go look now. And perhaps we can cut them out together."

"Gladly." Otis untied his shop apron and offered the seamstress his arm. Then at the door he seemed to remember Miss Jones. He looked over his shoulder. "Is it all right with you, Miss Jilly? Especially in light of the fact that I see three fashionable young ladies strolling our way?"

"Customers?" Miss Jones's face brightened. "Go right ahead."

"Ah," Susan remarked, gazing onto the street, "now Lady Tabitha is joining their number."

Stephen saw Miss Jones's face lose some of its glow.

"Very good," she said, striving to sound cheerful, but it was apparent to him that she was intimidated by Lady Tabitha.

She'd no reason to be, of course.

Although not a classic beauty like Lady Tabitha, Miss Jones was much more attractive, in Stephen's view. Lady Tabitha lacked the vitality and genuine warmth Miss Jones had in abundance.

Now Lady Tabitha and several female companions, obviously members of the *ton*, walked warily into the shop, as if they weren't used to patronizing bookstores, much less bookstores on an inferior street.

Stephen backed up to a corner and pretended to examine some books, the better to watch the proceedings undetected. He had a feeling Lady Tabitha was a bored society girl with nothing better to do than stir up trouble.

"Welcome once more, Lady Tabitha, and welcome to your friends." Miss Jones looked up from her counter and smiled graciously at the new arrivals. "Do let me know if I can be of assistance."

Stephen thought Miss Jones was the perfect shopkeeper: friendly, helpful, but not overbearing.

"We're not here to shop." Lady Tabitha's voice held no warmth.

No surprise there, thought Stephen.

"That's perfectly fine with me," Miss Jones replied, recovering quickly from the new arrival's bluntly stated words. "I enjoy company."

Lady Tabitha's friends hovered around her, delicate

and beautiful, every one of them dressed like spring flowers. None of them smiled at Miss Jones. Indeed, they showed no appreciation whatsoever for her warm welcome.

"I'm fascinated by the story of Alicia Fotherington," Lady Tabitha said. "I'd like to see her journal."

Stephen noted it wasn't a request. More of a demand.

Miss Jones rose from her seat, only the tiniest wrinkle on her brow. "I'll be happy to show it to you," she said, carefully polite. Then she gave a short laugh. "Truth be told, my assistant had it last. I'm not sure where he put it."

She hesitated, and Stephen could tell she was wondering whether she dared go upstairs and look for it.

"I'll keep an eye on the shop for you," he said.

All the women turned toward him.

"Captain Arrow!" Tabitha exclaimed, and her face took on a certain animation it had lacked when she'd been unaware he was in the room.

"Lady Tabitha," he said with a bow. "And ladies."

"Thank you for your offer," Miss Jones said quietly to him, and then to the ladies, "I'll be right back."

The ladies apparently didn't notice she'd spoken as no one responded. They were focused on him alone. Stephen noticed that they were much warmer in their greetings to him than they'd been to Miss Jones. He already knew Lady Tabitha was self-possessed, perhaps a little vain—and interested in him—but he hadn't known her conceit extended to making other women who couldn't possibly compete with her advantages feel invisible.

Her friends were no better.

Stephen had always admired people in high positions who made their underlings feel important and had striven to emulate them. In the navy, it was how he got his men to give him their best efforts. He knew all his sailors by name, and he made sure to ask after their families. He brought them to his cabin for a brandy if one of them had a death in the family and did the same for a sailor who'd lost his best mate in a battle.

Once he'd brought a young midshipman into his cabin for a drink when he'd received a letter stating his family had lost his favorite childhood dog to old age. And on several occasions, he'd counseled men who'd received letters from sweethearts or wives who no longer loved them.

He was already regretting telling Miss Jones that Lady Tabitha was sporting.

Sporting, my eye, he thought.

He watched Miss Jones leave through the back door to the office and then upstairs and wished he could go with her.

"So, Captain." Lady Tabitha interrupted his thoughts. "Are you ready for the ball tonight?"

"Of course," he said, making no attempt to charm her or her friends. "A man has very little to do to get ready. We don't have to go out and purchase new ribbons and gowns for every event."

The women tittered.

Let them. He was impatient for them to go. He'd one last edge to smooth on his ledge, and then it would be done.

"Did you ever meet Admiral Lord Nelson?" asked one young lady.

"Yes, miss," he said gruffly.

"How many times?"

"Several." To hell with waiting for them to go—he'd smooth that last edge now.

Undeterred, another young lady posed a question. "Did you really capture a pirate?"

"I did," he said, focusing his attention on the ledge.

The women seemed to sigh as one, except for Lady Tabitha. She merely curved her mouth up a bit. She was clearly the leader of her little clutch of friends.

"Captain, you appear tired with our silly questions," she said. "Does going about in society bore you?"

"Largely." He looked at her with not an ounce of interest. "Although I do have friends I like to see at various events."

"Do you waltz?" asked one young woman.

"Reluctantly," he said. He wouldn't tell them it was because he felt waltzing should be reserved for people in love. It was the one romantic thought he'd ever had, and he preferred to keep it to himself.

Lady Tabitha ran her gaze over his shoulders and chest, quite as if he were a roast on the spit. "It appears you prefer to do manly things. You've built something for Miss Jones."

"A ledge for her window." He reluctantly stood. "So she can display her books. She hopes it will improve sales."

Lady Tabitha's smooth forehead wrinkled. "She couldn't hire a carpenter?"

Stephen shrugged. "I volunteered. We're neighbors, after all."

While he looked into Lady Tabitha's gorgeous but hard face, he was tempted to come up with an excuse to get out of their engagement that evening. But he'd made his promise. He'd do his best to get the Prince Regent to come to the street fair.

"It appears Miss Jones has few customers," said one of Lady Tabitha's friends.

"No wonder," chimed in another. "A lady running a bookshop? It isn't done."

"Especially an unfashionable lady," said Lady Tabitha smoothly. "Yet her assistant is no better. His shoes are an abomination. And so are his waistcoats."

Stephen frowned. "They're both exceptionally able people. If anyone can make a bookshop successful, it will be Miss Jones and her assistant. In fact, I think Miss Jones would be helpful tonight at the ball."

"Do you?" Lady Tabitha hardly batted an eye.

"Yes," he said. "She could talk to Prinny about books and the history of the street. He's quite bright beneath his debauched exterior, and her excitement about the street fair will no doubt pique his interest."

"But is she of good family?" asked one of Lady Tabitha's friends.

Stephen couldn't resist a little lecture. "Ladies, in

battle, a man's character is measured not by the depth of his pockets or his bloodlines but by the reach of his heart."

"Yes, but does that mean she's of good family?" asked the same young lady.

Stephen stared at her, not sure what to say that wouldn't be insulting.

But he was saved from answering when Miss Jones walked back into the shop empty-handed. Her cheeks were pink.

Had she overheard any of their conversation?

He hoped not.

Seconds later, he was relieved to see she was embarrassed about something else.

"I'm so sorry," she told Lady Tabitha, "but I can't find the journal. I assure you, I realize its value as a piece of history concerning Dreare Street. Otis must have stashed it away in a safe place. When he comes back, I'll ask him where it is."

"Will you come to tea when you do find it?" asked Lady Tabitha.

Stephen was taken aback. The lady's tone was suddenly friendly.

He believed Miss Jones was surprised, too, as she stammered her acceptance.

"Very good, then." Lady Tabitha opened a fan and began to waft it slowly across her face. "And Miss Jones, I'd love for you to join us tonight. At the ball."

"Really?" Miss Jones's eyes lit up with pleasure.

"Yes. Meet us at my aunt's at half eight." Lady Tabitha cast a very brief glance at Stephen.

He forced himself to throw her the ghost of a grateful grin. He wasn't surprised when her mouth curved up again in that self-satisfied way she had about her, like a cat with cream.

Miss Jones seemed to hesitate. "I'm grateful, but I don't think I should."

"Why not?" He was suddenly anxious for her to go. He'd be able to tolerate the evening with Lady Tabitha and Lady Duchamp much better with her there.

She lifted one shoulder in a careless shrug. "I'm rather a homebody. I prefer not to go out."

"You'll be among friends," Stephen reminded her.

"Captain, I appreciate your intentions, but I must stand firm."

He restrained a sigh. She was the most stubborn woman of his acquaintance. "You're the one who started this whole idea of the street fair," he reminded her. "And you were distinctly regretful you weren't part of the activities that took place last night at my house."

He knew he had her there. He saw her pause.

"Miss Jones," Lady Tabitha said in a lively manner, "no more discussion. I expect to see you at my aunt's."

Stephen was glad Lady Tabitha had shown a rapid improvement in her attitude toward Miss Jones. But he wasn't a fool. She must have sensed his support of the bookseller and was trying to impress him.

He didn't care what her motivation was as long as Miss Jones could go to the ball.

"Very well," said Miss Jones with a shy smile. "Thank you."

Lady Tabitha shrugged. "Shall we go, ladies?"

They all fell in line and trailed out after her.

But then Lady Tabitha turned around. "Miss Jones," she said, "I hope you won't feel awkward about my mentioning this. But the truth is, I don't want you to feel out of place tonight. Shall I send over an appropriate gown? It would be no trouble."

"Why, that's thoughtful of you," Miss Jones said slowly, as if she had to think about it. "But I can't ask you to go to such lengths on my behalf. Really."

"I promise you, it won't be an inconvenience." Lady Tabitha waited without smiling.

"All right, then," Miss Jones said warmly. "I'd appreciate that very much."

Lady Tabitha turned to him next. "Dear Captain Arrow," she said in an overly familiar way, "you won't mind meeting us at the ball, would you? We won't have room in the carriage. My friends are staying with me until then, and now we have Miss Jones coming, as well."

"It would be no inconvenience at all." He made a restrained but polite bow to the departing ladies. "See all of you tonight."

When they were gone, Miss Jones turned to him. "It's completely inappropriate that I go," she insisted.

He laughed. "Why so?"

"I'm not out in society."

"So? You'll be the guest of Lady Tabitha and Lady Duchamp."

She still looked uneasy.

"And you'll be with *me*," he said.

She looked up at him then, unguarded for once. It

was as if that thought appealed to her, the idea of being with him. Something inside him twisted near his heart.

Plain and simple, he wanted to kiss her. But would he ever be able to again?

CHAPTER FOURTEEN

Mere seconds after Lady Tabitha and her cronies left Hodgepodge, Jilly found herself wanting to kiss Captain Arrow.

It was difficult to *not* want to kiss him. He was so handsome, after all, and thoughtful when he chose to be. And when he looked at her as if she were the answer to his every craving—as he was doing now—everything in her strained to lift herself up on her toes and press her lips to his.

He was nearly impossible to resist.

But resist she must.

It took all she had.

She turned away from him. "I think you'd better go," she said briskly. He'd go and she'd make a cup of tea and become a serious shopkeeper once again.

But he didn't move.

"Captain," she warned him.

He grabbed her hand. "Must I?"

Dear God. It was the answer she'd hoped for in her daydreams.

But this was real life!

She couldn't possibly look directly at him. She'd

look at the books over his shoulder instead. And she didn't know what in the world to *say*.

"I don't want to go, Miss Jones." His voice was husky. "You don't want me to, either. You want me to stay. Here. With you."

Still, she couldn't move. Or speak. This couldn't be happening again.

But it was.

He ran a thumb over the back of her palm. "I do believe you're thinking what I'm thinking."

She bit her lip and risked a glance at him. "And what is that?"

He was mere inches away. With a slow, deliberate movement, he turned her to face him. "You're thinking we should take inventory," he said. "Of all the books."

Inventory.

"Oh." She swallowed. "Right."

Heavens, that hadn't been what she'd been thinking at all! Her heart hammered in her chest, and her palms were damp. In the distance came the rumble of a wagon, the call of one workman to another, and the joyful voices of children singing a nursery rhyme she'd sung herself years ago.

But no sound, no intriguing book title, no shelf that needed dusting, could distract her from the realization that she and Captain Arrow were alone, in her store—

The store that almost always saw no customers.

Otis, too, wasn't due back for a goodly while.

"You're thinking we should take inventory," he

went on with a lazy yet heated grin, "because you've only done it at least a dozen times this week. Thirteen would be good. Thirteen times would assure you that you're using your time wisely."

She nodded, still mute.

"We should start here," he whispered, pulling a tendril of hair off her cheek.

"Here?" She could barely get the word out.

Slowly, he pulled her down with him to the floor. "*This* table," he whispered in her ear.

Books were stacked so high upon it that no one could see them from the door.

She swallowed. "I know what you're about to—"

And then he kissed her below her jaw.

Oh, sweet heavens! She gulped and blinked. "Captain," was all she was able to say before he kissed her again, this time on the edge of her mouth.

The edge.

It was too much to be borne. She needed to be kissed full on the—

Oh, now he was kissing her.

Was he ever!

"Don't worry," he murmured against her mouth. "It's your slowest time of the business day. And if by some slim chance, anyone comes in, we'll freeze and not say a word. They'll soon leave."

"Are you sure?" she said, her limbs weak with desire and, she must admit—

Fear of the unknown.

"I won't let anything untoward happen to my favorite bookseller," he said, "I promise you."

Those were exactly the words she'd needed to hear. She allowed herself to lean into him, luxuriating in the pleasure of feeling his broad, muscled chest beneath her palms.

But then she pulled back. "This is crazy," she whispered, and clung to his shirt.

"I know," he said. And in one swift movement, he lowered her gently to the floor. He wrapped one arm around her waist and put one broad palm behind her head, to cushion her.

It was the most cozy bed she'd ever lain in.

He kissed her, then pulled back a fraction of an inch from her lips. "It makes it that much more exciting, doesn't it? Knowing we're taking a substantial risk . . . all for a kiss."

She practically melted at the look in his eyes, at the sound of the word *kiss* on his lips.

He kissed her again, the rough skin of his jaw so pleasant against her own skin. She couldn't help herself. She moaned.

Their kisses grew deeper. She ran her hand over his back, and he caressed her breasts through the thin fabric of her gown.

She sucked in a breath. No one had ever done that to her before. Certainly not Hector. She closed her eyes and let herself be caressed. It was the only word for it.

Caressed.

"If this is inventory," she murmured, making one, last feeble attempt at being businesslike, "I—I like it very much."

He laughed against her mouth.

He shouldn't laugh. She was the owner of Hodge-podge, and it was broad daylight. Yet she was on the floor of her store with him, and if anyone walked in—

Why, if anyone walked in, she'd be run off Dreare Street, wouldn't she?

But she couldn't care very much at the moment. Captain Arrow was making her feel so very good. She couldn't even properly describe how she felt—just that she wanted to keep doing what they were doing.

"You're the most delectable bookseller I've ever known," he said, and pulled down the edge of her bodice.

"I am?" What a world was opening up to her, here on the floor of Hodgepodge! She was almost greedy with need, wrapping her arm around his neck and pulling him close for an openmouthed kiss.

"Yes, you are." He trailed hot kisses down her neck and shoulder. Then he nuzzled his chin and mouth into the lacy edge of her bodice.

"What are you doing?" she whispered.

"What I've wanted to do ever since I first laid eyes on you."

She felt him nudge aside the thin fabric there. Coolness struck. And then heat and—

Oh, God. He was suckling her breast. She closed her eyes, rocked by a deeply pleasurable sensation that flickered between her legs.

What they were doing was so *improper*. A volume of Shakespeare was nearby. And several fussy dictionaries. But she couldn't care. Oh, no, she was in a blissful state.

She'd never wanted a customer less than she did at this moment.

She arched her back. "Please don't expect this to happen again," she whispered into his golden curls, her hands caressing his tapered shoulders.

"Oh, no." He ran a finger in a lovely circle around her exposed nipple. "I wouldn't dare hope. It was entirely a matter of impulse you won't repeat."

"Exactly," she said with a sigh.

And then felt bereft.

Because she wanted this to happen again. Very much.

Someone walked by the store, whistling, and they both froze.

But of course, the person walked by without even slowing at the door.

"Thank God," she said softly.

"Yes, thank God. I haven't had nearly enough of you." He cast his eyes up, and she saw in them a glint of amusement vying with desire.

From the modest neckline of her gown, he released her other breast and ran a hand over both of them appreciatively. "You're gorgeous," he said admiringly, then raised his eyes to hers again. "I want you to remember what we did here when you come into the store each morning."

"I will," she whispered.

He lifted her skirt, but she didn't care. In fact, it felt delicious to be so exposed.

Delicious and wicked.

His kisses now became even more ardent, and his hand . . . his hand played delightful games up her legs, all the way to her softest flesh.

And then his fingers began to move there. He made little circles with his thumb over the nub of flesh guarding her most intimate place. She groaned with delight, lost in intense, delicious feeling. She felt wild. Free. Yet also at the center of everything, as if the whole world spun around them and not the sun.

All the while he kissed her breasts, her mouth, and then his fingers began to play more. She arched to bring him closer, and as she did, she began to slip into another world.

"More," she moaned. "Oh, please. *More.*"

And then she was floating free, suspended in a wave of infinite pleasure.

The front door of Hodgepodge opened and the bell tinkled.

Captain Arrow's mouth clamped over her own, and she rode pulse after pulse of sensation, her eyes wide, staring into his—he wouldn't let her look elsewhere.

I promised you, she saw there.

And she believed him. As she sank back down to earth, she didn't care that anyone was at the door.

"Miss Jones?" Lady Hartley's voice boomed.

Keep looking at me, Captain Arrow's eyes said.

She was slack, at peace, more relaxed than she'd ever been in her life.

She smiled at him, and he smiled back.

"Miss Joo-oones!"

Behind the table stacked high with books, they maintained total silence.

"Where are you?" Lady Hartley called out.

A big sigh came from the door. "Very well, then. I won't be coming back *here* to borrow a cup of sugar for our tea," Lady Hartley tutted. "Leaving a store unattended. Only a very irresponsible person would do so."

Captain Arrow looked down at Jilly, his eyes merry now. She bit her lip to keep from laughing.

And then the door slammed shut.

Captain Arrow ran a hand down her flank. "Well, now," he said. "About that inventory."

She let herself laugh then.

It was the first genuinely carefree laugh she'd had in years.

CHAPTER FIFTEEN

A full thirty seconds passed after Lady Hartley departed, then Captain Arrow tugged on Jilly's hand and pulled her up from their shelter behind the book table.

She knew her hair was a mess and her mouth was slack and her spine wasn't as rigid as usual, but the realization of what she'd done with him still hadn't hit her hard enough to allow her to regain her usual decorum.

However, it was coming toward her, slowly, from the fringes of her conscience, like a cat wending its way down an alley and then detouring at several more side streets before arriving home, especially when Otis appeared at the door, much earlier than expected.

"I forgot my sample handkerchiefs!" he cried, and went dashing upstairs to retrieve them.

Jilly and the captain exchanged a look as he sped by. It had been a close call. She strode to her father's mirror and straightened her hair. She also adjusted her apron and told herself it was time to return to business.

She might be a wanton, but she was, first and foremost, a bookseller.

Meanwhile, Otis came back downstairs, mentioned that they were out of bread, a lapse he would remedy, and went racing out the front door again.

When he was gone, the captain said, "I'm going to be working on some house repairs." He spoke plainly, leaving her no opportunity to indulge in embarrassment. "And if I have time, I'll begin the next booth. So if you need me for anything before this evening—"

"No," she stammered. "I'll be fine." She attempted a polite, professional smile, but it was difficult to look at him the same way ever again. "You take entirely too much upon yourself, Captain."

He laughed. "Very well. I will acknowledge that you're perfectly capable of taking care of yourself."

He said it like a caress.

She finally blushed.

"Thank you," she managed to say crisply. "You've given me my ledge." *And taken me to the moon and back with your hands and mouth.* "I'll spend part of the afternoon arranging books on it to my liking. I'm quite particular."

"I've noticed," he said, his mouth teasing.

What did he mean by that? she couldn't help wondering.

"And then with the time I have left before the ball," she forged on, "I'll check on Susan and Otis, look for the diary again—I really must find it—and I might pay a visit to the Hobbs family."

"You'd best stay out of it," he said with no heat in his

manner, which was a good thing because she would have objected strongly.

"Out of what?" she asked, attempting an equally light tone.

"Out of the Hobbses' business."

Hmmm. For a man who had just pleasured her so well, he was amazingly able to inflame her senses in an entirely different way.

"I don't plan to interfere," she said, heat rising up her neck. "I'm only offering my friendship to Lavinia. Nothing more."

He merely gave her a look that said he knew better—and waved good-bye.

She watched him walk back to his house and felt very guilty all of a sudden for wanting to convince Mr. Hobbs—in a subtle way, of course—of the error of his ways.

And then she felt terribly alone when Captain Arrow opened his front door and shut it behind him.

When he was with her, she was so focused on him she lost all sense of reason. But when he was gone, she couldn't ignore that voice in her head telling her that her life could go terribly wrong at any time if she were foolish.

Hector could find her.

She sighed and began to search the shop for the diary. Would she ever be able to truly relax? In the moments after she'd been suspended in total pleasure, she had. Her limbs were still weak from the captain's caresses, but deep in her heart, she was troubled.

Would every new, wonderful experience be tainted by the dread that her husband would find her?

Every day she was around Captain Arrow, her resolve to hide from life—because she *must*—weakened.

Meanwhile, she conceded that perhaps a small amount of her anxiety stemmed from the fact that the diary had gone missing. She couldn't lose it—somehow, it gave her comfort. It felt like a connection to a solution of some sorts to Dreare Street's woes. Hadn't she gotten the idea for the street fair from its pages? And she loved reading about someone on Dreare Street who'd been happy. It gave her hope.

It would be so frustrating never to see the journal again when she'd only read the first third!

She also had to admit that Lady Tabitha's friendliness was bothering her, as well. Perhaps it was catty of her to think such negative thoughts, but the femme fatale's generous invitation to accompany her and her party to the ball and provide Jilly a gown made no sense, coming as it did on the heels of the very cool welcome she'd given her when she and her friends had first walked into Hodgepodge.

In short, Jilly couldn't trust the woman, although Lady Tabitha had given every indication she was trying to be helpful.

"Ah, well," she said hours later when it was time to turn the sign in the window over to read CLOSED. She was unsettled. Perhaps her jealousy of Lady Tabitha's good looks and confidence was making her overly sensitive.

She still hadn't found the diary, but she had managed to make a beautiful display on the new ledge. Every moment of her pleasure in the endeavor had been tinged with a heated memory of Captain Arrow's form leaning over the ledge, making it with careful hands and looking up at her with laughing eyes.

She closed her eyes and pretended he was holding her hand again, telling her that if she needed him, he was nearby. And then she let herself go over every moment of their scandalous liaison on the floor of Hodgepodge.

She opened her eyes and drew in a breath. She was leaning against the door jamb, her face up to the late afternoon sun, which had come out for a moment from a swirl of clouds and smoke overhead and warmed her lips the way she imagined the captain's lips would.

If she weren't careful, she thought as she pushed herself off the jamb and began walking down the street toward the Hobbses' residence, she'd make a fool of herself and fall in love with Stephen Arrow. He was the least likely man to ever settle down with one woman, and—

It was a moot point anyway.

Why even daydream?

She was married.

Once again, the untenable nature of her situation reared its ugly head, mocking her attempt to live a normal life. She would never know *normal* again.

A minute later, she was at Mrs. Hobbs's door and about to knock on it.

"Miss Jones!" The voice came from behind her.

She turned and her breath caught in her throat. There was Captain Arrow, walking toward her with a slow grin and a twinkle in his eye. "I know what you're up to," he said, "and it won't be easy. I'm here to offer my support."

"You are?"

How could she not daydream about lying with him again and allowing him to kiss her senseless when he said things like that?

He knocked sharply on the door. "I told you I'd partner you in this whole endeavor. And things may go better with me here."

" 'Better?' " Her warm feelings once more dissolved instantly at his implication. "I'm perfectly capable of handling the Hobbs family myself."

He cocked a brow. "I know, but are they capable of handling *you*?"

"What's that supposed to mean?" she replied in an affronted whisper. "*I'm* not the one who allows people to hang out my window. *I* don't go about indiscriminately—"

"Yes?" His golden irises almost disappeared, and he looked at her as if he were making love to her again.

He was like a harpist plucking the exact right string to make her core thrum with desire for him, even against her will.

"Never mind," she said. "I'm a respectable—some might even say *boring*—bookseller."

"Are you finished?" His tone was amused yet somehow gentle, as if he knew exactly what she was feeling, that her insides were melting, and that she wanted to slide against him and—

Never mind, she told herself. They were highly improper thoughts. Ones she must forget.

She stuck her chin in the air. "Yes, I am." She refused to be stirred by him unless she chose to be stirred by him, which she most definitely didn't choose at this moment.

"Good." His eyes were locked on her own.

She felt stormy and weak inside, all at the same time. She wished he'd go away.

But then he leaned over and whispered in her ear, "You're never boring."

And blast it all, she wanted to kiss him all over again.

She whipped her head around to look stonily at the door and could swear she heard him chuckling.

The door opened then, and Captain Arrow took her firmly by the elbow. "We're here to see Mr. and Mrs. Hobbs," he said pleasantly to a ginger-haired butler with a stooped posture.

"Yes, we are," Jilly threw in for good measure, just so the captain knew she was perfectly capable of handling the situation.

"You people aren't allowed in," said the butler. "I can tell ye that right noo. So begone wid ye."

And he slammed the door in their faces.

"He's Scottish," said Jilly, feeling deflated.

"Yes, we know what that means," Captain Arrow said. "A warrior at heart. He'll never let us through unless—"

He knocked again.

The door was immediately flung open. "I said ye'd best begone—"

Captain Arrow stuck his foot in the door just as the butler tried to shut it.

"Listen, Sassenach—" the butler snarled.

"Only half English," Captain Arrow said equably. "I'm a Fraser on my mother's side." Then he reached into his pocket and threw the man a flask through the crack in the door. "Taste it. It's Highland whisky from Ben Nevis."

"I don't believe it." The butler sneered. "The English don't know anythin' about whisky. Ten to one it's that silly French brandy."

"Try it," Captain Arrow said.

The butler looked at him suspiciously, then lifted the flask to his lips. The look in his eyes said it all. "Only a true friend of the Scots would have Highland whisky," he said begrudgingly and opened the door wide. "Where'd ye get this?"

"I told you," said Captain Arrow. "My mother's people were Frasers. I've got more I'll be glad to share with you. Show up at my house any time and take your fill."

"You're not jokin'?"

"Certainly not," Stephen assured him, "and feel free to bring a friend or two. Now if you'd be so good—"

"Step right in," the butler said.

A moment later they were walking down a corridor toward a sitting room.

"I could have done that myself," Jilly whispered to the captain. "Without the flask."

"How?"

She speared him with a look. "I have my ways."

"Oh?" He squeezed her elbow. "Perhaps you could practice your—ahem—ways on me later."

Practice on him? She knew very well what sort of practice he meant, although—

Although she'd never, *ever,* um, practiced what she was sure he was imagining. She wasn't even sure what to do.

But I'd love to find out.

"H-how dare you suggest such a thing," she protested, but even to her own ears, her injury sounded feigned. Shocked and appalled at her own weakness, Jilly had to look away from her neighbor once again. He was much too good at stirring her up in improper ways.

He merely touched her lower back firmly and led her in a gallant fashion toward the Hobbses' sitting room, but she couldn't help recalling the purposeful yet careful way he'd held her on the floor at Hodgepodge, as if she were precious.

That memory softened her. It did more than that, actually—it bewildered her. Almost brought tears to her eyes.

Hector had never treated her so.

She'd never felt . . . womanly in his presence. Like a goddess adored. Yes, that's how Captain Arrow had treated her, like a goddess.

In the sitting room, she made the decision to allow him to help her with the Hobbses, after all.

Mrs. Hobbs rose from a chair, where she was knitting. "Welcome," she said with a broad smile.

"Sit down, Lavinia." Mr. Hobbs used a firm tone from his plush red armchair, where he was reading a newspaper.

Mrs. Hobbs did sit down, and she looked none too happy about it.

Her husband lowered his newspaper an inch. "I told Lavinia we don't have time for your nonsense, but she insisted we should see you. So say what you have to say and get out."

He put the paper back up in front of his face.

"Mr. Hobbs," Jilly said, "could you please lower the paper?"

He merely shook it.

"Mind if I take a seat, Hobbs?" Captain Arrow asked.

Mr. Hobbs lowered the paper and scowled at him. "If you insist."

The captain leaned back in a lovely Chippendale chair and pulled out a pair of cheroots. "Care for one?" He held it out to Mr. Hobbs. "They're the finest I've ever found in the Indies."

Without waiting for an answer, the captain lit the cheroots from a nearby taper—Jilly was impressed by his sangfroid—and the men both began to puff away. Mr. Hobbs looked like a grumpy dragon, Jilly thought, scowling and puffing, scowling and puffing.

Captain Arrow took what appeared to be a few

blissful puffs and let out a long sigh. He smiled and leaned over to Mrs. Hobbs and asked her about her knitting.

Good. Now Jilly could concentrate on Mr. Hobbs.

She cleared her throat. "Mr. Hobbs, you're a hard-working man."

"Yes, I am," he said, and rattled his paper.

She racked her brain. "You—you deserve to come home and have your home be your castle."

"Indeed, I do." He coughed, and a curl of smoke floated above the page.

Jilly took a chair, pulled it up next to him, and folded her hands in her lap. "I know you can't see me through your paper," she said, "but that's all right. There's so much fog on this street—we often can't see each other. Sometimes it tends to make one feel a bit . . . alone."

Silence from behind the paper.

Jilly squeezed her fingers together harder. "I just want you to know, Mr. Hobbs, that your family isn't alone. It might seem like it, but it doesn't have to be that way. And if you feel like your castle is under siege, there are actually people on the street who want to help you fight for it."

She waited, and he lowered his paper just enough that she could see one eye. "No one can help me," he mumbled around the cheroot.

Oh, dear. He sounded angry and despairing, all at once.

"But I think we can," said Jilly. "We can earn enough money from the street fair to—"

Mr. Hobbs dropped the paper in his lap and pulled the cheroot out of his mouth. "The bloody lease is just the beginning," he hissed. "My financial woes extend far beyond the requirements of that lease."

Mrs. Hobbs turned at the sound of his voice. "Mason?"

He looked at her. "These people can't help us, Lavinia."

He put the cheroot back in his mouth and the paper back up. Mrs. Hobbs's face fell. Jilly looked at Stephen.

Do you need help? his expression asked.

She gave him a brief shake of her head, but a part of her simply felt happy to have someone to rely on.

She inhaled a breath and went back to Mr. Hobbs. "I can't make any promises beyond the lease, Mr. Hobbs," she said in a firm, no-nonsense tone. "But one step at a time. *One step.* With the weight of the lease removed, you'll be able to think more clearly about the rest."

"The rest," he said contemptuously from behind his newspaper.

"Yes, the rest," she asserted. "Meanwhile, your wife and children can help with the fair. Anticipate success there, Mr. Hobbs. And with that momentum, you can go forward. Giving up isn't an option. In fact, we'd like you to help with the fair, too."

He lowered the paper. "No." His tone was still flat.

"Very well." Jilly stood. "But we do need Mrs. Hobbs and the children."

"Mason?" Mrs. Hobbs's voice was thin.

Mr. Hobbs looked at the frayed Aubusson rug then back at his wife. "You can help with the fair," he said. "But—"

"But what, dear?" Mrs. Hobbs asked him.

"Nothing." He stood and sighed. "Miss Jones, you're an interfering young lady."

"Thank you, sir," she said.

She heard Captain Arrow behind her give a small cough that sounded rather like a laugh. "You won't regret this, Hobbs," he said.

Mr. Hobbs's brows drew across his nose. "We'll see about that." He flung his hand toward the door, the cheroot still smoking between his fingertips. "Now out with you both."

"Thank you for coming," said Mrs. Hobbs with a happy smile.

"Come over tomorrow with the children," Jilly said, "and we'll talk about what you can do."

"I look forward to it," said Mrs. Hobbs.

Jilly hugged Mrs. Hobbs, then took Captain Arrow's arm. Together they strode out the door, past the butler, who winked at the captain, and out onto the street.

She looked at Captain Arrow, and he, at her.

At the same time, they laughed.

"Well done," he said.

"Thank you for sharing your whisky and cigars."

"My pleasure."

The biggest thing she'd noticed at the Hobbses'

was that she and the captain did well together. Not that she would tell him that. He'd be sure to remind her they meshed perfectly in another way, too—a way she was sure she should forget but already knew she wouldn't.

CHAPTER SIXTEEN

"So what's next, now that we've got the Hobbses on board?" Stephen asked on the street. Not that he cared overly much. All he wanted was to be next to Miss Jilly Jones.

"We're off to see Susan and Otis," she said. "I'm longing to see how their handkerchiefs are coming along, but don't you have those house repairs to make?"

He shrugged. "The needs of the fair take precedence." As did escorting an enchanting bookseller about Dreare Street.

"Are you sure?" She looked a little uncertain.

"Trying to rid yourself of me?"

"No, but I plan on stopping at Nathaniel's before I go to Susan's."

"Oh?"

She gave a determined nod. "He needs to help Susan."

"But he's a painter."

"I know." She bit her thumb. "I need to figure out a reason."

Stephen caught on. "Oh, so you want to play matchmaker?"

Miss Jones blushed. "Is that so wrong?"

"If love is meant to be, won't it bloom on its own?"

"I don't know," Miss Jones said. "Why leave it up to chance? I see nothing wrong with moving things along."

She gave him a chiding yet warm look—the kind that made him impatient to get her on the floor of her bookstore again—and knocked on Nathaniel's door. When the artist opened it, he was wearing an apron covered in speckles of paint.

"Delighted to see you both," Nathaniel said. "Do you want to see what I'm working on for the fair?"

"That's the entire reason we're here." Stephen glanced at Miss Jones. "Isn't it, Miss Jones?"

"Of course it is," she said, wide-eyed.

But he knew better.

At the far end of the spare garret, which was flooded with northern light because of an expansive window, Nathaniel pointed out several small paintings on an easel. The pictures were small watercolor renderings of various housefronts in Mayfair, done with great charm.

"They're beautiful," Miss Jones said, her whole face lighting up.

"Very nice work," he added. "Do you plan to paint any Dreare Street façades?"

Nathaniel laughed. "Of course not. Who would buy them?"

Miss Jones winced only slightly. "Someday, someone will. Dreare Street won't be hopeless for much longer."

Stephen had to admire her optimism—that and her dedication to her cause, which he'd now committed to making his own. He wasn't sure it was the best thing to do. But it was too late to turn back.

"Sorry, Miss Jones," Nathaniel said. "Old habits die hard."

"You're completely forgiven." Miss Jones smiled at him. "I'd tell you to start your Dreare Street collection by painting the captain's home, but he won't be with us for long. Once the fair succeeds, he'll be able to sell his house. You'll be on to a new adventure, isn't that right, Captain?"

She looked up at him with sparkling eyes.

"Yes, indeed," he replied, but the idea didn't fill him with much satisfaction. And Miss Jones didn't appear particularly perturbed at the thought of his leaving, either.

Nathaniel scratched his head. "To tell the truth, if I painted the captain's house, I'd need paper twice this size to capture the rambling qualities of it."

"It does appear as if the wings were tacked on one at a time," Stephen agreed.

Miss Jones asked about Nathaniel's daily work habits. When he was finished detailing them, down to an explanation about how he cleaned his brushes in the evening, she said, "It's been lovely stopping by, but we've got to visit Susan and Otis now. They're working on a project together. Oversized handkerchiefs for the street fair. Would you like to come with us to see them?"

Nathaniel shook his head. "Thanks, but I'm a bit

busy." And he was, obviously. He had a dish of wet paint nearby.

Stephen could see Miss Jones thinking rapidly.

"Oh, dear," she said. "I was hoping you could help."

"Help with what?" Nathaniel picked up a brush and began dabbing it on his latest creation.

Miss Jones folded her hands in front of her. "Susan is in need of someone to take Thomas to the park this afternoon while she and Otis work. But I understand. You're too busy. I'd ask Captain Arrow, but he's going with me to find Pratt and the Hartleys."

"I am?" Stephen said.

"Remember, we're going to see the theater troupe?" She smiled in a forced manner.

Obviously, he was supposed to go along with her.

"Oh, right," he said, recovering. "We are. As soon as we leave here, as a matter of fact. I'm on my way to hire a hackney."

"But—" Miss Jones insisted.

"No *buts*," Stephen told her. "We've got to cross Waterloo Bridge to get to the Royal Coburg Theater. Unless, of course, we give up on the whole idea. Thomas and I will have a lovely time in the park."

He could tell she longed to make an awful face at him, but Nathaniel was watching. "Oh, no," she said. "We really must go."

Stephen couldn't help but smile. "Is that a promise? I won't go unless it is."

"Of course." Miss Jones took his arm and sighed. "Good-bye, Nathaniel," she said to the artist. "I look forward to seeing more watercolors soon." And then she began subtly pulling Stephen toward the front door.

"Yes, ah, good-bye, Nathaniel," he said over his shoulder.

"Don't look back," she whispered.

"I can see you're an expert at this matchmaking business," he whispered back.

She ignored him and stared resolutely at the door. He could see how agonized she was as they got closer and closer.

"I suppose I could take the boy to the park," Nathaniel called out to them, just as they'd reached the front door. "A small break wouldn't hurt."

Miss Jones turned around, her face alight with joy. "You would? That's so kind of you."

Nathaniel scratched his head. "Yes, well, I'll do it." His face brightened. "Thomas likes birds, so we can go bird-watching."

"I know Susan will be so appreciative." Miss Jones nodded her head vigorously.

Poor fellow, thought Stephen. Nathaniel had no idea of the trap he'd just walked into, although Stephen must admit that taking a little boy on a walk would be a nice diversion for anyone.

Outside, Miss Jones's violet-blue eyes lightened almost to periwinkle. "Now we've got to go see Susan," she said with relish, "and tell her Nathaniel volunteered to take Thomas on a walk."

"And after that, we'll get that hackney and go to the theater," Stephen reminded her.

Miss Jones stopped walking. "But we don't need

to, really. I was just saying that to give Nathaniel an excuse to help."

"But you gave me your word we'd go together." Stephen was firm. "Besides, it couldn't hurt to check on Pratt and the Hartleys."

"All right," she said. "But—"

She hesitated.

"But what?"

She wouldn't look at him. "Nothing."

Ah. A blush was creeping up her high cheekbones. "If you're worried about your virtue," he said softly, "don't. It's safe with me."

She turned. "Is it?"

The vulnerability in her expression touched him.

"Of course," he assured her.

She brightened immediately. "I'm glad, Captain. Thank you for . . . for understanding. I know we"— she hesitated—"I mean"—she blew out a breath— "oh, dear, what I'm trying to say is that . . . I *am* a respectable bookseller."

"An indisputable fact I haven't forgotten," Stephen said, squeezing her hand. "Why don't you go see Otis and Susan, and then meet me out here at the top of the street when you're done."

"Oh." He could swear she looked almost bereft. "You won't come with me?"

It must have been a shadow that had passed over her face from a cloud overhead. There was no way Miss Jones would be bereft at the thought of his leaving.

"No," he told her. "I'm going to wait for a decent hackney."

And then he turned his back on her and began walking.

Don't look back, he told himself. *Give her a bit of her own medicine.*

He even started to whistle.

"Captain?"

He stopped in his tracks, smiled, then schooled his expression to be neutral. Slowly, he turned around. "Yes?"

"Thank you for getting the hackney." She plucked at her skirts, appearing almost shy.

"You're welcome," he said gruffly.

She gave him a crooked smile.

When he turned again to the top of the street, his chest felt heavy with something important.

He wasn't sure what it was, but it was taking place around Miss Jones.

Miss Jones.

Miss Jones.

He could say her name a long time without ever losing pleasure in the saying. Something was important about that. It filled him with wonder. And warmth.

He could hardly stand the five minutes he'd have to wait to see her again.

Miss Jones looked out the window almost the entire time they were in the hackney. Her profile was mesmerizing. Stephen enjoyed watching her bob up and down gently with the rhythm of the wheels, too. Her feet were pressed tightly together and her hands folded neatly in her lap.

She was such a lady.

Such a *tempting* lady.

He looked out his window, too, only occasionally sneaking peeks at her. The one time he spoke to her was when they crossed Waterloo Bridge. "A fine view, isn't it?"

She finally looked at him. "Yes," she said. "Very fine."

And that was that.

When they reached the theater, they couldn't find Pratt and the Hartleys in the crowd. They'd arrived too late for the dramatic performance, but they caught a pantomime and enjoyed the subsequent harlequinade immensely. Miss Jones especially laughed at Harlequin's antics when Pantaloon chased him across the stage and pummeled him so hard with his hat that Harlequin snatched it and punched his fist through the crown.

After it was over, they went backstage, where they did finally meet up with Pratt, the Hartleys, and the small, elite acting troupe known as the Canterbury Cousins.

"So nice to see you, Captain!" Lady Hartley said. She took his arm possessively.

"Shouldn't you be working on the house?" Sir Ned frowned. "The damned bats need to be got rid of, and the beam in the breakfast room and in Miranda's bedchamber are still rotting away. Why'd you come here?"

"The house repairs and the bats will have to wait." Stephen held his annoyance at bay. Of course he should have stayed home and seen to his own affairs.

But he wasn't going to have an obnoxious distant relative tell him what to do.

"The street fair is *primo,* Sir Ned," Pratt said in his melodious accent. "Miss Jones and Captain Arrow have taken it upon themselves to oversee the planning. You are *uomo vecchio* already, eh?"

"What's that supposed to mean?" Sir Ned narrowed his eyes.

"You are an old man." Pratt smiled his beautiful white smile. "You forget things."

Sir Ned's mouth dropped open. "I'm not an old man!"

"Then shut your lips." Pratt extended his palms toward Sir Ned. "In my country, people who talk too much get no wine. No women. No songs."

Surprisingly, Sir Ned did stop talking.

Miss Hartley stared at Pratt in wonder, then took her father's arm. "Yes, Papa, we need Miss Jones and Captain Arrow. They need to get the actors to come and perform for free."

"Free?" a red-bearded man said. "We can't perform for free."

"But sirs," Miss Jones said, "we've no money to pay you. Consider this an opportunity to become better known around London."

"Sorry, we're too good a troupe to work for no pay," said another actor.

"But Prinny's coming!" Miss Hartley said.

The actors all looked at each other.

"The Prince Regent?" the red-bearded man said in a disbelieving tone.

Stephen cleared his throat. "Yes," he told the actor. "He's coming. We're to make the arrangements to-night."

The actors took themselves off for a moment and came back.

"We'll do it," said the red-bearded man. "We'll start with the balcony scene from *Romeo and Juliet*. You'll need to provide us with a balcony on set, of course. It's quite an impressive performance."

"We'll make sure we've got a balcony," Stephen said, regretting that it was one more carpentry project he'd have to oversee before he got to the rotting beams.

"*And* make sure you've got the prince, too," one of the actors reminded him with a laugh.

Stephen made the obligatory chuckle at the man's attempt at wit, but he was bothered. Building the balcony would be a hassle, but that wasn't going to be nearly as difficult as getting the Prince Regent to come to Dreare Street.

"Isn't everything about the fair so exciting, Captain?" Miss Jones said in the carriage on their way home.

"Very." His lingering doubts about the street fair dissolved then. One look at her grin of delight and he realized that even if she'd wanted the moon, he'd move heaven and earth to help her get it.

CHAPTER SEVENTEEN

The gown Lady Tabitha sent over to Jilly to wear to the ball was of expensive cut but almost austere, a gray muslin with a modest neckline and only the smallest ruffle at the hem. Lady Tabitha had judged her size well, at least. In addition to the gown, she'd sent over a simple shawl in pale gray and a pair of serviceable French slippers in the same color.

"They may be too practical for a night of dancing, but they're a very soft kid leather, Miss Jilly," said Otis. "You won't trip in them. I believe the whole outfit shrieks understated wealth."

Jilly observed herself in the looking glass in her sitting room. "Oh, Otis. This outfit is perfectly proper but dull as dishwater. I look like someone's chaperone. Or a very well-dressed lady's maid. Admit it."

"Well—" He winced, unable to disagree.

"Do you think Lady Tabitha did this on purpose?"

He bit his lip. "How can we even think such a thing? She's enabling you to go to a fine ball. She didn't have to show you such attention at all."

"I know." Jilly was positively flummoxed by the

lady's attention. "But it's a shame I can't wear one of my old gowns."

"But you made a pretty sum selling them."

"I know." Jilly sighed. "But I know just the gown I'd have worn tonight." It was a deep green silk creation that went well with her eyes. Captain Arrow would have admired it, she was sure.

But she must stop thinking about what gowns he would like to see on her. It was a futile pastime, and she was beginning to question her own judgment. She was married, and he was a rake. Even if she were unattached, she should steer clear of him.

She fingered her neckline. "I need something to offset the spare look of this gown."

"It's a shame you can't wear your diamond pendant," said Otis. "It was quite distinctive. Some harpy probably owns it now."

"It's no use lamenting," Jilly said. "My old wardrobe helped us purchase Hodgepodge."

"That's true."

Her observation appeared to have the intended effect—Otis seemed happy again. He helped her dress her hair in a simple, elegant style, à la Sappho, and handed her a lovely fan.

She was ready.

He gave her a hug. "Your mother's fan will distinguish you—that and your beautiful eyes. *They* are your jewels. You need no others."

She almost teared up at his sentimental foolishness. It wasn't until he opened the front door of Hodgepodge to escort her across the street that she became nervous.

She was going out and would be seen by the finest of London society. Every step she took across the street reminded her she was leaving a relatively safe haven and venturing into dangerous, unknown territory.

She must stay calm.

Otis dropped her at the front door of Lady Duchamp's house and kissed her cheek. "You'll do splendidly," he said with a proud smile.

"Thank you. I wish you could come." She waved good-bye to him a bit wistfully.

When the butler allowed her admittance into the house, she immediately sensed a cold atmosphere that the lavish furnishings did nothing to erase. She followed him to the drawing room and sat there alone for a good ten minutes. Finally, she got up and peeked out into the hall.

"May I help you?" he asked.

"I was simply wondering . . . did I arrive too early?"

"No," he said. "The young ladies should be down momentarily."

"Thank you." She gave him a brief smile, sat back down on a hard sofa, and waited another five minutes.

Finally, the ladies arrived, and without any sort of welcome or apology, Lady Tabitha told her it was time to go. The other three women clutched their fans, shawls, and reticules and followed behind Lady Tabitha. Jilly took up the rear.

At the carriage, she was also last to enter and

squeezed in next to a young lady with a half-smile on her lips that faded when Jilly sat next to her.

The atmosphere was quite strained, so Jilly tried to soften it with a smile and an innocuous compliment. "All of you look lovely tonight."

No one responded—instead, they began speaking of a picnic to take place the next day near Hampstead Heath—and the carriage lurched forward.

Jilly felt her face turn red.

During the rest of the ride, she sat silent and listened to their fast-paced conversation about eligible gentlemen, other women they despised (they never mentioned a one that they liked), and even talk about their experiences kissing.

"I'd like to get Captain Arrow alone in the garden," tittered one of the ladies.

Lady Tabitha glowered at her. "He's mine, Serena."

Serena sat up. "Oh, I didn't know."

"Who couldn't want him?" Lady Tabitha said, and for the first time, she looked at Jilly. "Miss Jones, tell us what you know of him."

Her heart sped up as all of them turned to stare at her. "Well," she began, "he's a captain who found the peacetime navy a bit dull, so—"

"Do you have a *tendre* for him?" Lady Tabitha asked, her mouth curved in a sly smile.

Jilly sat up higher. "Of course not," she lied.

"Why not?" asked Serena with a disbelieving chuckle. "Who else on Dreare Street is handsome and eligible?"

Jilly considered her words. "I'm not in the market for marriage. My business takes all my time."

"You're wise to know your limits," said Lady Tabitha, a half-smile pasted on her lips.

The other women giggled.

Obviously, they knew as well as Jilly that Lady Tabitha's remark wasn't meant to be complimentary.

"Actually," she said coolly, "owning Hodgepodge allows me to go well beyond the limits imposed on most women. I'm not forced to marry where I don't want to. I can pick and choose my companions based solely upon whether I enjoy their company."

The other women's faces dropped a little at that, and she couldn't help being satisfied at dampening their condescending attitudes, even if only for a moment.

She was glad when the carriage stopped a moment later in front of a brightly lit mansion. Despite the sour company, her palms dampened with nerves and a bit of excitement. She didn't belong at the ball and shouldn't be at the ball.

But I'm here, she thought, and felt herself buoyed by a burst of courage. *And I dare anyone to tell me I don't belong.*

This time the ladies allowed her to be the first to disembark. She stood outside the carriage, looking up at the house, and wondered if the captain were there yet. The realization left her slightly breathless.

Then she wondered if Prinny had arrived. What would she say to him? How would she convince him to come to the street fair on Dreare Street?

"Here," said Serena, and placed her reticule and shawl in Jilly's arms.

Then the next two young ladies laid their shawls and reticules on top of Serena's.

Jilly was so stunned, she simply stood and watched Lady Tabitha put her things on top of the pile. "Leave them in a safe place," she said, and looked at Jilly with a gleam of malice in her eye. "Or better yet, sit with them in some corner."

And then the four of them strode off, laughing.

So. That's why Lady Tabitha had asked her to the ball.

To humiliate her.

But why? What had Jilly ever done to her?

The lights radiating from the house became large, blurry circles, but Jilly blinked forcefully until they returned to normal.

She would love to dump the women's precious shawls and reticules on the ground, but she wouldn't stoop so low. Slowly, she marched into the house, ignoring everything to the right and left of her.

"Excuse me," said one older woman. "Are you one of Lady Langley's maids? I need someone to repair my hem."

Lady Langley was giving the ball with her husband, the Earl of Langley.

"No, madam," whispered Jilly.

She didn't belong here.

She shouldn't be here.

The woman looked at her curiously but not unkindly. "Then who are you?" She swept a casual eye over Jilly's gown. "I'm sorry, but I didn't take you for a guest."

Jilly raised her chin. "*Au contraire,* madam, I *am* a guest. My name is Miss Jones. But I'm happy to help you with your hem."

She was so humiliated, she could barely speak.

The woman's eyes softened. "I'm sorry, my dear. I saw you with all those shawls and reticules . . ." She trailed off, her cheeks pinkening.

Jilly swallowed. "It's all right. If you don't mind leading me to the ladies' retiring room, I can assist you there."

"Very well. And on the way, you can tell me about yourself. I'm Lady Courtney. I'm a widow."

"I'm so sorry," Jilly replied.

"Don't be." Her eyes twinkled when she looked at Jilly. "He was the most unpleasant man I've ever met. But at least he left me a great fortune."

Jilly almost winced at the woman's bluntness. "D-did you have children?"

Lady Courtney sighed. "No. I think it's why he hated me so. I suppose I can't bear children."

"I'm sorry," said Jilly. "And sorry to say sorry again. I—"

Lady Courtney waved her hand. "It's quite all right, dear. I didn't want his children."

Jilly was astonished at how closely the woman's feelings about her husband resembled her own about Hector. She had an impulsive desire to confide the truth to her, but of course, she knew she couldn't.

She spent a few minutes helping Lady Courtney

and was grateful to find enough conversation that she'd had to reveal nothing about herself beyond her name. Lady Courtney seemed to have forgotten her earlier interest in her. The ladies' retiring room was filled with many of her friends, some of whom asked after her health. Others queried her about her travel plans for the summer months.

Pinning the countess's hem gave Jilly a few solitary minutes to think. A great yearning coursed through her to have a friend who really knew her, who could accept her—despite her failings.

She'd failed very badly at marriage, hadn't she?

She'd left.

No matter how much Hector deserved to be deserted, a tiny part of her believed that perhaps it was somehow her fault that he was so . . . so bad.

It was stupid, really. But it was still there, that little, niggling voice that told her other women might have been able to turn him into a sterling husband.

Where had such a voice come from? She'd grown up perfectly happy, loved and approved of by her parents. She'd liked herself on the whole—and still did—save for a few flaws in her character that she'd never been able to stamp out. Stubbornness was one. So was her quick temper. And a tendency not to think before she acted. Impulsivity had landed her in a number of scrapes.

Such as kissing the captain.

She'd made mistakes. Many of them. One was going along with Lady Tabitha when her instincts had warned her to be wary of the woman. She blinked back more tears. Tonight she mustn't be broken and dispirited. She must be brave, strong, and somehow in her gray muslin gown . . . enchanting.

The Prince Regent wouldn't notice her, otherwise. He might be drunk much of the time, but she'd heard he was a perceptive man who appreciated beauty, wit, and charm.

"Thank you very much," Lady Courtney said when she was finished.

Jilly looked up from smoothing out the lady's hem and smiled. "It was my pleasure."

Lady Courtney held out a hand and helped her up. "I hope I see you about Town in the coming weeks, Miss Jones. You're an amiable young lady."

"Thank you."

And then Lady Courtney turned her back on her and left with another friend.

Jilly took a deep breath and forced herself to leave the haven of the ladies' retiring room, as well, but alone.

She decided to skip the receiving line and slip into the crowd. Perhaps she'd find Captain Arrow.

But the first person she saw that she knew was Sir Ned, who was at the punch bowl. When he looked up and saw her, he raised a brow in recognition. "Miss Jones, I need you to take this to Lady Hartley. She's on the wall next to the gallery. I'm off to the card room and it's out of my way to return in that direction."

Heavens. Did she exude a servile attitude? Or was she simply too kind for her own good?

She chose to think the latter.

"I'm sorry, Sir Ned," she said. "I'm off to the game room myself. Shall I see you there?"

The look of shock he gave her was most gratifying. She moved away, unable to resist a small, private grin, and almost ran into Captain Arrow and Miss Hartley.

Miss Hartley clung to his arm and had such a glow of happiness about her, she looked almost pretty.

"Why, Miss Joneth!" Miss Hartley's lisp became more pronounced when she was terribly excited. "Isn't this the most beautiful ballroom you've ever seen?"

Jilly met Captain Arrow's eyes. His gleamed with good humor and seeming delight that he'd encountered her.

It warmed her heart to know someone was happy to see her.

She returned her gaze to Miss Hartley. "Indeed, it is a beautiful ballroom. And you look lovely."

Miss Hartley smiled broadly. "So do"—she hesitated, her eyes widening as if she were seeing Jilly's gown for the first time—"ah, *you*. You look very nice."

Nice. It was hardly a compliment, but she knew Miss Hartley meant well. "Thank you," she replied with a forced smile.

Would her humiliation never end?

"I must say you're a breath of fresh air, the two of you," said Captain Arrow. "I've had enough feathers in my face to keep me sneezing for years. At least you two know better than to dress like giant birds."

Miss Hartley looked at Jilly and giggled. "He's so silly, isn't he?"

Jilly had to laugh back. "Yes, he is."

She was glad he'd taken the attention off her plain gown.

Captain Arrow slanted her a glance. "We're on our way to introduce Miss Hartley to several of my acquaintances. I told her I don't dance, but my friends do. Would you care to join us?"

He held out his free arm, and she took it. "Thank you," she said, "I'd love to."

All the while they walked through the crowd, she noticed other women looking avidly at her consort. Yes, she was sharing him with Miss Hartley, but he was the handsomest man in the room, without a doubt. And she—

She'd lain with him, and allowed him to kiss her in most inappropriate places, and he'd made her—

She couldn't say what he'd done. But the memory brought heat to her cheeks.

"Are you all right, Miss Jones?" Captain Arrow whispered in her ear.

She felt a thrill down to her toes. "Perfectly," she said, feeling very happy. She wouldn't examine *why*.

At one point, they brushed by Lady Tabitha and her friends, who were surrounded by young bucks. Even so, Jilly saw Lady Tabitha and Serena pause in their conversation and watch them walk by. Jilly liked to think that perhaps they were miffed that she was with Captain Arrow and not they.

But it doesn't matter, she told herself. *I can't have him. Who am I to act so proud?*

Nevertheless, she couldn't help but be gratified to know she might have unsettled Lady Tabitha.

A moment later, she and Captain Arrow dropped off Miss Hartley with the captain's gentleman friends, one of whom escorted her onto the dance floor.

Lumley winked at Jilly. "We must dance. It's dangerous to linger long with Captain Arrow."

"Later," the captain said, conveniently ignoring his friend's teasing. "We're in the midst of an interesting discussion."

And then he led her away—but not before Lumley managed to get her to agree to dance with him in the next hour.

"Of course," she called back to him over her shoulder.

A moment later, she and the captain were finally alone in the crowd.

"You look stunning tonight." His tone was intimate.

"Thank you." She couldn't help it—she was gratified by his attention. Opening her fan, she looked over it in a teasing manner. "You're an adept flatterer, sir."

"I'm not joking." His golden eyes smoldered into hers. "No matter what you wear, you're beautiful, even if it's an ordinary blue-sprigged muslin gown . . . with a simple fringe of lace at the neckline."

She could hardly breathe. He was referring to the gown she'd worn that morning, the one he'd partially removed to pleasure her.

"You're very kind." And he was, but she felt a strong need to keep their conversation as plain and unromantic as possible.

He seemed to sense her reticence. "I see you're no longer with Lady Tabitha and her cohorts."

It was a convenient change of subject.

"Yes," she replied. "We parted ways soon after we arrived."

"Any problems there?"

"No." She had no desire to let him know of her humiliation. "At least I gained entrance to the ball-room, thanks to her invitation."

Captain Arrow looked at her with an inscrutable expression. "I'm not sure I believe things were easy between you."

"It's no concern of yours," she said smoothly. "I can take care of myself. Meanwhile, we have to devise a plan to catch the Prince Regent's attention."

"There is no plan. I'll simply introduce you, and then you shall charm him into coming to Dreare Street."

"Captain," Jilly remonstrated. "We need a better arrangement than that. I'm not the charming type."

"Which is actually why I find you so charming," he said low.

She swallowed and looked up at him. "You shouldn't say things like that."

"Why not?"

She bit her lip and looked away. "Despite what happened earlier today, I'm not in the market for flir-tation."

"Be that as it may, I find it hard to resist flirting with you." His tone was quite sincere.

She looked back at him, so handsome and impres-sive in evening dress. "I'm a substantial person, Cap-tain. I—I can't play about as if life were a mere game. It's serious business to me. I must make my living at the bookstore. I'm a woman alone, and I . . . I want to stay that way."

"Why?" He came closer. "Why, Miss Jones, should someone as warm and lovely as you want to stay alone?"

She stared up at him. "Because there's no pain."

Around them the crowd grew thicker and louder. He stared at her a moment. "I knew there was something you weren't telling me," he said, and pulled her by the hand to the garden doors flung open at the back of the ballroom. "Come with me."

She dug in her heels, which was impossible, really, on the marble floor, but she managed to stop their forward progression. "Please. Don't. You mustn't listen so closely to everything I say. I only meant, I prefer my simple life to the complications that must come with having a . . . a larger life."

He looked at her with a grave expression. "Simple life? That's an interesting way to describe hiding." He dropped her hand.

She froze for a moment, flustered at his choice of words.

Hiding.

He couldn't know. And as far as she was concerned, he never would. It really wasn't fair that she must keep her guard up at all times. But it was the price she must pay for her freedom.

"Remember our purpose," she said, striving to keep her tone light. "We're going to have a street fair to end all street fairs. Dreare Street will wake up. People will notice it again but in a good way. You'll be able to sell your house. I'll get more customers. We'll move forward with our lives."

"You're right." His tone was dry.

Now their aloneness in the middle of a vast crowd of merrymakers no longer felt cozy and warm. Something felt sad. Off.

"Shall we go see Prinny?" she suggested in a festive manner, but her heart was heavy.

"I suppose so," the captain answered testily.

He was angry she wouldn't go to the garden with him, but didn't he know why?

She'd surrender. And that was where her greatest danger lay.

CHAPTER EIGHTEEN

Stephen always enjoyed a challenge. His most difficult was Miss Jones. Yes, he'd merely wanted a scorching flirtation, and the events that had transpired at Hodge-podge had convinced him they had one, but he still wasn't satisfied.

He wasn't sure why. But something in him wanted more from her. Much more.

But what exactly?

He craved touching her, but he also liked sparring with her, telling her about his life, laughing with her, and simply *being* with her. He wished more than anything that she'd tell him about herself, but she'd made it clear she wanted to be left alone.

The secondary challenge of convincing the Prince Regent to visit the unluckiest street in Mayfair seemed easy in comparison to the problem that was Miss Jones.

Yet twenty minutes after Stephen's revealing conversation with her—and their mutual commitment to gain access to the royal—they still hadn't succeeded.

"He's surrounded by a most annoying crowd," Stephen said. "Most of them drunk and belligerent if anyone dares attempt to break into their circle."

"There's even a circle around the circle," Miss Jones observed, an adorable pucker on her brow. "Did you see the look on their faces when you told them you were one of Prinny's Impossible Bachelors and must speak to him? They couldn't have cared less."

She bit her thumb and stared at Prinny's minions, political and otherwise.

"What are you thinking?" Stephen asked her.

"What *you're* thinking."

"You have no idea what I'm thinking."

She blushed. "You're thinking we'll use your naval strategies to get to him."

"Is that so?" He couldn't help admiring her bravado. "Tell me more about my thoughts, Miss Jones."

"Very well." He heard the catch of excitement in her voice. "Imagine him, Captain, as the pirate's galleon you have to capture. And he's surrounded by a fleet of smaller ships, all with loaded cannons."

He chuckled. "You're mad." A beat passed. "But I like the way you think."

She grinned. "When you've devised the plan"— she nudged him with an elbow, probably to remind him not to get too close, physically or otherwise— "you'll know where to find me. I'll be with Lumley, taking him up on his offer."

And then she took off.

"Don't waltz with him!" Stephen called after her, feeling oddly protective. He didn't want any man getting ideas about her, not even Lumley.

But she must not have heard him. She was already wending her way through the crowds.

Reluctantly, he returned his attention to the Prince Regent. It only made sense that he'd have to stage a diversion. That would call off the smaller "ships"—the sycophants and political advisors—and then he'd take the prince broadside in an all-out attack, using every weapon he had at his disposal.

The best one, of course, was Miss Jones.

While he was cogitating, an imposing male with a broad grin approached.

"Harry!" Stephen clasped his good friend on the shoulder, and they shook hands.

"Glad you're on English soil again," Harry said heartily.

He was followed by a pert brunette who smiled from ear to ear when she saw him. "Stephen!" she cried, and hugged him round the waist.

"Molly Traemore." He hugged her back then held her at arm's length. "You're stunning tonight. More beautiful than I've ever seen you. And I think I know why."

Molly nodded happily and looked down at her stomach, her hand pressed to it with tender care. "We didn't want to write. We wanted to tell you in person."

"But you've been noticeably absent from our home since your ship came in," Harry said with an arched brow. "That usually means you're having too much fun to be bothered."

Molly tapped his arm with her fan. "*Are* you?"

"Yes," Stephen said, "if you call having a house on an unlucky street and a meddlesome neighbor embroiling me in a scheme to make it prosperous again entertaining."

"That wouldn't be Dreare Street, would it?" Molly asked.

"Yes, it is." Stephen looked over his shoulder at Miss Jones dancing with Lumley. "And there's the meddlesome neighbor."

Harry gave a low whistle. "Now I understand. Even from here, I can see she's a match for you. Look at those eyes. They quite twinkle."

"And I like the way she holds herself," Molly added. "I can tell she'll take no nonsense from you, Stephen."

Stephen's chest tightened. "It's not like that at all."

"I said the same thing about Molly." Harry cast an amused sideways glance at him.

"Don't start—" Stephen told him in his best warning voice.

Harry laughed. "I'm not one of your sailors, Captain. You can't make me walk the plank for noting that you've *never* stared at a woman the way you're looking at your meddlesome neighbor right now."

"Traemore—"

"Shush, you two," said Molly, avidly watching Miss Jones. "I saw her in the ladies' retiring room pinning the hem of Lady Courtney's gown." She clasped her hands together. "Now I know why I can't keep my eyes off her. She looks like a lady's maid let loose at a fine ball." She turned to Stephen. "*Is* she a lady's maid?"

"No." Stephen gave a little laugh. "She's a bookseller."

"Whatever she is, she makes an enchanting picture!"

Molly exclaimed. "Everyone's watching her and Lumley. See?"

She inclined her head to the crowd lining the dance floor. The observers *did* appear charmed by Miss Jones, who'd just passed under Lumley's arm. Her eyes were, indeed, twinkling merrily, and she had a most infectious smile. Lumley was clearly happy having her as his dance partner, even though her gown couldn't be considered luxurious, as the other ladies' could.

Stephen saw Lady Tabitha eyeing his neighbor with open scorn and a bit of frustration.

He turned to see if Prinny and his cronies were watching her, but they were still ignoring the goings-on around them. Raucous laughter spilled from their group. Stephen could see only the top of Prinny's head. It was as if the royal were inside a fortress three-people thick.

"Who *is* this neighbor of yours?" Molly asked him, her eyes curious.

"Miss Jilly Jones," murmured Stephen. "But I'd rather everyone think she were someone else."

"Why's that?" Harry still had his gaze on Miss Jones on the dance floor.

"We need to bring her to Prinny's attention." Stephen turned to Molly. "I'll explain later," he said softly, "but you've given me an excellent idea. I need you to tell your friends she's posing as a woman of unremarkable but respectable birth. Tell them she's actually the direct descendant of an old line of Celtic kings, is extremely wealthy, and doesn't want anyone to know her origins."

"But she's descended from kings!" Molly exclaimed.

"Not really—" Harry said.

"Darling." Molly sent him an arch look. "I know. I was acting."

"You're good." Her husband chuckled. "Very good. Now go follow the captain's orders, will you?"

Molly kissed his cheek—Stephen's, too—and scampered away, as best a lady expecting a child could scamper with a bit of scintillating gossip to spread.

"Congratulations, old man," Stephen told Harry. "I can't believe you're going to be a father."

"Thank you," Harry said. "I never thought I'd say this, but I couldn't be happier."

"I'm glad for you, truly." Stephen paused. "But don't wish the same fate on me. I see it in your eyes. You've joined the ranks of contented married couples and want me to be just as happy."

"Can you blame me?" Harry shrugged. "Maybe you're ready to settle down yourself. You've left the navy, after all."

Stephen shook his head. "Because I want to do something new. It's been a long, rewarding career. I've been at it almost fourteen years."

"Since you were a pup. Will you *ever* consider marrying?"

"It's not in my plans, no," said Stephen, his gaze still on Miss Jones.

"It wasn't in mine, either, as you'll recall." Harry gave one vigorous rub to Stephen's shoulder. "Just know I'm here if you ever get confused about anything."

"Confused? Me?"

"Oh, I forgot," Harry said, his tone dry. "A navy captain can't afford to get confused." He paused, a serious expression on his face. "I'll say it again. I'm here if you ever need counsel. It's hard to fathom, I know, but I've got experience now in matters of the heart. So does Nicholas."

"He's still in America with Poppy?"

"Yes." Harry grinned. "I'm better at it than he is, though."

"Right," said Stephen. "I'll be sure to tell him you said so when he gets back and we find out he's the father of a set of twins."

"If he is, then I'll concede my position as chief married blatherer," said Harry. "I'm sure Molly's going to have a boy, just one this time, and his name will be Harry junior."

They both chuckled and lapsed into a comfortable silence. Stephen wasn't the least bit annoyed with Harry for being nosy. True friends were allowed to be. But he seriously doubted he'd need counseling of the heart from anyone.

The dancers began another quadrille, and after it was over, there was a general stirring over at Prinny's group. The Prince Regent himself emerged, fists on hips, face flushed, and his eyes bright.

He stared at Miss Jones on the dance floor. "I want that woman who looks like a lady's maid!" he cried. "Bring her to me!"

Harry gave Stephen a subtle thumbs-up. Then Molly, who was on the edge of a group across the ballroom floor, caught their gazes and blew a happy kiss in their general direction.

"That kiss was for me, I think," said Stephen.

"It was for *me*," Harry insisted. "But I'll share it with you." He angled his head at Prinny's group. "Come on. Let's see what happens with your lady's maid."

Stephen wondered what Miss Jones was thinking when Lumley took her arm and began to lead her over to the prince. Lady Tabitha and Molly managed to wend their way over, as well.

Stephen and Harry got there ahead of them all.

"Harry," the prince said fondly a moment later. "Look at you. So happy with your beautiful bride and, soon, a child."

Harry put his arm around Molly and squeezed her close. "Yes, very happy," he said.

Prinny turned to Stephen next. "And Arrow!" he cried. "You ended your career in the navy well, capturing that pirate as you did."

Up close, Stephen noticed the Regent's cheeks were even fatter and rosier than last time he'd seen him. "Thank you, Your Highness," he said, standing at attention as he would have in uniform.

The prince appeared genuinely happy to see Lumley. "Still unattached, are you?"

"Indeed, Your Highness." Lumley gave him a gracious bow.

"Then who's the lovely lady on your arm?" Prinny eyed her with avid curiosity.

"She's Miss Jilly Jones of Dreare Street," Lumley said with a great deal of enthusiasm.

"Good evening, Your Highness." Miss Jones swept the royal a low curtsy.

"Oh, yes, Dreare Street." The prince chuckled. "The unluckiest street in London." He got two inches from her face. *"Just the address a Celtic princess would choose for herself."*

And then he burst into guffaws. So did his advisors.

Miss Jones's brow puckered. "I'm not a Celtic princess, I assure you. And I do live on Dreare Street. I own Hodgepodge, the bookstore."

"Yes," Prinny said, "and Marie Antoinette had her little village to entertain herself. It must be so delicious to play bookstore owner."

Miss Jones blinked. "It is, I assure you. And I don't believe in bad luck."

"She believes in creating her own destiny," Prinny called over his shoulder to his friends and advisors. "Isn't she endearing?"

There was a chorus of affirmatives.

He looked back at her with tender regard. "I would expect no less of a Celtic princess."

"You'll recall *me,* Your Highness, from a ball in Brighton," interjected Lady Tabitha. She curtsied in a most elegant manner.

The prince swept his gaze over her. "Yes, Lady Tabitha. I recollect our meeting."

She gave him a sensual smile, the same one she'd bestowed on Stephen at Hodgepodge.

But the prince didn't seem to notice. His eyes were back on Miss Jones. "Oh, let's cease the pretense now, as precious as it was. State your real name, my dear, and tell us why you hide beneath this disguise as a woman of lackluster origins."

Miss Jones's cheeks were pale. She looked genuinely nervous. "I'm still not sure what you mean, Your Highness."

"She's not disguised, Your Highness," said Lady Tabitha with a little laugh. "She truly is a lackluster little nobody."

The prince gazed sternly at Lady Tabitha. "You were *not* asked to speak. You've also no idea what you're talking about."

He made a quarter turn so that she was no longer in his line of vision. It was the ultimate insult—the cut direct, and given by the Prince Regent himself!

There were several gasps.

Stephen watched with morbid fascination and not a little satisfaction as Lady Tabitha turned bright crimson, turned slowly, and strode away.

Prinny lowered his eyebrows. "I don't care how beautiful the woman is, how dare she insult the daughter of a long, proud line of Celtic kings?"

His cronies all agreed in equally loud voices.

At the break in attention focused strictly on her, Miss Jones managed to dart a questioning look at Stephen.

Play along, he willed his expression to say. *This is that diversion you begged me to create.*

She widened her eyes only slightly. Stephen watched as she lifted her chin and her gaze grew more direct. Good for her. She was gathering courage. Ignoring the confusing circumstances.

She would have made a fine sailor.

Who was he fooling?

She would have made a fine admiral!

When the prince finished chortling with his colleagues, Miss Jones cleared her throat. "Dreare Street, Your Highness, is actually a very pleasant street on which to live. In fact"—she bestowed a genuine smile upon him—"we're having a street fair soon."

Prinny drew in his many chins. "Really? No one has those anymore."

Miss Jones tossed her head. "*We* do. I'd be honored if you'd make an appearance at ours, Your Highness, as our guest of honor. Would you, please?"

Stephen couldn't stop his lip from curving up. Miss Jones's voice was so throaty with hope and enthusiasm, who could resist her?

Prinny blinked.

Stephen felt his shoulders tense.

"Why, I'd be glad to, Miss Jones," the Prince Regent replied with spirit—and only a little bit of slurring in his speech. "But only if you stand by my side in that delicious lady's-maid costume." He waggled his brows at her.

"If you say so, Your Highness," she responded weakly.

"When shall it be?" Prinny gave a little hop of excitement. "A week from now, I'll be gone for at least a fortnight to Brighton. So it's either in the next seven days or not for a small while."

"It's this coming Wednesday," she blurted out. "Isn't that right, Captain Arrow?"

Their gazes locked. They'd planned to have the fair *two* Wednesdays from now. But it couldn't be helped. They'd have to have it sooner.

"Next Wednesday it is, then," said the prince.

"And please tell all your friends," Jilly asked him.

"And enemies, too," added Stephen. "We don't discriminate."

Prinny laughed a great big belly laugh. "You always were a card, Arrow. Very well. I'll tell all of London's Upper Ten Thousand to come. For one day, my foes and I will be friends—on Dreare Street, of all places."

"Why not?" Stephen agreed.

Prinny kissed Miss Jones's hand with a great deal of fervor then retreated to his group of hangers-on once more.

Stephen was impatient to catch Miss Jones's gaze. When he finally did, he saw she was bursting with excitement. He felt it, too.

The deed was done. Prinny was coming to the street fair. In all likelihood, so would many of London's wealthiest shoppers. Perhaps they'd buy books. And oversized handkerchiefs. Meat pasties and paintings and mobcaps and beautiful gowns. And maybe . . . just maybe . . . one of them would buy his house.

God, he had to get those beams fixed by Wednesday!

He'd do it if he had to stay awake from now until then.

But he had something much more imperative to think about at the moment—Miss Jones, and getting her out into the garden before they left the ball tonight.

It was time to hold a celebration of sorts. And not only about the prince's announcement. It was time to celebrate the fact that she'd managed to turn an intended slight from Lady Tabitha on its ear.

It was also time to celebrate her voluptuous body, her smile, her boldness, her intelligent gaze, her kindness.

It was time to celebrate *her* . . .

If she'd only let him.

CHAPTER NINETEEN

Captain Arrow had a glint in his eye, a bold, take-no-prisoners look, as he wended his way through the small crowd gathered around Jilly.

"You're coming with me," he said in her ear.

Without hesitation—for she felt terribly uncomfortable with all the sudden interest in her—she put her hand through the crook of his arm.

"I'm sorry, I must go," she told the people staring at her and murmuring things about her royal Celtic origins.

It was such a relief! She still wasn't exactly sure how the diversion had happened, but Captain Arrow had made clear with that look earlier that he'd had everything to do with it.

He looked down at her now, his expression smug. "We've something to attend to in the garden, and this time I won't take no for an answer."

He was acting like a naval officer again, expecting instant obedience.

"I'm not one of your sailors," she retorted.

"Thank God," he said softly.

The inscrutable look he gave her then made her heart race. "Don't think—"

"That's right," he said, walking without hesitation through the flung-open doors to the garden. *"Don't think."*

She was confused. And tired.

And blast the man, intrigued.

He took her by the hand, and she stumbled after him through paths of stately trees and beautiful flowers. "Captain," she whispered. "I know what you're doing. But we can't. *I* can't."

He said nothing until they reached the darkest corner of the garden, where he stopped, turned toward her, and put his hands on her shoulders.

"You," he said firmly but gently, "need me."

She opened her mouth to say he was mad, but at that exact moment, he pulled a tendril of hair off her face. And then he gave a small tug and she was in his arms, her cheek pressed against his chest.

"And God knows I need you," he said.

She was ashamed at how moved she was by that eloquent yet simple speech, and by how quickly she submitted. She fell limp against him and let him caress her back, all while she stared at the outline of a small statue of a goddess holding an urn, and behind that, a cluster of lilac bushes.

They needed each other.

"You did amazingly well tonight," he murmured in her ear. "Starting out with that awful bitch Tabitha, and then being thrust into the situation with Prinny with no warning as to what the plan actually involved—"

She said nothing. She couldn't. She was letting herself drift. When one drifted, one took no responsibility.

One . . . let things happen.

She closed her eyes. He laid a kiss on her temple, a soft, slow, thoughtful kiss. When he pulled back, she sighed, and he nuzzled her neck then, moving her hair aside with his mouth, lingering on the soft spot below her ear and then her throat. She let her head fall back.

"You're perfect," he murmured.

She let a desperate little giggle escape. "I'm not perfect."

Not only that, she was in far, far too deep waters.

He put his hands on the wall on either side of her head and made her look into his eyes. "You're perfect," he said in a serious voice. "Accept it and move on."

He stared at her a moment, daring her to defy him.

"All right," she said, and, in an insane move, lifted her hand to his cheek. "You're perfect, too," she whispered.

He closed his eyes and then opened them. "Perfect for now, right?" His voice was gruff, but his mouth lifted at the corner.

She couldn't help a small smile, too. "Yes."

"That's fine with me." He wrapped both his arms around her waist and spun slowly around with her.

She looked up into his eyes and was lost.

Lost.

"Captain—"

"Stephen," he whispered.

"Stephen," she said.

But she couldn't say anything else. He was still the insouciant rake. But tonight he was something more.

So was she.

She could feel it humming around them, *through* them.

He looked down at her, and without a second's hesitation, she wrapped her arms around his neck and kissed him.

And he kissed her back.

She was caught in a heady, buzzing garden of delight, wrapped in his arms, tasting his mouth, smelling his skin, his coat, the lilacs—hearing the moans of pleasure emitting from his tanned, masculine throat.

This was what she'd imagined kissing to be.

This was heaven.

Stephen picked her up then, and she wriggled as close to him as she could, her mouth never leaving his.

"Miss Jones," he said in a husky tone. "I knew you'd be unforgettable. The very first time I kissed you, I knew."

"Jilly," she told him.

"Jilly," he murmured. "I need to get my coat off."

She helped him, and somehow they kept kissing.

He dropped the coat on the grass and laid her on top of it, their lips still locked. He endeared himself to her by doing his best to spread the coat out beneath her.

"We don't want to muss your lady's-maid costume," he said, grinning against her lips. "You've got to wear it again for Prinny."

She grinned back, but he kissed the grin right off her mouth.

She wanted to wrap up in that coat. She wanted to take his shirt off. She wanted to do so much more. In the confines of Hodgepodge, she'd had the yearning to meld into the man, to lose herself in him, but she'd never known it would overwhelm her to the point that she was greedy, avid, selfish and tugging, like a starving beast.

She looked up at him as she yanked at his shirt. The sickle moon hung above his shoulder for a moment, until he raised both his arms into the air and pulled the shirt off over his head.

She gave a small cry of pleasure when he came crashing back down on her yet managed not to hurt her in the least, his mouth demanding and his hands tugging at her bodice. She lifted her back to make it easier for him to shrug her gown down over her shoulders.

When she was free, he fumbled at her stays, unlacing them while she lay stunned, staring into the night, her hands roaming his back and the nape of his neck.

What was she doing?

Who cares? a wild voice in her head answered.

She let her fingers burrow into his hair as his lips began a slow perusal of her breasts, nuzzling in the cleft between them. But he avoided her nipples, merely slowing to gaze at them, to blow his warm breath over each of them—so delicious on a cool evening—and then moving onward and upward, to her face again.

Damn him for being a tease.

The sensation of her nipples pressed against his hard, sculpted chest while he kissed her mouth drove her even more mad with longing. But she was also happy. Happier than she'd been in years.

He caressed her waist with a hand, and then the edge of her breast and the full underside, all the while teasing her mouth with his tongue. She played back with equal abandon.

Finally, he covered her breast with his large palm and gave a gentle squeeze.

"You're more luscious than any tropical fruit," he whispered.

"I am?"

"Oh, yes." He held her arms trapped while he bent low and slowly circled her nipples with his tongue. She arched upward, and he pushed her down again, firmly but gently, with his thighs and groin.

His torture was exquisite. She wrapped her leg around his, and he took her nipple in his mouth then, suckling her breast.

She felt feral, right, pressed to the earth, to Stephen's skin—

To life.

She moved her head first left, then right, unsure how to bear the exquisite pleasure thrumming through her, crashing into her like waves at the point between her legs where the captain now steadily pulsed with his thigh. His hands, meanwhile, pulled her gown up her legs so she could do what he wanted her to do, what *she* wanted to do—

Spread her legs and let him lie between them.

"We've got to stop," she said, almost completely out of breath.

He raised his head from her breasts and looked at her. "Soon," he said. "But not yet."

"Not yet," she repeated, looking up at the sky again, the moon and few stars she could see taunting her with their light and distance.

She should be there. Or somewhere far away from Captain Arrow. In the light of the ballroom.

But, no.

She would defy the moon and the stars. The gossips waiting inside. The minister who'd stood before her and Hector and declared them man and wife, even as she told herself silently that she wasn't his wife— nor ever would be—no matter what was said in church by a silver-haired gentleman who spoke godly words over them, a Bible in his hands. Her heart—her soul—hadn't participated in the least.

She thrust herself up to meet the captain—Stephen. She ground herself into his hardness, her hands clutching tufts of grass.

"Your body is all I want," he whispered. "All I've ever wanted."

And then he went lower, and lower, until those golden curls on his head were brushing her softest spot and his mouth was exploring the creases where her thighs met her belly.

His hands glided up and down her legs, his breath was hot against her womanhood, and she wanted—

Oh, how she wanted!

The heat of his mouth upon her tender core took her by such surprise, she gasped aloud. But he only nuzzled closer, suckling her and licking her with sweet abandon.

She arched again, over and over, moaning without even caring who heard, oblivious to everything but him and her pleasure—

And when the sensation grew too much to hold, she floated away and then back down, enveloped by the musky man scent of his jacket beneath her. She sighed, a sigh that reached to the darkest corners of her being, the places where her fears dwelled, and brushed them away, like cobwebs.

When he lifted his head, Stephen had never seen a more appealing woman. Miss Jones—Jilly—was sated. Relaxed.

Unafraid.

She was dangerous this way. He knew how to handle her when she was obstreperous and unmanageable. But when she looked at him with a face that revealed so obviously that she'd been pleasured not a moment before, his chest tightened.

She was too perfect.

Too beautiful.

And then she smiled at him, a glorious, free smile lacking any awkwardness whatsoever.

It was as if he were being hit with a volley of cannon fire. She was a merciless, unrelenting foe, and she didn't even know it.

He'd never met an enemy like that at sea. Everyone on the waves knew what they were doing, why they were there—had intentions to vanquish.

Miss Jones was more like a force of nature, a squall spiraling into a hurricane, thoughtlessly ravaging the village that he'd built so carefully to accommodate one—just one—person.

Himself.

He was wrecked.

Yes, wrecked.

She'd wrecked him.

No one ever had before.

He didn't understand it, but he was glad. His scorching flirtation with Miss Jones had succeeded beyond his wildest dreams.

Which was part of the reason he was wrecked. His wildest dreams had been fairly stupid. He had, indeed, gone well beyond them, to a new territory of intense and confusing feelings—it was a place where he felt a new traveler without a single chart to guide him.

CHAPTER TWENTY

Jilly looked in wonder out the window of Hodgepodge. Light, blessed light, shone through the branches of the trees, making puddles of sun on the pavement. A cat—her cat, Gridley, a gift from Stephen—rolled ecstatically in one sunspot on the window ledge, nearly knocking over a row of books with his tail, but he managed to flick it out of the way at the last second.

Everything had changed since she'd been with Stephen in the Earl of Langley's garden.

There'd been no fog for the past five days.

Otis had sold six books to total strangers.

And she woke up every morning without fear.

The morning after the ball, Lady Tabitha had packed her bags and was gone from Lady Duchamp's by eight o'clock. A short while later, Otis had donned his town crier uniform and called everyone back to Hodgepodge for another street meeting—while Lady Duchamp was away on her mysterious morning carriage ride.

Everyone had stood in stunned silence when Stephen told them the grand news: the Prince Regent was coming to Dreare Street, and in exactly one week.

"*Everyone's* coming to Dreare Street," Jilly had said. "Everyone with money to spend, that is. We can do it—if we work together, we can be ready for them. The countdown starts today!"

The silence in Hodgepodge had seemed to last forever. But then Thomas had piped up with, "Hip, hip, hooray!" and everyone had erupted in cheers.

Stephen had looked at her with a spark of true excitement in his eye, and she'd had the strong impulse to laugh out loud and kiss him at the same time.

Since that morning, the view from Hodgepodge's window had been lively. Someone was always walking by to speak to Stephen or to stop in and ask her advice about a project they were working on for the fair. Either that, or they were carrying supplies back and forth, most of which could be found in Stephen's shed.

"Go!" Jilly cried now.

She stared at the heads and shoulders of the volunteer carpenters bent over the remaining three booths. Mrs. Hobbs's son and daughter hammered away on one. Nathaniel and little Thomas tackled another. And a pair of middle-aged maiden sisters tapped carefully at a third.

But that was all right. Two young men stood behind the pair, waiting to follow through with more arm power when the ladies' spirited attempts gave out.

It had been an amazing five days.

Of course, the best part had been the hours she'd spent with Stephen. When they were in public and he was near, she felt indescribably happy and tortured, all at the same time. The only relief she could find was seeing him in private, which was nearly impossible, except in small doses—doses too short to reenact what they'd done in the garden at the ball or earlier, on the floor at Hodgepodge.

But they had managed kisses. Short, passionate ones. Three times in his shed, once behind the bushes to the left of Hodgepodge, and twice in her office when Otis was out shopping.

But on both those occasions, a neighbor had come in to discuss a book or the street fair with her, and Stephen had had to sneak out the back of the building through a window in Otis's bedchamber.

He was staying extremely busy, painting the white stucco front of his house and repairing the two beams inside. And in between those chores, he was building a movable balcony for the actors, overseeing other construction, and organizing a team to beautify Dreare Street. That involved trimming hedges and trees and cutting back the giant holly bushes partially blocking the entrance to the street (which might account for why five strangers had ventured to Hodgepodge). It also meant quick coats of paint applied to many a front door.

Jilly oversaw organizing the merchants—what items to sell, what food and drinks to hawk—and the events to take place, including the dramatic skit and the children's parade.

"Amazingly, everything's proceeding nicely," she said to Stephen after the booths had been completed.

She was searching for Alicia Fotherington's journal in the bookshelves. "Even more astounding, no one's gotten into any arguments. Yes, two groups ran into each other in the fog this morning, but when a pile of lumber fell onto everyone's toes, no one complained."

Stephen spanned her waist with his hands from behind and whispered in her ear, "Even Mr. Hobbs is keeping quiet."

Jilly turned around and grinned. "I know. I'm very happy about that."

There was a beat of silence between them. The air became thick with a delightful tension. Stephen's eyes got that look, the one he'd had in his eye the very first day she'd met him. And her heart—well, it started racing. It always did when he was nearby.

"Let's go to your office," he said in a husky voice.

Oh, heavens. She wanted to kiss him so badly. Quickly, she looked over her shoulder out the window. No one was approaching. The white placard, the one on which she'd written TWO MORE DAYS UNTIL THE FAIR just this morning, was still propped in the window for the neighborhood to see.

Two days. It wasn't many.

It had been five days since the ball. Five days since Stephen had twice in one day—

She blushed to think of it.

"What's that face?" he asked her, pulling her closer. "Wait." He gave her the smile that heated her to the core. "Don't tell me. I know."

"Of course you don't," she said briskly.

"Yes I do," he said. He took one, slow look down the length of her. "I want you on my jacket again, too. Or here on the floor."

She was mortified that he could tell what she was thinking.

"Off with you now," she whispered. "I know for a fact Susan is on her way with Nathaniel and Thomas. They've taken to going to the park every afternoon for half an hour. They're staying up until all hours framing Nathaniel's watercolors and sewing caps. They drop the finished ones off here before dinner. Their apartments are terribly cramped as it is, and I have the office to store things."

"Are you saying they eat dinner together?"

She shrugged, but inside she was tremendously excited. "I think so."

Stephen tapped her mouth with a finger. "You matchmaker, you."

She giggled, and then she grabbed his finger—
And kissed it.

His face took on a whole new level of interest in her. He put one hand on either side of her head. "You shouldn't do things like that."

"I know," she said. "I can't help it."

He stared at her for an instant. She couldn't help smiling at him. She knew it was unwavering. She was happy. She liked being trapped by him. She liked *him*.

Very much.

He readjusted his stance, then narrowed his eyes at her. "You, Miss Jones, are an incredible flirt."

"I am?"

He nodded, his expression inscrutable. Then he put his fists on his hips and walked away a few feet. He stood still, looking out the front window. His back was so broad and strong. She never tired of looking at it.

He turned around then and came back to her. "What about Otis's handkerchiefs?" he said.

"Mrs. Hobbs," she said, wanting to melt into him, "is tacking on the lace while Otis puts together his special shoe collection."

Stephen gave her a crooked smile. "Does Otis truly believe anyone will buy his shoes?"

Jilly nodded. "Of course they will."

Stephen lifted her chin with a finger. "You're an awfully good friend to have."

She lowered her eyes. "Thank you."

When she looked up, he was gazing at her with something that frightened her and exhilarated her all at the same time.

"What are the Hartleys doing?" she asked, turning aside and moving toward the counter. "I haven't seen them since the ball." She looked over her shoulder and saw him pursue her with all the focused attention with which a hound pursues a fox.

And she loved every minute of it.

He leaned against the corner and folded his arms. "They're taking Miss Hartley to various picnics and musicales, doing their very best to ingratiate themselves to society." He arched a brow. "But Miss Hartley isn't at all happy. She tried to get out of going this morning by claiming a headache."

"Was she truly ill?"

"Not at all."

"Do you think she doesn't want to get married?"

"I think she wants Pratt," Stephen said knowingly.

"No."

"Oh, yes." Stephen grinned. "Did you see him moping about last night? Miss Hartley was at another ball. We tried to get him to assist us with removing branches from the street, but he was quite halfhearted about it. He's never like that when Miss Hartley is nearby."

Jilly put a hand on her heart. "But this is wonderful! Did he admit he was pining after her?"

"No," Stephen said, "but he couldn't stop talking about her, and about how rude her parents were, and why it was such a shame that she was stuck with them. And then he groused about all the dandies she'd meet on the Marriage Mart."

Jilly pushed off the wall and walked to the shop window. "Dreare Street isn't unlucky at all!" She whirled around to face Stephen. "Love is in the air! Look at Miss Hartley and Pratt . . . Susan and Nathaniel—"

She stopped speaking all of a sudden, realizing that she'd brought them to an awkward moment.

Their gazes locked. He didn't look away. He looked very, very serious. She blinked.

"I invented a ruse in which I'm supposed to be pursuing you," he said slowly. "But it's really not necessary anymore. I think Miss Hartley would run away if her parents insisted she marry me. She has a *tendre* for Pratt, and why shouldn't they be together? He's a decent man."

"You can tell the Hartleys the truth now," Jilly said, her hands clasped in front of her. She felt very serious, too. "That you're not pursuing me."

"Yes," Stephen said. "I could."

They stared at each other some more.

"Don't—" she couldn't help blurting out.

"I won't—"

They spoke at the same time.

He took a step toward her.

She held out her hand.

The bell at the front door jangled.

"Where is she?" a rough voice cried.

Jilly turned—

And looked into the cold, stern face of her husband.

CHAPTER
TWENTY-ONE

Stephen's heart pounded in his chest. Something was wrong. Something was terribly wrong. Jilly was shaking like a leaf. She walked swiftly behind her counter and stood there, her nostrils flared, her cheeks pale, her mouth half open, as if she were struggling for breath.

She didn't even seem aware of his presence anymore.

That magical moment between them—when they'd spoken at the same time and reached toward each other . . .

It was as if it had never happened.

Threat hung in the air, dissolving that special memory to mist and propelling Stephen into full-blown defensive mode. His training at sea during wartime saw to that. And he was prepared to go on the offensive if the situation should require it.

He assessed the man standing at the door. The danger came from him, obviously, but Stephen had yet to know why, and he wanted to know—very much.

He wanted to know who was scaring Miss Jones.

His Miss Jones.

The fellow was impeccably dressed, in a fine coat

and waistcoat and a diamond stickpin in his intricately folded cravat, yet somehow the clothes sat poorly on him. He was perhaps two or three years older than Stephen, about the same height but slightly thicker at the waist. His brown curls were glossy but hung lank at his temples in a style that suggested he wasn't sure if he were a farmer, a Corinthian, or a man of business. His lips were thin and mean, and his chin jutted like a bull's. Without blinking, his small, brown eyes focused with a terrible intensity on Jilly.

She stared back, almost blankly.

It was as if the Jilly Stephen knew weren't there any longer.

This is the man, Stephen thought, *the man she fears—*

The one that Otis had been prepared to clock with a shoe.

He had the incongruous thought that he wished Otis were here now, pulling off one of his outlandish shoes. Jilly would have rebuked him—or not—but at least there would have been movement, words spoken, instead of this awful silence.

"Get your things." The man's voice was low, almost a growl.

Jilly flinched.

Stephen stepped forward. "Who are *you*?" he asked sharply, prepared at any moment to fight. He cast a discreet glance at the man's waist. His coat gaped, but Stephen couldn't tell if he was armed or not.

Every ounce of his being clamored to protect the woman behind him.

Out of the corner of his eye, he looked for a weapon of some kind. But all he saw were books. Book bindings could hurt if they landed on a temple correctly, but they weren't nearly as useful a weapon as a pistol.

At least he had his fists.

The man looked at him with contempt, yet he didn't appear interested in a fight. "I'm Hector Broadmoor," he said flatly, "and I'm here to retrieve my wife."

His wife?

Stephen's mind couldn't register what the man was saying. "She's not here, obviously." He looked about the room, and when his gaze passed over Jilly, she raised a shaky hand to her eye and wiped away a tear.

"Go away, Captain Arrow," she said in a voice he didn't recognize.

It was low. Ugly.

Despairing.

He shook his head. "What's going on?"

He had the same feeling he had on a ship when he heard a low, mournful whistling through the rigging, the sound that signified a storm was brewing, the kind that required the men to be at their most alert—to murmur prayers when the darkness fell and the swells grew large and cavernous, slapping against the hull, taunting the sailors with their tentacle fingers.

Jilly stared at him. "Please," she said. "Leave."

Stephen spread his feet and put his hands on his hips. "Explain to me what's happening, Miss Jones." His heart was going faster than it ever had, yet he felt as if he were moving in slow motion.

"There needs no explaining," the man at the door said, almost complacently. "She's my wife. And her name's not Miss Jones. It's Mrs. Broadmoor."

A wave of sickness washed over Stephen. He stared at Miss Jones—at Jilly—and she looked back with a mournful expression in her eyes.

It couldn't be.

It simply couldn't be.

"Is it true?" he managed to say. His mouth was drier than the bottom of a barrel of grog let loose among his sailors.

She hesitated but a moment, then nodded.

It all went rushing out of him then, like a waterfall, the bundle of emotions he'd felt about her—all of it, from the very beginning: the annoyance, the desire, the concern, the anticipation, the tenderness.

He was emptied in a moment, back to his old self, the one who hadn't really known who he was until after his mother had died and a village neighbor had told him his core family had never existed.

"All right, then." He looked back at Mr. Broadmoor, then one more time at Jilly.

Her brows, those exquisite black wings, were flung far out above her violet-blue eyes, which were wide with grief.

And perhaps shock.

Although . . .

Although she'd known he was coming, hadn't she?

It was why she'd steered clear of Stephen, or at least *tried* for a while to steer clear of him—

She'd known.

He turned away from her and walked slowly past the man at the door. He felt small. Invisible.

And profoundly stupid.

CHAPTER
TWENTY-TWO

Jilly watched Stephen go.

His leaving was inevitable, but it hurt her more than she had imagined possible. She'd thought giving up Hodgepodge would be the worst thing. But it wasn't.

Seeing Stephen look at her as if they'd never met? Seeing the joy leave his eyes? The respect? The regard for her?

It was like someone tearing out her heart.

She swallowed and looked around her, seeing her bookstore with the eyes of someone who knows she must go away forever. There were books everywhere, stacked neatly on the shelves. Too neatly, actually. A thriving bookstore wasn't so blasted tidy.

Her father's large, oval looking glass reflecting the street was shiny and clean, but the street was still hazy with fog. Looking into that oval mirror with its ornate frame, she wished she could walk into that murky otherworld and *stay*.

This world was too painful.

Gridley, her cat, sprawled out on the ledge between two books. He seemed to sense her looking at him because he turned his head and blinked.

Little tears threatened her then.

Gridley.

He was hers, but Hector would never let her take him with her. Besides, Gridley belonged here, at Hodge-podge.

"Get on with it now," Hector said in a threatening tone.

She jumped. "I will," she said. "Just . . . just give me some time." Her knees felt extremely wobbly.

He laughed. "Yes, you've had quite a shock, haven't you?"

She refused to answer.

"You're probably wondering how I found you." His voice was smug.

She put a curl behind her ear. "No, actually, I'm not."

Hector narrowed his eyes and advanced a few steps. "It was easy. I knew you'd not be able to hide long. You wanted to be found."

Again, she said nothing. But he was coming closer, so she had to move. She walked out from behind her counter. "I've some things to pack," she said.

Not much, really. She couldn't take the books, of course.

She wouldn't want to, either.

They belonged to Otis.

She felt a sudden jolt of power.

Hector had no idea.

It was the plan she'd shared with Otis, her worst-case-scenario plan. He'd balked, said it would never happen, not on his watch, but it was happening.

And she was very glad she'd thought ahead.

Now, when Hector thought she would be ripped away from all she'd managed to build up around her on Dreare Street, she would leave behind at least something . . .

The bookstore, for Otis.

"Yes, you wanted me to come after you," Hector said, and now he was a mere foot in front of her. She could smell his sour breath.

She raised her chin. "I'll be back in a moment."

"You'd better make it quick," he said.

She turned her back on him and marched up the stairs, hating him every step of the way.

When she found her bag and began stuffing it with the meager clothing she'd allowed herself to bring, she was no longer shaking with shock.

She was furious.

Why, a voice inside her said, did she have to give up her life for a churlish, stingy man with no heart?

She went quickly through the sitting room, leaving everything in place for Otis, and had the fleeting thought that she'd never found that diary again, the one that had belonged to another wife who'd lived long ago, happily, it seemed, at 34 Dreare Street.

At Captain Arrow's house.

She flicked the curtain back for a moment and stared at the white stucco front of his home, freshly painted. The pirate flag was no longer hanging from the roof.

She was back to thinking of him as the captain.

She could never think of him as Stephen again, not without inciting a little hitch in her breath and a burning behind her eyes.

She let the curtain fall.

It was time to go.

As she descended the stairs, she couldn't help feeling a bit of triumph. Whatever Hector was doing to her now, he couldn't erase all that she'd accomplished while she'd been away from him.

There was Hodgepodge. And Otis would run it.

Otis.

He'd be so—

Upset.

She inhaled a ragged breath. Who would take care of him? Who'd notice his shoes?

She stopped for a moment outside her office, closed her eyes, and pressed her fingers over them.

A comforting thought came to her. Otis would find friends. He already had friends. Susan. Nathaniel.

He'd been with them, actually, more than he'd been with her the last few days. He'd been humming about the sitting room in the mornings when he'd made breakfast, and he'd come home whistling at night.

Otis, she felt in her gut, would be all right, as difficult as it would be for them to part from each other.

But would she be all right?

Would she?

She opened her eyes and stared at her office desk, but what she was seeing was a picture of Captain Arrow's face, of the front door of Hodgepodge opening, of Lavinia Hobbs, Susan and Nathaniel, the Hartleys, Pratt, the Hobbses' children and Thomas, and all the other people she'd met since she'd arrived on Dreare Street.

Even Lady Duchamp. Jilly had never found out where she went each morning.

She'd wanted to know.

Now she never would.

Drawing in a deep breath, she entered the store again. It was time to go. Time to leave everything behind.

"Miss Jilly!"

Otis was there, his chest heaving and—God love him—his shoe in his hand. The other one was missing, presumably thrown at Hector.

Hector flung his finger in Otis's direction. "That oaf hit me in the eye with his demmed slipper."

"Yes, and I'll do it again!" Otis roared. "You've no right to come here and destroy our peace."

Jilly raised her hand. "It's all right, Otis. Don't worry about me. We knew this day would come."

Her loyal friend looked at her, his eyes hurt and his mouth sagging. "I don't want you to go." His voice trembled.

"I have to," she said, and knew she had to be strong for him. "You'll be fine. You've got Hodgepodge."

"What?" Hector's face reddened more than usual.

Jilly looked him in the eye. "You can't get this, Hector. It belongs to Otis."

Hector twisted his head to stare down Otis. "You cur. How did you manage that?"

Otis lifted his chin. "I don't care what you call me. And I didn't manage anything. Your wife was looking out for her best interests, and if I can help her do that, I will."

Hector narrowed his eyes and leered. "Aye, you take this moldering place. I'll take *her*."

Otis's eyes filled with tears.

Hector had known exactly what to say to hurt him. For a stupid man, he was surprisingly able to sling barbs.

Jilly wished she could hit him over the head with one of her large atlases.

The street was busy. Several children ran by the shop window. An elderly couple strolled down the other side of the street to watch the fair planners hard at work painting someone's front stoop.

"Hello, Miss Jones." A cheerful young man stuck his head in the open door. "How are you today?"

She gave him a wan smile. "I'm well, Gerald. Thanks for asking."

"Good." Gerald grinned. "Seeing your sign puts an extra spring in my step. Especially when we've got to do more hedge cutting next door to Lady Duchamp's. She's doing her best to be unpleasant. Yesterday she instructed her maid to toss a huge pot of rotted potato peelings out the windows on top of our heads while we were working."

"Oh, Gerald!" Jilly was horrified.

"No matter," he said. "We managed to get out of the way. Probably because her maid hates her, too, and called out a warning to us." He put his hand up in a friendly farewell and departed.

"Who's Lady Duchamp?" Hector asked.

Otis glowered at him. "Someone not nearly as wicked as you."

Jilly cleared her throat. "She's my neighbor across the street. She's not particularly friendly. She has a niece, Lady Tabitha."

"I wonder if we'll see them about Town," Hector said.

Jilly started. "What do you mean?"

Otis's eyes grew wide.

"We're staying here." Hector looked her up and down. "In fact, we'll be on Grosvenor Square. I rented a town house for the rest of the Season. I want Prinny and his cronies to know you're no Celtic princess. You're just Mrs. Broadmoor, a lying wife who needs a good comeuppance."

"So that's how you found me," breathed Jilly. "Someone at the ball—"

"She never stopped being Lady Jilly!" Otis cried. "And who wouldn't lie to get away from a blackguard like you?"

"Yes, indeed." Hector gave a short laugh. "You stepped right into it, Miss *Jones*." He was apparently ignoring Otis. "Maybe if you'd been a little less noticeable at that ball, you'd still be hidden from me. But no, you had to claim to be descended from Celtic kings."

Jilly swallowed. Captain Arrow had made that up, but she'd asked him to devise a strategy. So they could get to the prince . . .

So they could get him to come to the street fair . . .

So they could save Dreare Street . . .

So she could live here—happily ever after.

It hadn't worked that way, had it?

She gazed out the window and saw Gerald, Pratt,

and Miss Hartley laughing and merrily slapping paint now on a front door and some shutters on the house next to Lady Duchamp's.

The *happily ever after* hadn't worked for her, but perhaps it wasn't too late for everyone else.

"I'll go with you to Grosvenor Square," she said to Hector in a subservient voice, to pacify him. Her mind was working very fast. "Which house is it?"

She had to know if he was lying. Perhaps he really intended to take her straight back to the village in Somerset.

"Number 54," he said, "right next to Lord and Lady Beechum's residence. They're high in the instep, so the broker tells me. And she's a gossip."

So. It was apparently true that they'd be moving onto Grosvenor Square. Her husband was really enjoying himself at her expense, but she knew this day had been coming.

Was running away worth it? a voice in the darkest corner of her mind teased her. It had been silent ever since that night in the garden with the captain.

Now it was back.

Another jolt of misery overcame her as she recalled the look in his eyes when he'd learned the truth.

You made a very foolish mistake, the same dark corner mocked her. *You should have accepted your lot, the way other women do.*

She reached out a hand and steadied herself on the edge of a shelf. "Let's go," she said in a shaky voice. "I'm ready."

"But Lady Jilly—" Otis wasn't bothering any more with the *Miss Jilly's*. They were back to how things were in the village she'd lived in for all her life. She was a lady and always had been.

She managed to get past him without looking into his eyes and gathered a few things from the counter: her shawl, the book of poetry she'd just begun, and the little journal she'd kept. She'd ceased with the silly story about the captain and Miss Hartley and their dozen children. Now she was writing about her own hopes for the future, hopes she'd considered realistic—as Alicia Fotherington had.

"I'll be fine," she told her friend in firm tones.

It pained her to ignore Otis's concern, but she couldn't tell him her plan. She had to leave.

Now.

Before the rest of Dreare Street heard the truth.

If she stayed hidden in the house on Grosvenor Square, perhaps no one else would find out her true situation, beyond Captain Arrow. And she already knew he would tell no one.

Jilly was betting on the fact that Hector was a supreme liar and was lying now. They might go to Grosvenor Square but she doubted for long. He wouldn't want the whole of London society talking about how his wife left him. He had pride. Far too much of it.

This sojourn in Grosvenor Square was probably the most frightening revenge he could think of. He'd probably devised the idea on the journey to London.

He'd hate to part with the funds required to keep up a house in Mayfair, so she was sure they wouldn't linger for the entire Season.

No. He was merely attempting to torture her with the possibility of extended shame. She had no doubt.

In his own twisted way, he was quite brilliant. Jilly would be mortified to have to live in London and know that everyone would be talking about her, the daughter of a viscount who'd fallen so far that she'd pretended to be descended from Celtic kings *and* pretended to be an unmarried lady.

Despite her authentic pedigree, she'd not be invited to parties because of her deceit. Either that, or she would, so the party-goers could see the disaster of her life up close.

It didn't matter, really. No doubt Hector planned on keeping her confined to the house, which would suit him. He was exceedingly dull and at home had shown no interest in attending musicales or village dances.

And if, for some reason, he did intend to parade her about society?

She'd claim illness. She knew Hector would be willing to believe her. She could claim an attack of nerves—he'd like that, as he would have induced it—and she could lounge around in a fragile state for the time being.

Because all she needed was two days.

After that, everyone and their cousin could know she was Hector's wife.

She just couldn't have Prinny learn about it until after the fair. He wouldn't come, otherwise. And if he didn't come, no one from the Upper Ten Thousand would come.

So she must keep the street from finding out. If Lady Duchamp discovered her secret, the whole of London society would know by the day's end.

She'd do whatever it took to keep Hector content for two days.

Two miserable days.

And somehow, she'd also come back to Dreare Street on the day of the fair.

How? the awful voice in the dark corner of her mind asked her. *How will you get back here when you've already failed so miserably at your plan to be free of Hector?*

She didn't know.

But right now, she couldn't think of that. Time was running out. Someone, soon, would come by and ask why the carriage had been outside Hodgepodge. They'd ask Otis why Jilly had left in that carriage with a strange man. Already, she was sure Lady Duchamp was peering out her window and wondering what was going on. At this very moment, she might be calling for her cane and her shawl and demanding to have the front door thrown open so she could cross the street and see what the commotion was about.

Jilly had to leave before that happened.

But first she had to convey to Otis that he needed to make up some kind of excuse for why she was suddenly gone.

"Mr. Broadmoor," she said, for that's how he preferred to be addressed by her in public and sometimes in private, depending on his odd moods, "if you don't mind, I'd like to leave immediately. Please tell the coachman to prepare the horses."

"The coach is ready," Hector said.

"Very well." Jilly was unsure how she'd be able to get Otis alone.

She looked at the window ledge. "I'd like to take the cat with me." She strode over to Gridley and scooped him up. "You won't mind, will you?"

"Of course I bloody well mind!" Hector scoffed.

"Are you sure I can't have him?" Jilly feigned true distress.

She'd already determined she'd miss Gridley, but he was better off here, basking on his shelf.

Hector made a face. "Put the cat down, and let's go." His voice tightened menacingly.

"No." She turned her back to him. "Please. Not yet. I—I need to hold him a moment longer."

Her back felt rigid, exposed to Hector's malice. She cradled Gridley in her arms. He blinked up at her lazily, his mistress who fed him a small kipper every morning, along with a dish of cream.

A tiny tear pushed its way out of her eye and trickled down her cheek.

She heard Hector's impatient release of breath. "Get that cat away from her," he ordered Otis. "Why haven't you done so already, you lummox?"

Jilly resisted the urge to turn around and tell Hector to shut his mouth—that was her dear friend he was maligning!—and waited.

Otis stumbled toward her, around two tables, in the

process knocking a stack of prettily bound books to the floor.

It's a small price to pay, and they can be cleaned and restacked, Jilly thought, still in shopkeeper mode.

When he got to her, their eyes met, and Otis froze for a moment.

"Hurry up!" Hector shouted.

Gridley twisted in Jilly's arms.

"Here," Jilly said aloud for Hector to hear. She thrust Gridley in Otis's arms. "Good-bye, Gridley." She petted him slowly, doing her best to appear reluctant to leave him.

"Say I was called away for family illness," Jilly said in the merest of whispers. "I'll be back for the fair. Get the captain's help, meanwhile. Tell him . . . tell him I'm sorry."

Otis's eyes were still wide and she saw some pity in them. But she also saw a glimmer of hope, which he swiftly extinguished.

Good, Jilly thought. *He understands.*

Perhaps he understood more than she cared him to.

"I'll miss you, Lady Jilly." Otis gave a big sob. "Oh, how I'll miss you!"

Heavens, he was playing his part too well. But it was what she loved about him, wasn't it? She threw her arms about him, and Gridley squirmed, pressed as he was between them. When she pulled back, Otis gave a long moan of despair. The cat's tail whipped back and forth in a frenzied motion. He wanted back to his ledge and peace.

Jilly couldn't blame him.

She straightened her back, and looked at Otis with a great deal of affection. "I must go now, dear friend. Good luck with Hodgepodge."

He suddenly seemed to remember he was holding Gridley and let him slip to the floor.

When he stood again, he took Jilly's hand and raised it to his lips. "Good-bye, Lady Jilly. Best of luck to you."

His voice was a mere whisper now. The real grief had come back to replace the staged.

She felt it, too.

Oh, how she hoped her new plan would work! She'd still be stuck with Hector—who'd be furious after he found out—but at least Dreare Street would have a chance to be happy.

She went to Hector, and with everything she had in her, forced herself to place her hand on his arm.

"You'll never see her again, you idiot," Hector said to Otis, and strode with her to the door. "Good riddance," he said, looking back. "And may your bookstore go up in flames."

To prove his point, he flicked his smoking cheroot through the air.

"No!" Otis shouted, and went scrambling after it.

Hector merely laughed.

Jilly thought she couldn't feel any worse at that point. But when she headed straight for the carriage, she somehow knew Captain Arrow was watching her.

The shame she felt was so great, she could barely hold her head up.

She entered the carriage swiftly and was relieved

when the coachman cracked the whip seconds later. They were on their way.

When they rolled out of Dreare Street onto Curzon Street, she clenched her hands in her lap. She'd be back, she told herself, in two days.

She *would* be back.

CHAPTER
TWENTY-THREE

A few moments earlier, Stephen stood at a bedchamber window at 34 Dreare Street and looked out at Hodgepodge. It was the same window Jilly had leaned out when he'd first met her, the one where she'd dropped bags of water on the bull's-eye he'd painted on the street below.

Impulsively, he looked out and down, as if somehow he could recapture that special day, the first day he'd met Miss Jones. The bull's-eye was still there but fading now. Good thing. He'd have had trouble selling a house with a silly bull's-eye painted in front of it.

Dropping bags of water had been a foolish thing to do. So was hosting a night of theatrics. So was being a drunken idiot with his friends.

But none of that compared with the stupidity of falling in love with a woman who was married.

Yes, he'd fallen in love—real love—for the first time in his life. He'd been infatuated too many times to count, but love?

Never.

Not until Miss Jones had come along, with her notes

of protestation about the noise he was creating and her earnest knocks on his door, pleading for peace.

Hah.

She'd gotten her revenge, hadn't she?

He'd never have peace again.

Now he looked at Hodgepodge, at the fine carriage and two matched bays standing in front of it. Mr. Broadmoor—and Jilly—were obviously wealthy.

Stephen should have known.

He'd no idea why he felt compelled to watch, but he did.

She walked out of the bookshop.

She.

It was the only way he could refer to her without feeling as if his heart were being ripped out of his chest.

Her face appeared serene if serious, her chin was up (no surprise there), and her back was straight. It was only a moment between the shop door and the carriage, but would she look over at him?

Surely she knew he was watching.

No. She kept her eye on the carriage door, and moments later the vehicle was rolling away.

He turned from the window and ran both hands over his face, then stood silent, looking at nothing.

All he could see was her face when she nodded, admitting it was true—

She was that man's wife.

"Damn you, Jilly Jones!" Stephen cried into the empty bedchamber, then swiftly punched a hole in the wall.

Relishing the pain, he staggered from the room.

What else could he destroy?

"Captain Arrow!" It was Lady Hartley coming up the stairs. She froze in place, her hand on her skirt. "What has happened to your hand?"

Miss Hartley peered over her shoulder.

He looked down at his hand. It was mainly chalky white, but there was a streak of red on the knuckles.

Blood, of course.

When he looked up again, he'd tucked all traces of emotion away. "A small accident while I was working. Nothing to be concerned about." He certainly didn't want *them* to know what had happened to Miss Jones. He forced himself to smile politely. "Where's Sir Ned?"

"At the club." Lady Hartley gave a careless arch to one brow. She sounded bored and resentful. "Miranda is about to go out with that cook of yours to purchase more paint. But I believe I'll stay here."

"Am I?" Miss Hartley asked brightly. "I thought you and Papa said I couldn't—"

"Yes, well, I've changed my mind," Lady Hartley replied.

"Thank you, Mother!" Miss Hartley turned right back around and ran out the front door.

When the door slammed behind the daughter, the mother threw Stephen a meaningful look, which he completely ignored.

"Yes, well, I'm going out, too," he said to her.

"Have you finished all the house repairs?" Lady Hartley leaned back dangerously over the stair banister, her arms extended to either side, her bosom shoved forward, and her head thrown back, presumably to show herself to advantage.

"No." He was terribly far behind.

And he was also trapped on the stair landing.

She sniffed and ran her hand up and down the railing. "What a shame. Sir Ned has met someone who might be interested in purchasing the house if you can restore it to excellent condition."

She sent him a coy look.

Stephen was becoming rapidly bored with her infatuation. "Does this person know about Dreare Street's reputation?"

"His name is Lord Smelling. He'd like to come by soon to discuss the matter."

"Well, Lord Smelling will have to wait." Stephen couldn't care less that he sounded terse.

Lady Hartley laid a hand over her heart. "My goodness. You're certainly prickly today. Shall we tell him you're busy with the fair?"

"No. The fair's the last thing on my mind at the moment. Good day, Lady Hartley." Stephen escaped past her down the stairs.

"Captain!" Lady Hartley's voice was shrill. "What *is* on your mind? Could it be *me*?"

He flung open the front door only to see Otis already there, with his hand raised as if to knock. "Captain!" he cried. "I must talk to you! It's an emergency."

"I know about Miss Jones." Stephen could barely eke out the name.

He navigated around Otis with little more care

than he had shown Lady Hartley and sprinted down the front steps.

"Where are you off to?" Otis cried.

Stephen shrugged and kept walking. All he could see was red. Covered by black. Smothered by red.

And the blasted wisps of fog still hanging on the shrubs and branches of Dreare Street.

He had no idea where he was going. This was new terrain for him, loving a woman—

And then losing her in the bargain.

"Wait for me! I beg of you!" Otis called after him.

He kept going.

"If you have any decency in you at all, you'll stop right there, Captain!"

Stephen stopped. He'd never heard Otis sound so commanding.

When he turned around, the ex-valet was striding toward him with his fists clenched and his face determined.

He looked a bit like Admiral Lord Nelson.

"I'll have you know something," Otis said in a trembling voice. "There is no finer woman on earth than Lady Jilly—"

"*Lady* Jilly?" Stephen gave a short bark of laughter. "What other revelations will there be today?"

Otis narrowed his eyes at him. "Stop being an ass."

Stephen shook his head in wonder. "Did you just call me an ass?"

Otis raised his chin. "I most certainly did. If you're the man I think you are, you'll cease your judgment of Lady Jilly until you have all the facts."

Stephen's jaw worked back and forth as he tried to contain his anger. "I don't need the facts," he said low. "I know them."

"Not all of them," Otis said, unperturbed.

Stephen could feel his face become a mask. "Tell me, then."

He didn't want to know.

He didn't *need* to know.

In the navy, they called it making excuses. Excuses were for the cowardly.

Stephen didn't like cowards.

"If you knew her husband, you'd understand," Otis said.

They were walking toward the top of Dreare Street. To their left, Miss Hartley and Pratt were talking and laughing and walking toward Curzon, as well. The paint could be found a few blocks over, and Stephen had arranged that they'd receive a tremendous discount for buying so much. Up ahead, several children were already practicing the street parade. And to their right, an older man was walking his dog.

"I already suspect he's an ass." Stephen swung his arms with more than his usual vigor. "But it doesn't excuse—"

"What do you know of it?" Otis interrupted him. "You're not a woman. You're not at someone's beck and call. You command your own destiny."

His voice was bitter.

"Perhaps I do," Stephen replied just as bitterly. "And what I'd like right now is to leave Dreare Street. I've someplace to be."

"Mr. Broadmoor"—Otis ignored him and went on—"was thrust upon Lady Jilly as a mate. Her father decided on his deathbed he wanted to see her well placed before he died. Mr. Broadmoor's a very distant cousin. The viscount sent for him, but Lady Jilly refused the man. Not many women would do that, but Lady Jilly knows her own mind."

"I'm aware of that."

"She explained clearly to her father that the man was a scoundrel, that he'd tried to ravish her the minute her father's back was turned. And then her father confessed that all the property was entailed to Mr. Broadmoor and that if Lady Jilly didn't marry him, she would be thrown out along with all us servants. Jilly thinks her father was hastened to his death by her revelation about the man's character. So she felt both guilt about his decline and worry about the servants—both of which compelled her to meet Mr. Broadmoor at the altar."

Stephen released a sigh. "It's a sad story, I'll grant you that. But it doesn't excuse the fact that she pretended to be unmarried and—"

He wouldn't say any more.

Otis threw out an arm in front of him, and Stephen was forced to stop. He gave the man a sideways look. "You're playing with fire, you do know that, Shrimpshire?"

"I don't care." Otis frowned. "*You,* sir, are the one who pursued Lady Jilly, who told the Hartleys she was your intended. Have you conveniently forgotten that fact?"

"No, I haven't." His voice was clipped. "But I'd like to."

"You're no innocent, Captain." Otis's tone was tart. "*You* were playing with fire. You've made that your favorite pastime, haven't you? And now it's come to burn you."

Stephen sighed again. "I'm well aware of that fact. Perhaps it's why I'm so—"

He groped for words.

"Angry," Otis supplied for him.

"To put it mildly."

They walked in semicompanionable silence another ten seconds before Otis spoke again. "Lady Jilly had time to tell me only a few things before she was taken away. The first is that she intends to be back here for the fair. She told me to seek your help meanwhile, and to tell you"—he hesitated—"that she's sorry."

Oh, how those words fell like cold pebbles on the hardness of Stephen's heart.

Sorry.

What good was that?

It was all very nice to be sorry, but it didn't change the fact that she was married, he was not, and she'd never bothered to tell him, even though she should have. They'd been friends—*more* than friends.

He had no idea what to do with a *sorry*.

"Right," he murmured, and looked anywhere but at Otis.

"I hope you plan to continue leading us with the fair, Captain," the bookstore clerk said quietly.

Blast it all. Stephen felt like taking a swing at a

wall again. Why did he always feel compelled to do his duty? "I told you. I was about to go somewhere else." The words came out softer than he'd have liked. He felt completely dispirited, worse than he'd ever felt in his life.

"I don't believe you," said Otis.

Stephen glared at him.

Otis raised his hands. "All right, I believe you. But after an hour or two, you'll come back."

Stephen couldn't disagree. He knew he wouldn't abandon the street. It wasn't in his nature to quit before a job was done. Nor was it in his nature to be a scoundrel.

He was tempted to throw his head back and groan aloud. Couldn't a broken man take time out to feel *any* self-pity?

Otis smiled and looked hopeful, damn him.

"You're right," Stephen muttered. "I'll be back."

Otis slapped him on the back. "I knew you'd not disappoint us."

Stephen almost rolled his eyes, but two small children were staring at them, their brightly painted whirligigs temporarily forgotten.

"Are you ill, Captain Arrow?" asked one small girl.

He forced himself to shake his head and appear . . . bright.

Yes, bright.

He could do that.

"No, Rebecca, I'm not ill," he said.

She gave him a grin that lit up the whole street.

"Good, Captain. We can't have you ill before Wednesday."

"That's right." He winced and hoped she took it as a smile.

She and her companion ran off with their whirligigs spinning madly.

"Their mothers are making those for the fair," said Otis. "The children must be testing them."

Stephen looked after them. Every family on the street was involved, weren't they?

Everyone but Lady Duchamp and Mr. Hobbs.

He certainly didn't want to be lumped in with Lady Duchamp and Mr. Hobbs, did he?

For that reason and that reason *alone,* he told himself, he'd be back sooner rather than later. There was still much work to be done.

CHAPTER
TWENTY-FOUR

Jilly was not one to feel sorry for herself. She knew she was more fortunate than most. She'd been born a lady. She'd grown up in comfort and had been well educated. She'd had parents who'd loved her dearly, a village full of kindly neighbors, and a loyal friend in Otis. But at the moment, riding along the streets of Mayfair in a luxurious carriage with Hector, she was tempted to believe she was the unluckiest woman in the world.

Hector spent most of his time staring out the window, his cane between his legs, his hands resting upon the brass top. But she sensed he was keenly aware of her every move.

And no wonder. She was his wife, and she'd run away from him.

The whole world would agree he had every right to treat her suspiciously.

Finally, he turned to look at her. "You must realize you'll be punished."

She felt a roiling fear and loathing rise in her. "According to your God, I'm a sinner, I'm sure."

He scoffed. "And who is your God?"

"Not yours, that's certain," she said, not blinking.

He turned his face toward the window again. "I saw how that golden-haired man looked at you in that decrepit bookstore of yours, you harlot. You're lucky I've taken you back."

"You don't have to," she said quickly. "You could have left me there." She paused. "We could get a divorce."

Divorce was the ultimate shame. But she'd rather live in shame than live with Hector.

He leaned forward, and she pressed back against the squabs.

"Over my dead body," he said viciously. He leaned back as well and studied her. "Your lack of denial about your wrongdoing speaks volumes."

"Tell me what you intend to do," she said.

Why should she bother to deny anything? She didn't care for his good opinion. And she'd already lied by omission to Captain Arrow.

She'd had enough of lies—

And of running away. If she were to be stuck with Hector, this time it would be on her terms, as best she could make them. Most would say it was a laughable idea that she could hope to hold any advantage over her husband, but she had one thing he didn't: a fully developed sense of irony. There was always another layer to observe in their pathetic interactions. At the very least, she could attempt to find the bitter truth of their incompatibility an amusing pill to swallow.

But she would dare to reach for more. She couldn't go back to being the woman she'd been before she'd run away to London. She'd learned something in Town—how to take care of herself, to ignore those dark corners of fear lurking inside. Even now they clamored to be heard.

But she'd pay no heed to them.

She wouldn't.

If Fate demanded she forsake everything else, she refused to lose the only thing left her—her newfound confidence.

Hector leered at her. "I know the first thing I shall do. I've quite missed it."

Jilly's face flared hot. She knew very well what he was on about. Having him touch her was what she dreaded more than anything. Hector couldn't complete an act of intimacy. Something was dreadfully wrong there. But he could humiliate her very easily. He'd done so every night of their marriage. He'd watch her strip off her clothes for bed while he sat and watched.

And then—

She couldn't bear to think about what he'd made her do then.

She blinked rapidly. "I won't," she said. "I won't touch you that way ever again, Hector."

Hector laughed. "Why not? You're a slut, my dear." His face grew dark. "And I can make you do whatever I say."

"Not this time," she said. "This time I'll hurt you back if you dare try to coerce me. And I won't be quiet. I'll tell, Hector. I'll tell the neighborhood that you hit me because you can't"—she paused—"you can't perform your husbandly duties."

She'd never said that out loud.

He narrowed his eyes. "You wouldn't dare."

"I have nothing to lose," she said. She leaned forward and poked his chest with a finger. "If you insist on having me back, it will be on my terms. Is that clear?"

He sat in stony silence a moment, then said, "Fine. But at least I'll have the satisfaction of knowing that you can't have your little life on Dreare Street. I've the law on my side. We're married and shall stay that way. I plan to make certain you don't have a shilling to run away with, but if somehow you manage to escape anyway, I promise I won't be so discreet the next time I'm obliged to find you."

What could she say to that?

She *was* stuck.

They walked into the town home on Grosvenor Square, her meager belongings in a small piece of luggage which, of course, Hector made her carry herself. The hired butler shut the door quickly behind them.

"We're not receiving." Hector thrust his hat and stick into the man's hands.

"Very good, sir." The butler eyed Jilly with curiosity.

She gave him a small smile, bolstered by a strong sense of relief. They weren't receiving guests. Her suspicions had been correct. Her husband was merely toying with her, keeping her here in London. How many days did he intend for them to linger before returning home?

She would challenge him to find out more.

At dinner later that evening, she began her quest for more information. "Where shall we go first tomorrow? The park? Bond Street? Or the British Museum?"

He looked up from his turtle soup. "Nowhere."

She ladled a few more spoonfuls herself. She had no appetite, but she wouldn't give him the satisfaction of knowing how upset she was. Her heart was in pieces over Captain Arrow. Their relationship had come to an ugly end, and she simply couldn't reconcile herself to that fact. More than any desire she had to bring prosperity to Dreare Street, she looked forward to seeing him at the street fair so she could—

She didn't know.

How did one make an impossible situation better?

And what did it matter when she and the captain hadn't made any sort of declarations anyway? She was going on feeling, that instinct she'd had this morning that theirs was more than a mere infatuation.

Something bigger had loomed between them. It had been the same in the garden. It wasn't something they'd asked for, but it was there as sure as the moon was in the sky.

There was love between them.

Love.

The very idea made her eyes burn with unshed tears. She gulped them back with a hefty swallow of ratafia.

"And the day after?" she asked Hector smoothly.

He put his spoon down and glared at her. "You're not going anywhere."

She gathered her courage. "Then why are we here? Why not return home immediately?"

"Because I've business here."

"What sort of business?"

"It doesn't concern you."

"It does. Every penny you have belonged to me first. I certainly hope you haven't run through all of it."

There was no account, no property left that Hector hadn't already pilfered from. She'd gambled what little resources she'd had on that one attempt to be free—

And she'd lost.

There was still the satisfaction, however, that Otis had Hodgepodge. She hoped he could make something of it. Perhaps if he earned enough, he could open up a store for gentlemen's fashions, as well.

Hector stood from the table. "I don't have to explain anything to you."

But she needed more information. She couldn't make plans to leave for the day on Wednesday without some sort of knowledge of Hector's schedule.

She rose, too. "I accept that, believe it or not," she said. "And I would be glad to accompany you wherever you go. If we must stay together, we should make the association as painless as possible, don't you think?"

It took everything in her to say such conciliatory things to him.

Hector simply smiled. "I don't think so. I'd rather keep you like a caged bird in this house, tantalizingly close to your beloved Dreare Street. The servants have strict instructions to keep you under lock and key while I'm gone."

Gone.

Did he mean for an hour? For a day? Or several days?

She had no idea.

But *gone* was a good word. With Hector out of her path, she'd find a way out. She was sure of it. She wasn't Lady Jillian, daughter of Lord Harris and his wife, Lady Harris, for nothing.

Mama, she prayed silently. *Papa. Be with me.*

She needed a way to live—*truly* live—despite her miserable attachment to the man standing before her with a cruel look of satisfaction on his face.

"Very well," she said. The knowledge that she was a lady made it easier for her to swallow all the rude retorts that came to mind, that and the fact of some sort of looming absence on his part.

Slowly, silently, she ascended the stairs to her bedchamber and locked the door. She didn't care what the servants thought about the arrangements. She'd made sure she was at the opposite end of the hall from Hector.

The single night rail she'd packed still smelled of her sitting room above Hodgepodge, a sweet, homey smell that brought Otis's face instantly to mind. She inhaled its fragrance and let the tears come.

She wanted to go home.

As foggy and unlucky as Dreare Street was, it was her home, and she missed it with every fiber of her being.

Stephen was there.

Captain Arrow, she corrected herself.

If he were gone, would she still feel the same sense of home she did on Dreare Street?

He was to leave soon, as soon as he could sell his house.

A great sadness pressed down on her.

With trembling fingers, she crawled into bed and pulled up the coverlet. She was sure she wouldn't sleep—she still had no idea how she'd get to the street fair undetected—but she fell into a deep, dreamless slumber.

Stephen never went to bed that night. First, he convinced a very shy Nathaniel, who'd finally finished his watercolors, to supervise the merchants and oversee the schedule of events at the fair now that Miss Jones had been called away due to family illness. Then he assisted Pratt and his crew with the building of a new watering trough at the stables—one that would be fit to refresh Prinny's horses. After that, he helped Susan and Otis devise a system of strings and clothespins with which to display Susan's mobcaps and gowns in her booth.

He then went on to work all evening, aided by Pratt, replacing the rotted beams in his house with new ones. It was a sweaty, laborious chore, but it kept his mind off Miss Jilly Jones.

Although deep inside, he was worried. He didn't like her husband at all.

He hoped she was safe.

Those unwelcome and disturbing thoughts about his diminutive neighbor kept coming to him as he hammered and sawed. They plagued him while he and Pratt secured posts against the walls and laid temporary, load-bearing beams on top of those posts. They assailed him as he removed the old, rotted beams and replaced them with new beams. In the affected bedchamber, he made sure the path to the attic taken by the bats was completely blocked, as well.

No matter how long and hard he worked, images of an unprotected Miss Jones beset him, continuing when he and Pratt took down the temporary beams and posts and when he sheepishly plastered over the hole he'd punched in another bedchamber wall earlier in the day.

When the Hartleys came home at four in the morning from a rout, he'd sent Pratt to bed and was just beginning to clean up. His unwelcome guests were fast asleep and the sun was rising into a murky layer of fog when he swept up the remainder of his carpentry mess.

The task complete at last, he stood outside the house and looked up at what he could see of it through the fog. The paint had dried on the stucco façade. He'd also managed to fix a hanging shutter. The chimney, where it had crumbled slightly, had been repaired, as well. The bull's-eye would have been hidden beneath a layer of fog now, but he'd managed to remove it, with a little extraneous help from several neighborhood boys who got on their hands and knees with scrub brushes to move the job along.

And now . . . now Lady Hartley's contact could come see the house, and if that person didn't want it, perhaps someone at the fair would.

He looked over at Hodgepodge. There was no light from the sitting room. Otis must still be abed. All of Dreare Street appeared to be.

Perhaps all of London was.

It was just he . . . and the fog.

A roiling, unnamable emotion overcame him, and he marched through heavy shrouds of white vapor to Hodgepodge.

He'd put it off long enough. He had to find out where Miss Jones was.

Now.

"Fifty-four Grosvenor Square," Otis said a few minutes later, still in his nightcap. "But Captain, you can't see her. Her wretch of a husband won't allow it, I'm sure."

"I know he won't." Stephen turned on his heel to go then looked back. "Thanks, Otis."

"You're welcome." The unlikeliest of bookstore clerks had a fresh wrinkle on his brow.

Stephen grinned. "Don't worry about me." But then he grew serious. "It's Miss Jones we need to be concerned about."

"And I am!" Otis cried. "I didn't want her to go. I hit that blackguard in the eye with my shoe, but"—he hesitated—"I didn't know what else to do. I've been up all night thinking about it."

His expression, already heavy with lack of sleep, drooped even further.

"You did the best you could," said Stephen. "I'll let you know what I find out when I return."

Otis smiled. "Very well. Godspeed."

When Stephen arrived at the town home on Grosvenor Square in a hired hackney, all was quiet. He instructed the driver to wait on the corner. He sat in silence for an entire hour. In that time, the street lightened substantially. Another quarter of an hour went by before he saw any activity on the premises.

Someone flicked aside a curtain in a front window. A minute later, Broadmoor exited the front door on foot. Other pedestrians were out, not many, but a few. There was a chimney sweep, two young bucks who appeared to be headed home after an evening out on the town, and a nurse with three young children heading in the direction of the park.

Stephen was sorely tempted to knock on the door and demand to see Miss Jones, but he suppressed that temptation, slipped out of the hackney, and began following his quarry at a safe distance.

A little while later, Broadmoor entered the Pantheon Bazaar, lingering over a stall featuring men's silk hats and another that boasted cures for all men's ailments. After wandering for another ten minutes, he raised his cane in greeting to someone in the crowd.

Stephen's heart beat faster. Who was he meeting?

A woman emerged from the milling shoppers, and Stephen's first thought was that the two were a well-matched pair. Broadmoor was decked out in the fine garb of a gentleman, but he came across as low class. The woman wore an elegant gown and was quite beautiful—but in a hard way.

They appeared to be in intent conversation. The woman nodded repeatedly. Broadmoor gestured with his cane, as if he were giving her directions to another place.

After a few minutes, they went their separate ways.

Stephen continued following Broadmoor out onto the street. The man approached a line of hackneys and spoke to one driver, then moved down the line to another. He entered that vehicle, and it rolled away.

Stephen ran to the first hackney driver. "Could you follow the one that just left?"

The driver shook his head. "Only if you pay me more than that cheapskate was willing to. I've got a toll to cover, you know."

"Of course," said Stephen and named a fair price, which the driver accepted. "Can you catch up with them?"

The driver shrugged. "I'm sure I can, although I know where he's going."

"Where?"

"To a cottage in Kensington. He wanted me to wait there a few hours, but he wasn't willing to pay the extra money for that, neither. What does he think I am? Desperate?"

Stephen warred between the desire to know exactly what cottage Broadmoor was heading to and why—and an overwhelming need to see Miss Jones.

The need won.

"Keep the money," Stephen said to the man, "and I'll pay you triple that if you can tell me what the other driver says when he gets back. I'd like to know the address of that cottage."

"Fine by me," said the driver. "I'm here every day at this time. Ask for Jack." He tipped his hat.

"Thank you, Jack."

Stephen felt a sense of satisfaction that he'd soon learn more about Mr. Broadmoor. But it was nothing compared to the surge of happiness that overwhelmed him.

He was happy because he was going to see Miss Jones.

CHAPTER
TWENTY-FIVE

When Jilly woke up that morning, her first thought was of Stephen. Did he miss her at all? Or did he hate her so much for her deception that he'd already put her out of his mind?

She was entirely miserable recalling the events of the day previous. There was no denying she'd hurt him—badly. She felt guilt, but even more she felt overwhelming sadness.

They could never be together.

Why couldn't she accept that fact and move on?

With a sigh of despair, she swung her legs out of bed. She had no choice but to endure.

Yes, she was miserable and lonely, but on the bright side—if she could call it a bright side—at least she wasn't afraid of Hector anymore. She'd lost too much already to be afraid of a paltry man like him.

As she dressed, she wondered what Otis might be doing at the moment, not only Otis but the rest of Dreare Street.

A thought which reminded her of Stephen.

Everything always came back to him.

She felt a hitch in her throat, the kind that signified

imminent tears, but she choked them back. A moment later, she was thrilled to descend the stairs to the breakfast room to find Hector gone already.

"Did he say where he was going?" she asked the butler, who'd turned out to be a kindly old gentleman.

"No, madam, he didn't."

She bit into a piece of toast, surprised that she felt any appetite. But she did, a slight one. Her heart felt a tiny bit lighter without Hector near.

She took a sip of good, strong tea. "Did he say when he'd come home?"

The butler shook his head. "Sorry, madam."

"Thank you." She smiled at him, but her heart sank just a little. It was awful to be trapped here in the house, unsure of her husband's whereabouts. She felt a bit like a bird in a cage, which is exactly what he'd hoped she'd feel like, she remembered now.

The butler cleared his throat. "Mr. Broadmoor said you're to receive no visitors. But a man came by a few moments ago while you were still upstairs."

Jilly put down her cup. "A man?" Her heart beat hard. "To see me in particular?"

The butler nodded. "He was very angry when I told him no."

"What did he look like?" She could barely breathe. Had it been Otis?

Or Stephen?

"He was distinguished," said the butler. "Quite handsome."

"Young handsome or older handsome?" she blurted out.

"Young. But he was covered in plaster and sweat. I told him to leave the premises immediately, or I'd pull out my master's pistol."

He lifted his coat to show Jilly he meant what he'd said.

She gasped. "Why would you threaten anyone with a pistol? That's ridiculous!"

The butler appeared rather uncertain. "I don't like it myself. But Mr. Broadmoor demanded I be armed at the door. I must admit being required to wield a loaded pistol on Grosvenor Square doesn't sit well with me."

"Nor with me!" Jilly stood. "Is he still . . . around? This man you speak of?"

The butler shook his head. "No, he's not. He made sure to tell me that he could easily have removed the pistol from my hand as he'd done so from many a pirate, but that he doesn't like to break the arms of old men."

Stephen. It had to have been he!

"He also told me not to worry, that he wouldn't be back," said the butler. "And he insisted that I not admit anyone else, either. He recommended, in fact, that the mistress of the house stay in her bedchamber and lock the door if a threat looms so large that I'm required to wield a pistol."

"Oh." Jilly could barely speak above a whisper. Slowly, she moved past the butler into the corridor, past a coat of arms hanging on the wall, then past a large mirror in the entryway which reminded her of the one in Hodgepodge, and to the right, into the drawing room. She pulled back the heavy red velvet curtains and saw what she dreaded—

Nothing.

The square looked completely empty, save for a bird which sat on a bush nearby.

She'd missed him.

It felt the veriest tragedy to be so close yet not see each other.

She had the overwhelming urge to run out the front door and go back to Dreare Street. Perhaps Stephen would be there.

But would he even speak to her?

And what would Hector do when he found her gone?

Both of those were questions she didn't like to contemplate.

And then there was the matter of her excuse for not being on Dreare Street. Otis would have told her neighbors by now that she was attending to someone in the family who'd fallen ill.

She couldn't afford for anyone to find out the truth.

She bit her lip. For now, she was stuck here on Grosvenor Square. She must resign herself.

The butler hovered at the door. "Madam? Perhaps the man was right. An aged man such as myself has no place protecting the house in the master's absence. I think it would be prudent for you to retire to your room until he returns."

Jilly blinked. "I—I'll consider it. Thank you."

"Perhaps a book from the library to take with you?"

A worried frown creased his brow. He certainly was insistent, poor man.

Well, what did it matter where she went in the house? She had nothing to do. And if it made the butler feel more at ease, she would relieve his mind and go upstairs.

"Very well," she said. "I'll find a book and retire to my room."

The elderly servant moved back a discreet distance and let her pass. In the library, she spent a few listless moments searching the shelves then, with little conviction, pulled out an old history of London. As she flipped through its pages, she had another wistful thought about Alicia Fotherington and that missing diary.

She'd so wanted to finish it.

If she couldn't be happy in her own life, she might as well seek out stories of people who had been.

Holding the chosen book close to her chest, she passed the butler again.

"Don't forget to lock the door, madam."

"I promise," she assured him, a heavy ennui settling over her.

The air was stale as she ascended the stairs and walked down the plushly carpeted hallway to her bedchamber.

Boring was the word that came to mind as she passed silent, shut-off rooms. Her life was going to be very, very boring.

When she arrived at her bedchamber door, she

sighed. The room was nothing special, although it did overlook a small garden. She opened the door and pulled it shut.

"Don't forget to lock it," a familiar voice said behind her.

Jilly froze.

Good heavens. She let the book fall from her fingers to the carpet. Stephen stood there—sweaty and dirty and the most glorious sight she'd ever seen.

She most certainly wasn't bored anymore.

Stephen didn't know what to think when Jilly turned to face him and let the book she held fall to the floor. Her mouth fell open and her brows arched high, but then her shock dissolved and her eyes filled with tears. Big, fat tears.

She put a trembling hand to her mouth and smiled.

"Stephen," she whispered.

"Jilly."

A beat passed.

Did she know? Did she know how his heart had been cut to pieces by her deception? Did she know that he loved her in spite of it? That he had to be near her—with her—even though . . .

Even though they could never be together.

She took a halting step toward him.

It was enough for him. He took three steps forward and pulled her into his arms. When she looked up into his eyes with such utter trust, such pleasure at his mere existence, he allowed himself the luxury of staring into her own violet-blue depths for no reason other than that she was his.

Whatever the world thought, she was his.

His alone.

"You shouldn't be here," she said.

"I know," he said low.

There were so many reasons he shouldn't be there. Yet he couldn't resist pulling a tendril of hair off her face and wrapping it around his finger.

"I bribed a stable boy to point out your window. Thankfully, the trellis held."

She smiled. "I'm so glad you're here."

"I had to be," he said simply.

"Will you let me explain?" She laid a palm on his cheek.

"No. I already understand. I knew as soon as I saw him."

Her face softened even more then, and she let her hand slide down his cheek and fall useless to her side.

There was another silence.

And then he bent low—

And kissed her.

It was like coming home.

She wrapped her arms around his neck, and he pressed her even closer. But it wasn't enough. He picked her up—she didn't resist—and laid her on the bed.

"Come," she said, and held out her arms to pull him close again.

Without a second's hesitation, he settled himself

over her. He held her face in his hands a moment, and they gazed at each other again. Would they ever get enough of staring?

He didn't think so. He could look at her forever.

There was so much between them, so much unsaid that needed to be said. But it was dwarfed by that important, unnamed thing between them—something he'd felt with no other woman—which demanded no thinking, which required nothing but their presence. The closest they could come to satisfying the yearning that the nameless thing created in them was through touching—and just *being*.

Being together, that is.

Together.

As one.

For several minutes, he saw, felt, needed nothing but Jilly's face, her lips, her skin, soft against his own.

There were a few quick, passionate tugs on clothing, yanking off of shoes, interspersed with hot, hot kisses.

And before he knew it, they were both naked, and he was kissing her breasts, suckling them, running his tongue and teeth over them. She moaned and threw her legs wide, and he teased her with his fingers while she caressed him to the hardness of steel.

And then in the midst of warmth, softness, hardness, exquisite sensation—and bursts of color from tossed pillows, a scrunched emerald gown, ebony hair, and ruby lips—he thrust into her.

She cried out.

He immediately stopped, his chest constricting. "What is it?"

She swallowed. "Hector couldn't do this," she whispered.

"Oh, my God," Stephen said, understanding. "I'm so sorry—"

"No," she said. "Don't be. I'm glad . . . it was you."

"Jilly." He kissed her forehead with tender care, feeling the enormity of the trust she'd placed in him.

She encouraged him to continue by arching her back, kissing him madly, and caressing him all over with her hands, even with her thighs and calves, which she rubbed with great tenderness against his own legs and back, twining herself close to him, like ivy wrapped around a railing.

When she cried out with satisfaction, he kissed her, and her moans subsided in his mouth. It wasn't until then that he took his own pleasure, and her attention was both hot and sweet, entrancing him more than he thought possible.

When they were finished, he collapsed to the side of her and took her in his arms.

"I love you—" he said.

"I love you—" she said at the exact same time.

He chuckled, and so did she.

But then her expression, still soft, grew serious, too. She ran a finger down his cheek. "I'll carry you in my heart for the rest of my life," she whispered.

"And I you," he said. "Forever, actually." He smiled.

"Wait," she said with a matching smile. "I meant forever, as well."

"Good," he said gruffly. "I couldn't bear it otherwise."

She gave him a slow, tender smile then and closed her eyes. She snuggled close, and Stephen wrapped his arms around her, his eyes on the ceiling.

Jilly fell into a light doze, and still he cradled her.

He didn't know what he was doing. All he knew was that he had to do it. He wasn't himself anymore. He was himself and Jilly.

Yet they couldn't be.

So what was he to do? Walk around the rest of his life with a heart severed in two by her absence?

She was *married*.

He closed his eyes, choosing not to think, to remain instead with that important thing that connected them.

He chose to remain with Jilly.

He shook her awake a quarter of an hour later.

"I need to go," he said. "It's just after noon."

She sat up and leaned back on her hands. "I didn't even think of Hector—"

"It's all right." Her breasts were full and beckoning to him with their pert tips. He caressed them with his palm, missing them—missing her—already. "Your door is locked. It's easy enough to get out of here through the window."

She bit her lip. "You're quite resourceful."

"Once a man has climbed rigging to the top of a mast on a heaving sea, scaling a wall a few stories high is nothing."

They grinned together.

And then he kissed her.

When he pulled back, he saw it in her eyes, the wistfulness he felt.

"Oh, Stephen," she whispered.

He looked at her unblinkingly. "Don't think about it," he said gently.

She swallowed. "I'll miss you. Can you come back?"

He stopped breathing for a moment. "I'm not sure I can. We were very fortunate this morning." He slid out of bed, pulled on his breeches, and felt the world closing in again.

"I'm going to be there tomorrow," Jilly piped up almost gaily. "At the fair."

He paused in his dressing and smiled. "That's what Otis tells me."

She nodded. "I'll find a way."

"What if Hector comes, too?"

She winced. "That won't happen."

"All of London will know about the fair, if Prinny's claims are true. And how do you expect to escape here?"

She jumped up, completely naked, and came to him. Pressing her hands on his chest, she said, "Don't worry."

He took her wrists. "I can't help but worry about you with that—that dog."

She reached up and kissed his lips. "That sweet thought alone will sustain me until I see you again."

He took her face in his hands and kissed her one last time. "Take care," he whispered.

Saying good-bye was not an option.

She hovered over him as he opened the window

and crawled out. He found a foothold on the trellis and clung to the window sash for a few more precious seconds.

"Be careful," she whispered.

He winked. "Don't worry. Now go. Otherwise, you'll serve as a wicked distraction and I'll fall to my death."

"Oh, no." She put her hand to her mouth. "We can't have that."

He waited patiently for her to retreat.

It was the saddest thing he'd ever seen, when her face finally disappeared from view.

Because who knew when he'd see her again?

CHAPTER TWENTY-SIX

When Jilly woke the next morning, the first thought she had was of Stephen, of course. But the second wasn't of Hector.

It was about the fair. She wondered if Alicia Fotherington had felt the same way when she'd woken up on street fair mornings—excited, happy.

Jilly hopped out of bed and went through her morning ablutions as fast as she could. She still felt a pleasant ache between her legs where Stephen had left his imprint upon her and wished she could keep that feeling forever.

But she couldn't. This she knew.

She was married to Hector.

Oh, if only her husband never had to intrude upon her thoughts! He was like a pesky fly buzzing around a picnic. No, make that a bee, she thought, a bee which could sting and cause the picnic-goers to scatter, their food and drink untouched.

Yes, Hector was a bee, an angry, buzzing bee, too. When he'd returned yesterday afternoon from wherever he'd gone, he'd been in a sour mood. Which wasn't unusual, but he seemed particularly agitated about something.

When she'd asked, he'd refused to divulge the source of his ill temper.

All afternoon, Jilly had hoped he'd become more pleasant. She'd be able to manage him better then, she supposed.

But he never did. And then she remembered, he was in a perpetual foul mood. Perhaps she'd simply been away from him too long to remember how pervasive it was.

Meanwhile, stepping around his temper as best she could, she racked her brains to find a way to go to the street fair and hoped that somehow, a golden apple of opportunity would fall in her lap.

But nothing had happened. No special sign that Fate was on her side had appeared.

At dinner that evening, Hector had sawn through his roast beef with the same grim expression on his face he'd worn all day.

"Are you sure there's nothing you'd like to share with me?" Jilly had paused in her own sawing—the cook at the residence wasn't particularly adept.

"No." Hector lowered his brows. "And I'd appreciate it if you'd mind your own business."

"Oh," she said, used to being insulted by him but shocked that he'd uttered a word as nice as *appreciate*. "Sorry." And popped an overcooked carrot in her mouth.

Her husband threw down his fork. "You seem particularly cheerful for a woman who's had to spend all day inside."

And who has to eat this awful meal with a cad, she added silently.

She shrugged, instantly regretting letting her happy state of mind show—not that she was truly happy because no matter what, she was Hector's wife and would remain so. But she'd had a taste of happiness, all the same, with Stephen.

In her own bed, too.

"I'm simply trying to do my best to be a good wife," she said, vowing not to allow the maid to wash her sheets for at least another few days.

Hector wrinkled his brow. "Why the change of heart?"

She lifted her wine glass to her lips in a bid for time to think. "Because I'm resigned to my fate," she said eventually. "We're married. We might as well make the best of it."

He produced a small, triumphant smile. "That's better. You keep thinking that way and I'll eventually let you leave the house. Not this one, mind you." He raised a serviette to his lips and wiped them. "But when we're back at the village."

She let her face fall in dramatic fashion. "Are there to be no outings, then, for me in London?"

She knew his mood would soften if he saw her tormented.

And he did appear to relax a bit. He leaned back in his chair and studied her as if she were some great scientific experiment he'd invested no feelings in. "Exactly," he said. "You shall stay inside."

"Will you stay with me?" She did her best to sound the perfect balance of subservient and not overly so—or he'd guess she was up to something.

He gave a short laugh. "I'm afraid not. I've business every day that we're in London."

"How long will that be, do you think?" she asked lightly, as if she really didn't care.

"I told you, the rest of the Season," he replied equably, "but if my business concludes sooner, we'll depart."

"Oh?" She tried to look halfway dainty when she asked. He loved when she was dainty, meek, weak, or mewling.

"It could be as soon as next week," he said.

She laid a hand on her chest. "Next week?"

He nodded. "Why does it matter?"

She shrugged again. "It really doesn't. I was simply—" She hesitated and then shook her head. "Never mind. It's not important."

"What?" His tone was short, threatening.

She looked at him from beneath her lashes. "I was hoping . . ."

"Yes?" he asked, his face reddening.

She looked down at her plate and blinked. "I was hoping," she said softly to her plate, "that I could go out and purchase you a present."

He slammed his goblet on the table. "A *present*?" He looked perfectly gobsmacked.

She nodded quickly. "It's all right," she said. "It can wait."

He shook his head. "Why would you get me a present?"

"I told you," she said patiently, "I'm trying. If we're to be married, we may as well be on good terms."

He narrowed his eyes at her. "I don't believe you."

Which was exactly what she'd feared.

But she knew what to do.

"Very well," she said, and stood. "I won't purchase this present. Forget I ever mentioned it."

"Tell me what is," he demanded, loosening his cravat as if preparing for a fight. "And *sit—back—down*."

Trembling (she was discovering she could be a very good actress when she had a lot at stake), she sat. Then she raised her chin and looked at a point on the wall behind him, as if she were very, very shy.

"It's a private gift," she whispered.

"Oh?" An edge entered his voice, the worst kind of edge. The one that meant he was thinking of the bedchamber.

"Yes," she said, "something for which you've been longing." She clenched her fingers in her lap.

He gave a little laugh. Really, almost a giggle. She had to restrain herself from flinching at the sound.

"Tell me," he said slowly and leered at her.

"If I do, then it's no longer a surprise," she said almost coyly.

"Tell me!" he barked.

She ran a finger over the tablecloth, slowly, thoughtfully, and then she looked up at him. "It's a whip," she said. "With our initials engraved—entwined, actually—on the handle."

There was utter silence.

And then Hector leaned back in his chair and laughed. He laughed until he cried, and she sat there and watched, hoping, hoping . . .

When he was finished, he looked up at her. "Go get your little whip," he said, wiping at his eyes. "I want you to present it to me on your hands and knees."

He continued chuckling, but she knew he was serious—perfectly serious.

She stood again, pretended that her dignity had been wounded.

"You'll take a stable boy with you," he said.

There was no lady's maid, of course. He'd not seen to her comfort in the least.

"The big one," he went on, still amused. "His name is Jared, and if you make one false move, I'll tell him to pick you up and throw you over his shoulder. And you'll not like what I let him do to you—in front of me—when he gets you home."

Jilly felt a wave of revulsion sweep through her and almost buckle her knees.

"I understand," she said quietly. "May I go now?"

"Yes," he said. "Get a good night's rest. Tomorrow night we'll christen your little gift. Although it might have to wait. I might be gone for a day or two. I haven't decided."

"Really?" She tried to look terribly disappointed.

"Yes. But remember what I said." He wagged a finger at her. "One wrong move, and Jared is going to be a very lucky man."

She turned then and walked out, her relief at being

able to escape her husband for the day fortunately greater than her disgust, which was profound.

And now, as she bounded down the stairs the next morning, she vowed that she'd let nothing Hector could do to her get in her way. Somehow, she'd rid herself of Jared. He didn't appear very bright, and even if he were, she was brighter.

She'd spend her day at the fair. With Stephen.

On her beloved Dreare Street.

CHAPTER
TWENTY-SEVEN

In the early hours of the morning of the fair, Stephen was with Jilly again, and she was all over him. It was pure heaven—

Until he smelled her breath.

Good God.

Onions?

His eyes popped open.

"Captain!" Lady Hartley was in his face, and she was stark naked. She laid a kiss right on his gaping mouth.

He sat bolt upright on the pillows, wiped his lips with the back of his hand, and pointed at the closed bedchamber door (which he should have locked, he realized a little too late).

"Get out, Lady Hartley," he said in low tones. "Get out before I call Sir Ned in here."

She pulled a sheet up over her breasts. "You wouldn't."

"Yes I would."

She stuck out her lower lip. "But Captain—"

"Your behavior is entirely inappropriate," he said.

She turned to him. "Do you not find me attractive?"

He couldn't say no. He was too much of a gentleman.

"You're *married*," he said. "That makes all the difference."

Dear God, listen to him! A wave of guilt ricocheted through his chest.

Lady Hartley's brow puckered. "Are you sure?"

"Yes, ah, married women are off limits. It's a vow I made long ago to keep, come hell or high water."

"Oh, all right. If that's all it is."

"Yes," he muttered, and looked away from her. "Please go. Before we cause a scene."

She tittered. "Very well."

He heard her stand, and then she began humming.

"Are you decent yet?" he asked her.

"No, you naughty man." He could hear small sighs emanating from her as she dressed.

"Please hurry." He could barely contain his impatience. It was a terrible way to wake up in the morning, even worse than being called to watch on board ship in the middle of the night after a day-long storm that had already left everyone weary.

He heard her sigh and then she thumped on her heels over to the door. "You can look now, Captain."

Slowly, reluctantly, he turned toward the door.

She was wrapped in a voluminous silk dressing gown. "Just remember this," she said, fingering the cleft between her breasts, "*married* women are experts at sneaking about. And we have the experience you're looking for, without the diseases."

"Oh," he said brightly, "that's a high recommendation. Makes me want to give up my lightskirts right away."

She nodded sagely. "I thought so. If you ever change your mind . . ."

She left the statement unfinished.

"Right." He gave her an uncomfortable half-smile and waved her off.

But she paused in opening the door.

"I forgot to mention," she said. "Lord Smelling will be here today, and he's prepared to make you an offer you can't refuse."

"Is that so?"

"Yes." She began to chuckle. "It's really quite amusing. He prefers country living, you know. Can't bear London. But he's got a shrew of a second wife, who insists he purchase a home in Mayfair for her mother to live in permanently, and the daughter occasionally, when she visits Town. So he decided it would be an awful joke to buy a house on Dreare Street. He hopes the bad luck will rub off on them both."

He sounded rather a stupid man, Stephen thought.

"I wonder what Miss Jones will think of having another old harridan as a neighbor?" Lady Hartley asked him.

Ah, Miss Jones. His heart gave a sharp twist of longing.

The baronet's wife didn't wait for a reply. "At any rate, Lord Smelling is willing to pay through the nose to get his hands on this house." She pursed her lips provocatively and waggled her brows. "Are you certain you wouldn't like to celebrate with me?"

Dear God. The poor woman looked like a clown from Astley's when she did that thing with her eyebrows.

"Positive," he replied. "You *do* understand."

He attempted to look noble—

Which he wasn't.

He'd slept with a married woman only the day before.

He must have succeeded in his effort, however, because Lady Hartley fluttered a hand in front of her face, as if she were terribly hot. "Oh, thank *God* for men like you, protecting the motherland with your commitment to principles!"

And then she gave a mighty gasp which subsided in a strange wail, almost as if she were—hell's bells, he didn't even want to *think* what it sounded like— and pulled the door shut behind her.

He threw himself back on the bed, aghast.

The sooner the Hartleys left the premises, the better.

He released a pent-up breath.

On further thought, the sooner *he* left, the better, too.

"It couldn't be a prettier day, Captain!" An hour later Mrs. Hobbs went scurrying past him outside his house, carrying one of many pots of flowers the neighborhood ladies had assembled to beautify the special section of the street designated for Prinny and his advisors to occupy during the theatrical performance.

"Yes, Mrs. Hobbs," he called after her. "And we had not a shred of fog this morning."

"Surely a good sign, *capitano*!" called Pratt to him from the bottom of the balcony Stephen had built for the Canterbury Cousins. Pratt was rolling the contraption to the center of the cobblestones with several other men, Nathaniel among them.

Stephen looked up and down Dreare Street. As far as he was concerned, it looked spectacular. Every house was brightened by paint. The doorsteps had been cleaned and swept. The trimmed hedges and trees were perfectly lovely. Newly cleaned windows shone, and the faces of his neighbors were bright with optimism.

He felt a surge of pride.

And defiance.

They'd raise the money, they would, and send that money man, Mr. Redmond, packing.

But Stephen must admit, he also felt a bit of melancholy. He'd grown to like this place. Yes, it was damned foggy most of the time, but the people—well, they were sterling. Everyone, that is, except Lady Tabitha, Lady Duchamp, and perhaps Mr. Hobbs.

On the bright side, at least Lady Tabitha didn't live here on a regular basis. And Lady Duchamp was old—and perhaps in pain—and so rude she was almost entertaining. She could be forgiven her godawful disposition on both counts. Mr. Hobbs at least had a fine wife and children to recommend him.

Despite his best intentions to avoid thinking about personal matters while he was cast in the role of leader of the street fair, he allowed himself to glance at Hodgepodge.

Immediately, the deep, dull ache near his heart began. Would Jilly get here today? She deserved to see what her wild idea had wrought. And if she did get to come, what would he do when she had to leave again?

It was a hopeless, painful situation, yet his whole world now focused on those moments when he might see her, *be* with her.

It was a damned foolish way to live. He'd told innumerable sailors with broken hearts to move forward. There were plenty of fish in the sea, he'd reassured them.

Yes, there were plenty. But there was only one Jilly.

That's what his sailors had tried to convey to him, too, about the women they'd pined after, but he'd never been able to understand until now.

Love gone awry was a miserable thing and not as easily got over as he'd presumed.

Now Otis was fussing about the flower pots he'd set outside, waving and smiling at passers-by, but Stephen could sense his tension. Every few seconds, he began to whistle off-key and cast furtive glances down the street.

He was waiting for Jilly, too.

Stephen strode over to him and watched him twist a pot forty-five degrees.

"I want *this* bloom facing the Prince Regent." Otis pointed at a bright pink blossom.

"He'll no doubt appreciate that," Stephen said.

The bookstore clerk stood straight and made a face, then bit his lip, and—

Didn't speak.

It was so unlike him, Stephen thought. Dear God, they were both pathetic, weren't they?

"I miss her—" Otis said.

"I hope she'll get here—" Stephen interrupted him.

Both of them crossed their arms over their chests and looked up the street.

"You love her, don't you?" said Otis.

"Yes," Stephen answered, and released a weary sigh.

Otis sighed even louder.

Neither of them said a word as Nathaniel came running up. "Here, Otis," he said, and handed him a small book. "Miss Jones wrapped this up by accident with my book on the canals of Venice."

Otis looked down at it. "No! It's Alicia Fotherington's diary!"

"Yes, well, I meant to give it to you ages ago. But I've been"—Susan walked by with an armful of frilly mobcaps she'd sewn, and he sighed—"I've been preoccupied."

He followed her with his eyes.

"Do you love her?" Stephen asked.

"Yes." Nathaniel sighed and crossed his arms over his chest, too.

A beat of silence went by, and then Stephen shook himself out of his bleak reverie. "I've got to check on the stables." He slapped Nathaniel on the back. "Grab her while you can, my friend, before someone else does."

He began to walk off, but Otis stopped him. "Please

take this, Captain, and keep it safe for Miss Jones." He handed him the diary. "With so many books in one place, it's very easy to misplace one. I know she'll appreciate your protecting it."

Stephen paused a moment, then took the slim volume. "Very well. If she comes looking for it, it will be at my house, on the mantel in the drawing room."

He tucked it in his pocket and remembered how avidly Jilly had read from it. The whole idea for the street fair had come from the diary.

But really, the inspiration had come from Jilly. She'd chosen to believe the undertaking was possible.

"I know what you're thinking," Otis said. "The street fair was *her* idea."

Stephen nodded and shrugged. "Yes, well." What else was there to say?

Otis crooked his finger at him. "I've made her a surprise."

He walked with a great deal of panache into Hodgepodge, his green shoes glinting with paste emeralds, his coattails swaying gently.

Stephen followed, amused and touched, of course, by Otis's devotion.

The ex-valet unrolled a long cloth banner with a giant message painted on it.

He winked. "I've enlisted two young men to hang it from the roofline right after the theatrical performance."

Stephen nodded, not sure what to think.

"So?" Otis waited.

"Good," Stephen murmured. "Yes, I think she'll like that."

Or not.

He wasn't sure. She was a modest sort of book-seller (*modest,* not boring, as she'd once proclaimed herself to be).

Otis smiled. "On your way, Captain. We've got a fair to put on."

"All right, Jared." Wearing her drab muslin gray gown for the Prince Regent's amusement, Jilly rode with the stable boy in the shiny black carriage Hector had bought with her father's money. "I had to wait far too long to leave the house, and I've no time to waste. Can I bribe you to leave me alone or not?"

He squinted at her. "It depends, mum."

"How about this much?" She showed him some money. The amount she'd had in her reticule wasn't very impressive. But she'd not wanted to take any from Hodgepodge.

He shook his head. "Double that."

"I don't think so." She pointed the candle taper in her reticule at him. "I'd hate to put a hole through my new reticule, but you either take this exorbitant amount of money and go get blindingly drunk at a pub, or I'll be forced to shoot you."

"Right," he said, holding on to the top of the carriage window. "Put that way, I think I'll go get blindingly drunk."

She smiled. "Good man. I'll find my own way home. Did he say if he'd be back today or not?"

"He never committed one way or the other. But if he does come back, it won't be until late this evening, mum."

"Oh, in that case—" She cocked her head at the carriage door. "Get out."

"See you later," he said, stuffing the money in his breeches.

"Good-bye," she said, then leaned out the window. "Do you know where he went, Jared? Tell me the truth, or I'll put a ball in you."

"To see his fancy lady!" he called to her as the carriage began to roll away. "Although I'm not sure which one!"

"Right! Thanks!" She waved at Jared with the candle taper, and his face fell.

She sat back on her seat and sighed. Why was she not surprised? Hector had a fancy lady. No, not one fancy lady—more than one.

Poor fancy ladies, she thought and couldn't help an hysterical giggle.

She leaned out and told the driver to take her to Dreare Street. She might have gotten a late start, but she had the rest of the day free, and she was going to take full advantage of it.

She'd become Mrs. Broadmoor again tomorrow.

For today, she was Jilly Jones, fair organizer and woman in love.

The driver tried to drop her off at the top of the street, but there were so many elegant carriages lined up with members of the *ton* descending from them, she had to walk an entire half block to the entrance.

She caught her breath at the marvel of the scene. The massive holly bushes were neatly trimmed back, and on either side of them stood two little boys wearing miniature town crier outfits. They'd donned the same sort of black tricorne hats Otis sported as a town crier. In fact, one of those hats probably belonged to Otis.

And they rang hand bells, all while encased in important jackets that were only two or three sizes too big for them, like the hats.

"Welcome to the Dreare Street fair!" they both called out to the fine gentlemen and ladies milling by.

The crowd, Jilly saw, was impressive, and amused by the two young boys.

They entered the street happy.

And she hoped they'd spent loads of money.

When the boys saw her, they grinned and rang their bells harder.

"Miss Jones! You're back!" cried one.

"Yes, I am." She gave them both hugs.

"Just in time," said the other. "The Prince Regent's arrived. He yelled at all his advisors to get these people out of his way. He's heard about Otis's shoes and wants to see them."

"But the people are still coming," said the first boy, gulping so much air, he hiccupped.

"That's lovely news," said Jilly. "And you're doing a splendid job."

She blew them kisses and entered the street. It looked beautiful—both dignified and cheerful. The sun was shining, and everywhere she looked, people were smiling.

At the far end, she could see Stephen's house standing tall and proud (and yes, a bit rambling, with all its crazy wings). Nevertheless, it was impressive. And to its left was Hodgepodge. She could see the roof where she and Stephen had sat and had their picnic—and where he'd kissed her for the first time.

She inhaled a breath. Even the air smelled good today.

She was back with her friends. She'd play proprietress of Hodgepodge one last time. And if Prinny thought she was really a Celtic princess, then so be it.

She'd play the part. It was a small price to pay.

Her heart brimmed over with happiness. It had only been going on an hour, and the fair was far better than she could ever have imagined.

But then she heard loud exclamations from the crowd at the far end of the street, near Hodgepodge and Stephen's house. It was where the theatrical performance was to take place later that afternoon.

Much to her dismay, the random yells became a dull roar that assailed her ears and didn't stop. It could mean only one thing.

"Fight!" one of the little boys cried.

The two small greeters left their assigned stations and went running into the crowd.

CHAPTER
TWENTY-EIGHT

Yes, he was anxious about Jilly, but at least everything was going swimmingly at the fair, Stephen was pleased to realize—until the fight broke out during the performance of the famous balcony scene from *Romeo and Juliet*.

Prinny had insisted on holding the theatrics well before anyone had planned. It was supposed to be the culminating event of the day, to take place *after* the booths had been nearly emptied of merchandise, food, and beer. Stephen reassured his neighbors they'd have plenty of time to sell their wares later—meanwhile, Prinny's quirks must be indulged.

But when two men, one lanky and one short, rushed at the wooden balcony structure in a blur of motion, hitting and punching each other in the middle of the scene, Stephen felt a sharp pang of alarm.

The street fair was in crisis.

The disturbance was fairly minor, yes, and could be curtailed. Stephen had a security force in place, consisting of Pratt, Lumley, and several other of his gentleman friends, all of whom were expert pugilists.

It was simply a matter of waiting a moment or two to let them do their jobs.

"Your mangy cur ran between my legs, then turned around and bit my ankle!" the short brawler cried to the other.

"He's not *my* mangy cur," the lanky one yelled.

Juliet scrambled down the balcony. Romeo caught her around the waist and hastened her to safety on the edge of the crowd.

The brawlers tumbled over the balcony, fists flying, and landed first on Pratt, who'd rushed forward to contain them. Somehow the balcony fell over—much to the crowd's dismay and then delight when they realized no one had been crushed. Meanwhile, the fighting went on. Pratt let fly with his fists, as did Lumley, who promptly shoved the lanky fighter. The lanky one then stumbled and landed on one of Prinny's advisors, whereupon the advisor, a thin, snooty man, fell backward and sideways, landing against the side of Prinny's chair.

Prinny's arm flew up, and he dropped his goblet of wine.

A splash of the red stuff landed on his chin and cravat.

Blast, Stephen thought. A bit of bad luck.

The two arguing men, who'd by now landed in a tangle near Prinny, stopped fighting and scrambled away on their hands and feet, like crabs, back into the sea of people. Lumley and Pratt stood with chests heaving and disappointed looks on their faces.

The crowd shifted uneasily.

"We'll start the scene again, Your Highness," Stephen said calmly. "Please accept our apologies for the damage to your cravat. We'll get you a fresh one."

Prinny looked down at the blot on his fine white linen. "This cravat," he said through narrowed eyes, "is my lucky cravat. It was given to me by my best mistress. But it's ruined, thanks to the antics here on Dreare Street. Now I'm sure to lose my bet on the cockfight I'm attending this afternoon." He pushed himself out of his chair. "Never mind about the performance. As far as I'm concerned, these theatrics are *over*."

The crowd began to murmur but stilled again when a huge banner was unfurled above Hodgepodge:

THREE CHEERS FOR MISS JONES,
OUR FAIR'S FOUNDER

Stephen winced as he read it. Oh, well. He'd forgotten about that. On the roof of the bookshop, the boys who'd strictly followed Otis's orders to lower the banner after the theatrics yelled, "Hurrah!"

For the first time since the day's events had begun, Stephen saw Jilly. Wearing the plain gray gown she'd worn to the ball, she stood in front of Hodgepodge, directly below the banner. Her face paled and her eyes widened as she, too, read the words.

There was a deafening silence, which Stephen wished he knew how to end. But he had no idea what to say, how to *fix* things.

For the very first time ever, his leadership skills failed him.

"There you are, Miss Jones." The Prince Regent's annoyed voice broke the silence. "You *did* come up with the idea for the street fair, didn't you?"

Jilly stood, hands clasped, and stared at the royal. "Y-yes, Your Highness. I—I'm so sorry. It was supposed to be *fun*."

"Fun?" Lady Tabitha pushed through the hordes and stood before her. "It was hardly *fun*."

Jilly flinched when Lady Tabitha looked her up and down as if she were a loathsome creature.

"Her name isn't really Miss Jones." Lady Tabitha spoke in a bold voice. "And as I told you at the Langleys' ball, Your Highness, she's not descended from Celtic kings. Her true name is Mrs. Broadmoor. She's a runaway wife, and she's been bamboozling you all."

Bamboozling you all.

Runaway wife.

Stephen felt the harsh accusations sear him like a knife. It was a dreadful moment. Otis gave one, long whimper that sounded almost like a howling dog.

Jilly stood as if turned to stone.

Prinny stared at her. "Is this true? Are you married, Miss Jones?"

She blinked once, then nodded. It was the moment that finally broke Stephen's heart.

All the smug, wealthy residents of Mayfair began to talk, to disapprove. To be horrified. And it appeared so did everyone else—everyone except Stephen. He felt too depressed to speak or move.

The Prince Regent stared at the banner on the roof of Hodgepodge, and after that, he shifted his gaze to the overturned balcony. "This has got to be the un-luckiest street I've ever had the misfortune to visit," he pronounced.

The affronted royal walked several houses up the street to the brightest and shiniest of the retinue of wait-ing carriages and entered it. The entire crowd watched as it drove up the street, out the entrance, and bowled away.

And that's when the mass exodus began. Stephen knew it signaled the end of all of Dreare Street's hopes—and of Jilly's dreams.

All around him, people began walking fast toward what they could see of Curzon Street. A few ran. Some even dropped the whirligigs they'd bought for their children, afraid they were tainted with bad luck. Others cried out, looking for loved ones, as if there were a chance they'd gotten sucked into an invisible vortex of bad luck.

All this, while Stephen and the other residents of Dreare Street stood silently and watched.

When the last fair-goer had fled, almost as one, the ones who remained on the much maligned street turned back to Hodgepodge—and Jilly.

But, Stephen noted with a halt of his breath, she was gone.

CHAPTER
TWENTY-NINE

The fog came in that night around eight o'clock, worse than it ever had since Jilly had been in London. She stood at her bedchamber window at the house on Grosvenor Square and tried to peer through the cloudy vapor that swirled outside, but it was impossible to see anything.

She wished she could see right now what the people on Dreare Street were doing.

Were they eating their suppers? Were the Hobbses slowly ladling their turtle soup and wondering how they'd pay their lease? Perhaps some neighbors were crying. Others might very well be cursing her for getting them into this mess.

All of them, she was sure, despised her for lying to them.

No doubt they'd never want to see her again.

She'd lied to them.

She'd lied to Stephen.

His face swam before her eyes. He'd looked so sad and cold and unapproachable when Prinny had asked her if she were married.

It seemed almost as if she'd imagined his sneaking into her bedchamber here and . . .

And making love to her.

Genuine love.

She'd felt it. It had seemed as palpable as the bed pillows they'd crushed beneath them. As sturdy and strong as Stephen's face when she'd touched him.

Tears pearled beneath her lids, but she pushed them back. She would never let Hector see her cry. It would make him too happy.

Today when she'd scurried out the back door of Hodgepodge and returned to Grosvenor Square via back alleys and other people's gardens, she decided she would never, ever lie about being married to Hector again. And she would never, ever try to be happy, either.

It was too painful when the happiness was snatched away.

She turned to her bed, prepared to sleep her life away—at least until she had to face Hector again. She had no idea if he'd return that night, or the next day, or the one after that.

She did know, however, that he'd return eventually.

He was a nightmare she couldn't wake up from—ever.

Lord Smelling sat at Stephen's table that same evening. The fog was so thick, the earl, who'd come to the street fair, had been forced to stay the night. Indeed, the fog had never been thicker since Stephen had moved to Dreare Street.

"So have we come to an agreement?" Lord Smelling asked him. "Shall I buy 34 Dreare Street and house my mother-in-law here? And occasionally, my wife?"

He looked at Sir Ned and Lady Hartley. All three of them broke into loud guffaws.

Sir Ned slapped his hand on the table. "I assure you, Smelling, they'll be *miserable*!"

Lady Hartley shook her head. "Yes," she said, hic-cupping, "absolutely wretched. Who knows when an-other beam will rot?"

"Or another neighbor will fall on hard times or break a bone," added Sir Ned.

"Or set off a riot," Lord Smelling said, latching on to the pastime of insulting Stephen, his house, and Dreare Street itself.

The laughter went on unabated until Miss Hartley spoke up. "I haven't been miserable here," she said quietly.

Her parents immediately straightened their faces.

Sir Ned glared at her. "What do you mean by such a ridiculous statement?"

Miss Hartley looked rather fierce, Stephen thought.

She tossed her head. "I like Captain Arrow *and* this house. You're the ones who make everyone mis-erable by being so rude. And if you hate this place as much as you claim, why are you still here anyway?"

"Miranda!" her mother scolded her. "To marry you off, of course."

"And to save money doing it," said Sir Ned. He leaned over to Lord Smelling. "I've not made my fortune—"

"By spending it!" Miss Hartley interrupted sharply. "How many times do we have to listen to your boasting about being a miser, Father?" She exhaled a great breath. "Listen, you two. I don't want to be married off to anyone . . . anyone but Mr. Pratt."

Stephen was quite impressed by her newfound boldness.

"Mr. Pratt?" Lady Hartley's mouth dropped open.

"But he's a nobody," Sir Ned protested.

"He's a ship's cook, for heaven's sake," Lady Hartley said. "With trousers hitched up to here." She indicated her neck and gave the tiniest giggle.

Her husband responded with a small chuckle. Then Lady Hartley giggled again—and he chuckled—and Stephen was just about to knock their heads together.

"Not only that, he can't make a sunnyside egg without breaking it," said Sir Ned. "Only on Dreare Street would you find a cook who couldn't do that."

He was busy shaking his head and biting down on his lower lip to suppress more chuckles when his daughter leaned forward and narrowed her eyes at him.

"I'd rather be with a nobody who's kind and amusing," she said, "than with people who treat others shabbily, the way you and Mother do."

She pushed back her chair and stalked from the room.

There was a vast, awkward silence.

As a good, albeit put-upon host, Stephen went to his sideboard to see what he had to offer to diffuse the tension. His brandy and whisky were all gone, thanks to the theater troupe, who'd demanded *something* for their wasted time. All he had left were a few West

Indian cheroots and some ratafia, which he offered to Lady Hartley.

"No, thank you," she said, her cheeks pale. "I must see to Miranda."

And she left the room looking for the first time like a mother concerned about her child instead of a vain flirt.

"Well," said Lord Smelling a moment later, smoke curling around his head, "what's your answer, Arrow? Shall you sell me your house?"

Stephen considered him, triple jowls, florid face, and all. The man was offering him a substantial amount of money for a house the earl didn't care for . . . a house he was going to use to make his wife and mother-in-law miserable.

Should he accept? He'd be able to leave Dreare Street and start life over with his pension and a substantial amount of money in his pocket if he did.

He stood, strode to the window with his cheroot, and looked out at the black night and the fog. No matter how much he strained to see, everything was hidden from view, which was a disappointment. Until now, he hadn't realized how much he'd enjoyed looking out the drawing room window at Hodgepodge.

He would miss Dreare Street. Much had happened to him here. He'd fallen in love. But if he remained without his favorite bookshop owner nearby, he'd feel lost. Looking out his drawing room window would become painful.

It already was.

He inhaled once on his cheroot and blew out a

plume of smoke. As he did so, he realized with great certainty it was time to go.

He turned around to face the men.

"I'd like another day to consider it," he said, surprised—nay, shocked—at his own answer.

Where had *that* come from?

A large furrow formed on Lord Smelling's brow. "Are you certain?"

"Don't think you can get him to offer more by playing coy," Sir Ned said nastily.

Stephen felt his intense dislike of Sir Ned bubble over. "It's best that you leave tomorrow," he told him. "I'll let you stay until I give Lord Smelling my answer, and then you'll have to find a hotel to stay in if you care to remain in London. I agree with your daughter—you're a rude miser. I want you and your opportunistic wife gone. By the way, your daughter deserves better parents. At least your wife is attempting to be one now by speaking with Miss Hartley. You should join them."

Sir Ned's mouth fell open. "How dare you speak to me this way! Why, you're nothing but an earl's by-blow!"

"Better that than a fool," Stephen said back, still feeling a twinge of shame to have been so deceived by his mother, her peers in the village of his birth, and by Earl Stanhope himself. "Now douse your cheroots, please, sirs, and retire for the night."

There was much muttering from Sir Ned and actually very little objection from Lord Smelling. He looked at Stephen meekly on his way out. "Now, don't let this small misunderstanding spoil our deal," he said.

"I told you . . . I'm still considering it," Stephen replied, feeling prickly. He didn't like Lord Smelling, either, and was rather discomfited by the fact that he was still considering his offer.

But he needed the money.

He needed to *leave* Dreare Street.

But he needed Jilly more.

I'm here if you ever need counsel. It's hard to fathom, I know, but I've got experience now in matters of the heart.

Harry's words, spoken at the ball, came back to him. Stephen couldn't believe it, but he did need his friend's advice. Tomorrow, he'd seek him out. Until then, he'd simply go by instinct.

A small tap came at Jilly's window.

She closed her eyes.

Could it be?

She looked over, and—

She'd recognize that chin and that golden brow anywhere. Stephen was gazing at her from the window, his face only partially visible through the fog. She raced over, opened it, and he clambered through.

She could hardly believe he was there. "How did you find me in all this fog?"

He winced and grinned. "It wasn't easy."

"I'm so glad you're here." She pressed herself against his chest. "What a day."

"When you disappeared like that without saying good-bye—"

She pulled back and looked up at him. "I'm sorry. I simply couldn't stay. Everyone was staring. The street fair was ruined, and then Lady Tabitha . . ." She trailed off with a little shudder.

"I wonder how she found out?" Stephen wrapped his arms around her and rubbed her lower back with his hands.

"I don't know," Jilly said, delighting in the sensation. "But it probably wasn't very difficult. She could have spoken to the previous owner of Hodgepodge. I signed documents under my true name, but then the seller moved to Kent, so I thought I was safe. Perhaps she followed one of us here and did some snooping among the servants. Or she might even have talked to Hector."

"Who knows?" he said. "The damage is done."

Jilly lowered her eyes. The humiliation of being thrust into the open with her lies, in front of all her Dreare Street neighbors, was still very strong in her. "It doesn't matter," she said. "I can't go back. Hector says we're returning to the village very soon." She paused and swallowed. "I might never see you again."

"I would hate for that to happen."

It was such a simple statement—but it said everything.

There was a beat of silence. She saw her own pain reflected in his eyes. And in those seconds of grief at what would soon be, the most natural thing in the world to do, Jilly intuited, was to breach that sad place with a kiss.

Stephen was already reaching for her when she moved toward him. She luxuriated in the heavenly feel of his mouth against hers, and then she took him by the hand to the rug in front of the hearth. She sank to her knees, and he did the same. They stripped each other of their garments, loving care obvious in every pull of a tie or push of cloth back to reveal warm, scented flesh.

But when it came time for their coupling, they were both fierce, clinging—

Desperate to have each other.

To *be* each other.

To meld as one.

When it was over, although limp with satisfaction, Jilly didn't feel content in the least.

Neither, apparently, did Stephen.

She'd rolled to her side to look at him. He was her favorite view, after all. He was staring at the ceiling, but when he saw her watching him, he reached over and caressed her hip.

It was lovely. Intimate.

But no peace came.

The ormolu clock on the mantel chimed the hour—it was midnight. Heavy fog and a thick silence lay over the house, over London.

There was only this room with its one flickering candle, and them—

And no place left for her feelings to hide.

"If I have to be wrenched away from the life I want," Jilly blurted out, "I might as well *truly* leave."

Stephen's hand stilled at her waist. "What do you mean?"

So this is what had been building in her!

"I could live in another country," she said. "No one would ever know I'm a married woman."

It was so simple. She wondered why she'd never thought of it before this moment.

Abruptly, Stephen sat up on his side, leaned on his elbow, and faced her. "Another *country*?"

She nodded. Bit her lip.

And then she realized there was something else inside her, something even bigger than what she'd just said.

"You and I could go together," she breathed.

The words hung in the air . . . huge, shimmering, powerful.

She waited, suspended, it seemed, floating.

They were alone, just they two, with her great, glorious idea.

But as the seconds ticked by on the clock, it dawned on her that he'd said nothing back yet. And he should have by now. He should have grinned widely—right away—and said something like, "Of course. Why didn't *I* think of that?"

But he hadn't. In fact, he was staring at her, *through* her, actually. Surely he was simply in shock at her great, glorious idea. If he really loved her, wouldn't he move mountains to be with her?

Of course he would.

But her heart began to skip oddly. And her breathing—well, she *wasn't* breathing at the moment. She couldn't. Her lungs felt as if they were being filled with cold water. Her whole body was cold. Her fingers, her arms and legs, her feet—everything in her shivered with the cold.

Why didn't he *say* something?

His gaze finally met hers, and she knew.

She knew it was over.

"We have to face the truth," he said carefully. "We can't have a future together. We'll have to say good-bye for good."

She blinked. How did one deal with one's world—one's dreams—collapsing into dust in a fraction of a second?

Stephen sighed and rubbed her upper arm.

She flinched and pulled back from him. "What's stopping you?" She almost didn't recognize her voice. It was bold, angry, some might say slightly hysterical, but she knew better. It was the true Jilly. She wasn't hiding from anyone anymore.

She was done with hiding.

"Why won't you go with me?" she asked, her heart hammering in a steady, hard rhythm. "Because I know you can. You can do anything you want, Stephen Arrow. You're a free man. Not only that, you're the bravest man I know."

He said nothing.

She rose to her knees, then stood, the soles of her feet pressed firmly against the rug, her breath coming in great, even lungfuls.

He stood, too, and faced her.

"I love you," he said plainly. "And I know you had every reason to lie about your marriage. But there's a part of me that can't—that can't let go of that."

She tossed her head. "Just because you were lied to by your mother and your village about your father—which they did to protect your feelings, by the way, so you're utterly selfish holding it against them—you're willing to let me go?" She scoffed. "That's not love. That's an immature boy who hasn't learned to grow up."

She strode away from him, and with shaking arms, thrust the window up and pointed out.

"Get out," she said.

His face was still, his expression inscrutable.

When one loved, one didn't *hide*. It was a lesson she'd learned too late. But now that she knew, she couldn't go back.

"You have to know this pains me to the core," he said, pronouncing every word as if it were a shard of glass he must swallow. "You're everything to me."

She kept her eyes on his, daring him to look away. "*You're* the one who pursued me, who entangled me in that foolish web you created to keep Miss Hartley at bay. You've come here twice now and made love to me in my bedchamber, practically under my husband's nose. We were in this mess together—or so I thought. I've told you how sorry I was for deceiving you, but no. My explanation isn't good enough for you. *I'm* not good enough." She lifted her chin. "What do you know about what's right and wrong? You've never been in my position and will never understand what it's like to be a woman afraid."

Once more, she thrust her finger at the open window, at the dense fog hanging there like a shroud. "I never want to see you again," she told him. "Don't attempt to contact me."

She couldn't be there to watch him go. She left, taking her candle with her. Downstairs, she shook the kitchen boy awake, and told him to take a lantern and walk a straight line out back until he reached the stables, where he should rouse a groom immediately. She needed to get to Otis, to Hodgepodge, and to Dreare Street—

The fog, Hector, and Stephen Arrow be damned.

CHAPTER THIRTY

There was something wrong with him. Stephen knew that now, as he stumbled through the fog toward Dreare Street. He'd never realized it before.

He was a coward.

He winced just thinking of the word.

Coward.

He'd always used it to describe other people. But it was what *he* was.

Good God, and he'd been so sure of his identity. He was a tested warrior, a former captain in the Royal Navy who'd earned high honors. He'd fought and won battles against merciless enemies.

He also had supreme confidence on land. With women, especially, he was assured of his prowess as a man.

Until now.

For another quarter of an hour, he wended his way, slowly, instinctively, through the blinding vapor. On the sea, fog could be both a helpful friend or one's worst enemy. It allowed one to hide from danger. You could slip right by an opponent's ship, and they'd never know you'd come near. But a dense fog could also lead a ship to the rocks and almost certain death.

Stephen had come to find out, however, through his lengthy experience with it, that fog wasn't the real challenge. Fear was. The test came in his own response to the primal fear fog induced. Fog was a great separator, the reminder that in the end, you were alone to either give in to the fear—or not.

Until now, Stephen had chosen to be soothed by the notion that he was ultimately his own man. Finding out that his mother and his entire village had perpetuated a myth about his beginnings only affirmed the fact that he lacked an anchor, was sailing through life on self-generated power, answerable to no one, his destiny in his own hands.

But now in the midst of the mist, he had the odd sensation of being panicked. His natural fluidity—his calmness in the center of the white blindness—was shaken.

He was glad when the fog began to ease slightly, enough that he could see a few feet ahead of him in the dark. A well-lit carriage crept by, the horses whinnying in fright, the driver calling encouraging words to them. Stephen watched and wondered who would take a carriage out this late at night and in such conditions. A doctor on the way to see a patient? Some drunken fool on the way home from a rout?

Who else would dare?

When the last ring of the horseshoes on the cobbles faded in the distance, he was left behind, a solitary shadow figure on an empty street.

He remembered Jilly's cozy bedchamber, the rug, the low fire, and he wished he were back there with her.

But once again, he was cast adrift. It was what he knew best. There was to be no more Jilly. And no more Dreare Street.

When he arrived back at Number 34, the house was dead quiet. He felt much too empty—raw, actually—to sleep. He knew if he tried, the sheets would feel like sand, the mattress like gravel.

He lit a candle from the mantel and saw a small, bound book lying next to it.

Alicia Fotherington's diary.

Otis had given it to him earlier to keep safe for Jilly.

He picked it up, took it to a chair, and sat down to read. He'd nothing else to do, and reading would remind him of her. At first, the entries in the diary were cheerful. But little by little, the tone changed.

Lyle just added on a second wing, he read. *Our elegant little house is getting larger and larger. Lyle makes it very clear why. He's preparing the house for our children. But—it pains me deeply to say it—I've not been able to conceive. Every day that goes by, he acts more like a disapproving father, not a loving husband.*

All these years later, Stephen felt sorry for Alicia. A little while later, she wrote:

A chill fog this morning seems to match my growing sadness about the lack of a babe in our lives. I don't believe Lyle loves me anymore. Indeed, I think he might have taken up with someone else. He comes home with the scent of her on his garments.

Stephen read swiftly. Alicia had his complete attention now: *The third wing is complete,* she wrote. *It is to house* her. *He pretends he feels pity for her. She's been widowed these two years. But I know why she's here. She's my cousin. How could they do this to me?*

Stephen gazed into the candle flame. Poor Alicia Fotherington. How different these later entries were from the first ones, where she'd had such hope about her new life as wife to Lyle. As he turned the pages, more and more entries mentioned the unrelenting fog.

The sun had just come up when he began the last entry:

I'm a far distance from the woman I used to be. There's nothing left here that I love. The house is a rambling mess of wings that reminds me every day that I've failed in my duty as a wife to bear my husband children. My beloved street fair is long gone, chased away by the strange, clinging fog that seems peculiar to Dreare Street only this past year. I've decided I shall run away, but before I do, I must save some money. It will take me at least a year of my gritting my teeth and pretending I don't know what's going on, but I'll do it. And then she'll have to move out. They won't have me here to guard her reputation anymore.

And that was the last thing Alicia Fotherington had to say.

Stephen closed the book and thought about Jilly, about Alicia, about all women who'd been mistreated by unloving mates.

It was a sad thing, profoundly sad. But there was nothing he could do about it, although everything in him raged against cowardly beasts like Lyle and Hector.

He stood, looked out the window, at the fog creeping up his steps—steps Lyle and Alicia had traipsed two hundred years ago—and wondered what had happened to the pair. Had she succeeded in running away? Had Lyle died a slow, lingering death—alone?

Stephen knew it was wicked of him, but he hoped so.

It came to him that Hector was still alive, and at this very moment, he was probably sleeping a fine sleep. Soon he'd wake and have a hearty meal and continue living his comfortable life, all the while causing Jilly tremendous pain.

It wasn't right.

And it wasn't too late, either.

Stephen couldn't do anything about Lyle, but he *could* do something about Hector.

He'd find him. And he'd make him pay.

The next morning Jilly kept her hand on the counter, straightened her spine, and prepared herself for another disappointment. Otis was outside with his bell, calling a meeting at Hodgepodge. She insisted he wear his town crier regalia to do it, too. Reluctantly, he'd agreed. He'd stood silent, forlorn, while she placed the tricorne hat on his head and wished him luck.

Now he rang.

And rang.

And rang.

Through the fog, he called, "Emergency meeting at Hodgepodge!"

At one point, he came to the bookstore window and stared at her mutely. She knew what he was thinking. No one was coming. He should stop *now*.

"I can't bear thinking of you enduring any more rudeness directed toward you," he'd said earlier as he'd reluctantly put his arm through the magnificent scarlet coat she'd held out for him. "The ignominy you've suffered already is more than I can bear."

She'd smiled at him and said firmly, "*I* can bear it. I'm stronger than I realized. And so are you."

She'd patted him on the back then and sent him on his way.

While she waited now, she wondered what Hector would think if he'd arrived home last night and this morning would find her gone. No doubt he'd come straight to Hodgepodge. This time, however, she wasn't going to go back with him.

No more hiding.

She had to fight back.

This was her only life, and she was going to live it without fear.

This time, she was going to tell him to go away. And if he tried to pick her up over his shoulder and force her to go back, she'd scream and thrash and pummel him.

But she didn't think it would go that far. Because if Hector did show up, the first thing she'd do was stand behind her counter, where Papa's small pistol was now sitting in a drawer. She'd never thought she'd use it when she'd taken it with her from home, but she was a different person now.

No longer manipulated.

No longer hiding.

She was going to fight to stay at Hodgepodge. She'd cling and cling and cling until something or someone managed to tear her away.

She clung now to hope while the bell rang.

The first to show was Susan, with Thomas. At the door, she looked tentatively at Jilly. "Are you all right?" she said, her voice stricken, her eyes wide.

"Yes," Jilly said, even as she felt a great sadness wash over her about Stephen.

"I'm so glad you're back!" Susan opened the door wider, and Thomas came running in, his hair wet and slicked neatly over his head.

Jilly felt an immediate surge of happiness. At least one family was welcoming her back, the very first one who'd greeted her when she'd arrived on Dreare Street.

Thomas hugged Jilly around her legs. "You went away yesterday. My mother couldn't even sing me to sleep last night, she was so sad."

Susan hugged her next, a long, lingering embrace. When she pulled back, understanding passed between them.

"Are *you* all right?" Jilly asked her. "Even though you couldn't sell your gowns and mobcaps?"

Susan grinned. "I'm fine." She colored. "I hate to say this right now in the midst of your suffering, but even though I sold only one gown in the time the fair was open, things are *very* good. I sold that gown to a fine lady named Lady Harry, and she told me she'd tell all her friends in Mayfair about me. She's a friend of Captain Arrow's."

"Wonderful!" Jilly said, even though her heart ached at hearing Stephen's name.

"That's not all," Susan said. "Nathaniel proposed last night. I know we don't have much to live on, but he loves me, Jilly. And I love him."

"I love him, too!" said Thomas.

"I'm so happy for you both." And she meant it. Jilly hugged Thomas, then Susan. Genuine happiness had created a new glow in her friend's eyes.

"But now we're worried about you," Susan said, squeezing Jilly's fingers.

"Please don't worry about me. I'll be fine, no matter what happens here."

The worst had already happened. She'd lost Stephen. As far as she was concerned, everything else that occurred in her lifetime would be manageable.

"The only reason we didn't arrive sooner," Susan said, "was that Thomas was in his bath. And then we couldn't find his shoes."

"Yes," Thomas piped up with the droll disinterest of a child. "Mother was quite frantic to get here. She told me I didn't even have to make my bed first."

Jilly and Susan laughed. In the distance, Otis rang his bell and called, "Emergency meeting at Hodge-podge!"

She felt a pang of doubt return. Would anyone else come? But she suppressed it by grinning at Thomas. "Let's go find your bird book, shall we?"

When she led him to the back table, the door opened again.

It was Pratt, Nathaniel, and several other young men who'd helped with heavy lifting and cleaning the street in preparation for the fair.

Her heart skipped a beat at the sight of them. She smiled and said simply, "Thank you for coming."

Nathaniel and the young men gave her shy grins and didn't say much. Nathaniel made a beeline for Susan. The other fellows shuffled in awkwardly and didn't appear to know what to do with themselves. But Jilly directed them to the delicious scones and pot of tea she'd made for anyone who cared for some.

Pratt, on the other hand, came straight to her and raised her hand to his lips. "I am very glad, my dear lady," he said in his lovely Italian accent, "that you've returned to your home. We were concerned about you."

"Thank you," she said.

A frown creased his brow. "Have you seen Miss Hartley yet this morning?"

"Not yet." She sensed his disappointment. "But I do hope she'll come to the meeting, even though she's not actually a resident of Dreare Street."

"How could you think I'd stay away?" a voice came from the door. It was Miss Hartley, and she smiled softly at Pratt, and then at Jilly.

He strode over to her and kissed her hand as well, but he lingered extra long.

She dimpled. "I'm so glad you're back, Miss Jones. And Mr. Pratt"—she took a deep breath—"you're a wonderful man, just the way you are."

He smiled modestly. "Thank you. And you are a wonderful lady."

They both stared into each other's eyes, and Jilly and Susan exchanged an amused glance.

The next people to walk in were Mrs. Hobbs and her tall, pale children. Mrs. Hobbs looked gravely at Jilly, and she felt her stomach clench. The children looked quickly away from her when she greeted them and went immediately to find Thomas.

Mrs. Hobbs came to Jilly and took her hands. "I've something very important to say." Her mouth was set and firm.

Jilly felt a slight burning behind her eyes. She knew she'd disappointed her friends—she'd hated to lie to them—and now one of them was going to call her to task.

"Miss Jones," Mrs. Hobbs said in a low, serious voice, "you've deceived us."

"I-I know." Jilly sighed. "I'm so sorry."

Mrs. Hobbs put up a finger. "There's someone at the door who wants you to know how he feels about your being here on Dreare Street under false pretenses."

Jilly looked over and saw Mr. Hobbs there. He gripped his tall hat in his hands and looked at her with a baleful expression.

She cleared her throat. "Thank you for coming to visit, Mr. Hobbs."

It was the first time he'd ventured into the store.

He glowered and stepped around two lads eating scones and came to stand in front of her. "Miss Jones—for I cannot think of you as Mrs. Broadmoor—what you did was extremely . . . unconventional."

She bit her lip. "I'm sorry. Really, I am."

He clenched his jaw. "But I can't help thinking that a woman who was trying to help her entire street—however nosy she was—must have had an excellent reason for hiding her identity. I want to do all in my power to help you if your aim is still to pull Dreare Street out of the pit of foggy despair in which we now wallow."

Jilly blinked, not sure she was hearing correctly. Was *Mr. Hobbs* saying he wanted to help?

Evidently so, because the very edge of his mouth curved upward.

"T-thank you," she stammered. "I'm overwhelmed."

"Don't be," he said flatly. "I was a pompous ass. It took my wife threatening to leave me last night, the same way you'd left your husband, to make me see how wrong I was."

Mrs. Hobbs had a twinkle in her eye. "That's right," she said, lifting her chin. "I told him if Miss Jones can succeed on her own selling books, I can do the same." She pulled a piece of paper out of her pocket. "And I think I know how."

"What is it?" Jilly asked.

Mrs. Hobbs smiled. "A receipt for a special tea. And Jilly, I made it up myself. I may not be very good at following other people's receipts—my meat pasties were a disaster yesterday—but I'm excellent at following my own intuition. And I know, my dear, that we have a winner here. You must trust me on this, the same way we've trusted you."

"Oh, I will!" Jilly said.

"We'll tell you more about it during the meeting," Mr. Hobbs said, and took his wife's hand in his own and kissed it.

Jilly bit her lip. Mr. Hobbs's loving gesture was very sweet. One might even say adorable. She met Susan's eyes again, and hers were shiny with emotion, too.

Within several minutes, the room had filled up. Lady Duchamp, of course, was missing, and so was Stephen (her heart skipped a beat knowing he was probably right next door), but everyone else had come.

She and Otis exchanged hopeful glances.

He indicated that he was going to keep an eye on the door and signal her if Hector came anywhere near—it was their plan.

Jilly cleared her throat and addressed the gathering: "It's so good to be here," she said, "and I simply want to state unequivocally that I'm sorry I misled all of you. I *am* Mrs. Broadmoor, and I'll acknowledge that openly now. But I don't plan on living with my husband, and I'd prefer you all call me Jilly. There's no place I'd rather be than with friends like you—if you'll accept me back here. I can endure the fog. I can endure the bad luck. But I can't endure being without you as my neighbors."

Nathaniel stood. "On behalf of the whole street, I think I'm safe in saying we all embrace you . . . Jilly.

Because from your very first day here, you've embraced us. And even though the fair went wrong, for an hour there it was working, wasn't it?"

He looked around. Everyone nodded their heads.

"I've never seen anything like it in all my years on Dreare Street!" piped up one ancient old man. "For the first time, I felt like Dreare Street was *the* place to be in London!"

Everyone cheered.

"Good," said Jilly. "Because we can't give up. We have only days left before those leases come due." She smiled gratefully at Mr. Hobbs. "I'm very glad to announce we have Mr. Hobbs working with us now. Together we can still raise the money we need. But even more important, we're going to get rid of Dreare Street's poor reputation once and for all."

After talking for another half an hour, a plan was hatched to everyone's satisfaction.

CHAPTER THIRTY-ONE

Stephen arrived at the little cottage in Kensington with a great deal of misgivings.

Who was he to interfere in someone else's marriage?

But he had to know.

Before he'd left London, he'd gone to see Harry, who'd instantly understood the crazy mess in which Stephen had landed himself.

"You've got it bad, my friend," Harry had said sympathetically. "But your plan is sound. You didn't need me to tell you that, although it couldn't hurt to hear it from someone who's been right where you are now."

And then he'd slapped his back, told him he'd take care of telling Lord Smelling to shove off, and wished him luck.

Stephen had gone to the Pantheon Bazaar next, where it had taken him an hour to locate that hackney driver, the one named Jack. But finally he had, and now he was here in Kensington.

He would get some answers.

A woman of uncommon beauty opened the shabby

front door. It was the same woman he'd seen with Hector at the Pantheon Bazaar.

"Yes?" Her voice was sharp and unpleasant.

Her beauty dimmed instantly. But he gave her a cordial smile.

"I'm Stephen Arrow. May I come in, please? I'm here on rather urgent business."

"Urgent?" She arched a brow. "Pray tell, what is so urgent that you'd knock on the door of a complete stranger?"

"Who's there, my love?"

Hector.

Stephen pressed his lips into a thin line and stepped over the threshold.

The woman's brow puckered, but she didn't tell him to move back. "Someone asking questions," she said over her shoulder. "A man named Arrow."

There was a stark silence. Then a clatter of a fork on a plate.

Hector came out of another room, chewing. "Not *you* again," he said with his mouth full.

"I'm afraid so."

"Get out," Hector said, pointing to the door.

Stephen widened his stance. "I'm not going anywhere. We can either hash this out inside, or go outside together."

"Go with the man," the actress urged Hector, fear in her voice.

Hector narrowed his eyes at Stephen. "Wait here then, Bessie."

In a great sulk, he followed Stephen outside.

Stephen faced him beneath a gnarled fig tree. "Tell me who that woman is."

"None of your business." Hector had spittle in the corner of his mouth.

"She's your mistress, isn't she?" Stephen asked carelessly.

Hector shrugged. "So what if she is? What wealthy married man doesn't have a mistress?"

"I'll grant you that some do. I also know plenty who don't," Stephen replied. "At the moment, I'm only concerned about you and yours."

Hector laughed. "You love my wife, don't you?"

Stephen refused to answer.

Hector tsked. "What a shame she can never be yours. Because I assure you, we won't divorce. And I won't let her go. Ever."

A bird whistled from the fig tree, and from the cottage next door, several children's voices could be heard arguing. A woman opened the door to that cottage and pointed outside.

"Go," she ordered.

A moment later, several children came out and went scampering off down the street.

Stephen watched them run, their bare feet flying. The world itself didn't care that the woman he loved was trapped in marriage to the wrong man and that he would be lonely the rest of his life.

There were so many stories everywhere. His was just one.

"You don't know what to do, do you, Captain?" Hector cocked his head, looking vastly amused at his discomfiture. "You can't ram me. You can't take me down with cannon fire. So why are you here?"

The children ran toward the next corner, laughing now—their argument already forgotten—and disappeared from view.

The words rushed into Stephen's head. *I am here to set Jilly free.* Like those children. The woman he loved shouldn't be tethered. She should be able to come and go as she pleased, to laugh, to run if she wanted to, by God.

To be her true self.

But what could Stephen do—other than kill her husband—to make that happen?

No matter how much he despised Hector, no matter how poorly the wretch had treated Jilly, Stephen couldn't kill the brute as a matter of convenience. He believed in justice, yes, but justice properly administered within the framework of laws. He was an experienced war veteran, but he would not be a vigilante.

Besides, he knew in his gut that Jilly, no matter how mistreated she'd been by Hector, would not condone his murder, either.

"I'm here to inform you that I *will* bring you down," Stephen said evenly. "It might not be today. But it will happen, and soon."

Hector laughed. "Go on, Captain. Back to your dreary little street. Alone."

And he went back inside, shutting the front door behind him.

Stephen seethed with frustration. He needed more information. He could travel to Jilly's village, but

Mayfair was closer. Perhaps he should start with Otis. He should know something more about Hector's background.

With a sigh, he mounted again. Slowly, he walked his horse down the street. He was reluctant to leave, knowing his quarry was there uncaught.

He must be patient.

And sensible. He wanted to get back to Dreare Street as soon as possible. But he'd had a long journey and another one still ahead of him. He'd make a quick stop at an inn one street over for some portable sustenance, some bread and cheese perhaps.

While the barkeep went back to the kitchen to get his order ready, Stephen nodded his head at a middle-aged gentleman sitting next to him with a pint of ale.

"You could use one of these," the man said to him, raising his glass. "You look much disappointed in something. Let me buy you one, stranger. My name's Mac McIver, at your service."

"Thank you, no," Stephen said, barely managing a polite response. "I need to get back to London."

Mr. McIver gave him a sideways look. "Why the long face, then? London is a fine place."

In a moment of weakness, and against all his good judgment as a gentleman—a military man, at that—Stephen gave in to impulse. "I'm in love," he confessed.

"Well," the man replied, "that usually induces more feelings of happiness than gloom."

"Yes, sir," Stephen said with a sigh, "normally you'd be correct. But she's married. She doesn't love her cad of a husband, nor he her. She loves me. But as a gentleman, I can't do anything without compromising her honor, or mine."

Thankfully, the barkeep returned then with Stephen's food, wrapped in paper. He paid for it and put the package under his arm. "Good day," he said to Mr. McIver.

He was rather embarrassed and anxious to be gone.

The stranger touched his arm. "Your dilemma isn't unique," he said low, "but it's unsalvageable in most cases, no?"

Stephen nodded. "Right."

"If I may be so bold, might I know the names of this man and woman?"

Stephen shook his head. "I'd rather not say." It still stung deeply to recollect that awful moment in Hodgepodge when he'd first realized Jilly and Hector were married. "They're not from here anyway."

Mr. McIver grinned. "I envision him as a Ferdinand. Or Brutus. The villain always has such a name in the Gothic novels my wife is fond of." He chuckled. "If he doesn't live here, then tell me, lad. Just the first name will do."

Stephen shrugged. "It's Hector. The lady's name I'll keep to myself."

Mr. McIver drew in his chin. "My goodness," he said. "I know a Hector. Are you sure they're not from around here?"

"No, they're not, I assure you."

Mr. McIver looked at Stephen with a great deal of pity, almost as if he thought he were lying.

"What is it?" Stephen couldn't help feeling a bit defensive.

The old man twisted his mouth in a faint grimace and patted his hand. "I feel for you, lad."

"Yes, I know you do." Bitterness crept into Stephen's voice. "Thank very much. But I'll survive."

Just barely.

Mr. McIver leaned close to him. "You came to see Bessie Brompton, didn't you, and you found Hector there," he whispered knowingly, and looked up to make sure the barkeep wasn't listening. "Don't worry. Your secret's safe with me."

The hairs on the back of Stephen's neck stood up. "What do you mean?"

Mr. McIver shook his head. "You're not the first to fall in love with Bessie. Hector comes and goes, sometimes for months at a time. They've been married at least ten years, but"—he paused—"everyone knows Bessie has her occasional suitor." And then he winked.

Married.

For ten years?

"The Hector you refer to . . . his surname is Brompton?" Stephen could barely get the words out.

"Why, yes," said Mr. McIver. "Of course. Hector and Bessie Brompton."

Brompton.

Broadmoor.

The names were very close.

"Got married in our village church." Mr. McIver

cocked his head at some unknown point. "Everyone from here gets married there."

Stephen forced himself to regain his outward composure, although inside he was still reeling. "I'm sure you have the wrong Hector. What does he look like?"

"Why, he's got an ugly scar right by his mouth."

It *was* the same Hector!

"I really must go," Stephen managed to say. "But thanks for the kind ear."

The man nudged him. "Forget about Bessie," he said with sympathy. "Surely there are other women who'll capture your heart. Go find one in Town, eh?"

He slapped Stephen on the back once and went back to his ale.

Stephen walked out of the pub with a smooth brow and calm manner, but his heart beat a wild tattoo against his ribs. When he mounted his horse, he wheeled it around and cantered in the direction of the small spire down the street. Hector's doom would be found right here—in Kensington, where he kept his real wife.

It would be the same place that Stephen would confront him with the truth—and here that Jilly, the woman both he and Hector had wronged, would find her freedom.

"No, you may *not* come in," Otis said loudly to Lady Duchamp, who'd arrived at the door of Hodgepodge while everyone who'd attended the emergency meeting was discussing the new plan to bring prosperity to Dreare Street. "Not if you plan to make trouble."

Lady Duchamp arched one eyebrow. "Are you afraid of me, you sartorial disaster?" She eyed his tricorne hat and scarlet coat with scorn.

Jilly and everyone else froze at the overheard conversation.

"I'm most certainly *not* afraid of you," Otis said with dignity. "So do come in and make your standard dramatic entrance—it's getting to be quite boring, by the way—and fire your best volley. We shall *sink* you, my lady, if you dare! That I promise you."

He leaned toward her, his voice trembling with emotion.

"You've been consorting with that ridiculous sea captain too long." She pushed Otis aside with her cane and entered the shop. "Stop your eating and drinking. The news I have shall make you all sick to your stomachs."

Everyone stared, but then a young man next to her bit into his scone and stared fixedly at her. He swallowed loudly and took another bite.

Her eyes narrowed. "That's at your peril."

"I'll take my chances," he said low, and kept chewing, like a cow at its cud.

"How can I help you, my lady?" Jilly's tone was businesslike.

Lady Duchamp stuck her withered chin in the air. "As some of you know, I own several buildings on this street. But until now, none of you have guessed that *I* own the ground beneath your feet. You pay your leases to *me*. Mr. Redmond is my accountant."

There was a stunned silence.

Then Mr. Hobbs stood. "What of it? We don't care who owns the land beneath our feet. We'll pay you and be done with it. And there's nothing you can do about it."

There were murmurs of assent from all around.

"Oh, yes there is." Lady Duchamp smiled, and it was an awful smile, to say the least. "As of yesterday, I've changed the terms of the lease."

Jilly felt her stomach sink. "What are the new terms?" she called out, refusing to let any fear enter her voice.

The old woman's smiling face suddenly went stony. "The money is due in three days."

"No, it's not, my lady." The young man with the scone wiped his mouth. "We have a whole week."

Lady Duchamp poked him in the chest with her cane. "Not any longer. Of course, I wanted the money due today. But the attorneys said it would take three days for the paperwork to go through. Good-bye, all of you, for good. Might as well pack and leave."

The whole room fell deathly silent as Lady Duchamp walked out the front door again. Everyone turned around and looked at Jilly as if she'd know what to do.

The old bat had been right. Jilly *did* feel like throwing up. But she wouldn't let any of her friends know.

"So we have three days now instead of seven," she said briskly.

"But we *need* seven," Nathaniel said.

"We don't have them. " What else could she say? "We'll simply have to adjust to the new schedule."

Everyone but Otis—how good a friend he was!— looked rather doubtful.

"Right." Jilly blew a tendril of hair off her face. "This is only a temporary setback. Let's disband for the moment and regroup here at two this afternoon."

The group stood and moved to the door, quiet again.

Deflated.

Like her. But she remained stalwart until the last of them left. And then she sank onto a stool.

For the first time, she truly felt defeated. "What are we to do?" she asked Otis. "Nathaniel is right. We really *do* need a week."

Otis stared at her a moment. On his face, she read worry. But there was something else, something that buoyed her.

"Follow me," he said, and stuck out his arm. "I told you once I'd save you at your darkest hour, and I will. I know *exactly* what to do."

And he marched her over to Lady Duchamp's house and knocked on the door.

CHAPTER THIRTY-TWO

Jilly was surprised to see that Lady Duchamp answered Otis's knock herself. "It didn't take you long to come begging, did it?" The old lady smirked. "This should be quite diverting."

"We're not begging." Jilly stepped into the entryway. "We're confronting. And if you call confronting your foe diverting, then I suppose it is."

Once inside, Otis stared at Lady Duchamp's feet. "Those are *my* shoes," he said flatly.

Jilly saw she was wearing a pair of aquamarine-colored slippers with golden ribbons.

"Yes," the old woman said. "What of it?"

"Give them back." Otis spoke sternly, and Jilly was surprised at his vehemence.

"Absolutely not," said Lady Duchamp. "They're mine, fair and square."

"You threatened them out of me at the beginning of the street fair," Otis said. "You said you'd find a way to shut it down. I capitulated then, but I'm here to tell you we won't be threatened by you anymore."

Lady Duchamp huffed. "Come to my drawing room. I don't endure fools in my entryway."

They followed behind her at a snail's pace, which frustrated Otis no end, Jilly could tell. He'd been so full of fire at the door, and now . . . now the tension was seriously dissipated. No doubt Lady Duchamp was aware of that fact as she shuffled along.

"She's the only person I know," Otis whispered to Jilly, "who can make frailty a devastating weapon."

Jilly squeezed his arm. "Your time for speaking will come soon enough," she whispered back.

He bit his lip and endured, but once in the drawing room, Lady Duchamp rang for tea and proclaimed that no one was allowed to speak until the niceties were observed.

So Otis must tap his feet another five minutes.

Finally, both he and Jilly held a brimming cup in their hands.

"Now I shall proceed," Otis said.

Lady Duchamp glowered. "Not until you take a sip and offer your compliments."

Otis made a face. But he did as he was told and set the cup down. "Lovely blend," he said to his hostess with feeling.

"Why, thank you," she began, then stopped herself.

Otis also looked mortified at his sincere compliment.

"Speak your foolishness now, so I can return to being alone," Lady Duchamp muttered around her own teacup.

Jilly was eager to hear what Otis had to say.

He looked first at her—with a mixture of pride and affection—then at Lady Duchamp. "Your power over the street has ceased as of today," he proclaimed in a pleased yet defiant manner.

"Is that so?" offered Lady Duchamp.

Otis nodded, and picked up a biscuit from a plate. "I followed you this morning."

She sucked in her cheeks. "How rude of you!"

"As if *you* are not the same?" He huffed, then put his hand on his breast. "Now that I know your tragic history, you'll not only quit your stranglehold on the neighborhood, you'll return my shoes."

"Never!" she cried.

Otis pointed the biscuit at her. "You're just the same as the rest of us sad sacks on Dreare Street, my lady. You can deny it no longer."

Lady Duchamp's white-powdered cheeks paled even further.

"Do explain, Otis," Jilly said softly. "And gently, please, if it involves tragedy."

Otis sent a dark look at Lady Duchamp. "Oh, she can bear it. She's a stalwart old thing."

Lady Duchamp tried to look insulted, but she had a difficult time maintaining her pique, particularly when Otis let down his own defenses and bestowed a pitying look on her.

Jilly sighed. "Otis? The story, please?"

"Oh, right." He placed a hand on her arm. "You wouldn't believe it. I found Lady Duchamp depositing a daisy from her garden onto the front door step of a spectacular mansion on Dover Street. After she left, I knocked on the door and inquired. It seems she's been leaving a flower on the stoop for almost four decades.

In the winter, she'll leave hothouse blossoms. The butler's favorite are the pink peonies."

"No!" said Jilly, and looked at Lady Duchamp.

She appeared to be shrinking, having made herself into a small ball (with delicious shoes) in the corner of the settee.

"Yes," insisted Otis. "I found out from the housekeeper that Lord and Lady Duchamp used to live there as a young couple. They were very much in love. But the earl came to an early demise. Fell off a horse."

"I'm so sorry," said Jilly to his widow.

Lady Duchamp scowled at her. "I told you bacon-brains my history."

"Yes," said Otis, raising his finger. "But you didn't tell us that Lord Duchamp didn't die from a fall off a horse. He died in your own bed with his longtime mistress, someone you'd no idea existed."

Lady Duchamp waved a hand. "Pure faradiddle."

"I think not," said Otis. "The houseboy who found him is now the butler at the Dover Street house. I told him you intend to destroy the lives of everyone on Dreare Street because you're so damned unhappy. He decided it's time for you to put the appalling circumstances of your husband's death behind you. So he told me all the details."

Lady Duchamp's hands began to shake.

Jilly immediately dropped to her knees in front of the settee and held the old woman's hands. "It's all right, my lady."

Otis's face softened, and he moved over and sat next to Lady Duchamp on the settee. "The butler also told me that your husband left you penniless. It seems he spent much of his fortune on his mistress and her home, a fabulous mansion in the countryside of Kent. You were forced to leave your beloved home and all your false expectations and move to Dreare Street because you were too ashamed to ask your family for financial help."

"I was the worst thing that ever happened to this place," Lady Duchamp said proudly. "Even worse than the fog."

Jilly patted her hand. "How did you rebuild your fortune?"

Lady Duchamp glared at her. "None of your business."

"Her parents had loads of money," Otis said glibly. "So after they died, her penurious circumstances ended. She bought up a great deal of Dreare Street."

"I couldn't very well leave it. I had to serve as a scullery maid in this very house." Lady Duchamp shuddered. "After I received my inheritance, I dared not move to another part of Mayfair and risk becoming a laughingstock. My mistress had lavish parties, and I was always afraid a member of the *ton* would visit the kitchens to compliment Cook and—and see me washing out a huge pot lined with pig grease and bits of potato, or some such thing."

"Oh, my lady!" Otis cried.

There was a brief, pregnant pause.

Otis reddened, and Jilly bit her lip, wanting to laugh. She knew it was wrong of her, but she could swear Otis was feeling soft feelings toward Lady Duchamp, which was outrageous. But somehow . . . appropriate. She had no idea why it should be so, but it was in a strange—ahem, *very* strange—way.

Lady Duchamp glared at Otis, but her mouth was soft, almost pleased. "Get on with it," she demanded. "And keep your pity to yourself."

"Very well." Otis sniffed, straightened his spine, then stuck out his chin, which was his storytelling posture.

"It was the shame and the heartbreak," he whispered, "that made Lady Duchamp the way she is now. She bought out the land lease from the previous owner so she could make an entire street miserable along with her."

"Can you blame me?" Lady Duchamp said hoarsely. "It worked like a charm for decades. And then that silly captain moved in, and you two—all at the same time—and everyone started cheering up. It couldn't be borne. So I consulted with my attorneys and accountant and found a way to rid myself of all of you and start over with new people on the street. The damned lease is what did it. I'd forgotten all about it."

Otis wagged a finger at her. "It's time you stopped this nonsense. That house on Dover Street was never your home. Dreare Street is. And you can have the family you never had as a married woman."

Lady Duchamp sucked in her teeth. "You don't want me as family."

"Certainly we do." Otis glared at her. "But not Lady Tabitha."

"She's a witch with a capital *B*," Lady Duchamp agreed. "But she comes by it honestly."

There was an extended awkward silence.

Jilly finally rose. "Well, we'd best go. We have to work on our new plan to save the street."

Otis stood, and he pulled up Lady Duchamp. "Are you still going to give us only three days to pay our leases?"

She shook her head quickly. But she was as prune-faced as ever. "No. You may have the entire week."

Otis bent in—then pulled back—then bent in and kissed her cheek. "Thank you, my lady."

Jilly dared to lean in and hug her. Lady Duchamp flinched, and she was brittle as a dried stick, but she endured the embrace.

When Jilly pulled back, Lady Duchamp stood staring at the wall, her cane between her hands. "I don't really need that lease money," she admitted.

She wouldn't meet either of their gazes.

Otis looked at Jilly with wide eyes.

Jilly looked at Lady Duchamp. "P-pardon?"

Lady Duchamp knocked her cane on the floor. "Are you two deaf?"

"Oh, no, my lady," Otis said in a rush. "You're saying we don't have to pay you any lease money."

"Exactly." She glared at him. "But don't go asking for those shoes. They're mine. And I demand five more pairs, all different colors. But not yellow. I despise yellow."

He lifted his chin. "Very well. It's a small price to pay."

"Otis," Jilly remonstrated with him.

Otis put up his hand. "I'll have plenty of time to make more shoes. And as I'll be taking Lady Duchamp about Town again—I refuse to let her hide anymore—all the *ton* shall see my shoes on her feet. Which means I shall do very well, indeed."

The old woman narrowed her eyes. "Very well. Begone."

Jilly took Otis's arm and paused at the door. "We have a special event going on soon at Hodgepodge, and you shall be one of our guests of honor."

"Pish-posh," she said, waving her cane at them.

But the arc she made with it was not nearly as pronounced as it had been when she was their enemy.

"You *did* save me, Otis," Jilly said, leaning on him on their way across the street. "My darling, you saved the entire street, including Lady Duchamp."

He expanded his chest. "I told you I had it in me."

"I never doubted it for a minute." Jilly squeezed his arm. "There's only one thing we have left to do. Save London from its misconceptions about who we are."

"And the sooner we do that, the better," Otis agreed wholeheartedly.

Of one accord about their mission—even their steps were synchronous—both of them jumped at the booming voice of Lady Hartley.

The lady came running toward them from the captain's house. "Where has Captain Arrow gone?" she demanded to know.

Neither of them had any idea, of course.

The baronet's wife pressed a hand on her heart and

widened her eyes. "I'm *so* surprised. He left without telling me anything."

"Whatever could you mean?" asked Otis.

Lady Hartley tossed her head. "I thought we had an understanding, the Captain and I."

"Understanding?" Jilly was flummoxed.

Lady Hartley looked at her with a bit of pity. "For a married woman, you're awfully naïve."

"I am?"

"Yes, you are." The annoying woman snorted. "Isn't she, Otis?" She elbowed him in the ribs.

"No." He glared at her. "She's not."

Lady Hartley abruptly stopped chuckling, glared at the two of them, and stalked back to the captain's house.

Otis gulped. "She wasn't saying—"

"I think she was," whispered Jilly.

They both started walking again without saying anything further about it. Jilly did her best not to think of Stephen. But seconds later, she paused right outside the bookshop window and stared.

Dear heavens. Forgetting about him would be awfully hard to do when *he was inside Hodgepodge at that very moment.*

CHAPTER THIRTY-THREE

Stephen looked up when Jilly walked in with Otis.

She stared at him, unblinking. Otis tiptoed away, and Stephen heard the door at the rear of the store open and shut again.

They were alone.

"Hello," he said to her. He was busy making her that outdoor easel she'd wanted, the one she'd told him about when they'd lain in bed together at the Grosvenor Street mansion and daydreamed about improvements they'd like to make at Hodgepodge.

Out of the corner of his eye, he saw her walk slowly over. "What are *you* doing here?" she whispered.

Every muscle in him was tense. He put down his hammer, stood up, and took her by the arms. "I'm here to be with you," he said.

She looked at him with hurt eyes. "It's too late."

Ah. Those were the words he'd dreaded hearing.

"I understand why you're angry," he said. "I deserve to lose you. You trusted me—and I disappointed you."

She said nothing back.

His whole life revolved around this moment. "You

were right." He squeezed her arms. "I was acting like a boy, still pouting over the fact that I didn't have the ideal family I so desperately wanted. But that's no reason not to trust you. And not to understand why you had to lie."

Her face softened a fraction. "I'm no longer interested in going to another country. I don't want to spend my life hiding. Everyone has accepted me here, so . . . I'm staying at Hodgepodge."

There was a brief pause.

"I'm glad," he eventually said.

She looked at him a long time. "Lady Hartley claims you and she have an understanding. I know she's been living at your house this whole time. And . . . and men have needs."

She looked away.

Good God! Would that meddlesome woman never leave his life?

Gently, Stephen drew Jilly's face back. "You don't think that Lady Hartley and I would ever—"

He couldn't possibly complete *that* sentence.

Jilly shrugged. "You're a rake," she whispered. "You never claimed to be anything else."

"Well, I am now," he said firmly. "I'm not the same man anymore. Not since I've met you. I *love* you, Jilly Jones. You're the only woman I ever want to be with again."

Jilly shook her head. "I don't know if you understand. I'm staying in England. And so we can't be together. I love you. But I can't hide anymore."

"I understand," he replied softly. And he did. "But I have some news for you. It's going to shock you, so perhaps you should take a seat."

She stared at him a moment. "No," she said. "Tell me now."

He hesitated, as well. "If you're certain."

She nodded.

He took a deep breath. "Jilly Jones—"

"Jilly Broadmoor," she said in a choked whisper.

He felt his eyes burn, just the merest fraction. "No," he said, swallowing. "You're not Mrs. Broadmoor."

She looked at him as if he should be sent to Bedlam.

"Hector *is* married"—he hesitated—"but not to you. To someone else."

Jilly flinched, but he took her shoulders and held her. "The charlatan was married eight years before he married you," he said as kindly as he could.

She seemed to stare right through him.

He gave her a gentle shake. "It's true," he assured her. "I left him today after confronting him and his wife. He lives in Kensington. He was with you because he was evil. He was already married, but he wanted *you* as his property, as well."

She gave a little cry.

Stephen gathered her into his arms. "He's been taken to gaol."

"What about his other wife?" Jilly whispered. "Is she all right?"

Stephen's heart filled with more love for her than ever. "Don't feel sorry for her. She knew about the whole arrangement. He was siphoning money off to her."

Jilly wiped her eyes with the back of her hand and stared at him with an intent gaze. "This still doesn't change things between us. You're only with me now because it's easy. But when you had to choose me or life in England, you chose England."

He nodded again, stricken at the memory. "I had a feeling you'd say that. But I've told you. I'm not the same man anymore. You were right—all those things you said about my not being willing to grow up made perfect sense. You'll have to trust me that I resolved to try again to win you—come what may—before I knew this news about Hector. I can never prove it to you, otherwise. But it's the reason I went after him. I'd decided that he deserved a comeuppance. And then I was going to come to you and ask your forgiveness. After that, I was going to ask you to move with me to Italy or America—or any other place you wanted to live."

Her brow puckered, and he waited patiently.

"Will you trust me?" he said eventually.

She looked at the ground. Then she looked back up at him. "I'm sorry, but I need more time. I'm so confused."

His heart clenched. He had so hoped that today, she'd be his again. But he understood. "I'm sure the news about Hector has completely thrown you."

She nodded shakily. "There's so much to think about. Can you wait?"

"Of course," he said, not wanting to burden her

with his fear of losing her. She really had had a shock, and he wasn't going to compound it with his own worries. "Now go upstairs and see Otis. Tell him the wonderful news. And get a cup of tea."

She gave a shaky laugh. And then for a moment her face was radiant—as if she finally comprehended the truth.

"You're free, Jilly. *Free.*" He let go of her hand reluctantly and watched her walk to the door in the back. This was one battle he couldn't win by being aggressive.

She opened the door, turned around, and looked at him one more time.

And then, smiling shyly, she shut the door behind her.

Dear God, he prayed, *next time it opens, let her come to me.*

CHAPTER THIRTY-FOUR

Jilly realized that even though there was so much more fun to be had at their new special event now that the lease money wasn't a problem anymore, they still had the biggest dilemma of all to solve—changing Dreare Street's reputation.

She was pleased to see that not a single resident of Dreare Street dropped out of the new plan. Everyone, it seemed, still wanted Dreare Street to be known as a place of prosperity and good cheer.

The first thing they did was enact a name change, which they'd achieved with the permission of the Lord Mayor of London. Lady Duchamp blustered only a moment or two when the sign went up at the top of the street:

READER STREET, it read through wisps of fog.

"It's the same letters as in *Dreare* but all jumbled around," Thomas explained to Lady Duchamp. "We've got a bookshop here, so it makes sense. Especially because we're all readers, right, my lady?"

And he held a book upside down to prove the point.

Jilly linked arms with Susan and laughed at that.

Nathaniel put Thomas's book down, picked him up, and swung him around.

Not long after, they enacted the next part of the plan, which was crucial to the success of their mission.

"There must be gossip," Jilly reminded everyone later that day at Hodgepodge, "*lots* of gossip about a certain tea with, um, certain properties."

She blushed. Every other woman in the room did, as well. But the men—the men had almost predatory looks in their eyes.

"When can we get some?" an elderly gentleman cried.

"Yes," said Pratt, "I want some now."

"I'm making a new batch this evening," Mrs. Hobbs said, "just for the neighborhood."

"Don't worry," said Mr. Hobbs. "I'm reopening my tea company, right here on Dreare—I mean, *Reader* Street. And we'll specialize in this particular exotic blend of leaves from a remote corner of China."

"We've had crates of various teas sitting around our house for six weeks now," Mrs. Hobbs said, "ever since Mr. Hobbs shut down the company. I figured I'd at least *try* to do something with them."

"I'm very glad you did," her husband said smoothly. "At any rate, this tea is combined with Lavinia's special extra ingredients—"

"I only add—" she began excitedly.

"Shush, my dear." He patted her hand. "It must be our secret."

"Of course." Mrs. Hobbs looked well pleased.

"Although I'm glad to share the final result." She wagged a finger at the crowd. "And don't forget, ladies. This tea is beneficial to *all*."

"It's what they call an aphrodisiac," said Mr. Hobbs. "If Hobbs's special blend doesn't spark romance between you and the person you love, nothing will."

All the women blushed again.

And the men pulled at their cravats or cleared their throats.

Jilly tried not to think of Stephen.

"Which is why," she went on, "we needed to get the word out to the *ton*." She looked at Miss Hartley.

"It was so easy," Miss Hartley said. "I told Lady Gallagher about it last night at the Fordhams' ball. She's an awful gossip. The whispering began, and all night long, I could see the word being passed. By the end of the evening, I've no doubt at all that everyone knew that if they come to Hodgepodge this Friday at noon and say the secret word, the special tea will be made available to them."

"What *is* the code word?" asked Pratt.

Miss Hartley turned toward him, her eyes wide. "Throb," she said in a sweet, yearning voice.

Pratt leaned toward her. "You're much too good for me, *bella*," he whispered.

"No I'm not," she cried.

"Miranda!"

Jilly and everyone else jumped.

"There you are." Sir Ned was at the door with Lady Hartley. "Captain Arrow has said no to Lord Smelling's offer to buy the house, but he still insists we move into a hotel."

"Why we must depart is beyond me," said Lady Hartley. "I showed him the letter from our attorney giving us permission to stay here, and he tore it up, said he'd take us to court to dispute it if he had to. And then he said it would be a moot point anyway. I have no idea what he meant by that, but he has a strange light in his eye. A *very* strange light."

"Now say your good-byes," Sir Ned ordered his daughter, "and meet us in the carriage."

Miranda stood. "No, Mother and Father. I'm not leaving Reader Street."

Her mother sneered. "It's Dreare."

"No, Reader," Miranda insisted.

"Dreare," said Sir Ned.

"No, Reader!" said the whole room as one.

Lady Hartley made an ugly face. "You people can rot on Reader Street for all I care. Come, Miranda."

Miranda shook her head. "I'll stay with Susan or Jilly if I have to, but I'm staying. I'm going to marry Pratt if he'll ask me—and I have high hopes he will after he tries the Hobbses' aphrodisiac tea."

Lady Hartley's eyes lit up. "Aphrodisiac tea?"

Pratt suddenly broke into a big grin. "I can't wait to try it. Not that I need it with your daughter. She sets my heart racing with *amore*."

Miss Hartley smiled broadly. "Really?"

Lady Hartley waved a dismissive hand. "Ignore him, Miranda. Love is for the lower classes."

"And so is this *amooray* you're talking about!" Sir Ned blustered.

Without a word of warning, Pratt got down on one knee in front of Miss Hartley. "I need no special potion to ask you to marry me," he said, gesticulating wildly at his heart and then Miss Hartley's sweet countenance with his hands. "I'm a free man. I can ask any time I desire, no?"

Jilly felt a pang of remembrance. She hadn't been a free woman for such a long time—

But now she was.

She wished she could be as happy as she'd been when she'd first heard the news of Hector's fraudulent behavior, but all she could think about was Stephen and how they weren't talking and about how she was so *confused*. He was being so patient—

Waiting for her.

Gently, Pratt took Miss Hartley's hand. "Will you marry me, my dear Miranda?" he asked in a ragged whisper.

"Ye-th!" she said, and burst into happy tears.

"She shall *not* marry you!" Sir Ned cried.

"You can't expect our daughter to marry a nobody," Lady Hartley snarled.

"He has a name, Mother," Miss Hartley gritted out. "It's Pratt."

Her mother rolled her eyes. "He must have another name to go with it."

"Of course he does!" Miss Hartley said hotly, then blinked confusedly at her new love. "Don't you?"

Pratt lifted his chin. "Yes, I do. It is no one's business but mine and Miranda's, but I am Lucio Basso, Conte di Cavour. Your daughter has made me very happy."

"Conte di Cavour?" Sir Ned stumbled over the title.

"Indeed," said Pratt coolly. "I go by the name Pratt when I travel with my friend Captain Arrow. Until now, I preferred the vagabond's life and enjoyed seeing the world incognito. But now that I've met you, my love"—he cast a doting glance at Miss Hartley—"I'd like to take you home. To my castle."

Miss Hartley gasped. "Oh, dear! You're not really Pratt?"

Lucio shook his head. "Are you disappointed, dearest?"

She looked a trifle worried. "Not really. Not if it means you'll still fry eggs for me each morning."

"Of course I shall. I am an Italian count, my love, of excellent family, and I can do anything I want. Even serve as cook on a ship if I so choose." He turned to Sir Ned and Lady Hartley. "I suggest you two depart. We will talk to you at some other time. Perhaps when you become kinder, I shall invite you to my home in Sardinia."

He turned his back on them and kissed Miss Hartley to much applause.

"Miranda?" Lady Hartley called weakly.

Miranda lifted her head for just a moment. "Later, Mother," she called breathlessly.

And she went back to kissing her count.

Sir Ned and Lady Hartley's mouths dropped open, and then they turned quietly away and left.

When Lucio finished kissing Miss Hartley, his gaze roamed around the room until it landed on Nathaniel. "I am a great collector of fine art. Your paintings bring me much happiness. Would you care to sell me your entire collection? We have many rooms in my home."

Nathaniel beamed. "I'd be glad to."

Lucio smiled at Susan. "And before I take my bride back with me, I would love for you to sew her trousseau. I pay very well and shall spread word of your great talent throughout my country and to any expatriates who live here in London."

Susan blinked rapidly. "Of—of course, Lucio. I mean, Count. Thank you very much."

"You must call me Lucio," he said, and was about to open his mouth to say more when there was a mighty rumble and groan that literally shook Hodgepodge.

Some women screamed, and there were shouts from the men.

The crowd gathered at the window. And then there were more cries, this time of astonishment.

Jilly almost fainted when she saw what was happening. Stephen and his friends, including Lumley and Lord Harry Traemore, stood outside in the street with a team of four large draft horses. Several ropes led from the horses' harnesses to Stephen's house. They ran through the front door and several windows and now—

Now a portion of 34 Reader Street had fallen to the ground. The rest was leaning very precariously. Jilly could see it wouldn't take much more to pull it all down.

Otis threw open the door and ran outside. All the

people in Hodgepodge did the same. Jilly was caught in the crowd, but she was desperate—*desperate*—to get to Stephen.

Finally, through all the chaos, she was able to reach Stephen's side.

Everybody was talking, yelling, pointing, gesturing, and some were simply staring in awe at the destruction.

Stephen grinned when he saw her, and his eyes lit up like a little boy's, as if he'd just played a prank and was laughing at the results.

She'd never been so confused in her life.

"What have you done?" she cried. "Your house! You worked so hard on it. And—and you had a buyer. You could have sold it and taken the money and—"

"Stop, Jilly." He took her by the shoulders and stared into her eyes, his own filled with so much strong yet tender feeling that she had to burrow into his chest and cling to him because it was too, too much. Her own raw emotions were about to burst from her, but she couldn't let them.

Not now, not in front of all these people.

He held her close and stroked her hair. "It's what I want to do," he said softly into her ear. "I read Alicia Fotherington's journal. And I figured out why Dreare Street—I mean, Reader Street—is so filled with fog."

She looked up at him. "Why?"

He chuckled. "It was the perfect storm. First, it has to do with where the house is situated on the street in relation to the prevalent winds."

She laughed. "Always the sailor, aren't you?"

"It will never quite leave me," he said with a grin. "And it also has to do with all the wings Lyle Fotherington built on. He made the house so big that it blocks in all the fog that would otherwise blow away. The journal made it clear that the street never had such a preponderance of fog until he built those wings." He paused. "We must face the truth, Jilly. My house is the reason for the fog."

"Your house is a bottleneck?" She shook her head. "It's a crazy theory, but—"

He put his chin up. "Just you wait. When you wake up in the morning tomorrow, I'll bet you there won't be any fog, or at least no more than they have on Half-Moon or Curzon Streets."

She blinked back tears. "I trust you. But why, why would you give up your house so that we'd have less fog on Reader Street?"

He took her face in his hands. "For you, my love. I wanted to make you happy. I wanted to bring sunshine to the front door of Hodgepodge, so that Gridley would have more days to bask in it, so you'd have more reason to stand in the door and not huddle by the hearth. So people could see Otis's waistcoats from a distance. So shoppers would come wandering down the street this Friday, when your new plan is set in motion, and buy books. I wanted to make this street a cheerful, sunny place, to match the warmth and love I've already found from *you*."

She squeezed her eyes shut a moment, but two teardrops formed anyway and made her vision blurry. "I love you, Stephen Arrow," she whispered.

"I love you, too, Jilly Jones."

She couldn't wait any longer.

She reached up and kissed him full on his handsome mouth.

He grabbed her around the waist and kissed her back.

A draft horse whinnied.

"Back up now, time for the next pull!" Lumley cried.

Friends, dogs, neighbors, lovers, and family tumbled past Jilly and Stephen, all in an effort to see the big house come down.

Stephen squeezed her close. "Good luck, bad luck— what does either one matter when you're with the people you love?" he shouted above the creak of the horses' harnesses and the general tumult as the ropes attached to the house stretched tauter and tauter.

Jilly gave a little hop of anticipation—

And the street was the happiest it had ever been.

EPILOGUE

"Who knew?" said Jilly, wrapping her leg around Stephen's torso. "Who knew a first anniversary could be so blissful?"

"I did." He pulled her close and kissed her once on the mouth. "It's even better than the wedding."

Where he'd fulfilled that old romantic notion of his and waltzed with his new bride—and her alone. The nuptial celebration had taken place a mere week after the bookstore event at Hodgepodge had initiated a whole new way of life on Reader Street. The tea had sold out, the sun had shone, and the energy of the neighborhood—and the scandalous tea, no doubt—had even brought Prinny back.

This time, Jilly sold him a book, and when she did, he assured her he'd be frequenting her shop on a regular basis.

Now, almost a year later, she and Stephen were nose to nose in her bed above Hodgepodge. Otis had moved into Lady Duchamp's house and was now called her secretary, although Jilly had to wonder if there was something more between the two eccentrics.

When they weren't yelling at each other, Lady

Duchamp actually kept Otis's life in order—not the other way around—by watching over his books and organizing the correspondence generated by his new business venture, a shop for men in the building vacated by Susan when she, Nathaniel, and Thomas had moved to a bigger house right next door to Hodgepodge after their wedding.

Otis's shop was small and posh and simply called Otis. He sold his shoes, handkerchiefs, and men's waistcoats there. In fact, his signature pieces were all the rage among the dandies in Town. Some were even beginning to call a new style of tying their cravat the Otis.

He'd offered to sell Susan's gowns, as well, but now that Nathaniel was a successful artist—Lucio's patronage had gone far to establishing him—Susan had decided to make custom garments only occasionally, and only for Lady Harry and other very rich customers, from a lovely sewing room in her home. She really preferred to sing while Nathaniel painted one floor above her in a lovely studio. After all, a new baby was on the way, and singing while she sewed her baby's first clothes and Thomas played at her feet made her happier than anything.

The Hobbses were so rich now from the still-brisk sales of their aphrodisiac tea, Mrs. Hobbs and her children were no longer quite so pale. They'd had a lovely holiday in Italy and returned rather pink. And Mr. Hobbs—well, he no longer wore that grim expression or that horrible black cape. He was a happy man who got splendid sartorial advice from Otis—who

understood his conservative nature and trod very
carefully in selecting him clothes that suited his new,
brighter self. Jilly suspected the tea, both as commod-
ity and beverage, had nothing to do with Mr. Hobbs's
transformation. Mrs. Hobbs was the reason for his
good cheer, and Mrs. Hobbs alone.

"You're daydreaming," Stephen said, pulling a lock
of hair off her shoulder and putting it behind her, the
better to reach her breast with his mouth.

"I suppose I am," she murmured, and then gave a
little moan.

He was doing naughty things to her.

She *loved* when he did naughty things.

"I was just thinking about Lucio and Miranda," she
said. "I can't believe she's a countess now. But it's so
delicious that she is."

"Yes," Stephen murmured against her belly now.

Jilly sighed. "Sir Ned and Lady Hartley were wax-
ing on about the wedding, how big everything was at
Lucio's castle, how shiny and magnificent. I'm so sorry
we missed it, but at least the Hobbses were there."

"At least," said Stephen, nudging aside her leg.

Jilly gasped at what he was doing.

And for the next several minutes, she floated away
on a cloud of pure bliss.

When she returned, it was Stephen's turn, and she
took her time showing him how much she could never
tell him exactly how much she loved him—because it
was inexpressible, at least with words, wasn't it?

She did the best she could with her mouth.

He apparently understood, judging from the lazy kisses he bestowed on her afterward.

Life was good, she thought, as she flicked back the curtains and saw the big, empty space that used to be 34 Dreare Street. It was now a small park for the neighborhood children to play in. Stephen had seen to that. Every bit of money he'd gotten from selling Alicia Fotherington's small but valuable collection of jewelry and gold coins—which she'd stashed in a corner of the attic and was discovered by Otis during the cleanup—went to beautifying the lot.

Jilly liked to think of it as Alicia's present to the world.

She hadn't told Stephen yet, but soon . . .

They'd need that park for their own family.

Stephen watched his naked wife at the window and smiled at the wonderment of it all. He was a married man. God, he was like Harry and Nicholas now!

It still shocked him.

But then again, it didn't.

Looking at Jilly, he realized it was the most natural thing on earth for him to be married to her.

She was everything he'd ever wanted.

He got out of bed, as naked as she, and came to stand behind her.

"Shall we go to the roof again tonight?" he said in her ear.

She loved when he spoke in her ear. She said it tickled.

"I'd like to go now," she said, looking back up at him. "In the sunlight."

They had so much more of that these days.

"Why, Miss Jones!" It was still his favorite name for her. "You do mean clothed, don't you?"

She shook her head, a mischievous twinkle in her eye. "No one can see us if we stay far enough back from the edge."

"Oho," he replied with a grin. "I seem to remember long ago that you said anyone who wanted to look up there could see us from that perch where we had that first picnic."

They'd since had many more.

She bit her lip. "I *did* say that, didn't I?" She giggled. "Perhaps I wanted you to kiss me that day."

"Oh, I'm sure of it," said Stephen.

She pretended to slap him. "You were always so sure of yourself."

"Still am," he said, and laid a kiss on her neck.

She pulled back and held his hand. "Are you certain?"

He nodded.

"I'm glad because soon things will be different." Her face had changed. Something about her eyes.

He didn't know what to think.

But then he did.

Somehow he did.

Without saying another word, he picked her up in his arms.

They stared and stared at each other, little tears coming to both their eyes—and then Jilly laughed.

"Put me down, you handsome sailor. I'm going to beat you to the roof."

He swallowed and did as he was told. But he couldn't move. Or think. Or breathe. She was the only one who could make him feel not sure of himself.

Well, she and the—

He couldn't even say it yet, he was so stunned. He watched her climb the ladder, and then he saw her raven hair swing down.

"Hurry up, Captain," she cried, "and don't forget the bags of water!"

Read on for an excerpt from Kieran Kramer's next book

If *You* *Give* *a* *Girl* *a* *Viscount*

Coming soon from St. Martin's Paperbacks

CHAPTER ONE

September 1, 1820

"I'm bored with the relentless horde of money-seekers." Charles Thorpe, Viscount Lumley, held up a missive written in a feminine hand to show his three best friends. They were seated in a private room at their club. "This one came to Grandmother first, but she's off on a world tour. She's asked me to handle the matter with a delicate touch because a goddaughter is involved."

"How many goddaughters does she have?" asked Lord Harry Traemore.

"I've no idea," Charlie replied. "I think something like sixteen. She usually throws money at them, and do they ever show their gratitude by visiting or writing her regularly? No. They only write when they need money. I intend to provide no financial remedy to this one. I'll offer my sage counsel, and that's that."

"You can't do it," Harry told him, and then bit into a large drumstick and swallowed a gulp of claret.

Stephen Arrow, former captain in the Royal Navy, chuckled. "First sign of tears, and you'll be pulling out your wallet, Charlie old man. You can't resist a sad tale."

"Arrow's right," added Nicholas Staunton, the Duke of Drummond. He slapped Charlie hard on the back. "Besides, you don't know how to solve anything *without* money."

Charlie scowled. "I do, too."

The other three Impossible Bachelors looked at each other and burst into guffaws.

Charlie felt a deep, black rage form in his chest. He stood. "None of you knows what you're talking about."

Harry put his glass down very carefully and looked soberly at him. "We know you better than anyone, except for your mother. And I can tell you this: The main reason you're in such black moods these days is because you've got nothing to prove to anyone. You don't have to. You're too bloody rich."

"You need a challenge," Arrow said.

Charlie's soul sagged, even as his chest was still thrust out. His best friends were right.

"You don't know what you're made of, apart from your money and properties," said Nicholas.

"I believe I do," said Charlie. "But it seems as if the

rest of the world doesn't. All they see is my wealth. Especially debutantes and their mothers."

They all gave a shudder at the thought of debutantes and their mothers. They hadn't been named Impossible Bachelors for nothing.

"Arrow's right," said Harry. "You need a challenge." He put his palm out. "Give me your wallet."

Charlie balked. "That's—that's crazy." And kept it in his coat.

Stephen laughed. "See? You're lost without your blunt."

Charlie scowled. "Every man requires some money in his pocket."

"We'll give you your fare to Scotland and back," said Nicholas. "As for the rest, you'll have to manage to help your grandmother's latest supplicant without it."

"No," said Harry quietly and stood. "This is serious. I say let's take all of it."

Charlie stared at him.

"Yes." Stephen grinned. "Let's see you survive without a tuppence in your pocket."

Charlie opened his mouth, but he didn't know what to say.

"Why not, Charlie?" Nicholas challenged him. "You know you'll eventually get it back. This is a lark, and nothing more. So you might suffer a bit finding your way up to the Highlands. But it won't last forever."

"And maybe you'll learn what you're made of," added Harry.

"Stern stuff," said Arrow, thumping his chest with a fist.

"We're not best friends with a coward," Nicholas said softly, almost menacingly.

"Nor with a bland, forgettable gentleman," said Arrow with a yawn.

"We're best friends with a viscount of tremendous character," Harry pronounced.

"A man who can solve problems using his own ingenuity," added Nicholas.

"What's his name?" Charlie said with a little chuckle and drained his glass of brandy.

Everyone had a comfortable laugh at that. But not for long.

Harry gave him a stern look. "We're serious."

Charlie looked back and forth between the three of them. "So am I."

A feeling of excitement gripped him. Without hesitation, he reached into his coat pocket and removed his wallet.

"I'll take it," said Harry.

Charlie slapped the leather billet into his palm.

"Next time you see it, you'll be a different man," said Arrow.

"Who knows what adventures you'll have meanwhile?" asked Nicholas.

"I wish I could go with you," said Harry a bit wistfully.

"Huh," said Charlie. "You can't fool me. All three of you can hardly wait to get back to your wives and the beds they're keeping warm for you."

The others exchanged looks.

"He's right," Stephen said with a sigh and pulled

out his pocket watch. "It *is* well after midnight. But knowing Jilly, she's waiting up for me."

Charlie snorted. "Jilly, Poppy, and Molly. My God, you say their names every chance you get. Not that I don't adore all three of them, but really, lads."

"What can we say?" said Nicholas with a shrug. "We're sickeningly happy with our lovely spouses."

"And children, I might add," said Harry, who was the proud father of a boy and a recently arrived baby girl.

Charlie chuckled. "Yes, I can see why. Miniature hotheaded bachelors and gorgeous debutantes in the making. But I've noticed you've fathered interesting debutantes-to-be. Not the simpering kind."

"That's a nice way to describe the little hellions," said Nicholas, who had two very active twin girls. "I've no doubt Stephen's boy or girl will be just as rambunctious when he or she arrives."

"Any day now." Stephen grinned.

They all took a moment to savor the fact of the charming small people who'd so recently entered their lives and who were soon to come.

"Right, Uncle Charlie," Harry said, "do your present and future godchildren proud. Us, too."

"I swear I will," Charlie replied. "Just don't expect me to come back legshackled." He arched a brow. "I've got a survival instinct you fellows apparently lack. After all, I'm the last Impossible Bachelor standing."

With that, he saluted them and left the cozy chamber within their club. It was the same room in which they'd encountered Prinny and his mistress, who'd appeared from behind a panel in the wall that long while ago. So much had happened to the other Bachelors since then. Charlie was ready for something to happen to *him,* even if it was just an escapade to the far North.

He shivered in his coat when he opened the club door to the dark London night and trotted down the steps. He'd done it thousands of times before. But this time, when his right boot hit the pavement, he made sure to note that it was his first step on a journey to Scotland—

And what he dared to hope would be the adventure of a lifetime.

CHAPTER TWO

October 8, 1820

High in the left turret of Vandemere, the smallest and most decrepit castle in northwest Scotland, Daisy Montgomery pushed a letter back into its envelope and stared into space. "I've been given a viscount," she murmured.

A viscount?

But she hadn't *asked* for a viscount.

She pressed the envelope to her mouth in an attempt to stave off her disappointment. Her highest hope had been that the household would receive a trunk full of money (God, how she'd hoped for that!) or at the very least an invitation to journey down to London to visit Lady Pinckney, Ella's godmother.

But to be delivered a viscount, Lady Pinckney's own grandson?

Such an outcome hadn't figured into any of Daisy's plans.

Standing in the quiet, she couldn't help but wonder what to do with him.

A small mouse appeared beneath her window, one

of Ella's pets, no doubt. "If you're hungry, I've got nothing," Daisy told the tiny creature, who somehow managed to look disappointed, too.

"Almost everyone in this house is hungry," she murmured, and looked at the tattered lace at her cuff. And then at the aged red velvet curtains at the windows. She walked over to them and put her palms on the rheumy panes. Peering through them, she detected Ella circling the back garden, her golden hair an aureole about her stunning face, her modest gown pieced together from hand-me-downs not doing a thing to diminish her beauty. It was typical of Ella to be in search of lovely flowers, no matter how much her stomach must be growling this afternoon.

Dear Ella.

An unwelcome image overcame Daisy: her lovely, good-hearted stepsister being swept away into a dark miasma. Or perhaps the dark miasma was simply Ian McLeod's imposing black carriage.

Daisy bit her lip. She hated dark miasmas *and* Ian McLeod. With a passion—a strong, firm passion that wouldn't tolerate either one of them entering her life and sucking Ella out of it.

But as close as Daisy was to allowing somber forecasts to sink her resolve, she determined—out of sheer stubborn conviction—that negative thoughts wouldn't break her. Perhaps the mouse had something to do with it. He was in a much worse predicament than she, waiting for crumbs and worrying about who was his friend and who wasn't.

Even though they were in dire straits at Castle Vandemere, Daisy clearly knew which people she could call friends. And which ones she could not. She swallowed the bitter knowledge that her own mother and sister weren't her friends in the least. But she couldn't bear to call them her enemies. It didn't seem right. She'd never give up trying to find out why they were the way they were, but now was not the time to dwell on their discordant natures.

As for the viscount, *he'd* be on her side, wouldn't he? He'd have no choice.

He was hers for the nonce.

A small frisson of excitement assailed her, which she chose to interpret as nerves. It wouldn't do to be excited about being given a viscount. It simply wasn't done.

But she couldn't help striding away from the window with an extra spring in her step. He was to be at her beck and call. No one had *ever* been at her beck and call.

She, of course, was always at Mother's and her elder sister Perdita's. It was the only way to deal with them. Otherwise, they picked on Ella, and Daisy had promised Barnabas she'd always protect her stepsister, no matter what.

Yes, no matter what.

For a moment, looking into her own reflection in the aged looking glass above her bureau, Daisy saw that her expression was a bit wild and felt well pleased. According to the village gossips, she was a pale imitation of Ella. Ella was a pocket Venus, and Daisy was merely a bit on the short side. Ella had long, shining

golden hair; Daisy's was the color of the last of the
winter hay that old Joe pulled out from the back re-
cesses of the barn. Ella had eyes so vividly rob-
in's-egg blue that one wondered if she were a fairy,
whereas Daisy's were slate blue with a tint of sober
gray mixed in.

Not that she cared that she was overshadowed. Ella
was her great solace. Ella was her sister—her sister of
the heart.

And for her, Daisy would do anything to save her,
even if it meant . . . she'd have to use a viscount to do it.

But you'll need a clean guest room first, a sensible
voice in her head reminded her.

And after that, a fine dinner to serve him.

Surely, when you were given a viscount, you made
outrageous requests—

No. *Demands.*

Yes, demands!

No. *Requests.*

She'd be mannerly and charming. She must win
this viscount over just in case her requests were unusual ones. Which meant she'd have to have a new
gown.

And that fine dinner.

Which would entail an immediate trip to the village for one of Mrs. Gordon's ready-made frocks
and one of Peter Poole's whiskey-and-brown-sugar-
encrusted hams.

But they had no carriage.

Or money.

Fie on the money—she'd get everything on credit—
and she'd have to ride a horse.

"Hester!" she called at the top of her lungs. And
then decided not to wait. She ran pell-mell down the
stairs. "We need to saddle Blue!"

Hester looked up from the book she'd brazenly
removed from the library, her dust cloth forgotten.
She always said the Scots believed in education for
all (and made this pronouncement often when there
was housekeeping to be done). "Ye canna be wantin'
Blue," she said disbelievingly.

Blue hadn't been ridden in five years. It was because he was old and wicked and ran away every time
anyone tried to approach him with a saddle, even Ella.
But today was important. Blue was needed. Daisy
would harness him. "Yes, I do," she told Hester. "I require a carrot. The fattest one we've got."

"We have no carrots."

"Lumps of sugar?"

"No."

Daisy shoved her curls out of her face. "But Blue
and I must gallop to the village for a ham and a gown,
and you must prepare a bedchamber," she said. "We've
an important visitor arriving. A viscount. Sometime
very soon. Perhaps even today. He sent me a note from
an inn four days' journey away, and today is the sixth
day. I wonder why he's been delayed? The weather's
been fine enough."

Hester's face paled. "A viscount? Today? Och, and
I haven't polished the silver."

Hester always said she hadn't polished the silver when she was agitated. Everyone knew she hadn't polished it in years—Daisy had taken on that chore. Still, she knew it gave Hester succor to say so.

A knock sounded at the door. Once, and then again. The knock was solid, impatient. And unfamiliar.

"Oh, God, it's he." Daisy's heart leapt.

Hester gave a little gasp and her eyes widened. "But what brings a viscount here, of all places?"

"His grandmother is Ella's godmother." Daisy quickly swept a dead bug that Jinx, the grey tabby cat, had brought in under the worn Aubusson carpet and straightened an oil painting. "I wrote to her."

"You *did*?" Hester scuttled after her toward the door.

"Barnabas gave me her address before he died," Daisy whispered in rushed tones.

Hester gasped. "But you said god*mother*. This is a viscount we're to entertain."

"I know. The godmother, Lady Pinckney, is traveling to Italy, apparently. She's sending her grandson in her stead."

"Oh, dear." Hester put a trembling hand against her softly powdered cheek. "We're in for it noo, lassie."

"What is it?"

"Don't ye know ye should never trouble trouble until trouble troubles *you*?" Hester swallowed and touched her lace collar. She was the most superstitious person Daisy knew.

"But we *do* have trouble." Daisy strove for patience. "It's Ella. We must save her from Ian MacLeod. He's about to ask her to marry him. I heard him and Mother discussing the matter at the kirk bazaar."

Hester harrumphed. "At which neither of them bought one of my famous bannocks."

"He said he'll pay Mother a great sum for her, and you know Mother will take it, especially now that we're down to our last sovereigns. The only thing holding her back—"

"Oh, aye." Hester nodded vehemently. "The mourning period. The year ends . . . why, a month from today."

There was a sad silence as they both remembered jolly Barnabas, Ella's late father and Daisy's step-father.

"How yer mother could be sae cruel," Hester said, "throwing a puir, sweet girl with a father barely cold in his grave to a weasel like Ian. I dinna care how large a property he has."

She hesitated, looked at Daisy from the corner of her eye.

"*Hester.* You can't mean that you'd be all right with Ella marrying Ian."

"Noooo." Hester rubbed her nose. "But think of all the improvements he'd make to Castle Vande-mere if he married her. I myself would love a bolt of shiny black bombazine." She looked down at her housekeeper's uniform. "This old thing is faded to grey."

Daisy huffed. "Piles of gold don't change the fact that he's cruel to his tenants and doesn't love Ella a bit. I'd rather see you in *our* faded grey than *his* black bombazine any day."

"Ye're right," said Hester. "Besides which he's ugly as a stoat. I'd have to close my eyes to kiss the likes o' him." She added the last bit with the vigor of someone who knows she's been thinking selfishly and hopes she'll be forgiven.

The impatient knock came again. Louder this time.

The flowers on the massive hall table almost seemed to stir, although there was no breeze. Jinx, sauntering through the hall with her tail a question mark, suddenly leaped into the air as if she'd seen a ghost. Afterward, she stood stricken, her pupils large and black, her legs splayed.

Daisy exchanged glances with Hester.

Already things were different, and all because of the viscount. Daisy knew this deep inside, in that illogical place she kept hidden because Mother often told her (in that scornful manner of hers) that when you were English, you were sensible. Scots were the barmy ones. Not the English.

She released a breath. "You get the door," she told Hester calmly. "I'll be in the drawing room. We'll worry about dinner later."

"What I should do about your mother and Perdita?"

"Stall them if they wake. Tell them the vicar wants them at the kirk immediately to wash the altar cloths."

Hester chuckled. "They'd never in a million years—they'll say they have colds and hide in their beds."

"Exactly." And with that, Daisy stuck her chin in the air and left Hester to do her duty.

Daisy had her own duty to perform, and rather than rely on a new gown and a ham, she'd have to lean on her wits and her natural charm to see her through, even though the natural charm, according to what her mother and Perdita had told her, had never been anywhere in evidence.

But still . . .

She *must* try.

Ella's future depended on it, and that was all that mattered.

Daisy shut the drawing-room door behind her and strode immediately to the chair in front of the window and sat. The sun's rays behind her would cast her face in shadow. The visitor—her viscount—wouldn't see right away that she was plain, the plainest of all three young ladies in residence at Castle Vandemere. Perdita insisted on wearing the latest fashions no matter the cost, so a stylish observer's eye was diverted from her perpetually churlish expression. And Ella was so beautiful she could dress in a burlap sack and turn heads.

Daisy, in her simple mourning dress of gray muslin, fixed what she hoped was a pleasant smile on her face and prepared to wait. There was a deep voice in the hall. Clipped. Cold. Very masculine. And then Hester's thin, rabbit-y answer.

Oh, dear. Couldn't Hester work up a bit more nerve?

And then Daisy swore she heard an unfamiliar feminine giggle.

No, that would be *two* unfamiliar feminine giggles.

She clung to the sides of the chair, her palms

sweating, her nails like talons. Her pleasant smile was gone. She'd never been good at playing a part anyway.

Daisy Alice Montgomery! Her late stepfather's voice came to her. *Be brave.*

And she must be charming.

She loosened her grip, adjusted her curls. Hoped for a sudden boost of radiance to infuse her person. Perhaps she'd sneak out the double French doors and go saddle Blue, after all. She'd get that ham and slip into a new gown and gallop back.

If Blue would cooperate.

What she wouldn't give for a carrot at this moment! Or a lump of sugar. Which treat would be more likely to get that stubborn old horse to cooperate?

But she didn't have time to debate the matter. The door was flung open not a second later.

Hester walked in, her eyes wide and blinking, her hand curled to her mouth. "Viscount Lumley of London," she gasped bravely, "and his . . . his sisters!"

And then she scuttled off.

A second later, a man strode through the door. Apart from his clothes, which at one time had obviously been in the first stare of fashion—from his muddy black hightop boots to his snug but ripped buckskin breeches to the coat (with no buttons left) which fit him like a glove (Daisy noted the complete absence of a cravat over the stained white shirt)—he looked almost exactly like the dramatic depiction of Sir Lancelot in the large, florid oil painting in the servants' hall.

Almost.

Obviously, in his state of disarray, he was more

like Sir Lancelot's bad twin. But he had the same deep brown hair—wavy and thick—and eyes the tawny brown color of the hazelnuts heaped in the white ceramic bowl in the kitchen. And like the Lancelot in the painting that Daisy had admired for years now (she'd imagined kissing him when she was younger), this man's jaw was square, his nose aquiline. His bearing was proud; his stance, assured.

Except for that ghastly black eye and a bloody scab on his nose, he was handsome. Far too handsome for his own good. Daisy had never seen such a handsome man (who'd obviously been in a brawl. Or two).

Her heart raced not at his good looks, she told herself, but at the lack of warmth in his manner and the scowl on his countenance. He also reeked of cheroots and stale ale.

Most shocking of all, he was accompanied by two women, one clinging to each arm. They were lightskirts, wearing too much rouge and their necklines scandalously low. They could be nothing else. Daisy had been well sheltered, but even *she* knew when a woman wasn't a lady.

"H-hello." She stood and looked back and forth between the two women, both of whom were about her age.

"I'm Isabel. *Lady* Isabel," said the tall, slender one with rich auburn hair and a dimple on either side of her mouth.

"You may call me Lady Oleander," said the shorter one with light brown hair, a curvaceous figure, and long, lush dark brown lashes.

The women giggled.

Daisy shut her gaping mouth and looked full-on at the gentleman.

He returned her gaze with cold equanimity. "And I am your viscount," he said softly, in a take-no-prisoners tone.

She put her hand on the back of a chair to steady herself. It was even more than she'd expected. Never in her entire life had she been exposed to such . . .

Such excitement.

Such awful, *horrible* excitement.